PRAISE FOR EVELYN ROGERS' PREVIOUS BESTSELLERS!

THE FOREVER BRIDE

"If time travel were an option, it's romance like *The Forever Bride* that would have millions of readers going back in time to search for the love of their hearts! Ms. Rogers is a topnotch storyteller!"

—*The Literary Times*

"Ms. Rogers weaves a believable story and gives her characters depth and personality. Her detailed love scenes simmer with sensuality."

—*Romantic Times*

"Fans will be scrambling to get their hands on *The Forever Bride* and will cherish the story of Robert and Meagan. Definitely a keeper! 6 BELLS!"

—*Bell, Book, and Candle*

"A reading treat you can't put down. Another triumph for the talented Ms. Rogers!"

—*Rendezvous*

"A first-rate reading experience that has the right amount of magic to make it shine."

—*Affaire de Coeur*

D0963936

DEVIL'S KISS

He wanted to take her here on the ground, sharing sex as wild as the land surrounding them. Instead he held her close and covered her face with kisses.

"Who are you?" he whispered.

Her answer was a shudder that trembled through her and into him.

Impatiently he pulled at the wide tie holding her bonnet in place and tossed the hat aside. He licked her throat. "What devil sent you here?"

She shook her head. "Please don't talk."

Thrusting his hands into the falling tumble of yellow hair, he kissed his way to her ear. "Who are you?"

"You're bad to do this to me," she said with a catch in her voice.

"I'm bad. And good." He kissed her eyelids. "Admit it."

She clung all the harder to him. "And good."

"Who are you?" he repeated.

"A crazy woman."

"You're driving me insane. Do you realize that?"

"No."

"Yes."

TEXAS EMPIRES:

Crown of Glory

EVELYN ROGERS

LEISURE BOOKS   NEW YORK CITY

*This book is dedicated to Chris Dunham,
booklover and friend.*

A LEISURE BOOK®

July 1998

Published by

Dorchester Publishing Co., Inc.
276 Fifth Avenue
New York, NY 10001

ISBN 0-8439-4403-X

The name "Leisure Books" and the stylized "L" with design are
trademarks of Dorchester Publishing Co., Inc.

Printed in the United States of America.

AUTHOR'S NOTE

Crown of Glory launches a series of books about the founding of empires in the early days of Texas. The years of the Republic of Texas were difficult for everyone, from the usually indomitable Sam Houston to the poor immigrants who came West expecting easy times and quick fortunes. The characters of this first book, all fictitious, are representative of the dreamers, the outcasts, the loners, and the fighters who peopled the Republic.

Like the characters, the town of Glory never existed except in the imagination of the author. The passing events, however, from the political and economic troubles to the tragic struggle with the Comanches, are as real as the history books allow me to make them.

Future stories will span the century, from statehood through Reconstruction, and edging toward the new century. Look for Cord Hardin's story in the spring of 1999. I welcome your reaction to *Texas Empires*. Write me at the address below, including an SASE for a reply, and please check out my website.

Evelyn Rogers
8039 Callaghan Road, Suite 102
San Antonio, TX 78230
http://www.romcom.com/rogers

Crown of Glory

Chapter One

New Orleans
October, 1840

On a misty autumn afternoon, Cal Hardin arrived
at the place of his birth with one purpose in mind:
to bury his mother, then get out of town as fast
as he could. His destination didn't matter. It never
had, as long as it was far from New Orleans.

He'd bought a fancy, angel-decorated vault to
hold her coffin—above-ground burials were necessary in the swampy soil—but he couldn't buy a
priest to say the final words. A long time ago, his
father had made that impossible.

Standing in the unconsecrated section of the
cemetery, Cal thrust all thought of Raymond Hardin from his mind. Today belonged to Margaret
O'Malley Hardin Broussard. In life she'd had far

too few special days; he would do all in his power to make sure that in death she was remembered with dignity.

"Poor Margaret," his Uncle Finbar O'Malley said, sidling close to his left side. He shifted from foot to foot and repeated, "Poor Margaret," then lowered his head in a silent good-bye.

"May our dear departed sister rest in peace," said Cal's Uncle Fitzgerald O'Malley, to Cal's right. Like his twin brother Fin, Fitz shifted from foot to foot, occasionally glancing around him as if he expected trouble.

The pair, with their short, spare figures and gray-streaked red hair, were as alike as two men could be, though Fin was the leader of the two and Fitz bore a small childhood scar in the center of his chin. They loved cards, whiskey and women, not always in that order, and avoided hard labor whenever they could. Nothing about them bothered Cal, except their forgiveness of past sins.

Some things he could never forgive or forget.

Over the twins' final whispered words, the ritual message of the mortician droned on. No one among the small crowd of mourners listened. Instead, they sent darting glances toward the departed's wayward, wandering son.

So much, Cal thought, for dignity. He pulled his hat low over his eyes. Whatever grief lay in their depths was his and his alone to know. Except for his uncles, he didn't give a damn about any of the mourners. Not even the black-veiled woman standing behind him in the mist, away from the plastered brick tomb that would soon hold Margaret's remains. Whatever had drawn the woman in black, it wasn't simple curiosity. She was far too intense.

Cal hadn't been able to see the woman's eyes through the veil, but he could feel her stare boring into his back. She stood motionless, like one of the surrounding vaults, burning with an emotion so searing he felt her heat.

With his thoughts on her and his eyes on the coffin, he suddenly felt he couldn't breathe. The reaction made no sense. Nothing and no one got to him, ever. Men called him cold, a hard son of a bitch. Women used softer, more seductive terms, but the results were the same. No one got close. No one wanted to.

The veiled woman at his back seemed neither soft nor seductive. He had an instinct for picking out his enemies. Whatever her purpose or past, she doubtless ranked high on the list.

"Lad, we have to talk."

Cal glanced at his Uncle Fin, and the sense of entrapment died as quickly as it had come. Must be the setting, he told himself, the mist, the sadness of the occasion. Besides, on the best of days, he never drew a relaxed breath in New Orleans.

This definitely wasn't the best of days. Cold and hard he might be, but he had loved his mother in his own way and he had the decency to feel guilty because he wasn't sure she had known it.

Fin tugged at his sleeve. "Are you listening, lad?"

At his other side, Fitz huddled close. "Aye," he said, "we have important matters to discuss." His voice sounded as frantic as his twin's.

13

The two of them, pink-skinned for all their fifty-four years, had been especially fidgety ever since Cal arrived at the cemetery. After a half hour of standing in the misty air, having shown their genuine grief, they were getting close to losing control. It seemed a strange reaction to the entombment of their sister.

Never before in his life had Cal attended a funeral. He wondered if they were all this other-worldly.

He glanced over his shoulder to see if the veiled woman was watching. She was gone. A strange sense of loss hit him, but it didn't linger. If she truly was his enemy, they would meet again.

What he couldn't figure was what troubled Fin and Fitz. A pair of ill-starred wheeler-dealers, they could have almost anything on their minds.

Before either of the twins could say more, it was time for the three of them, the lone pallbearers, to ease the casket into the waiting tomb. Maybe he should be saying something over Margaret's remains, a final good-bye from her only offspring, making up for what a priest might have said.

Whatever he had to tell her was not meant for strangers to hear. Besides, he should have talked to her last week, when she was still alive. As at so many other times in her life, he hadn't been around.

Hell, he'd barely made it to the cemetery in time for the burial.

The wooden casket slipped easily onto the waiting shelf. The mortician was offering him the swath of black velvet when carriage wheels crunched on the pathway close to the small gathering. Fin and Fitz jumped, and Cal could swear he saw terror in their eyes.

More puzzled than worried, he looked beyond them to the crepe-shrouded carriage slowing to a halt behind the empty hearse. The carriage door opened; a youth slowly emerged. Something in the slump of his shoulders and the way his eyes darted left and right, every direction but straight ahead, made clear that he wanted to be anywhere but here.

Cal got a good look at the eyes, startlingly blue and filled with contempt. They were Hardin eyes, both the color and the contempt. He ought to recognize them. They were the same eyes that stared back at him from the mirror every day.

He stiffened. Though he'd never seen Cordoba Hardin before, he knew his name, and he understood the reluctance that made the boy want to run. He would have been surprised if his half brother felt otherwise. Except for the accident of birth, they were nothing to one another.

For a moment they exchanged stares, and then the boy bent slightly at the waist. Someone must have summoned him, because he turned back to the carriage and gave his hand to a woman, who stepped gracefully to the ground. Behind her came a Negress cradling an infant against her bosom. All were dressed in black, except for the baby, who was swathed in pink.

While the uncles whispered among themselves, Cal kept apart, waiting for the rest of the Hardins to come to him, his eyes directed beyond them to the tall masts of a schooner anchored in an adjacent canal. These people had no place here. Let them see to Raymond Hardin's memory and leave Margaret O'Malley alone.

With an open, defiant stare at Cal, the boy held back beside the Negress, leaving the woman to step forward alone. She covered the distance quickly, oblivious to everyone but Cal.

"M'sieur Hardin," she said, her French accent still evident though she had been in New Orleans half her life. Or so he had been told by Fitz and Fin.

"Mrs. Hardin," Cal said, taking her extended hand.

"Please accept my sympathies for your loss," she said.

"I hadn't seen my mother for a long while."

"*Quel dommage*. And now you can never see her again."

Her voice was gentle, but the words sounded suspiciously like a rebuke. Raymond's third and final wife was not the mealy-mouthed weakling she appeared.

"I'm surprised to see you here," he said. "I should have thought you would have had your fill of cemeteries."

"*Oui*, it has been a sad week, first Raymond, and now your dear mama. I had hoped to see you at his burial. The tomb is close by. I can show you if you wish."

"I do not wish. I doubt if you really expected me."

"Another pity. We do what we must, *n'est-ce pas?*"

"We do what we must."

How civilized they were, each of them caught

in the present, caught as well by the past, talking as calmly as if Raymond Hardin hadn't been a selfish, arrogant bastard, as if he hadn't disgraced, abandoned, divorced the woman lying dead a few feet away.

What was this woman to him? A stepmother? Raymond must have laughed when he chose to marry a woman younger than his firstborn. But the laugh had turned on him. She must have exhausted him, lowering his resistance to illness. Normally a hardy man, he had been felled by a cough less than two years after taking the French beauty to his bed.

Had his own mother's death following so soon after been linked to his? Cal suspected it was so. She had always defended the bastard, forgiving all he had done. Maybe she had clung to life until the man she still considered her husband was truly gone.

He looked past his father's widow to Cord. He must be fifteen by now, the son of the second wife. The boy's Spanish Creole heritage was visible in the sharply hewn lines of his face, in hair blacker than Cal's, in the proud way he held himself.

And what about the baby, the only daughter, the lone child of wife number three? As if she could read his mind, Adrienne Hardin turned to the Negress and held out her arms for the newest progeny, the last that Hardin would ever bring into the world. Perhaps she wouldn't grow to hate his memory the way his two sons did.

The widow parted the blankets, and Cal stared down at his half sister. She was pink and fair, and she stared unblinkingly back at him with familiar blue eyes. He was thirty-two, too old and too hardened to be stirred by such a sight, though he saw that she was a beautiful child.

"Her name is Madeleine," her mother said. The name came out like whispered music.

"She'll be called Maddie."

"Perhaps. Your father called her Madeleine, and so shall I. She is but six months old. So young to be orphaned."

Cal could have pointed out that he was only eight when Raymond left, orphaned in an especially cruel way by a mother who turned inward with her troubles and a father who publicly called her a whore. But that might have sounded like self-pity, an emotion he had long ago left behind.

The mist thickened to a light rain.

Adrienne Hardin covered the child, then returned her to the Negress. "You have my sympathy, m'sieur, though I know you do not ask for it. If ever you want to talk, I will listen. This is what I came to say, and to offer my condolences."

She turned toward the carriage, followed by the servant. The brothers stood for a moment, their eyes locked, and then, after a second quick bow, Cord, too, hurried toward the shelter of the carriage. Cal watched as they rode away, doubting he would ever see another Hardin again. Where he should have felt satisfaction, he sensed only emptiness.

Around him the other so-called mourners headed for their separate conveyances. Show's over, he thought. He conferred briefly with the funeral official, but only to say the arrangements had been satisfactory. They should have been. He had paid a considerable sum for them months ago, when he sensed his mother was soon to die.

In truth, she had been dying for years.

As the hearse pulled away, its black plumes waving in farewell, he felt a momentary relief, glad the ceremony was done. And then he saw the veiled woman again. She stood in the roadway watching him, a small, indistinct figure in the rain, yet powerful, too, as if all the forces of the universe could not move her from her position.

Instinct and a sense of inevitability drew him toward her, but before he could take more than a step she whirled, her cloak billowing around her, and disappeared in the rows of tombs at her back.

Cal was not a fanciful man, yet he wondered if she had been nothing more than a specter, the Ghost of Unconsecrated Ground. If he had been able to touch her, would his hand burn or would it sift through shadowy air?

A sudden exhaustion took hold of him. The appearance of his almost-family, the veiled woman, the final good-bye all took their toll. He was right to hate New Orleans. Nothing good had ever happened to him here, not even his birth.

He turned toward his uncles, the last and most sincere of the mourners. "You wanted to talk?"

"Not here, lad," Fin said.

" 'Tis privacy we'll be needing," Fitz said, "before you take once again to the road."

Rain dripped from the flat brim of Cal's black, low-crowned hat. "There are none but the dead to hear us here. They won't be telling tales."

Two pairs of green eyes darted around the

vaults that held New Orleans' dead away from the water-soaked soil.

Fin's shouted "Down!" seemed to come from out of nowhere.

The twins hit the ground at the instant a gunshot exploded in the rain. Cal was right behind them, his pistol drawn. Fin's umbrella skittered along the ground toward his sister's tomb; then all was still as the explosion echoed in the clouds of thick mist.

"Are you all right, lad?" Fin asked.

Cal squinted through the rain in the direction from which the shot had come, but he could make out nothing except a line of silent vaults. Slowly he stood, expecting at any moment to feel the slam of a bullet, but the silence held. Hurriedly he checked out the area where the shooter must have stood, but the rain had already obliterated any footprints he might have left.

If the shooter was a man. He thought of the black-veiled woman. She had disappeared in another direction, but she could have circled back to where she could get a good shot. Even someone so small as she could fire a gun if she were angry enough or hurt or burned with the fires of revenge. Given the right motivation, a woman could be far more dangerous than a man.

Suddenly the scene ceased being otherworldly. The gunshot had been very, very real.

He returned to his uncles. "Maybe we weren't the targets," he said. "Maybe a gun went off accidentally."

Fin held up the retrieved umbrella, pointing to the hole in the side. "We were the targets right enough. That's what we've been trying to tell you. There's someone in New Orleans will nay rest easy until we join our beloved sister in her tomb."

"All right, let's talk. What's going on?" Cal asked.

The three of them were back in the Vieux Carré house he had bought years before for his mother and uncles. Dressed in dry clothes, they sat before a healthy fire, doubly warming themselves with snifters of Irish whiskey.

Fin took a swallow of the potent drink. Fitz did the same.

"Someone wants us dead," Fin said.

"He's shot at us before," Fitz said.

"How do you know it's a man?"

As usual, Fin took over. "Get on with you, lad. What sort of woman would be firing a gun in a cemetery?"

Cal couldn't see how the location mattered, but he let the question go.

"Anyway, we've seen him. Not a good look, mind, but enough to know it's a man."

"How many times?" Cal asked.

"Twice. Both following soon upon the game of chance. No matter what you hear, lad, we didn't cheat. 'Tis a mystery for sure how we won. That king of hearts surprised us as much as anyone."

Cal held his patience. Eventually they would make clear what they were talking about.

While Fin talked, Fitz got up to refill the glasses. Cal waved him away. His glass remained close to full.

A log snapped in the fire. The twins jumped.

"Relax," Cal said. "You're safe."

"Easy for you to say," Fin said. "You've not been the target—ah, but I forget. With your traveling ways taking you to high places and low, meeting the ladies, making money so fast it must set your head in a whirl, you've probably stirred up an enemy or two."

Cal wasn't fooled by the observation. Even dodging bullets, the pair wanted to know the particulars of his nomadic life.

"This game of chance," Cal said, ignoring the hint. "You want to tell me more?"

"We were at the pub," Fin said, "working as usual, serious-minded about the business so that we can pay you back someday. We've got plans. We're not the wastrels you suppose."

"The game," Cal prodded. As far as he was concerned, they owed him nothing, having taken care of their sister all these years while her only son roamed the country.

"Some of the regulars have taken to settling in on a Saturday night and indulging in a round or two of cards. That night—oh, it must have been close to a month past—we were persuaded to join them. Now we know you don't care for us gambling, being somewhat poor at it as we've proven often enough, but it would nay have been sociable, us being the proprietors and all, to decline."

A man of few words, Cal would have liked to hurry Fin on, but he'd never figured out how to do it.

Fitz made another round with the whiskey, while Fin continued his recollection.

"A stranger entered, determined to sit in. Nary

a drop of Irish blood in him, not like our usual clientele, but he had money and who were we to toss him into the night?"

"Who indeed?"

"Chase, he said his name was. We found out later he has a tailor shop over on Royal Street. Had, that is. After the shooting—"

Fin lapsed into reverie.

"This shooting," Cal said. "Was it aimed at you or at Chase?"

"In time, lad. In good time. There's much to tell about the cards. They fell first one way, then another, Fitz and me more than holding our own, which ain't the usual way, even with us backing each other up, playing the one hand. The hour grew late, and we'd had a wee bit of grog. Chase pulls a piece of paper from his pocket and drops it on the table. Says he'll put it up against all our winnings. Naturally enough, we agreed."

"Naturally. Did you bother to read the paper first?"

"Do you take us for fools? Tell him the stakes, Fitz."

"Land," Fitz said in a hushed tone, as if he'd offered his nephew a magic word. "Almost five thousand acres of prime land, a place called the Double T. The deed spelled it out clear as you please. A league and a labor, it said, but Chase explained it for us. And we were risking no more than fifty dollars. A man could hardly go wrong with such a wager as that."

"The game was draw," Fin said. "Chase dealt the cards down right fast enough, his hands moving so quickly we could scarce keep up with 'em, but then, we'd had the wee bit to drink."

"Three kings, that's what we held," Fitz said. "And two little nothings, a deuce and a trey. We passed the nothings, or thought we did, and asked for two more. Then we shuffled the hand and spread the cards. We were looking at the same three kings and a pair of deuces."

"A winner," said Cal.

"There was one thing wrong." Fin glanced at his brother, then back at Cal. "We made a mistake when we passed the cards. We threw away the trey, but instead of the deuce, we tossed the king of hearts. We had already said our good-byes to the deed. But there the king was, nestled with its mates and the deuces backing them up. When we laid them down for all to see, there were those had seen our foolish mistake. They took to muttering. Already the talk of cheating had begun, though how they figured it we could not understand."

"There's those will always question the good fortune of others," Fitz said, shaking his head at the sad state of humanity.

"What was Chase holding?"

Fin spoke up. "We never saw. He got a look at the full house and tossed in his cards. Word of the cheating spread fast. We ain't got the best reputation for winning, you see, but we've scarce had one for cheating, you may be sure. We've got one now."

Fitz set down his glass. His eyes darted around the room as if seeking out intruders. "That's not the worst. Some say we're killers, too."

Cal decided it was time for a swallow of whiskey. "Let me guess. Chase was killed."

"Aye, shot in the back not two days later," said Fin with a solemn nod of his head. " 'Twas said we were seen nearby. Truth was, your dear mother was lying in her sick bed needing our help. We were at her side the evening of the killing, but the poor lass was too feverish to come to our defense, and we had only each other to swear our innocence. There's those who doubt the veracity of Irishmen, as you no doubt ken."

"We're lovers, not killers," put in Fitz. "Anyone around would tell you so if they weren't enjoying the lying rumors."

"Why would you want Chase dead?"

"He was considering charging us with cheating him out of his land. That's the word, you understand, though he seemed to us glad enough to pass the title on."

The twins lapsed into a rare silence.

"When did the shooting turn to you?" Cal asked.

"After the brick came through the window. A week after Chase had been laid to rest. We had it replaced—the glass that is—at great expense but we're not asking for recompense. 'Twas the note wrapped around the brick that caused alarm. We were to pass the title on to the bank, declaring in writing that someone would come calling for it afore long. Naturally we threw it away."

"The note, you mean."

"Aye, we were nay taking such nonsense seriously."

"Until the shooting started."

"Twice now. Not counting today."

Cal rubbed at his head. "The woman at the cemetery. Had you ever seen her before?"

"What woman is that, lad?"

"The one in black. With the veil. She stood apart for a while, and then she was in the roadway where the hearse had been."

The brothers looked at one another. Clearly they had no idea what he was talking about. He was thinking too hard, connecting her with the O'Malleys' troubles. Maybe she really had been a ghost.

Again he rubbed his head. He never had headaches, but he had one now.

"Have you reported the incidents to the police?" he asked.

"With rumors going around we're shooters ourselves? We had nary a witness to our troubles. The authorities being what they are, they would say we were trying to turn suspicion away from ourselves."

Sly looks passed between the brothers. Having seen those looks before, Cal took another swallow of whiskey. His head pounded. For all the bad news they had imparted, he knew the worst was yet to come.

Fin was the one who presented it. He smiled, his pink cheeks cherubic on either side of his drinker's veined nose.

"When your dear mother died, may she rest in peace, an idea came to us, like she was talking to us from the Great Beyond."

Cal finished the whiskey and debated asking for more.

"It's fate, that's what it is," said Fitz, "the king of hearts being the deciding card, and us long calling you King Cal, being named as you were by our dear sister for King Callaghan in the great Irish past."

Never let two words suffice when twenty were available, thought Cal. No, he amended, make that two hundred and twenty.

"We're asking yourself to sell out all that's in New Orleans," Fin said. "We know the place is painful to you. Come with us to Texas. 'Tis a Republic in its own right, a new country, a new land. Think on it. Five thousand acres of rich grassland waiting for us, little more than fifty miles from the coast. 'Tis the new paradise, or so we've heard."

"Have you heard of the Comanches, too? Of the Mexican Army threatening to invade again? Times have been hard in this country the past few years, but nothing so hard as in Texas."

He could have gone on, having considered investing in property there himself after the Panic of '37 hit the United States. But he had found the risks too great. Besides, he preferred life in towns, especially those he had visited in the East. There was nothing approaching civilization in Texas. With the riffraff pouring across the borders, he doubted there ever would be.

"If this shooter was serious," he said, trying to inject a note of reason, "he could have taken you down anytime he chose. Today, for instance. The three of us made easy targets. He wants nothing more than to frighten you."

"We're frightened, right enough," said Fitz. "For all you know, nephew, he could be a very bad shot. Which doesn't mean he won't get us eventually, given enough opportunity. Even a bad shot hits his target on occasion."

Fin nodded in agreement. "You're a man used to owning things. Despite all you've said, the pub was never ours. We didn't mind caring for your ailing mother, setting you free to wander, and the watering hole was a joy, most of the time. But circumstances have changed. The Double T answers our prayers."

They prayed poorly, Cal thought, but they knew how to twist the tatters of a man's conscience. He looked from one brother to the other. Beguiling though they could be and as close to warming his heart as anyone, Fitz and Fin would never get him to Texas. They clearly were in trouble, and somehow he would get them out.

But not by running to Texas. The idea was far too absurd.

Chapter Two

"Gone to Texas!"

In a rare fit of temper, Eleanor Chase slammed her hand against her father's desk. Like the rest of her, the hand was small but strong. Everything on the desk shook.

"How dare he?"

Alone in the room, she spoke to herself, which was no problem since she also answered herself.

"Because he's a scoundrel, that's why, no better than his cheating, murderous uncles."

The *murderous* got to her, even though it was her own word, and she caught her breath.

"Oh, Papa," she whispered, "why did you get yourself killed?"

She sounded as if he were at fault. He wasn't. Nobody asked to be shot in the back. Or cheated out of his land.

She collapsed in the chair and stared out the street window of her father's office. A week had gone by since she'd gotten her first look at her enemies, a week since her life had changed. Outside the window, the world went on as if everything were the same.

Her particular view was of the fashionable people of New Orleans trailing past, men and women alike dressed a shade fancier than their counterparts back in Richmond. Some stopped to stare at the CLOSED sign on the tailor shop door. A few shook their heads sadly at the black crepe that lined the window.

Henry Chase had been a good tailor—a popular one, too, according to his well-kept records. It was so little for Ellie to know about him. He'd left Virginia right after her birth, after the death of her mother, leaving the upbringing of his only child to Ellie's spinster aunt.

Aunt Abigail had been affectionate and properly instructive, everything a mother would have been. But she hadn't been a real mother, and she could not have been close to being a father, no matter how hard she tried. Before his death three years ago, her uncle had attempted to fill the void, and she had loved him for it.

But she hadn't loved him like a father, not with her real Papa still alive. As practical as she was most of the time, Ellie was also a dreamer. She had dreamed of the real thing. Before settling into matrimony—she shuddered at the thought—she had made the long journey from Richmond to get to know her mysterious father, traveling with a Virginia family that was moving to New Orleans.

She had arrived too late, even for his burial.

And all because of two unscrupulous saloon-keepers who were now beyond her reach, and because of a no-doubt equally unscrupulous devil named Callaghan Hardin.

The Virginia family had moved on to Baton Rouge, and Ellie was left with nothing but business records and bolts of wool, with half-finished clothing in a tailor shop that would never be open again. She had spent the days since her arrival closing accounts, working with the bank in paying and collecting debts, ending up with more money than she would have supposed. Papa must have been a fine tailor indeed.

And she had made inquiries about the shooting. The police knew little, or at least claimed such, but talk on the street had taken her to Finbar and Fitzgerald O'Malley, to the funeral of their sister, to the nephew who was to help them escape from their crimes.

What a strange thing a New Orleans cemetery was, with its white tombs crowded one against another, no order to their placement, no uniformity to their design. The graveyard of her mother's family, the Davenports, was green and restful, the marble headstones simple and discreet above the graves of her grandparents, her mother, her only uncle, and now Aunt Abigail.

There was nothing simple or discreet about New Orleans or its citizens, especially Callaghan Hardin. He truly looked like a devil in his black suit and black hat, dark hair thick against his shoulders. There was the devil, too, in his blue eyes. Other women might have called them heavenly blue, but not Ellie. When he looked over his shoulder at her during the funeral, they had glinted with the fires of hell.

What she hadn't seen in those blue depths was any sign of mourning over the loss of his mother. But then, if the preachers back home had it right, devils felt no grief.

She refused to excuse the evil black clothing because of the funeral. At least he had arrived in New Orleans in time to attend. Henry Chase had gone to his final reward with no blood kin to weep over his grave.

She sprang from the chair. This maundering and fulminating was getting her nowhere. She forced herself to walk up the back stairs to the apartment where her father had lived alone for so many years. One large room used primarily for sleeping, with a table and chairs at one end near a cookstove that looked unused, his quarters were comfortable but far from luxurious. Papa must have taken his meals elsewhere. He obviously did no entertaining. He must have been a lonely man.

Settling on the floor beside his bed, she opened the wooden box she had found earlier atop his wardrobe and removed the ribbon-wrapped letters inside. They were letters she had written him through the years. He had saved them all, even the childishly scrawled notes from when her education had barely begun. From their worn look, she could tell he had read them often, but he had seldom answered. Aunt Abigail had said he was a man of few words.

But that was no excuse. She was his only child. Surely he must have loved her.

The tears came. She forced them back. Papa didn't need mourning. He needed vengeance. Did the O'Malleys kill him? Maybe. Did they cheat him of the land he had recently purchased? Almost certainly. Aided by Cal Hardin, they were now reaping the reward of their crime.

In honor of her father's memory, she had to get that title back.

Gone to Texas! The sign, common across much of the South, had been posted early this morning on the O'Malleys' saloon door. Even back in Virginia, Texas was notorious as the refuge of scoundrels and thieves and debtors from the United States. After today's departure, three more names could be added to the Republic's list.

She had to get the rascals back. Or somehow get herself to them. The very idea of vengeance stunned her, being alien to her nature and all she had been taught. She had been educated in music, needlework, literature; raised to marry a wealthy gentleman, serving as his likewise gentle helpmate all her life.

Goodness, she could even play the harp, her talents honed for long winter evenings when the wind howled outside the plantation house windows and her loved ones gathered close.

But now was not the time for harps or other gentleness. Now she must scheme and lie and cheat as boldly as her enemies and, like them, show no sign of remorse.

But how? Stroking the stack of letters, she sat on the floor beside her father's bed and put her considerable powers of concentration to work.

* * *

Late the next day Ellie sat in the shadows behind her father's desk and watched the two women enter the tailor shop. They had tried to get in at the same time, but the portal was far too small and their girth too wide. The woman in green graciously gestured for the woman in purple to go first, which she did.

Purple, as Ellie promptly dubbed her, was the taller of the two, but not by much. Both had six inches on Ellie's five-foot-two, and they outweighed her by a hundred pounds. A great deal of the weight came from the mass of red hair piled atop each head, the layers of kohl thickening their lashes, and the formidable bosoms that Ellie eyed with envy.

At fifty, more or less—Ellie could only guess their ages—they were handsome women in their overblown way, their gowns a satiny texture that caught the light in a sensuous way. They must have been beautiful as young girls.

All in all, they were exactly what she had expected, not in the least simple or discreet. She smiled to herself. The O'Malley boys were doomed.

Green was the one to spot her in the shadows.

"Miss Chase?" she said. "Is that you hiding in the dark?"

Ellie sat forward, letting the light from the desk lamp fall on her.

"Miss Dollarhide," she said. "Excuse me, Misses Dollarhide, am I right?"

"We got word you wanted to see us," Purple said.

"We *received* word," Green corrected. "Ain't we ladies now?"

"I hope not," Ellie said.

She bit her tongue.

"At least I hope you haven't reformed completely," she amended, but the Dollarhides weren't paying her words any mind, giving all their attention to studying her as she had studied them.

"Not much to her," Green said to her sister.

"Doesn't have to be. Didn't we learn years ago size ain't important?

Green shrugged. "Miss Chase, you won't mind my being blunt, it's just us women here and all, but what in hell does a ladylike little snippet of a thing like you want with a couple of whores?"

"Former whores," Purple said. "And we weren't ordinary whores. We owned the place. That makes us madams."

"Which ain't—isn't—too far up the social scale."

"Ladies," Ellie said, "please take a seat. I've a business proposition to discuss with you."

"We're retired," Green said, settling in one of the chairs in front of the desk.

"Not our idea," Purple said, settling in the other. "The good wives of Charity, Mississippi, hurried us along."

"Charity, humph!" said Green. "When we went out of the business, they wouldn't let us even give it away."

Ellie wasn't sure she understood what they were talking about, but she thought it best not to ask.

"I appreciate your responding to my summons," she said.

"Your message asked us to come right away," Purple said. "It wasn't real clear exactly why."

Ellie swallowed. She was filled with all the confidence in the world that her cause was just, but she wasn't so certain about the course of action she wanted to pursue. She'd always been honest and straightforward, outspoken even, according to Aunt Abigail. She saw no need to change now.

"The *why* is a little complicated. Please be patient and hear me out."

"We don't have nothing on the social card for this afternoon," put in Green. "You got something biting under your corset, let's get 'er out."

"My father lost the deed to valuable land in a crooked poker game. Shortly after, he was shot in the back."

Her voice barely quavered as she spoke. She felt inordinately proud.

The hardness that had been in the women's eyes softened in sympathy, and Ellie began to like them.

"Were you two close?" Green asked.

"I didn't know him. My home is in Virginia. I came here before I . . . well, I came here so we could meet."

"Ran out on your ma, did he? There's men that'll behave that way."

"She died. Papa left me with her family. They're all gone now, and when I got here, so was he."

Ellie tried to put the situation as simply as she could, and to keep the emotion out of her voice. She almost succeeded.

The sisters clucked in understanding. Clearly they thought her a poor orphan left alone in the world, which wasn't exactly the case. She had all the land she could ever need back in Virginia, a lawyer looking out for her interests, and a man waiting to take her as his wife.

Bertrand Rutherford, a widower sixteen years her senior, was also ready to get her in bed, a fact he had hinted at more than once during the last year of their betrothal. The hints had been coming on a regular basis since Aunt Abigail was laid to rest.

Rumors said that for a long while a widow woman had been around to "satisfy his needs," as her friends put it. But like Aunt Abigail, the widow had gone to her final reward.

Ellie had a vague idea of what was to take place in his bed. What she didn't understand was what Bertrand's needs could be, since she didn't seem to have them herself. Whatever his needs were, it was her duty to let him have his way. As an honorable Southern lady, this she was prepared to do.

Unfortunately, he also wanted her to take over the handling of his six boys. She wanted a home and family, especially children, very much indeed, but not the wild, motherless Rutherford brood.

She also didn't appreciate the fact that Bertrand coveted her land. His was worn out from planting too much tobacco. Hers had been better managed, by both Aunt Abigail and the shrewd overseer she had hired.

If Ellie hadn't promised her aunt on the dear woman's deathbed that the oft-postponed nuptials would soon take place, she would call off the whole thing.

She didn't mind in the least postponing her return, especially for a cause that was so just.

"Was this your Daddy's place?" Green asked, looking around her.

Ellie nodded. "The men who cheated him in the game have gone to claim their ill-gotten gains. I suspect they were the ones who shot him, too. They're genuine rascals. And their nephew is even worse."

"How did a nephew get involved?" Purple asked.

"Apparently they asked his help in getting settled on the land. I'm only guessing since I wasn't in on their private conversations. I've seen them only from afar."

"Have you been spying on them?"

"I have."

The Dollarhide sisters nodded in approval.

"How do we figure in?" Purple asked.

"I want you to confuse them."

"Seduce them," Green said. "Is that what you mean?"

Ellie nodded. "Whatever way you can, make them want to leave their land and return with you to New Orleans. I'll be there to buy them out—with, of course, as little outlay of cash as possible. Whatever you get from them will be added to what I pay you. I plan to be generous."

Furrowed brows met her words.

"And the nephew?"

Ellie sat as straight as she could in the chair and smoothed her gown over very inadequate breasts. "While you're confusing the O'Malleys, I'll try to do the same with him. I know I'm not . . . well endowed, but you said yourself size wasn't important."

"We were talking about the size of men," Green said.

"The O'Malley twins are not very tall, that's true, but the nephew must be close to six feet."

"And we weren't talking about height," Purple said. She glanced at her sister, then back at Ellie. "Never mind, honey. I reckon you'll find out soon enough. Especially if you're intent on seduction."

"What makes you think we can do what you want?" Green said. "There's lots of women younger and prettier than us. There's those that say we're shopworn. Now don't look at me that way, sister, you know it's the truth."

Ellie thought over her answer carefully. "They've got a reputation for liking the ladies even more than gambling and hard liquor. There are card games where they're going, I suppose, and liquor, too. But women are in short supply."

"Not much competition, is that it?"

"I didn't mean it as an insult. Here in New Orleans, Cal Hardin would never give me a second look. I've never seen so many beauties in my life."

But he had given her a second look, and a third, at the cemetery. Curiosity, that was all. She had been covered from head to toe in black. Once she stripped—that was, once he got a look at her in regular clothes, he would lose interest fast enough.

Even in the wilderness where he was headed.

But now was not the time to exhibit self-doubt.

"As I mentioned a moment ago, this is a business proposition. I'll pay you well to act as my chaperones."

"We don't need the money," Purple said with pride. "Those Mississippi farmers knew how to show their appreciation for a job well done."

"Not to mention the ones just passing through," Green said. "Give me a traveling man to know how to have a good time."

Both women seemed lost in reverie, and Ellie feared she was losing their interest.

"It's my guess you're bored," she said. "Women of your experience"—she chose her words carefully—"women used to being appreciated by a variety of men, must hate spending so many hours remembering."

The Dollarhides studied her a moment, then put their heads together and began to whisper.

Ellie took a deep breath. She had either insulted them beyond all redemption, or she had assessed them accurately. In truth, she had no idea exactly how they had passed their days, or how they were passing them now. If Aunt Abigail knew she was even in the same room with them, she would be digging her way out of her grave.

Ellie was a Southern lady, born and bred. But Virginia was a long way away. If she had her wishes, the way would get even longer.

The two redheads separated.

"Let's say we're interested," Purple said. "Just where is this land where there are few women and even two broken-down old whores can catch a man?"

"I didn't say you're broken down. You're very

handsome. And you know it. So stop asking for compliments."

"Blunt, ain't you, honey?"

"It's my besetting sin. That's what Aunt Abigail always said."

"Not a sin in the least. We can't stand all the pussyfooting around most women think is charming. But you ain't answered the question. Where is the land you want so bad?"

"Texas."

"Texas!" Both sisters exploded at once.

Green patted her hair. "They scalp women in Texas."

"And cut off their titties," Purple put in as she hugged herself.

"Oh," Ellie said. Here was a detail of Texas life she hadn't known.

"I'm a good shot," she said. "We can go armed."

"Humph," the Dollarhides said in unison.

"It'll be exciting," said Ellie. "And I need you. If you don't go with me, I'll have to go alone."

"It's a stupid thing to do. I splotch in the sun," one said.

"We're indoor girls," her sister put in. "From what I hear, Texas is all outdoors."

"I can't promise it will be easy. If you're not up to the challenge, I'll just look for someone else. Or, as I said, go alone."

Ellie knew there could be no one in all the world as perfect as the Dollarhides, but she didn't think flattery would win them over, not with their scalps and important body parts in jeopardy.

They might not like being called cowards, however.

41

Evelyn Rogers

Again the heads went together and whispering commenced, while Ellie sat quietly, trying to look helpless and confident at the same time.

At last the heads parted.

"I'm Gertrude," Green said, "and this here's Mayveen. Call us a couple of fools, but if you're willing to take the risk, I guess we are too."

Ellie sighed in relief. "Mayveen and Gertrude Dollarhide, thanks more than I can ever say."

"Gert and May, that's us. No thanks needed. You'll pay us. We don't come cheap. And we have one more request, Miss Chase. We'd like our hair attached to our heads when we return."

"Call me Ellie, please. I'll do the best I can with the hair and"—she took a deep breath, putting herself in the mood of the occasion—"with the titties."

Gert opened her purse and pulled out a cigar, offering one to May. They were soon puffing away. Staring through the smoke, she said, "Let's get down to particulars, Ellie. It's gonna take a while to pack."

Chapter Three

Two weeks later Ellie and the Dollarhide sisters stood on the deck of the schooner *Valiant Voyager* as it sailed into the choppy waters of Texas's Lavaca Bay. Their destination ashore lay a little more than fifty miles to the northwest, halfway to the town of San Antonio.

Ellie's scant knowledge of Texas included a few details about the battle at a San Antonio mission called the Alamo and the location of the land her father had bought and lost.

According to one of the sailors, it lay near a settlement called Glory. He claimed to know little about the place except that he would guess it had been misnamed.

"Texians got a strange sense of humor, miss," he had declared. "Sure hope you aren't planning on going there."

Ellie had given him her best enigmatic smile. Regardless of what Glory looked like, if it was where she avenged her father, everything about it would be glorious indeed.

The sailing had been smooth; right away she had taken to the brisk sea air and the rhythmic roll of the ship. Gert and May had not been quite so sanguine about riding the waves, but they kept their food down mainly, they swore, by smoking cigars.

Despite their serious purpose, with the sunlight sparkling on the water and a cloudless blue sky stretching overhead, they arrived in a cheerful, confident state of mind. How could they not be cheerful and confident on such a beautiful day?

As the *Valiant Voyager* slipped deeper into the bay and anchored offshore, they got their first look at what had once been the thriving port of Linnville. Blinking twice to make sure of what she saw, Ellie felt her blood run cold.

On the first day out of New Orleans, the captain had described a pretty seaside town. But they were staring at a lone building that stood amidst burned-out ruins. The smoke from the fires was gone, but from the *Voyager's* deck they could see sadness and death hanging like a dark cloud over the destruction. There was nothing pretty in sadness and death.

The confidence and cheer died. So, too, did the laughter of the passengers crowded on deck and the chatter that had drowned out the caw of the circling gulls. Only the slap of water against the *Voyager's* hull and the snap of the schooner's sails broke the sudden silence as all eyes turned to the scene ashore.

"Damnation," said one of the mates standing close to Ellie and the Dollarhides.

"May God have mercy on us all," another added in a more reverent tone.

Mercy indeed, thought Ellie as she stared at the lifeless ruins, her vision blurred by tears. She had never known a town could die. Everything about the scene suggested it hadn't been a natural death. Like Henry Chase, Linnville had been killed.

Several small craft took the passengers ashore. In their somber cloaks and dark dresses, both necessary for the roles they had assumed, Gert and May trod first on what had been a busy dock. Now the warehouses were gone, and only a few men worked desultorily at clearing the debris.

"We're trying to get this back the way it was," one of the laborers said as the passengers and crew made their way from the boats. His work clothes and face were smudged with soot, and skin showed through the tears in his worn leather gloves. "Don't got much hope."

"You're Tom Higgins, aren't you?" the captain asked. "You sailed with me once." He looked beyond the workman. "What happened?"

Tom spat in the dirt. "Comanches."

Gert hugged herself, and May stared in horror around her. Ellie stood beside them, unmoving, her hands dangling limp at her sides as the men talked.

"When?" the captain asked.

"Last August. They rode down from the north

the way they like to do. Came through Victoria, killing and stealing, taking cattle and horses wherever they found 'em, but it was here they commenced to burning."

Another workman joined them, and the passengers and crew of the *Voyager* gathered round.

"Some claim it was vengeance they was seeking," the second man said. "For the killing at San Antonio a few months back. Rangers took down some chiefs that'd gone back on their word about releasing whites they'd been holding captive. Others say they were put up to it by the Mexicans wanting to take over again."

Tom shook his head in disgust. "Now, Daniel, the why of it don't matter much, 'pears to me. Linnville was a right nice place to live. Not no more."

Ellie could hold her silence no longer. "Were many lives lost?" she asked, death being uppermost in her mind.

"Counting those killed at Victoria, upwards of twenty-three, I heard. Most folks made it to boats out in the bay. They got to watch the looting and the burning and all the whooping going on. There was a lot of wailing out on those ships, I can tell you. They lost just about everything they had."

"Least they kept their lives," Daniel said. "Poor old Hugh Watts—he was the customs man hereabouts—stayed back to get his watch. Pure gold, and he was right proud of it. What he got was an arrow in the chest. Corset saved his wife from dying the same way. Always thought those contraptions was pure foolishness. Ain't so sure now."

Ellie looked at Gert and May and saw the horror in their eyes. It must be equally strong in her own expression, but she kept her eyes on them and her chin high, trying to be brave, grateful they couldn't see the shaking of her knees.

For all her determination, and the anger and hurt in her heart, during the sailing the journey had taken on an almost festive air. Now only the anger and hurt remained. This was a dangerous business she had undertaken. She must never forget it again.

"Will they be back?" asked another passenger, a hardware salesman from Tennessee who had spent much of the voyage on deck swaggering around Gert and May. Right now he was blinking his narrow eyes and pulling at his beard, and his voice came out no better than a squeak.

Tom tugged his trousers up an inch. "Not likely. We whupped 'em good up north of here, place called Plum Creek. They skedaddled clear out of the county. They're somebody else's problem now."

"This Plum Creek," said Ellie. "Is it near Glory?"

"It's up a good ways. Far as I know, Glory wasn't hit. Hard to tell if it was. It ain't much of a town."

Listening in silence, Gert and May backed away from the crowd, their heads bent close as they conferred with one another. Ellie gave them a moment of privacy, needing a moment herself to gather her own thoughts. All the beauty of the day was nothing compared to the ugliness that the sun shone upon here in the inlet of Lavaca Bay.

She came to a decision fast. She must do what had to be done.

With a nod of her head, she motioned the women down one of the deserted Linnville streets, out of earshot from the others. Wind off the water molded her skirts against her legs as she walked; behind her the schooner creaked and rocked in the choppy bay water. A gust hit her so strongly, it almost knocked her over. For the first time in her life she wished she were a man.

Someone as tall and strong as Callaghan Hardin—and just as unfeeling.

Turning to face the Dollarhide sisters, she took the wind full force against her face. She held her ground.

"You've done all I asked," she said, "and more. We're all using my mother's maiden name, you're wearing the clothes I bought, you haven't slipped once with cursing, and you've been very discreet with the cigars. Everyone thinks you're my maiden aunts serving as chaperones until I meet my fiancé. Miss Gertrude and Miss Mayveen Davenport, two spinster gentle ladies from a small plantation outside Baton Rouge. That's who you say you are and who can doubt it?"

Gert and May nodded, but neither spoke.

Now came the hard part.

"When the *Valiant Voyager* sets sail in a few days, I want you both on board. I'll pay you in full the amount we agreed upon. But I cannot ask you to go farther than this wretched town."

Neither sister spoke for a moment.

"You planning on being with us on that ship?" Gert asked.

"No."

"That's what we figured," said May.

Ellie's heart sank. They had already decided to leave. Her offer to pay them just made it official. Selfish person that she was, despite her most honorable intentions, she had held a small hope that they wouldn't go.

Gert pushed a bright red curl in place beneath her severe gray bonnet. "So what you're saying is, you're going to take off on your own while we hurry back to our safe little New Orleans abode. Ain't that what it sounds like to you, May?"

"Exactly what it sounds like."

"But—" Ellie began.

"We figured you'd come up with something like this," said Gert. "At first we decided to put it to you this way: you go, we go; you stay, we stay. But that would be putting pressure on you to do something you probably wouldn't want to do. You got a lot of self-sacrifice in you, girlie. Too much by far."

"Damned if you don't," said May. "And don't you two go to looking at me like I done something wrong. I've been holding back on the cussing for almost two weeks now. I got a pile of *damns* dammed up in me. Best to get rid of 'em when it's just us girls."

Ellie tried again. "But—"

"This is the proposition as we see it," said Gert, laying out a gloved hand and slapping it with the other to make her points. "You do what you think you have to do. Go or stay. As for us, we're staying. That man down there at the water already said the Indians have been run out of these parts.

49

Trusting souls that we are"—here Gert's eyes twinkled—"we believe him."

Ellie was certain the twinkle was covering up fear. The Dollarhides weren't stupid. They must be terrified.

At the same time, she felt a weight lift from her heart. They were wrong about her being self-sacrificing; right now she was the most selfish person she knew.

She really should be more assertive and demand that they leave. She really should.

"What we truly want," said May, giving her no chance to speak, "is a chance at those lying, murderous O'Malley boys. We know a trick or two about catching men. By the time we get to 'em, what with the scarcity of women in this pitiful country, they'll be ripe for the picking. We'll get that title for you quicker than I can get out of this corset you forced on me."

"Don't forget that fellow's wife. Corset saved her from an arrow, ain't that what we heard?"

"I'm not sure living's worth it if we've got to get trussed up like this every day."

They spoke as though underclothing were the most important matter on their minds.

Ellie could contain herself no longer. She threw herself into Gert's arms, and then into May's, giving them both the grandest hug she could manage. Backing away, she couldn't bring herself to look either of them in the eye. She had no right to be so joyous over the danger into which they had placed themselves.

Her joy was short-lived.

"What you've got to do," said the ever-practical

Gert, "is keep that rascally nephew occupied so we can work without interference."

Ellie nodded dumbly as she looked at the devastation around her, at the fallen buildings, the deserted streets. She had never heard the war cries of an Indian brave nor the wailing of souls in agony, but she could imagine them. Her sympathy went out to all the victims of the raid and even to the Indian chiefs who had been killed in San Antonio.

But she saved a portion of her pity for herself. In her heart she had feared her part in the plan would come to this. Cal Hardin was obviously a worldly man, tall, long-limbed, and darkly handsome, his face too long for its leanness, giving him a wolfish look. Everything about him exuded confidence, even his easy, graceful walk. Despite his grace, he had a way about him that made people step out of his path.

It was strange how she had noticed so much about him in such a short while, and stranger still how the details had stayed in her mind. No matter how devilish or wolfish or whatever he was, he was not without appeal. How she was to occupy the attention of a man like him was beyond her imagination.

The challenge was certainly beyond her limited charms.

" 'Tis not paradise we've come to, lads." Finbar O'Malley stretched his short legs beneath the saloon table and finished off his glass of whiskey. "Texas," he concluded, "is hell."

It was a sentiment the O'Malleys had expressed

more than once since getting a first look at their new home two weeks before: the cabin looted, stock rustled, fields unplowed.

"We've not seen a woman since we got here," his brother Fitzgerald said, as if that were the worst of their worries.

"At least not one that's unattached," Fin said.

"Gentlemen, I correct you."

Sitting between his uncles, Cal didn't bother to look over his shoulder at the speaker. It was just Sir Simon spouting off again. This was their second visit to the saloon during their short time in Texas. The first had been on their way to Goliad to buy replacement furniture for the cabin. Today, they were on their way back to the cabin with their purchases. Both times Simon Pence had occupied the same chair.

"There's the shopkeeper's daughter," the Englishman added.

He spoke in his usual laconic way, but there was a not-quite-hidden edge to his voice that Cal picked up on, as if Sir Simon were testing the O'Malleys in some way.

Fitz couldn't resist a rejoinder. "I meant one with some flesh on her. Something for a man to hold."

"Ah," Sir Simon said, "you value your women by the stone, I fear. Forgive me, by the pound. I forget where I am."

"Wish I could," muttered Fitz, so low that Cal almost missed his words. Following his brother's action, he drank the last of his whiskey and signaled for the bartender to bring another round.

Service being what it was in Glory's lone saloon, the bartender kept on staring into empty air, picking at his teeth with a splinter of wood. He owned the place. He worked when he chose.

"We've got a wagonload of goods waiting on us," Cal said, hinting that his uncles should let the liquor alone. They didn't respond, and he let it go. When was he ever anybody's conscience? He wasn't even his own.

A week, two at the most. That's how long he gave them to give up their dream of owning a Texas estate. Estates didn't exist in this godforsaken country. They were learning the facts for themselves, from the drifters, peddlars and homeless immigrants who crowded the roads that ran closest to their isolated cabin.

Cal looked around the dingy saloon with its scarred tables and counter, bare walls, sullen owner and a dozen disreputable patrons, a couple of them drunk, not a one without a gun strapped to his waist.

Except for Sir Simon. English gentleman through and through, he probably carried a lethal little pistol tucked inside his frock coat. How he had gotten here, and why, Cal couldn't guess and didn't want to know.

The best that could be said for the place was that none of the guns had been turned on the O'Malley twins, at least not yet. Cal figured that was beginning to matter less and less. A gambling man, he would bet anyone in the room that before the week was out his uncles would be making plans to sell the Double T and be gone, leaving all of Texas in their dusty wake.

"I'd give an acre of prime grassland to see a

handsome woman swish through that door," said Fin, who was never one to give up a subject without talking it to death.

"I'd throw in an acre from me half," Fitz said, "to see the same."

"Aye. I'm partial to redheads meself, being from Ireland and all, but I'm not unbending, you understand."

The sound of wagon wheels crunching against hard dirt drifted through the swinging doors; they came to a halt right outside.

"Perhaps your wishes have been granted," Sir Simon said. "Even now a voluptuous, fiery-haired temptress is descending from her carriage—"

He stopped as the swinging doors parted and a voluptuous, fiery-haired temptress walked inside. A mature temptress, Cal amended, her crimson hair peeking out in curls from beneath a plain gray bonnet, her voluptuousness covered by a dowdy gray cloak.

Youth had left her several decades before, but not, he suspected, her feminine wiles.

Reared to be a gentleman, he pulled himself to his feet. His uncles scrambled to imitate him, and one by one the other patrons did the same, more than one chair falling backward in the process. No one bothered to speak, not even a cuss word, which was uncommon indeed.

"Excuse me, kind sirs," the woman said, slowly drawing out each word, "we're in need of assistance." Unlike her speech, her search of the room was not in the least slow. Her eyes settled on Cal, but she spared a small smile for his uncles first.

"My niece has taken ill. She needs a place to lie down as soon as possible."

Instinct, tempered by experience, warned Cal not to respond. There was no need, with the way the rest of the men were hurrying toward the door. Even Simon had managed to stir.

She stopped them with the raising of one hand. Her eyes remained on Cal.

"You, sir, seem to be the cleanest-shaven of the lot, and I suspect, the most recently bathed. You also appear to be the most physically fit. Would you please help? I wouldn't want my niece to rise from her faint and take a fright."

"Our nephew'll give you all the assistance you'll be wanting," Fin said.

"We'll be right there by his side," Fitz said.

"You do relieve my mind," the woman said as she turned and walked back through the doors.

Cal tamped down his suspicions. Whatever was going on here at least relieved the boredom. With uncles and gamblers, Englishman and bartender trailing, he went outside to investigate.

Another mature temptress, much like the first, sat high on a rickety wagon seat, her arm supporting what appeared to be a child. It was hard to tell how old the child might be, what with the full cloak and bonnet covering her.

The back of the wagon was filled with trunks, and in the front a sway-backed draft horse hung his head low, nibbling at a lone stalk of grass growing out of the dirt road.

"I'm Miss Gertrude Davenport," the first temptress said, "and this is my older sister Miss Mayveen Davenport. She's caring for our precious

Eleanor, the daughter of our only brother, may he rest in peace."

Miss Mayveen grimaced at the *older* comment, Cal noticed, figuring he shouldn't miss a clue. They were telling too much about themselves. Generally that meant the telling was a lie.

He pulled himself up onto the seat beside the precious Eleanor. Miss Mayveen practically thrust her niece into his arms, then dropped unceremoniously to the ground on the wagon's far side.

"Could you lift her from this abominable conveyance?" Miss Mayveen said, batting her eyes up at him. "I'm sure once she gets solid ground beneath her feet, she will come around."

Miss Mayveen spoke as slowly as her sister, as if the two were having to consider every word. Stepping carefully around the muck and manure in the street, she joined Miss Gertrude on the rickety wooden sidewalk.

Pushing her bonnet back, Cal got a look at Eleanor's face. High cheeks, full lips, wide-set eyes thick-lashed, she looked like anything but a child. He took a moment to study her, liking what he saw. He might be an unfeeling cad, but he was human, too.

Putting one arm around her shoulders, he tried to put the other beneath her legs to lift her. She was as stiff as a board.

He leaned close to whisper, "Have you ever fainted? You're supposed to be limp."

One eye cocked open. Brown with long, thick lashes. The eye closed fast and the body fell limp. Too much so. The woman was small and she was wearing what seemed to be a steel corset, but as she draped herself against him he could feel an ample supply of soft curves.

She was definitely not a child.

Parts of him reacted, parts far from his mind. For once he was in agreement with his uncles. He had been away from women too long.

With little effort, he lifted her down, continuing to hold her after he was standing once again in front of the saloon. But she was having none of his embrace. In an exhibition of remarkable recovery, she shoved herself away and fell from his arms, landing on her feet with admirable agility, standing without so much as a single sway.

She was supple, he gave her that. Suppleness was a feminine trait he always admired.

He got a good look at both eyes. Both were brown, both long-lashed, both glaring at him. He was glad they matched. She wasn't a beauty, but she was close.

Fin and Fitz hurried to her side, but one glance from those eyes and they backed away.

"If you'll point me to whatever lodging is available," she said, tugging her feathered little bonnet in place over wisps of yellow hair, "I'm certain I'll be all right."

The uncles stepped forward, stumbling over themselves to apologize for Glory's only hotel.

Miss Gertrude Davenport smiled, and they both fell mute. "I'm certain it will be fine. We are not shrinking violets, sir, despite our genteel upbringing."

"Surely this establishment cannot be half so bad as you say," Miss Mayveen Davenport added.

The twins gestured for them to proceed down the uneven walkway that led to the Glory Hotel, and the entourage took off without Cal.

Miss Eleanor Davenport spared one glance over her shoulder at him. It was not a look of gratitude.

The look was like a dash of cold water. Cal had been right to regard the arrival with suspicion. He had never seen the aunts before, but he was certain he knew their niece. He didn't know where or when they had met or under what circumstances, but she was not a stranger to him.

Their acquaintance had not been intimate. That was the only fact he knew for sure.

Three women riding alone into a rough frontier town, feigning a problem they didn't have, stopping at the saloon for help instead of at the general store, speaking and acting boldly, showing no fear—something was definitely going on.

Something that involved him. Miss Gertrude Davenport had singled him out right away. He doubted it was because he came the closest to being clean.

Long after the others had returned to the saloon, he stood outside and tried to remember who the hell Miss Eleanor Davenport could be.

Chapter Four

"Hardin wasn't trying anything, was he?" asked Gert.

"You must've forgot the part about clinging to him," said May. "Remember? You were supposed to act like a pack of mad dogs was snapping at your skirts and he was your only hope of salvation."

The two were coming at Ellie from both sides, even while they stripped the bed in the room they were to share. They were at the back of the small hotel's second floor, which they claimed would be the safest place to stay. Women traveling alone, no matter their past lives, couldn't be too careful.

"What do you mean, *trying anything*?" Ellie asked. She was busy taking a few belongings from her horsehair trunk, shaking out the wrinkles, trying to concentrate on unpacking only the essentials, trying to forget being held in her enemy's arms.

But her ersatz aunts were determined to bring up every detail. They had already discussed how the O'Malleys didn't look like thieves or murderers, with Gert pointing out that the innocent-looking ones were the worst kind. Now they had moved on to Cal Hardin, who didn't look innocent of anything.

The sisters stared at one another across the bare, stained mattress. Their full figures were clad in similar throat-high gray dresses, exactly what maiden aunts would wear, but nothing short of black paint and masks could mute the color of their hair or the knowing look in their thick-lashed eyes.

"We got us a lambkin here," Gert said.

"The question is, do we lead her along slow or do we tell her the way of things?" May said.

"You may as well tell me," said Ellie, knowing they would anyway. Aunt Abigail had given her lessons in life about what made people behave as they did, but she knew the Dollarhides had different lessons in mind.

Gert shrugged, then groaned, massaging the small of her back. They had been two days in the wagon bought outside of the former Linnville, one day getting from the coast to the county seat of Victoria, including a harrowing ferry ride across the Guadalupe River, another bouncing along the road to Glory. The farmer they dealt with hadn't mentioned that the wagon had no springs and the horse could get up speed only when moving downhill.

Aunt Abigail would have said he was no better than a thief.

"Was Hardin rubbing his hands anywhere private?" Gert asked. "On you, not on him. He ain't the type to grab hold of himself, especially with a woman in his arms."

"Of course not," Ellie said, refusing to ask the questions that popped into her mind.

"I suspect he was rubbing you up against him then. He was holding you close enough, but I didn't see any foolishness going on."

"Careful what you call it, Gert. We made us a fine living with such carryings on. Most of the time it didn't seem foolish at all."

"You're right there. I was trying to go at the problem like a real aunt."

Ellie thought of Cal Hardin's solid body and of the practiced ease with which he'd held her. Foolish was not a word that came to mind.

Gert threw open the hotel room's only window and tossed the sheets outside.

"Burning's too good for 'em. We've got to get us some fresh linens. Ladies like us're too sensitive for anything less." She fumbled in the pocket of the cloak hanging from the bedpost, pulled out a cigar, and fired up.

Ellie looked at the mattress, at the bare walls, at the curtainless window. Unlike the inn where they had stayed on the road, at least the hotel's windows had glass panes instead of strips of cowhide to hold out the cool November wind. Or the panes would hold it out once the room was aired and Gert finished her cigar.

"I'll go down and see if I can't get us a few necessaries. Like soap and a pitcher of water and some clean sheets," May said.

"Throw in a chamber pot," said Gert. "I can see the outhouse from here. It's a good walk and the wind's picking up." She sniffed. "Blowing the other way. We better hope it stays that way."

May left, and Ellie sat gingerly at the edge of the bed, the skirt of her yellow gown billowing around her. The gown wasn't practical for the road, but the sisters had insisted she wear something feminine. The yellow silk, with its low neck and fitted bosom, was as feminine as she could get.

Under the circumstances she would have preferred black. She thought of her Papa and how he was lost to her, and she looked at Gert. The women were taking all this discomfort in great style, making jokes, pretending they didn't ache from head to toe. She must give them all the cooperation and the honesty that she could.

"I know men like to touch women. I'm not stupid. As a matter of fact, I'm engaged to be wed."

"You got you a sweetie?"

"I've got a fiancé waiting for me back in Virginia."

"It ain't always the same thing. How old are you?"

"Twenty-four."

"You don't look it."

"It's my size," Ellie said in disgust.

"Nothing wrong with the size of your body. You just need to learn how to use it."

Ellie knew that sooner or later she would be told exactly what Gert had in mind.

"I know you're wondering how I got to be a spinster," she said. "My engagement to Bertrand Randolph was arranged by Aunt Abigail a long time ago. We just never got around to the ceremony. When she was dying, I promised her I'd go through with it."

"You don't sound too eager."

Ellie went on to explain how Mr. Randolph's farm adjoined hers, how he was sixteen years older than she, a widower with a brood of six boys, how she had always wanted a large family and now she was to have one.

As she spoke, she avoided Gert's knowing eye.

Gert took a puff and blew the smoke outside. "You two done any touching?"

"He kissed me once. On the cheek. He said something about kissing me elsewhere, but Aunt Abigail walked into the room and he swore he was getting a speck out of my eye."

"You liked the kiss?"

"It was wet. I had to fight not to wipe my face."

Another puff. "I'll bet if Cal Hardin gave you a wet kiss, you wouldn't wipe it off."

Ellie thought of the arrogant way he had instructed her to go limp. He had known she was pretending. That gave him power over her, a situation she couldn't endure.

"I wouldn't bother wiping off his kiss. I'd shoot him instead. I know how. My uncle taught me. Before he took to his bed, we used to ride and shoot together. He said a woman needed many skills if she was going to get by."

"Kissing's one of 'em," said Gert, but Ellie ignored her. To prove she could do what she threatened, she went to the cloak she had hung on a peg, reached into the inside folds, and pulled out a small pistol, a pepperbox she had owned for a couple of years.

Gert choked. "That thing loaded?"

"No, but I've got the cartridges put away where I can get to them." She patted her bosom. "A corset ought to be good for holding something in."

"Shooting seems maybe a little drastic. If you're planning on keeping him occupied, that is, while we get the deed."

"It would keep him occupied, all right."

"It could also get you hung. I don't know the laws in Texas, not sure they have any, but killing's usually a hanging offense."

"Not if I were defending my honor."

"Honor ain't necessarily something you want to defend. And don't look at me like that. Cal Hardin is probably the rascal you think he is—most men are—but he's not without his uses."

Ellie wasn't sure she wanted to know what Gert meant. Just then May burst into the room, and she had no chance to ask.

"We got gentlemen callers," May said. "The O'Malley brothers are asking us if we care to dine. It seems there is only one small establishment that offers meals to travelers. It's too dangerous for ladies like us to go unescorted."

"I'm not so sure about that," Gert said, pitching her cigar out the window. "Ellie here has a gun."

May frowned and shook her head, then stepped aside to allow the O'Malley twins to enter the room. They were carrying the supplies that May had gone after. The chamber pot rested indelicately on top of the sheets.

The O'Malleys, no taller than the Dollarhides and outweighed by fifty pounds, were dressed in black suits, with high white collars pinching their necks, their red hair slicked back with thick pomade, string ties at their throats. They were grinning from ear to ear.

Ellie turned and stifled a cry. On the street in front of the saloon, she hadn't been up close to the cowardly thieves, hadn't got a good look at them. But they were close now. She could hardly stand to be in the same room with them.

Gert guided her to the window and stroked her back. "She's still a bit puny. We best not leave."

"No," Ellie managed. "You go on and eat. I'm not hungry. I'll stay here and rest."

The sisters put up a good show of protest, but in the end they left with the two brothers and Ellie was left to compose herself.

She finished making the bed, but sleep was beyond her. With twilight coming on, she grabbed her cloak, patted her corset to make sure her ammunition was readily available, then went downstairs. She slipped out of the hotel without being seen by the dozing clerk.

Glory's main street was deserted, except for a few horses, a wagon in front of the saloon and another in front of the general store. She turned her steps to the stable where they had left the draft horse. Her plan was to rent or, if necessary, buy a smooth-gaited horse. She would do almost anything to keep from getting in that wagon again.

A shadow moved in front of her path. A man. With a start she looked up into the eyes of her enemy.

"My apologies, Miss Davenport. I didn't mean to startle you."

The voice was deep and low and unfortunately familiar. It also sounded not in the least apologetic.

. . . if Cal Hardin gave you a wet kiss, you wouldn't wipe it off. . . .

Where in the world did that thought come from? She could hear Gert saying it now.

She took a backward step. Like the O'Malleys, her accoster was dressed in black, but there was so much more of him, at least in height. He loomed before her like the night.

"You didn't join your uncles for dinner?"

"How did you know they were my uncles?"

His question startled her almost as much as his presence. For a reason she couldn't imagine, Hardin was viewing her with suspicion, as if she were doing something wrong.

Maybe it was the fake faint. He had to wonder about that.

Her mind raced. She looked at the street, at the sky, at the walkway, anywhere but into his remarkable blue eyes.

"My aunts must have told me. I really don't remember."

She sounded stupid. But that was all right. Aunt Abigail had told her men didn't care for women who were smart.

"Of course," he said. "I didn't intend to startle you with the question."

She had the feeling that startling her had been precisely his intent.

"If you will excuse me," she said, trying to step around him. He gave her no ground.

"Please, Mr.—"

She paused, giving him a chance to introduce himself. She didn't want to make any mistakes again.

"Hardin."

"Mr. Hardin, I really must be on my way."

"To where?"

"The stable," she said before she could think. Her destination was really none of his business, and he was impolite to ask.

"I'll escort you. I'm not certain a lady is safe alone on the street."

If a lady was not safe, it was because of men like Cal Hardin, but Ellie was in no position to tell him so.

"Thank you, Mr. Hardin. You and your uncles are being most kind."

She had meant to sound gracious and demure, but the words came out with a sharp edge. He noticed. She saw it in his sidelong glance.

He fell into step beside her, taking his place between her and the street. A horseman rode by, gave them a curious glance, then galloped on. Otherwise, they were alone. Shadows were falling across the storefronts and in the distance the sky was purpled by the setting sun.

At such a time, Glory did not seem so bad.

But Cal Hardin seemed worse—taller, darker, more intimidating than ever.

Evelyn Rogers

"Tell me, Miss Davenport, what brings you and your aunts to Glory?"

The question was innocent enough, the sort of inquiry anyone might make. Ellie steadied herself, ready with her response.

"A wedding, Mr. Hardin. I hope to get married here."

"You're looking for a man? I imagine there are a few eligible bachelors around."

So much for innocent inquiries. Rascals were never innocent for long.

"I already have a man," she said with indignation. "A man I've known for years."

"My misfortune," he said. As if he would ever have been interested in a serious alliance between them.

"I was originally supposed to accompany him to Texas, but I was detained because of an illness in the family."

"Nothing serious, I hope."

As if he cared. He questioned her because he was curious, that was all, and naturally cautious. And she was the only female around.

"My father died." The catch in her voice was genuine. She couldn't lie all the time.

He murmured something about being sorry, but she was in no mood to take any sympathy from the likes of him. Besides, he neither sounded nor appeared the least bit sympathetic. Cal Hardin was a cold, hard man whose smooth manners covered the lack of a heart.

"Are your parents still alive, Mr. Hardin?"

"No."

She waited for him to describe his mother's re-

68

cent death and reveal something about his father. She had no idea who had sired the man, but she knew it had to be a devil like him.

"Where are you to meet this fiancé?" he asked instead.

Ellie smiled to herself. She now possessed another fact about him: he did not like to talk about himself.

"We were to meet here in Glory. He had money to buy land. It's long been his dream, and he liked the name of the town." She frowned. "I hope nothing has happened to him."

"He knew you would be traveling with only two women as your companions? Into Texas?"

"Bertrand is a bit impulsive."

The real Bertrand was about as far from impulsive as a man could get. They had, after all, been engaged for four years.

"He wanted to leave right away, but I couldn't manage to go so quickly. I assured him it would be all right."

Hardin was giving her far too many sidelong glances. She should have put on a decent bonnet instead of the silly little hat the Dollarhides preferred. That way her expression couldn't be seen so easily.

"We're almost at the stable," she said. "Thank you for the company, but as you can see, I was quite safe."

He made no move to leave. She considered pulling out her gun and ordering him away, but Gert and May would not approve. She was supposed to charm him into doing her bidding. They refused to believe that approach would never work.

He stayed close by while she made arrangements for a ride in the early morning. Luckily the stable hand was able to come up with a sidesaddle and a mare that would give her a good ride.

"You're going looking for Bertrand?" her unwanted companion asked when they were on their way back to the hotel.

"Bertrand will find me," she said.

"Unless something has happened to him."

"That's a terrible thing to say," she snapped, trying hard to look worried. With Cal Hardin standing so close, it wasn't difficult.

"Where are you and your fiancé from?"

"Virginia."

"Have you ever been in New Orleans?"

Her heart leapt to her throat. "Why do you ask?"

"Virginia is a long way from Texas. I thought you might have stopped there on your journey."

Ellie knew she was waiting too long to answer. She had taken to lying with surprising speed, but occasionally the details of the lies got her down.

"We changed ships, but you couldn't say I actually was in New Orleans. Is that your home?"

"I don't have a home."

His answer came so quickly, she didn't have to think about a reply.

"Everybody has a home."

"There you're wrong."

She stopped walking and looked at him, really looked at him for the first time since he had joined her outside the hotel. Twilight played across the lines of his lean face, and his eyes returned her stare with what was close to insolence. Or maybe he was daring her to argue with him.

She didn't know which was the case. She didn't care, or at least she shouldn't, but something about him stirred a feeling inside her other than anger, other than contempt, the two attitudes she was trying desperately to maintain.

"Mr. Hardin, we know nothing of each other besides the little we have allowed ourselves to reveal. Let's keep it that way."

If she had hoped to shake him, she failed.

He stepped close. "You have secrets, Miss Davenport?"

He dared to brush a tendril of hair from her cheek.

She jerked back. "Don't touch me."

"Fears, then. You have fears. Or perhaps Bertrand has spoiled you for any other man."

"You are too forward, sir."

"I've been told that before."

He took her by the wrist and pulled her into the shadows of a closed storefront. He stepped close, pinning her against the wall, not by actual pressure but by the strength that came from him along with his natural scent.

It was a man's scent, unadorned with bay rum. She had never smelled anything like it before. She closed her eyes. Lord help her, it wasn't unpleasant in the least.

"I demand you let me go," she said. "This is unconscionable."

"If you mean I'm without a conscience, you're right."

Deft fingers untied the neck of her cloak and eased the woolen cloth aside, exposing a pale throat and a pale bosom, barely visible in the early evening light. Ellie's quick intake of breath gave her more curves than she would have displayed under normal circumstances. She wondered how much he could see.

"You're a tease, Miss Davenport."

He saw too much.

"Never in my life have I been called such a thing."

"The men in Virginia must be fools to let you get away to Texas."

"I'm nothing special and you know it. You're making fun of me."

"A little."

Ellie wanted to cry. Why his words hurt, she didn't know.

"You're supposed to be protecting me," she said. "Who's to protect me from you?"

"No one, I'm afraid. Your aunts have been captured by my uncles—"

"Captured?" She felt genuine alarm, forgetting for a moment Cal Hardin's overwhelming presence.

"Not really. Fin and Fitz haven't enjoyed female companionship in weeks. Neither, I might point out, have I."

Which was why he was being so forward. It was exactly as the Dollarhides had predicted. She truly wanted to shoot him through the heart.

She decided to tell him.

"If I were a man, I would kill you."

"If you were a man, I wouldn't be with you like this."

"If you were a gentleman, you wouldn't either."

His answer was a continued stare. She wanted to squirm, but she feared that would look like an invitation of some sort.

The stare concentrated on her lips.

"Tell me, Miss Davenport, has Bertrand ever kissed you?"

It was a question she was fast growing tired of.

"A thousand times. A million. So many I lost count."

He brushed his lips against hers, stunning her into silence.

"Like that?"

He increased the pressure.

"Or that . . . or maybe . . ."

She pressed herself against the wall, not, Lord help her, to get away from him but to keep from falling in a swoon at his feet. His kiss wasn't exactly wet, but it wasn't exactly dry, either, and it was decidedly warm.

Her face flushed hot and her brain turned to mush.

"Stop," she managed, grateful to come out with a coherent word.

"I doubt if you really mean that."

She wanted to burst into tears of shame. Damn his evil soul, he was right.

She forced herself to look into his eyes. Drowning in a sea of blue, she grabbed at the first thing that came into her mind.

"How were you raised, Mr. Hardin? Did your father abuse your mother? I've heard that men who enjoy hurting women often come from such homes."

Ellie stunned herself with her harshness. The words must have originated with Aunt Abigail. Their effect was immediate. The hot, bold man who had overwhelmed her with his presence stiffened and turned cold, as if he were not made of flesh and blood, as if he were made of stone.

He stepped away.

"Forgive me, Miss Davenport. You are right. I am no gentleman."

Why she had the urge to apologize, she couldn't imagine. She hadn't been thinking straight since she'd stepped onto Texas soil.

She was busy summoning her dignity when hurried footsteps came at them from the direction of the hotel.

"Cal, is that you?" one of the uncles called out frantically.

"Praise the saints, we found you," the other one said in a matching tone.

The pair came to a halt in front of their nephew. Behind them Gert and May looked on.

"What's wrong?" he asked.

"A man rode into town not a half hour ago," Fitz said. "He spied us in the cafe."

"Walked right up to our table, he did," said Fin, "and announced to one and all that we matched the description of two desperadoes—that was the word he used, desperadoes—they were looking for back in the States."

Fitz grabbed his nephew's sleeve. "We're wanted for murder, that's what he said. They put a price on our heads, Cal. We're wanted men."

Chapter Five

Cal and his uncles spent the night on a creek bank just outside Glory, near the Victoria-to-San Antonio Road. He had slept under the stars many times; for Fin and Fitz it was a first. If they hadn't felt a rope tightening around their necks, he figured they would have complained more than they did.

Mostly they kept muttering the word *desperadoes* while they tossed and turned through the night.

The next morning they left early, the two uncles in the heavily laden wagon, Cal riding alongside on the black gelding he had bought weeks before in Victoria. At the cabin they would discuss what they were to do. Cal had a suggestion, but he knew it would take some persuading for them to agree.

They rode through countryside that Cal reluctantly admitted had potential. Rolling land hip-deep in grass and rich enough to support all the cattle and horses a man could run, provided he came up with a market for them; creeks lined with moss-draped trees and vines; endless blue skies; sweet air that carried with it the hint of the sea less than sixty miles away—all was here for a man willing to tame it.

He wasn't that man, and neither were his uncles. They needed regular doses of civilization, the way some people needed a dose of salts. They wouldn't get the civilization here. With the limited supplies available to them, they would have a hard time getting the salts.

At mid-morning their destination loomed on a far hill—a dog-run cabin, a barn and a fenced-in area for chickens.

There weren't any milk cows or horses to put in the barn, or chickens to put in the yard, or hogs to let roam free around the top of the hill. Except for a buzzard circling overhead, the only animal in sight was a mongrel dog sleeping in the passageway between the cabin's two halves. He'd shown up the first evening, acting as if he belonged. Cal didn't bother to feed or water him and he doubted his uncles thought about it. Still, the mongrel remained, looking no less healthy than he had at first glance.

Cal didn't care one way or another. Neither did the looting or the loss of the stock cause him concern. Despite the furnishings his uncles had insisted on buying, there was no way they were staying. The only problem facing them was where to go.

As soon as the horses were watered and staked out to graze, they put their efforts into unloading their purchases—two mattresses, a rickety dining table and a pair of matching benches, a horsehair sofa, a skillet and a stack of tin plates, and a bare minimum of utensils. Everything was a bare minimum. They'd been lucky to get what they had from a family who'd decided to sell out and travel farther west.

The only thing they hadn't needed was a place to sleep, the beds having been built into the cabin walls and impossible for the looters to steal. Bedlinens would have been a luxury. They were sleeping on the blankets they'd brought with them from New Orleans.

Likewise a stove was too much to expect. Cal started a fire in the fireplace and set a pot of coffee on a grate at the edge of the heat; then it was down to the real business of the day. How to put the matter to his uncles wasn't a problem. Blunt was the only way.

They were gathered in the north half of the two-part cabin, one large room that served as kitchen, dining room, and parlor. To the south, across the passageway, was the sleeping area.

On both sides of the passageway the clapboard roof was sturdy, the floors wooden, the hand-hewn log walls packed tightly enough with sticks and clay to keep out the November wind. Both halves even featured a sturdy stone fireplace and hearth. When they first got a look at the place, Fin and Fitz had talked about adding a lean-to behind each cabin half to give them extra room. For comfort, they were going to enlarge the porch across the front.

"A man could sit out on such a porch, watch the sunset and grow old with peace in his heart," Fin had said.

"The sunrise, too," Fitz had agreed, although he didn't mention how such a feat could be accomplished from the same west-facing chairs.

"If he didn't have to slop the hogs and feed the chickens, milk the cow, herd the cattle, tend the horses, and generally worry about how he was going to survive."

Cal's contribution had received nothing but scorn.

But that had been two weeks ago. They would have to listen to him now.

Slipping out of his black suit coat, he rolled his sleeves halfway up his forearms and poured them each a cup of coffee. The twins settled on the horsehair sofa, the only piece of furniture they'd bought that came close to offering comfort. Cal stood beside the stone hearth, leveling a look at them that said not only was he speaking first, for a change he was speaking the most.

"You've got two choices. You can keep on running or you can go back to New Orleans and defend yourselves."

Fin held up his shaking cup. "We've a price on our heads, m'lad. Do you have any whiskey for this?"

"After we've talked."

"You've grown harsh through the years," said Fitz.

Cal ignored the criticism. Besides, Fitz was right. Look what he had almost done to innocent Miss Eleanor Davenport last night.

Or maybe not so innocent. She came into town faking a swoon, and she had known how to defend herself with a few well-chosen words. Not to mention the fact she knew how to use a gun, or so she said.

He shook off the memory. He had enough problems without worrying about her. It could be he really did know her, as he had first suspected. He knew many women. None were important in his life.

Not like the O'Malleys.

"You didn't steal and you didn't kill," he said, turning the full force of his persuasive abilities on them. "But running made it look as if you had."

"It wasn't the rumors that put us on that ship," Fin said. "It was the shooting. Are you saying we should return as targets? The way we see it, 'tis that or be thrown into jail."

"Neither. I can set you up outside of New Orleans and start investigating what is really going on. It's what we should have done in the first place."

"We couldn't ask it of you, lad," Fitz said. "You've done so much already, and you still grieving the loss of your dear mother, rest her soul."

"We wanted our land," Fin said, more to the point. "Have you so soon forgot what it is like to want something so much your heart aches and sleep will not come?"

Both uncles looked at him with such earnestness, he was reminded of how hard it was to watch dreams die. Most of his had died when he was eight, and the rest were beaten out of him a few years later. But all that happened long ago.

He looked around the long room, at the crudely carved table and bench, the walls bare except for a couple of shelves and scattered pegs, the floor covered with only the dirt they had tracked in.

Even the lone window at the front of the cabin lacked real glass, a thin sheet of translucent rawhide filling the frame instead.

"Is this what you really want? I could swear you've been sounding disgruntled lately. Tell me if I'm wrong."

The pair fidgeted.

" 'Tis not as grand as we hoped," said Fitz.

"Grand is not a word that comes to mind when I think of Texas," Cal said. "Rugged, wild, poor, pathetic. Now those are terms I can believe. It's not a real republic, though they've got a president and congress. They issue money, too, but it's worthless. There's no law here, except for a Ranger that occasionally rides through. Glory doesn't even have a jail, and neither does Victoria, the county seat, for God's sake."

"If you're hoping to discourage us," said Fin, "you've picked a few poor points to do it."

Cal shook his head in exasperation.

Fitz looked at him slyly from the corner of his eye. "I can see why you're so quick to mention returning. You've a brother and sister there. 'Tis only right you get to know them better."

"Time is too short not to make amends," Fin said, picking up the old argument without a moment's pause. "Your own mother tried to tell you

Raymond Hardin was nay the villain you suppose."

But Cal knew that he was. He had the scars, inside and out, to prove it. For whatever reason she had chosen to deny the truth, his mother had been wrong.

"It won't work," he said.

"What in the world are you talking about?" asked Fin.

"You're not discouraging me about going back."

Fin shrugged. "We'll lay the matter to rest. For now. You've talked about running and about returning, but staying in Texas was nay one of your choices. Sure and we've sounded disenchanted, for that's exactly how we felt. But we hate to give up the land. 'Tis all we really own."

Cal knew that bringing up the fact that he had given them the New Orleans house and the saloon would get him nowhere. They thought wrongly that he had sold everything before they'd left. He hadn't had the right, even if he had wanted to. All the property was in their names.

"Then sell the Double T and buy a piece of land somewhere else," he said.

"Where are we to find a buyer? We've seen nary a soul who looked as if he had the money."

"There's Sir Simon," Fitz put in.

Fin snorted. "He's like all English, more talk than substance."

"Aye, you've got a point," Fitz said, and was about to add more when Cal waved him to silence. Someone was approaching the cabin. The dog barked once to show he agreed. Slipping a pistol in his waistband at the small of his back, he grabbed a rifle from beside the hearth and opened the front door.

His uncles watched with wide eyes.

"Are we under attack?" Fin asked.

"Has a posse come for us already?" Fitz asked.

"Saints above—" Fin began.

"Quiet," Cal said and watched a lone rider come up the rise to the house.

At the sound of hooves on the hard ground, both uncles crowded at Cal's back. The dog did not stir from his prone post.

"You've a keen sense of hearing," Fin said. "It comes from your mother's side."

"Since we don't know who our visitor is," Cal said, "why don't you two go on out and greet him for me? That way, if he's a desperado, the three of you can have a nice little chat. Talk about ways to break the law, compare your separate styles—"

"We get your point, lad," Fin said as they backed away. "No need to be sarcastic."

Cal stepped out of the house, silently watchful as the stranger reined his pinto mare to a halt. The man was not much past forty, Cal estimated, stocky with a ruddy complexion, a broad, flat face and a sharp look in his eye. Dust from the ride had settled on his dark suit and dark hat. He sat easily in the saddle, and deep lines grooved the corners of his eyes, evidence that he squinted often into the sun.

Except for a shotgun strapped to his saddle, Cal couldn't tell if he was armed.

"I mean no harm, neighbor," the stranger said as if reading his thoughts. "This is a friendly call."

Cal nodded a silent greeting.

The stranger looked at Cal's rifle. "Alden Fowler's the name. My place is next to yours, to the north."

Cal had heard the Fowler name from Simon Pence. The rancher had lost his wife and infant son years ago in a Comanche raid and pretty much kept to himself. So why was he calling now?

Dismounting, Fowler pulled off a worn leather glove and extended a hand. The men shook.

Cal introduced himself and his uncles, who were by now peering once again through the door.

Fowler nodded a greeting, then turned his sharp eyes back to Cal.

"I understand you and your uncles are settling in on the Double T," Fowler said.

Instead of answering outright, Cal asked him in for a cup of coffee. Behind him he could hear his uncles sputtering, but by the time Fowler walked up the front stoop and through the door, one was pulling down a cup from the shelf and the other had the coffee pot in his hand.

"Just the way I like it," Fowler said, accepting the cup as he dropped his hat on the table. "Thick and black."

"We could sweeten it with whiskey," Fin said.

Fowler shook his head. "I'm not a drinking man."

The uncles shook their heads in disbelief.

Fowler looked around the room. "I heard about the looting. Damned shame, that's what it is. Too many criminals are passing through these parts.

Still, I'm surprised Will sold out to you without a word of what he was up to. If he'd let his neighbors know, maybe we could have kept an eye on the place."

"Will would be the former owner?" Fin asked.

"William Gibson. One day he was here, then suddenly he was gone, heading back to Ohio with his wife and two sons, or so I was told. A few months later you men showed up."

"Was it Indians that ran him off?" Fitz said.

Fowler squinted at him. "We don't run from Indians here. Unless we're cowards. Will never seemed like a coward to me." He drank the coffee and again looked around the room. "Who actually holds title to the T?"

"We do," the uncles said in unison, and Fin added, "Cal here is helping us get set up."

"You mind telling me how you bought the place? You don't look like farmers or ranchers to me. No insult intended, understand. It's a hard life. A man has to be prepared."

"The deed was offered in New Orleans," Cal said before his uncles could answer. Any minute they would be blurting out the whole truth, at least as far as they knew it.

"Can't imagine how it got over there."

"Maybe Gibson's route took him that way."

"Of course. I should have figured it out. He sailed up the Mississippi. It would be safer for his family than traveling through Comanche country."

"I thought Texans didn't run from Indians," Fin said.

"We don't run from 'em, but we don't run into

84

a mess of 'em, either. Besides, Will isn't really a Texan, is he? Not leaving the way he did."

"You seem interested in Mr. Gibson's motivations," Cal said.

"There's reason. The truth is, I knew the man wouldn't last. As I said, it's a hard life out here. Texas isn't for everyone, as I'm sure you and your uncles will agree. I had made a generous offer to buy him out. I'm hurt he didn't accept, and puzzled, too. I was hoping you might clear up the mystery."

"If the land is so harsh," Cal said, "what keeps you here?"

"It's my home. Like most other Texans, I didn't have much before I came here. I was born to a Kentucky farmer with more children than money, working his whole life in dirt he didn't own. Here the land is mine. It's in my blood."

"We know what you mean, Alden," Fin said, warming up to him. "You got a league and a labor from the Mexicans?"

"I see you know something of our history. That was before the Alamo, of course, before San Jacinto. I'm one of the early settlers. I came here in '25."

He gave no sign anything bad had happened to him since, like losing a wife and child.

"See there, Cal," Fin said. "I told you a man could stick it out."

"You have plans to leave?" Fowler said.

"Maybe," said Cal, shooting a *keep quiet* glance at Fin and Fitz.

"I would be more than happy to make you the same offer I made Will Gibson."

"Why?"

Fowler set his cup down on the table and stared at him a moment before answering. Was he a thoughtful man, or quietly calculating? Cal couldn't decide.

"This is good land," Fowler said. "There's no use trying to lie about it. You're far too smart to believe otherwise."

Calculating for sure. The flattery gave him away.

"Good grass, fertile soil, access to water," Fowler went on. "The T is prime, but so is my place. That's why I called it Rancho Grande. Big Ranch, if you're not much on Mexican talk."

"Is it grand?"

"It's on the way. I have plans to set me up an empire. This country is going to prosper, especially when we get that sop Mirabeau Lamar out of the presidency and old Sam Houston back where he belongs. With Sam running things, a man willing to work hard, to sacrifice, to face danger can grow rich. In all honesty, Cal, when we shook I noticed your hand lacked the calluses you'll need. Perhaps you're willing to work for them. I'm guessing your uncles may not be."

"How much are you offering?"

Fowler looked at the O'Malleys. "A dollar an acre. You've got close to five thousand acres. I'm a generous man, and I want this land. I'll make it five thousand even, and I'll throw in compensation for whatever improvements you have made."

"Cash," said Cal, drawing the rancher's attention back to him.

"Cash. United States dollars. Not Republic of

Texas paper. I can tell you would be too smart for me to make such an offer, and besides, I have no intention of cheating you. I want the land."

Cal could see his uncles thinking. Alden Fowler was definitely up to something, but was it anything that would keep the deal from going through?

The truth was, he didn't care what lay behind Fowler's offer. He wanted to see the last of this place, and working hard had nothing to do with it.

He was about to start talking the when-and-where of the deal when the thinking look on the faces of both uncles changed to one of hesitation. They often came up with the same idea at the same time. What they were cogitating now did not bode well for a quick sale.

They would come around to seeing the sense of leaving. But it wouldn't be today.

He put Fowler off. "We'll talk it over and let you know," he said.

"I'll be back tomorrow," Fowler said. "Whatever objections you can come up with will be settled, I'm sure."

With that, the rancher left. Good as his word, he showed up at noon the next day for their answer. Cal had spent the intervening time with his uncles, talking and thrashing matters out. Fowler was sitting on the sofa where he had sat before and the twins were sipping coffee at the table and about to give their reluctant approval when Cal heard more company riding up.

The Double T, normally isolated, was getting

downright crowded these days. The dog didn't bother to bark.

Picking up the rifle, he went to the door. Under a flat November sun, a wagon and outrider came slowly up the rise. Cal shook his head, unsure he was seeing right. The Davenport sisters sat side by side on the wagon seat; their niece was on the horse. They came to a halt beside Alden Fowler's tethered pinto.

The aunts made quite a picture as they sat regally in the crude wagon, their flame-colored hair thrust beneath their staid bonnets. But it was the niece who got Cal's attention. She sat high and proud on her bay mare, the animal's size making her look even more delicate than she had two days before when he'd accosted her on the street.

But there was nothing delicate in the firm way she held the reins, nor in the ease with which she rode in the sidesaddle, her black riding habit gracefully draped over her legs and riding boots, her feathered bonnet waving in the breeze. Her cheeks were flushed, and her yellow hair was losing the struggle to stay in place.

She avoided his eye. Clearly she didn't want to be here. That was pretty much the way Cal felt. So why had she made the long ride? The Double T lay on an old Indian trail, far off the Victoria-to-Goliad-to-San Antonio road. Besides, all of them knew the O'Malleys were desperadoes with a price on their heads. That should have sent them fleeing the opposite way.

Cal was a naturally suspicious man. Everyone in Texas made him wonder what the hell was going on.

"Ladies," he said, keeping his eyes on Miss Davenport, "this is a surprise."

Her cheeks took on a deeper red. "It was my aunts' idea," she said.

"So you weren't just riding by."

She studied her riding gloves. "No. We asked at the store how to get here." She looked at him straight on. "You really weren't hard to find."

"We're not exactly hiding," he said.

She glanced past the cabin to the expanse of countryside. "Aren't you? It seems a perfect place."

"As you said, we weren't hard to find."

He looked at her lips, remembering the kisses they had shared. They were good kisses and they were her first, he was sure of it, which meant that anything beyond kissing that they might do with one another would be her first time, too. He'd had a few virgins throw themselves at him, but she was the first who tempted him to catch what was thrown.

Was that her purpose in riding out all this way uninvited? To throw and see what he would catch?

He reined himself back in, remembering how she had lashed out at him.

Did your father abuse your mother?

It was strange how she had unerringly chosen words that would hurt. Was it a lucky guess or prior knowledge? It had to be a guess.

Something stirred in the back of his mind, a memory, but before he could give it full attention, his uncles were out the door.

"Ladies, forgive our nephew," said Fin. "He's

89

forgot his manners. Please come inside."

"Why, thank you," Gert Davenport said. "See, Ellie, I told you they would be glad to see us." She glanced at Fowler's horse. "You've got another visitor?"

"We're having afternoon tea," said Cal, setting the rifle aside. "We were hoping for female company but had just about given up when you came by."

The sisters tittered. Their niece rolled her eyes, obviously unimpressed. He would have to work on better lies.

Fin and Fitz helped them down from the wagon, but before Cal could assist Ellie, she dropped to the ground on her own. She straightened her back, taking a moment to get her balance, but when he moved toward her, one sharp look kept him from drawing near.

"Mr. Hardin," Gert said, "would you mind unhitching our poor draft horse and seeing he gets some water? Ellie will take care of her own, but May and I have found the journey very wearying and are in need of assistance."

"What you need is some liquid refreshment," said Fin.

"We've got just the thing inside," said Fitz. "And we don't mean tea."

"We brought food," May said, "thinking you might be too distraught to think of eating. You men must keep up your strength."

The four swept inside. Cal made short work of the unhitching; then, leading both the draft horse and Fowler's pinto, he guided Ellie to the trough by the barn. With him at her left and the bay on her right, she seemed smaller than ever, the top of her bonnet waving close to his cheek.

Small and rigid. He got the feeling that if he touched her, she would crack. So maybe he ought to touch her and find out.

Standing close beside him, she studied the murky water as if she would read secrets on its surface.

"Have you heard from your beloved?" he asked.

She took a moment to answer. He could have sworn she was struggling to decide what he was talking about.

"Not yet."

"But you still have hopes. I know how much a woman needs the security of a man. Especially one who is strong although, as you said, impulsive."

"How absurd. I don't need—"

She broke off, her jaw clenched, and looked away.

"Tell me, Miss Davenport, are your aunts trying to get us alone? Or is it your idea?"

She gave him her frightened-doe look, then concentrated on stroking the bay's sweaty neck, watching the animal drink. Eleanor Davenport had a nice slant to her slender neck and an even nicer slope to her shoulders. Cal took special notice of the tendrils of fair hair tickling her nape.

Maybe she wasn't so rigid after all.

"As usual, Mr. Hardin, you are much too forward. And totally misinformed. But that's the way of men, is it not? Especially those who consider themselves strong."

He would not rise to the bait. "Cal, please. Mr.

Hardin is much too formal after all we have shared."

She glowered, her brown eyes casting off sparks. "We didn't share anything," she said. "Your interpretation of our last meeting is far different from mine."

She was lying, to him and probably to herself. Celibacy was doing crazy things to him. He wasn't sure he even liked the woman—he didn't know enough about her for that—but he wanted to kiss her again. He wanted to find out if she really tasted as good as he had thought.

He was contemplating telling her so when a gust of wind sent her bonnet flying. He hurried to retrieve it from the clump of shrubs where it was caught, taking his time walking back, watching the wind play in her fast-falling hair.

He also watched the way it forced her clothes against her body. Despite the number of women he had known in his life, the female sex always remained a mystery and a temptation. This small, feisty creature with the soft body and the hard eyes tempted him the most.

"There's hay in the barn. We can take the animals in there and you can put on your bonnet out of the wind."

He didn't wait for her approval, giving her no choice but to lead the bay after him.

Inside, the air was musty but not unpleasant. The open doors provided ample light, and toward the back of the barn broken slats in the walls let in rays from the noonday sun. When the animals were seen to, he turned to her. She had tied the bonnet back in place and tried to tuck her hair beneath its inadequate confines. The results made her look both vulnerable and enticing.

The *vulnerable* should have kept him at bay, but the *enticing* was far more appealing. Which she probably damned well knew. He had to keep reminding himself she was no innocent, except in the ways of sex. If she meant to arouse him, she was doing a fine job. But she'd aroused more than she had planned; her lying made him mean.

Cal was a man who saw connections. Did she have anything to do with the shootings in New Orleans? He couldn't figure how that could be so. Neither could he separate her from his uncles' turn of fortune in winning their land.

Fragile and tough, was she? He had to break her, to see how far she would go if he was ever to find out who she was. Baiting her with words wasn't getting him anywhere. He would have to try another approach.

He stepped close. "Ellie, we were interrupted before. Why don't we take up where we left off?"

Chapter Six

Ellie edged toward the open barn doors, putting her greatest efforts into keeping calm. Before she had gone more than a couple of feet, a gust of wind slammed the doors shut and she was left in semi-darkness with a very dangerous man.

The only thing she could think of to do was yelp.

"It's fate, Ellie," Cal Hardin said, not nearly so distressed. "Even the elements are conspiring to give us privacy."

The sound of her name on his lips caused her to shiver. She was trying her best to flirt, or at least show a semblance of cordiality, which she doubted he realized or appreciated. But the flirting was beyond her, and cordiality was scarcely the reaction he aroused in her. The man had a way about him that destroyed a woman's peace of mind.

Barely able to make out the details of his looming figure, she remembered all too well what he had looked like standing on the cabin porch, tall and lean and somehow graceful, though he scarcely moved. His open-necked shirt had been stark white against his sun-darkened skin, the muscles of his forearms exposed by the rolled-up sleeves, his flesh shadowed by dark hairs both on his arms and at his throat.

Most of all she pictured the piercing blue eyes looking at her. Wise eyes, or at least clever. No, make that wily and watchful. He knew she lied about the reason she was in Texas, and also the reason she and her "aunts" had ridden out from town. He just didn't know the why of their lies.

The mysteries surrounding her couldn't make her special to him. He probably had a host of women wanting to search him out and do him harm, so many they were a blur in his mind.

The concept helped stiffen her resolve. Underestimating her was his mistake. Somehow, some way she would bring him to his knees. She had only to get through the next few minutes, free herself of his oppressive presence, and victory would eventually be hers.

He moved closer. Her eyes adjusted to the reduced light, and she glared at him in open contempt.

"I'm carrying a gun," she said. "I'll use it if you so much as touch me."

"That's the second time you've threatened me.

I'll just have to risk it," he said without hesitation, taking another step toward her.

"Do women threaten you with shooting all the time?"

His answer was another step, which brought him dangerously close to touching her.

She backed toward the door and fumbled in the folds of her riding skirt, at last coming up with the small pepperbox she had brought with her from Virginia. She waved it in the air.

He raised his hands. "You've got me. I'm yours to do with what you will."

She aimed the gun straight at his black heart, hoping that in the dimness he couldn't see the barrel shake.

"I don't know what has you so upset," he said. "It couldn't have been the kisses."

"Little do you know. The truth is, they disgusted me."

"Liar. Besides, you don't shoot someone out of disgust. At least I never have."

"Oh," she cried. He really was a villain.

He upset her so much, she forgot the gun and her hand relaxed. In an instant he had her in his arms, the pepperbox held uselessly at her side.

"All right, big brave man," she said. She closed her eyes and lifted her lips. "Get it over with and then get out."

The world turned a couple of times on its axis before he responded.

"If you want a kiss," he said, "ask for it."

Her eyes flew open. "What?" she asked, staring at his bristled chin, not daring to look higher.

"Ask me to kiss you."

"You're insane."

"Insanely proud."

She squirmed to no avail. She got the impression that he liked it. She held herself still. "Proud of what? Your manly strength?"

His lips twitched. A smile? Fury? The man was difficult to judge.

"Proud was the wrong word. I just wanted you to ask."

"Never."

"That's a very long while, Ellie. And this is a very lonely land."

His words took her by surprise, speaking to something deep inside her, but before she could respond, he backed away, so unexpectedly that she swayed to catch her balance. When she lifted her hand to brush a wisp of hair from her forehead, her eyes focused on the forgotten gun and her jumbled feelings settled into a single humiliation.

She couldn't even shoot a man right.

"Next time, try loading it first," he said. "It makes a more convincing threat."

"How did you know—"

"You lifted it too easily for the cartridges to be in place."

Behind him, the horses shifted restlessly in their stalls. In the hay close to her left something scurried, something small and very much alive.

"Mice," he said.

"I'll load the gun and shoot them. I'm in a mood to shoot something."

The twitch turned into a very definite smile.

"I'd better leave. If you're like most women, you're a very bad shot."

"I'm not like most women."

"No, I don't believe you are."

The words were drawn out, reflective of his Southern birth, a heritage that had shown up all too seldom in their brief association. Regardless of whatever nefarious motives they might have, Southerners were invariably polite.

"Tell me, Miss Eleanor Davenport of Virginia," he added, "why are we adversaries?"

"Because—"

In her distraught state, the truth almost came out, but it was too soon for confession. The Dollarhides had not yet worked their charms on Fin and Fitz. When she told Cal Hardin who she was, she wanted to be holding the precious deed in her hand.

"I don't think you're a very good man," she said.

"There are different ways to be good."

Ellie's heart took a little twist. He was implying far more than she could interpret, but there was nothing on earth that could make her ask what he meant. No matter how much she wanted to know.

Stepping around her, he threw the barn doors open and blinding light flooded the barn. She blinked and he was gone, leaving her the choice of following after him or running away.

Right now she didn't have a choice. Tucking the gun back in its hiding place in her skirt, she followed.

When she entered the cabin, it was to a scene of domestic harmony that bordered on merriment. Gert was kneeling beside the hearth, stirring the contents of a pot at the edge of the fire, May was setting tin plates on the table, and the two desperadoes were drinking from cups obviously fortified from the bottle of whiskey in front of them. All were grinning.

A man she did not know sat on a sofa in what could only be called a disgruntled state, like someone who had stumbled into a party to which he was not invited. She felt very much the same way.

Keeping himself apart, Cal Hardin stood inside the door.

She took a moment to take in the cabin that should have been—and someday would be—hers. Once she adjusted to its plainness, she saw it had an efficient simplicity about it that suited the land on which it had been built.

She stopped herself. Who was she trying to fool? The house her father had purchased provided nothing more than the barest amenities for survival. She had begun a mental list of necessary changes when Fin and Fitz stood, their cups raised. The stranger on the sofa did likewise.

"Miss Davenport, allow me to introduce our neighboring farmer and rancher, Alden Fowler," Cal said, gesturing to the stranger. Then to Fowler he added, "Miss Davenport is here to find her wandering bridegroom. You haven't seen him by any chance, have you? I forget his name, but he's ambitious and impulsive and he's dashing enough to have caught a fair lady's eye."

Containing her irritation, Ellie gestured for the men to sit.

"Her aunts have been explaining the nature of their visit," Fowler said. "Miss Davenport, I wish you well. Texas is a vast land."

"Mr. Hardin jests at my journey," Ellie said. "It's clear he's never known love."

She dared look Cal in the eye. The look he returned mocked her. Not only had he not known love, he seemed to say, he didn't miss it in the least. She could not imagine such a man ever wanting to hold her in his arms, even if it was for no other reason than to tease.

A man who really wanted to hold a woman, and to kiss her, didn't expect her to ask.

In that moment, with everyone watching, she admitted to herself the disappointment she'd felt in the barn. She *had* wanted him to kiss her. She had wanted it very much.

Watching him, she brushed her fingers against her mouth and imagined his lips touching hers. His mocking regard turned to something far darker and hotter. She felt naked before him, all twisted inside, and not in the least ashamed.

"Would you join us, lass, in a wee nip to fight the winter wind?" Fitz said, and the moment between them was lost.

Averting her eyes, she shook her head, not trusting herself to speak.

"My uncles tend to exaggerate," Cal said. "Both the wee and the wind."

Did his voice really sound huskier than usual? Or was it just the roaring in her ears? The real wonder was that he could manage to speak. But then, he was much better at this flirting than she was.

"We're celebrating," Fin said, ignoring his nephew and concentrating on Ellie. "Your lovely aunts have assured us the situation at home is nay so bad as we were first told."

"We were about to inform our skeptical nephew of the particulars," Fitz said. "I'm sure whatever we say is no news to you."

Their voices droned on, but she was scarcely aware of what they said. Cal's silent stare shouted at her, even more than the questioning looks in the eyes of the Dollarhides. She forced herself to concentrate on the twins. They were the important ones here, not Cal.

"Our friends"—Fin smiled at Gert—"put questions to our talebearer of two evenings past. It seems we're wanted for questioning, not for committing an actual crime. And the sum offered as reward is little enough to tempt a bounty hunter. Fifty dollars for the pair of us. 'Tis almost an insult."

"But you're still wanted," Cal said.

"Aye. Should we ever visit New Orleans again, we'll be sure to visit the authorities and clear up whatever questions they have."

"You're planning to remain in Texas?" Cal asked.

Both uncles nodded.

"Our situation is looking up," Fin said. "Miss Gert and Miss May have found a place in town where they will stay while they wait for the wandering fiancé to appear. They've invited us to dine with them anytime we choose."

"Considering it's a two-hour ride, I don't imagine you will be accepting the invitation nightly.

You still have to live out here and work the land."

"In good time, nephew, in good time. Winter's coming on. We'll spend the cold months making plans."

"Hold up there," Fowler said, sitting at the edge of the sofa, his eyes hard. "I've been listening to all this without interfering, but no more. I don't know what happened in New Orleans, but I know what happened in this room not more'n an hour ago. We had an understanding. You were selling to me."

Ellie glanced in alarm at her aunts, but they still maintained beatific, pleased expressions. She couldn't imagine what they had to be pleased about. If the O'Malleys really sold out to Fowler, she would never get title to the land that she believed had cost her father his life.

"What you offer is tempting," Fin said. "Should we ever decide to sell, we will speak to you first."

But that wouldn't do at all. Ellie had to bite her tongue to keep from crying out. She looked around the room, at Fowler, then the twins, the Dollarhides, and lastly Cal. He was the only one who stared back, with that wily, watchful way that twisted her insides into a knot.

She couldn't look at him long. What was she doing in this alien land, far from everything she knew, a world away from everything that had always comforted her? There was nothing here that could give her solace, nothing save a long drink from the elusive cup of revenge.

But would it be sweet or bitter to her tongue? Sweet, she assured herself, but in her heart she really did not know.

*   *   *

Ellie put questions to the Dollarhides as soon as they were clear of the cabin. The women were puffing cigars as they bounced along on the wagon seat, looking as if they hadn't a worry in the world.

She reined the horse to the upwind side of the wagon. "You're glad the O'Malleys decided to stay?"

"They were about to sell out to Fowler. Five thousand dollars, mind you," Gert said. "Once the deal was done, we might be able to get the money from them, but that wouldn't get you the land. Fowler didn't look like the sort to hand the title over to you out of the kindness of his heart, not after paying so much cash."

"We had to convince them to stay," May said.

Ellie sighed. All this was getting very complicated.

"All right," she said, "I can see what you were up against. But what was all that talk about a fifty-dollar reward and them being wanted only for questioning?"

"I made all of that up. Had to." Gert exhaled a thick puff of smoke. "Fin took me out back to the pump for some water and said Cal had about convinced them to sell out, run and hide while he went back to New Orleans to see what was going on. That nephew's a wily one. There's probably some way he could get 'em clear of suspicion. I did some quick thinking and came up with the lies."

"You always were good at them," said May, flicking ash into the wind.

Even while she listened to the sisters, a thousand torments tore at Ellie—private admissions, longing, and shame. The greatest of all was shame. She had to blame Cal for her confusion. No one else had ever made her feel this way.

"Cal Hardin's wily all right," she said. "A wily bastard." In all her life she had never even thought the word *bastard*, but saying it out loud felt good. "A real bastard," she added for good measure.

The sisters looked at her.

"What happened while you two were outside?" Gert said. "We looked around, but you were gone."

"We were in the barn feeding the horses."

"The doors were closed," said May.

"The wind blew them shut."

"So what were you two up to?" Gert asked. "Anything else get fed besides the horses?"

"Nothing. The bastard"—she was truly warming to the word—"thinks he's a temptation no woman can resist, but I threatened to shoot him and he backed away quick enough."

Heaven help her, she had taken to lying so much, she was lying to the two people on her side.

Gert thumbed her bonnet farther back on her head. "We got to get that pepperbox away from you, honey. That kind of talk discourages a man. If I recall rightly, the plan was for you to get his attention while we were getting the deed."

Ellie didn't bother to dignify that remark with a response. Instead, she asked, "Do you think this is going to take much longer?"

"Hard to say. The O'Malleys are foolish, but they're not stupid."

"I don't get the difference."

"Stupid is not knowing what the hell is going on," Gert said. "Foolish is when you know it but don't particularly care, figuring whatever you want to do is worth the cost. We got to make them think that our company is more valuable to them than sweating away on some land that'll never make much money and will sap the life from them in the process."

"But won't they just sell out to Alden Fowler?"

"Not if we make it clear that if they sell to him, they don't get us," said May. "They don't seem the smartest businessmen we've ever met. Better yet, they're hornier than two bulls trapped in a herd of steers."

"That don't mean Fowler's not a complication," said Gert. "We've got to find out more about him. He must be real rich to offer five thousand U.S. dollars for that piece of nowhere they're sitting on."

"Maybe he's stupid and foolish both," said Ellie.

"He didn't look it. He's up to something. What we've got to do is find out what it is."

"What about Cal?" Her enemy's first name slipped out far too easily for comfort. Maybe the sisters would not take note.

She should have known better.

"Cal, is it?" May said right away. "You sure you told us everything that happened in the barn?"

Ellie sighed. She wasn't getting away with anything.

"Shooting a man, even just wanting it, invites

familiarity. It's the country. Manners and morals seem different out here."

The sisters exchanged knowing looks. Ellie decided to ignore them. She had too much to think about already, all of it focusing on getting back safely to Virginia as fast as she could.

With, she warned herself, her virginity intact. Until today, her virtue had never been in question. Now keeping it seemed as chancey as regaining the deed.

Alden Fowler was definitely a complication. Maybe she ought to double his offer to the O'Malleys and let them wander back into the hands of the New Orleans authorities. After all, she had always planned to give them something for the land, though the offer itself would have come from the Dollarhides.

But she had been thinking of a few hundred dollars. Doubling Fowler's offer would take all her remaining money, but it might be worth the sacrifice.

Unfortunately, she reminded herself, in New Orleans their nephew might very well get them off, leaving them rich and satisfied. She would have the title she was after, but she wouldn't have her revenge, and that was all she really wanted.

Truly, that was all. To get it she must be a warrior woman, right out of the mythological tales she had loved as a child.

She looked around at the expanse of rolling grassland, the far woods, the sun resting halfway down a vast sky. And she thought of the two-room adobe house she and the Dollarhides had moved into yesterday. Abandoned after the previous owner had been killed in a gunfight at the saloon, it lay off the main street of Glory at the edge of town, close to the big oak that was supposedly the town's hanging tree.

Like the hotel room, the house had a wooden floor and glass panes in the windows—few enough amenities, though it still surpassed the cabin at the Double T. They had bought their bed in the hotel, and a cot at Glory's lone store, Merse's Mercantile.

Ellie thought of the lace curtains in her room at home, of the high feather bed, of the thick rug that covered the polished floor. She thought of the towering oak outside her window, a tree meant for shade and beauty, not for death.

And she thought of the steaming cup of chocolate and warm bread that were served to her every morning.

After leaving her room, she had worked hard during the day, helping with the meals and the soap-and candle-making and the thousand other chores that went with running a plantation, even a modest one like hers.

But she had started the day with hot chocolate and warm bread.

Her breakfast this morning had been jerky bought at the general store.

Again she studied the land around her and yearned for more trees. Occasionally she caught sight of grazing cattle—wild or domestic, she couldn't say since she was able to see little more than their horns above the tall grass. She had heard there were herds of wild horses roaming the area as well, but she had yet to get a glimpse of them.

No matter. She wanted her friends near her, not wild animals. She wanted the harp she had learned to play as a child, the one that sat with grace and beauty in a corner of the parlor.

She wanted home.

Some warrior woman she was turning out to be. She must be losing her mind.

In Virginia, when all her mother's family had been laid to a peaceful rest in the family cemetery, she had looked at Bertrand and his children and thought of her father far away. With her fiancé and her lawyer making sure things went all right, she had told herself that the plantation overseer could manage affairs during the fall and winter until she returned.

All of that had been rationalization. She had wanted to get away. Not now. Distance turned Virginia into paradise and even made Bertrand Randolph seem not so bad. She had a fondness for his boys, undisciplined though they were. Though she and Bertrand did not love one another, he would always treat her with respect.

Which was something a man like Cal Hardin would never do.

She spent the rest of the ride trying to concentrate on Bertrand and on cups of chocolate, succeeding most of the time. When she got back to Glory and their small adobe home, she sat down to write her fiancé a letter. She had written him twice in New Orleans, to tell him of her father's death and then of her plans to travel on, leaving the purpose of the extended journey vague.

It was time to let him know she had arrived in Texas safely. She remained vague, saying only that she was clearing up her father's affairs.

The next day, after helping Gert and May scrub down the walls and sweep the floor, clean the windows, and air out the two rooms, she threw her cloak over her plain workdress and went to the store with her letter.

She didn't bother with a bonnet. The sky was gray and sunless, and she liked the feel of the autumn breeze in her loosely bound hair.

The storekeeper, Joseph Merse, greeted her with the assurance that the mail would start its long journey the following day, although it would be more than a month before Bertrand heard from her. All she had been able to assure him was that she was safe and well and would, she hoped, be returning home soon.

She didn't send her love. He would know it was a lie.

Setting about buying supplies, using a list the Dollarhides had prepared for her, she saw a young woman standing in the shadows at the back of the store. A faded blue gown hung loosely on her thin body, and her fair hair was braided into a knot at the back of her neck. She was pale to the point of whiteness, her expression otherworldly, as if she dwelt in an unseen place.

Ellie had noticed the woman yesterday standing in the same dark corner. She had smiled at the shadowy figure, as she was smiling now, but also as now, the woman had not responded.

"My daughter Katya will help you," Merse said

in a thick German accent. "You have only to give her the list."

Ellie had the feeling that if she approached her, Katya would flee. But the young woman held her ground, took the small piece of paper held out to her, and without looking up proceeded to gather the few items that were stocked at Merse's small store.

"It's nice to meet someone close to my own age," Ellie said as she followed the young woman around. "Do you mind if I call you Katya? I'm Eleanor. Most people call me Ellie."

Katya Merse gave no sign that she heard anything Ellie said.

"Perhaps you don't speak English," Ellie said.

"She speaks English good," her father said. "Better than me."

Ellie glanced over her shoulder at the father and saw a look of such sadness in his eyes that her heart went out to him. She looked back at Katya.

"Maybe later we'll talk," she said, "when you're not so busy. It gets lonely out here, I'm sure, without another woman to talk to."

She would have gone on, speaking inanely, saying anything to try to draw the woman out, but the door to the mercantile opened and she heard the thud of heavy boots against the floor.

Ellie tensed and turned, expecting to see Cal Hardin's mocking face staring at her, although why she thought that, she had no idea. Perhaps she feared his presence more than she did any other. Lately she had come to expect the worst.

Instead of the tall, lean darkness of Cal, she saw

110

a man of average height, his slight frame dressed in a black frock coat and black trousers, his sandy hair combed back from a thin, pale face. His eyes were a watery azure, not the vibrant blue of Cal's, and the look he cast her was of polite interest without a hint of disdain.

Vaguely she remembered him from her arrival at the saloon three days before. He had been among the men who crowded onto the rough walkway.

"Miss Davenport," he said. "I am happy to see your health has improved."

"You have the advantage of me," she said. "You know who I am."

"I know your name. It is not the same thing, is it? I scarcely know who you are."

He spoke with the suaveness she had come to expect from the few Englishmen she knew.

"But forgive me," he went on. "You raised a legitimate point. I am Simon Pence, late of York, wastrel son of a fine English gentleman and a mother who has long grieved over my dissolute ways. Please call me Sir Simon. My title is the last affectation I have in all the world."

Ellie couldn't keep from smiling, pleased to speak with a man whose mockery was turned on himself instead of her.

"I wonder, Sir Simon, exactly how much of that is true."

"All of it, I fear. The one sin that I have managed to avoid is prevarication."

He looked past her to Katya Merse, and the polite interest sharpened into something more intense.

But the courtesy was still in his voice when he spoke.

"Ah, gentle Kate, I see you assist your father as always. Let me help you with that sack of meal. It seems far too heavy for your delicate hands."

Ellie was certain she saw the girl's pale cheeks turn pink. When Sir Simon drew near, the girl set the flour down and backed once again into the shadows. He stared at her with troubled eyes.

"I fear I have frightened you. I meant no harm."

"Leave her be," the father said, sounding more resigned than gruff.

Sir Simon turned to Ellie, his bland smile back in place. "Allow me to help you in Fräulein Merse's stead."

Ellie had no choice but to accede to his request. They were headed toward the door when Cal Hardin strode in from the outside gloom, looming like a six-foot cloud before her, catching her by surprise.

She gasped.

His eyes flicked from her to Sir Simon and back to her. "Did I catch you doing something naughty, Miss Davenport?"

Ellie flushed. "Must you always be insulting?" she asked.

"Always."

"What are you doing here?" she said, refusing to be flustered by such rudeness.

His eyes narrowed, and the mockery was gone.

"I've come for ammunition. It seems I will need more bullets and powder than I planned. And a holster. I want to have my pistol close at hand."

"For heaven's sake, why? Have the Comanches returned?"

Like a cold wind, tension swept through the room. She had been no more than half serious, believing the war parties were far away. She could very well have been wrong. Holding her breath, she looked straight at Cal and waited for his reply.

"Comanches are not the only dangers in Texas. During the night, someone tried to murder us in our sleep."

Chapter Seven

"Vigilantes."

Fin pronounced the word as if it held all the evil in the world. Cal was inclined, for once, to agree with him.

Along with Fitz, Fin was sitting at the table in the adobe home the Davenports had rented. Gert and May were clucking in sympathy. Ellie sat apart, watching, but she had yet to put in a word.

Cal stood close to the front door, back to the wall and hat in hand, his attention directed to the niece. She was wearing a plain brown cotton dress with a shawl collar, fitted waist, and full, flowing skirt. Her yellow hair had been loosely pinned at her nape, making her look both vulnerable and desirable.

But looks could be deceiving. He remembered the smoldering eyes that stared at him yesterday with a heat that seared the soles of his boots. Today, her regard was closer to ice. Overnight she'd done some thinking, always a danger with a woman. He had better start wondering where she carried her bullets and whether she carried her gun.

"It was vigilantes, you may be sure," Fitz said, aware for the moment only of himself and his predicament. "Joseph Merse, a man wise in the ways of this land, said a few of the hotheaded citizens hereabouts banded together after the last Indian attack and styled themselves lawmen. But since the Indians haven't come back, they're pursuing every outlaw they can find."

"Anyone they decide is an outlaw," Fin said. "They have no plans to wait for a trial."

"It matters not how much money is on a man's head," Fitz said. "Fifty or fifty thousand, they'll hunt him down just the same, as long as he's a desperado."

"Trying to keep Texas free of crime, according to Merse," Fin said, "though none will put a name to the night riders." Fin shook his head in disgust. "How lawful is it to circle around a man's home and shoot up the night?"

Fitz stared solemnly at Gert and May, concentrating especially on May. " 'Tis part of no law I've ever heard."

The Davenport sisters trilled their sympathy. Cal searched for the same kind of emotion on their niece's face, but she sat still, for all the world unmoved by what his uncles described. Maybe the problem was that they had gone through the description a half dozen times, how after the moon had set the cabin was surrounded by night riders firing shotguns into the air.

A few had hit the cabin walls. Cal had come out of the front door firing both rifle and pistol. Even the mongrel dog had gotten into the action, drawing himself up beside Cal and barking as if he would tear the marauders apart once he decided to leave the porch.

But the night was dark and the riders had gotten away. Cal wasn't sure how many there were; he estimated three, though they had made enough noise for ten.

Had they really been vigilantes, good men gone bad for a noble cause? He wasn't at all sure. The only thing he knew was that they provided another reason to leave. Unfortunately, his uncles had not yet come around to the same conclusion. He should have dragged them outside with him and the dog.

He rested his palm on the gun handle at his side, trying to get used to wearing it so close. Most men strapped their holsters to the waist, but he'd adjusted his to rest against his thigh, using a leather thong to tie the bottom in place. Riding lower on his leg, the pistol was easier to grab in a hurry.

No coat of his would hide it, but he wasn't after a hidden gun. If anyone came at him, he wanted the bastard to know he was armed. Besides, he wasn't wearing a coat, having traded it for a fringed leather jerkin he'd bought from Merse along with the holster. A brown neckerchief was tied loosely beneath the collar of his buff linen shirt. He was dressed like a Texan ready for whatever battle came his way.

Unlike Ellie, he kept his pistol loaded. After last night, he would keep his back to the wall. In Texas a man had a better chance of surviving that way.

"You're awfully quiet, Mr. Hardin," Gert said. "What's your feeling about the shooting? You think it was vigilantes?"

"It could have been. We haven't made any enemies out here. Not yet, at least." His gaze shifted to Ellie. "Not as far as we know."

She lowered her eyes. Whatever she was thinking, he knew he would find it interesting. But he also knew she wasn't ready to reveal her secrets. He would have to get them out of her the best way that he could.

He knew a few good ways. But the two of them would need to be alone. The next time he got an opportunity like the one in the barn, he would make better use of it.

"I guess this means you will be wanting to leave," May said.

Ellie's eyes flew up to her aunt, as if in warning to be quiet.

"Would it matter to you if we did?" Cal asked, directing his question to the niece.

"Of course not," she said with an airy wave of her hand. "Why would your whereabouts mean anything to me?"

"No reason in the world. Even after all we've shared."

He had heard the expression "looking daggers at someone." He now understood what it meant.

The aunts looked on with the interest of cats

watching a pair of birds, undecided about whether to pounce on him or her.

His uncles were staring into space, their thoughts directed toward troubles they had hoped were far behind them.

"I'm sorry you were shot at," Ellie said, sounding not in the least sympathetic. "And I'm sorry you didn't hit anyone when you came out the door. Are you not a very good shot?"

Cal shrugged. "There are a few things I haven't done in a while, and shooting's one of them. I need a little practice, wouldn't you say?"

"I couldn't begin to know what you need," she said, the only one in the room who appeared to know he was talking about more than guns.

"There's a fence not twenty yards from the back of the house," Gert said. "Ellie, why don't you take Cal on out there and get him set up?"

"But—"

"Now, Ellie," May put in, "considering it might save his life, or the lives of his dear uncles"—here she fluttered her eyes at Fin and Fitz—"it's the least you can do."

A silent communication was passing between the women, almost as if the aunts were pushing their spinster niece onto him. Whatever the message, Ellie eventually acquiesced.

"Of course," she said, standing.

She smiled sweetly at Cal. He took it as a warning to stay alert.

"We may as well get this over with now," she added. "I'll get my own gun from the other room, and we can both practice. One never knows when an enemy will appear."

Outside, wearing a cloak over her gown and holding the pepperbox at her side, she walked with determination across the field that extended from the house to the tall oak tree reputedly used by the town for its hangings. With each step, her sturdy shoes hit the ground hard, and the hem of her garments picked up grass and stickers. Hat pulled low, Cal watched as she placed a row of targets on the top rail of a rickety fence that ran across the back of the property, twenty yards from the house.

The targets were varied—a large rock, a fallen branch of oak, a rusted tin, and a clump of dried-out manure. When she came back to his side, she didn't flinch or blink as she looked him in the eye.

"Cal, you've pretty much shown me I know little about dealing with men. You've teased me and taunted me until I can't think straight, while all I've done is wave an empty gun in your face. It's time I proved to you what I can do."

Standing halfway between house and fence, she loaded the pepperbox and fired at the manure. The clump broke, and a thousand pieces scattered in the air.

"Your turn," she said and stepped aside, showing no sign of distress over the noise of the explosion.

Here was a new side to the enigmatic Ellie, a side Cal liked. Damned if he knew why, but he did.

His bullet sent the rock flying; for good measure he immediately shot it again, catching his target in mid-flight. Like the manure, it broke apart.

"Show off," she said. Aiming carefully, she hit the tin. He got the branch.

They both stood in silence for a moment, letting the thunder of the shots die away. Overhead the sky was gray, and the few birds that had been visible when they first walked out were now gone.

"I guess we don't need practice after all," she said.

"Not from this distance."

"I can make it farther if you like."

"I had closer in mind."

She looked away. "I know you're not talking about target practice, are you? You mean kissing and other things. I should have reminded you yesterday that I am already betrothed to another. You seem to have trouble remembering it."

"We both do."

She didn't attempt to argue. "That doesn't make it any the less true. I'm spoken for, Cal. I gave my word."

"Where did you get the idea I had marriage in mind?"

That shook her, more than he had intended.

"Don't flatter yourself that I would consider the possibility you were serious. I meant only that I believed, or at least hoped, you would consider a woman in my situation with a certain amount of respect."

"Make that interest and you would be right. Respect is something a woman wants when she can't get anything better."

"Spoken like a man."

"That's the only way I know how."

He came at her. She did not back away.

"A man without honor," she said, glaring up at him as he drew near.

"You've figured me out," he said.

"No," she said, more sadly than anything else. "I figured me out."

"That puts you way ahead of me. I haven't the slightest idea what you are up to."

"I told you—"

"About Bertrand the Impulsive? You must have figured I was Cal the Stupid with that one."

"I can think of many ways to describe you, but stupid isn't one. How about Cal the Arrogant? Cal the Opportunist? Cal the Lecherous?"

"You're right about one of them." He brushed a curl from her cheek. "Guess which one."

Her shiver was visible, as was the anger in her eyes.

"You tear at me, Cal, and you know it. The only way I can defend myself is to accept the truth. If you passed me on a street in New Orleans, you wouldn't give me a second glance. In Glory I'm practically the only woman around."

"You don't think much of yourself."

"I don't think much of my looks. It's not the same thing at all. Your attentions could probably charm me out of my petticoats, but whatever you gave me of yourself wouldn't be flattering and it wouldn't last."

"You want things to last between us?"

"Heavens, no. It would mean my ruin."

Damn the woman. She had a way of enticing him, and yes, arousing him, then dousing him with a bucket of cold words. It was as if she had a load of special hate stored up inside her, not the general kind that came from women who had no use for men. Her hate was specific, its heat directed at only him.

She whirled from him and in that instant he knew where he had seen her before, the certainty so strong it rocked him on his heels. Thumbing his hat to the back of his head, he thought of the gunshot at the cemetery, the open vault, the mysterious woman in the black veil.

Beyond all doubt, that same woman stood before him now.

He remembered her last appearance in the roadway, at once as insubstantial as a specter and as solid as stone. And he remembered her turning away in a swirl of black wool. The veil was gone, but the cloak was there, as well as the burning anger. Instinct had told him they would meet again. Instinct had been right.

Now it needed to tell him what the hell was going on.

Ellie tossed her cloak onto the bed and with shaking hands packed the gun and its ammunition away in the trunk at the corner of the room. The house was empty, the aunts and uncles having disappeared, but it made no difference to her, not with her blood boiling and her insides in a turmoil she had never before known.

And all because of one impossible man.

Somehow he and his family were involved in her papa's death. This was a fact she must never forget.

She truly did not understand her reaction to him, or why she had traded barbs in a manner alien to her nature and to her upbringing, and more important, to her most immediate goals. Her one consolation was that at least verbally, she gave as good as she got.

How dare he tease and flirt with her, making her want things she shouldn't even know about, letting her know he knew far too much. She was nothing to him, less than nothing; otherwise he would have realized she truly wanted respect.

Not from him, of course. She'd had a long time to think yesterday, a long time to remember her shame. It was his touch that got her. She was lonely and she knew she was unloved. That much he must have sensed about her. He was lower than a snake, lower than a worm, and if he thought for one minute she truly wanted him to—

He came into the room and she turned, ready to defy him. But he gave her no chance. Tossing his hat on the bed on top of her cloak, he continued toward her, his stride long and purposeful, his arms unyielding as he pulled her into his embrace.

She grabbed the fringe of his leather jerkin for support and was starting to yelp when his lips covered hers and he swallowed the sound.

The lips were warm and firm and devastatingly persuasive. He seemed to swallow all of her, including her will, and in that split second of time, all her brave thoughts dissolved into incoherence. She wanted to fight him, but there was nothing left of her strength. The resultant void lasted for only an instant before something else took its place, an explosion of wanting that drove her to open her mouth in invitation to a deeper kiss.

With a groan, he responded and she tasted his tongue against hers.

It frightened her, this first encounter with true intimacy, but like her will, the fear dissolved. Simply put, she liked his taste, and she rubbed her tongue against his to taste him more. Instinct drove her on; she had no other guide.

His embrace tightened. Her arms stole around his neck and she stood on tiptoe, the better to reach his lips. She felt the pressure of his holster and gun against her waist. He lifted her off her feet, never once reducing the pressure of his kiss. Eyes squeezed shut against the glare of day and of reality, she clung to him with a fervor that stunned her even as it gave her the energy of a thousand urgings.

Urgings to do what? She didn't know except that she wanted more of him, more of his touch, his kiss, the feel of his hands at her back. Her body tingled and her blood raced. Her hands made frantic strokes across his shoulders as she tried to force herself inside his clothes.

The room was a whirl and Cal was the only thing of substance in it. She didn't exist except for the hunger he aroused. Then, suddenly, he was setting her down and loosening his embrace. It took her a moment to realize what was happening.

Her first instinct was to cling to him, to whimper, to beg him to kiss her again. Her eyelids fluttered open, and in the cutting light she saw things as they were. The urgings, never fully understood, fled, and in their stead flooded a sense of shame she understood all too well.

Head reeling, she tried to pull away, but he did not let her. She had to content herself with resting her hands against the front of his vest, lightly so that she could not feel the hard body underneath. But she could sense the separate breaths dragging through him, each one as ragged as her own.

"Ellie," he said softly.

She covered her lips with her fingers and looked up at him, but she could not speak. She didn't know what to think, and she didn't know what to say.

Cal did not suffer the same problem. "I was about to carry you to the bed. Would you have stopped me?"

She closed her eyes and in defense tried to form an image of her father in her mind, but she had never seen Henry Chase, not since infancy. The only face that formed was Cal Hardin's, a mask of hard lines and bristled cheeks and lips far more deadly than any gun. All the brave words she had thrown so proudly at him were as insubstantial as the wind. From him there was no escape.

"Would you?" he said.

She wanted to be righteously indignant, and later perhaps she could be. But not with him staring down at her with eyes that would see through any lie.

"I don't know," she whispered through her fingers. "I hope so. Please let me go."

He stepped away, and she felt a sudden chill. It must be the chill of dishonor, she told herself. She hugged herself. Today she had proven herself a disgrace to everything she believed in, to all she held dear.

She hadn't realized a kiss could be so powerful. It could truly be the ruination of a woman.

She backed away from him and turned to stare out the window at the fence where they had so recently shown off their shooting skills. Outside, she had matched his ability. Inside the house, he had been the one who knew what to do.

"Are you really Ellie Davenport?" he asked.

The question took her so by surprise that she almost answered, "Ellie Chase."

She fingered a strand of hair behind her ear. "I don't understand what you're talking about."

"I think you do. Those two women who came with you are no more your aunts than Joseph Merse."

Here was an accusation she hadn't expected. It seemed so distant, so impersonal after their explosion of intimacy, yet it hit at the soul of what she was and why she was here.

Her heart pounding in her throat, she managed to find the indignation she had been seeking. "They most certainly are," she lied. "How can you doubt it? They care for me and I care for them. That should be clear, even to a man like you."

"You don't look anything like them."

"We look as much alike as you and Fin and Fitz."

"I'll concede the point. But no other. Whatever brought you here, you should have come up with a better story than a fiancé named Bertrand."

At last she could come up with a truth; it gave her the strength to turn and face him.

"I am truly engaged to a man named Bertrand

Rutherford, although how I am to face him again after today, I do not know."

"You'll manage. If there really is such a man."

"Are you always so cynical?"

"Always. I've never known a reason not to be. Take you, for instance."

"I'd rather you not."

He laughed. Like everything else about him, his laugh was dark and seductive. "I didn't mean physically take you—"

"Neither did I."

"—although we didn't thoroughly explore that possibility, did we? I meant, you are not what you seem. You ride in with a preposterous story, pretending to be prim and proper and cold, when you're really much warmer and more human than that."

"Weak, you mean."

"Not at all. I thought you were going to rip off my clothes." She gasped, but he didn't stop. "You're a passionate woman, Ellie, if that's your name, and far lovelier than you imagine. I don't know how you contain all those feelings inside yourself. You should be six feet tall."

"I am nothing like you describe," she said, wondering as she spoke whom she was trying to convince. "You had me so angry, I wasn't thinking clearly. That's all."

But she knew her reaction had been much more. Tears came to her eyes. He must not see her cry.

She gave him a wide berth, grabbed her cloak, and ran from the room, ran from the house, ran down the street without giving the least thought to her destination except to put as much distance as possible between the two of them. She knew he followed; he was not the sort of man who let a woman have her way.

Peals of laughter and raised voices rolled out of the saloon. She thought she recognized a particular high-pitched giggle, but it couldn't be.

Of course it could. What she heard was the final degradation of the day.

Giving no consideration to the suitability of her actions, she shoved her way through the swinging doors. The smoke-filled room was bare of adornment. A bar was to the left and tables and chairs were scattered haphazardly across the sawdust-covered floor.

Except for the bartender, who stood at his post and picked his teeth, everyone was crowded at the far end of the saloon. She got only a rear view of the men; their backs formed a wall over which she could not see. Not that she wanted to. One man caught her eye, and she recognized Sir Simon Pence, the Englishman she had met that morning at the general store.

Could it have been only that morning? It seemed a lifetime ago.

He nodded with the dignity that went with his bearing. Tapping the shoulders of the men in front of him, he got them to turn. One by one, they stared at Ellie, a big grin on each grizzled face. Never in all her life had she seen such an array of disreputable humanity. She held her cloak close.

The men parted, forming a narrow cordon that led to the saloon's back table. They gave her no choice but to walk toward the laughter and the shouts.

But she pretty much knew who and what she would find.

The four of them sat at the table, Fin and Fitz across from one another, Gert and May the same. Coins and bills lay scattered before them, and Gert was shuffling a deck of cards with far more ease and skill than any supposed lady should have possessed.

The only thing for which Ellie could be grateful was that the Dollarhide sisters were not smoking cigars.

Which didn't mean they wouldn't light up any minute.

She thought about leaving, but she knew Cal was close behind her.

Gert was the first to spy her, and the shuffling stopped.

"Ellie," she said, not looking nearly as chagrined as she should have. "You finished with the shooting?"

"Gentlemen," May said, "allow our niece to come forward. Can't one of you get her a place to sit?"

May's trilled request resulted in a general scurrying, and a half dozen chairs were dragged toward her. She waved them away.

Sir Simon looked at her in sympathy; the rest of the men looked at her in ways she refused to analyze.

"Now don't go to scowling so much," Gert said. "We never done this before—"

A few of the men guffawed.

"Well, we haven't. But Fin and Fitz said they could teach us a few things about gambling, and we were wanting to get away from all that racket you and Cal were making in the back, and the next thing you know, here we are."

"We're winning, too," May said. She smiled coquettishly at the twins, her biggest smile saved for Fitz. "I'll say one thing for them. The Irish sure do know how to treat a couple of ladies."

The laughter grew. Ellie glanced at Sir Simon, whose pale blue eyes were filled with sympathy. She caught a sideways glimpse of Cal. His midnight stare held curiosity and a hint of what she feared was triumph.

The laughter faded. Everyone seemed to be waiting for her to respond. She wished with all her might that she could fall through the floor.

Chapter Eight

"I guess you think we went back on our word."

Gert puffed at her cigar in the safety of the adobe house. She was stirring some kind of stew in a big pot on the stove, inadvertently seasoning it with ashes from time to time.

"That's one way of putting it," said Ellie, who still burned with shame over the cowardly way she had fled the saloon without saying a word to her aunts. The worst part hadn't been the insinuating remarks that followed her hasty retreat. The worst part had been brushing past the wily-watchful Cal, feeling his eyes on her, suspecting he could read her mind.

The only thing for which she could be grateful was that he had returned to the Double T and wasn't around to torment her. Fin and Fitz were staying at the Glory Hotel until Cal brought word concerning the vigilantes' possible return.

May sat beside her at the table and took her hand. Like her sister, the woman was strong, and since she had a great deal of heft behind her, Ellie made no attempt to pull away.

In this one very long day, she had already lost far too much dignity.

"We were learning more about the boys," May said. "You can do only so much by sitting around and minding your manners. Besides, if we heard one more time how they almost got gunned down in their sleep, we would have quit then and there and headed back to New Orleans."

"Those Irish lads are single-minded," Gert said. "And we weren't what was on their minds. We had to do something to get them back to us."

"There's no doubt you did that."

"And there's no need to sound so miserable about it. If I didn't know better, I'd say you're edging close to sarcastic," said May. "I know how it must have looked to you, but you got to have a little faith. We've got your best interests at heart."

Ellie eased her hand from May's grip and looked from sister to sister. They truly looked concerned. She was judging them too hard. Going into the saloon was the kind of thing they would naturally do.

Maybe they were right. Maybe the only way to understand Fin and Fitz was to find their level and get on it. But why did they have to do so in front of a crowd?

She sighed. "I'm sorry. It's just that I've been around Cal too long. He takes a negative view of everything."

The sisters looked at one another.

"He can be won over," Gert said.

"By you," May said.

"Ha." They should have seen her and Cal in the bedroom an hour ago.

"So what did you find out about the O'Malleys?" she asked.

Gert put down the stirring spoon and joined them at the table. "They know how to have a good time."

The sisters shared a grin.

"They sure do," May said.

"I haven't had that many laughs since we left Mississippi."

"It felt good, didn't it, Gert? As good as when we took off our corsets this morning." May glanced at Ellie. "We had to. They was leaving deep red marks all over. We looked like someone had been whipping us, and that's one thing we never allowed."

"Don't look so worried, honey." Gert patted Ellie's hand. "We explained to them how we came from the wild side of the family and how we were the only ones brave enough to come out here with you."

May nodded. "We said we'd been on our best behavior but decided a couple of hours being ourselves wouldn't do any real harm."

"It loosened the boys up right fine," said Gert. "Finbar O'Malley can be a charmer when he wants to. He knows how to accept a woman the way she is."

May shook her head. "Fitzgerald is the real charmer."

133

"Fin."

"Fitz."

Ellie looked back and forth at the women in disbelief. This couldn't be happening. She closed her eyes for a moment. But of course it could.

"So they're charmers," she said. "Is that all you learned?"

The grins disappeared and Gert drummed the table with her fingers. "There's one thing you're not going to like. I might as well give it to you straight. Those boys are without doubt the worst card players we have ever met. There is no way they could have cheated your father."

May nodded. "Unless he was trying to lose the title on purpose, and that don't make a hell of a lot of sense."

"But I heard stories about the game. I asked around and people came to me at Papa's shop."

"Did you offer any money for 'em to drop by?"

"A little. And don't look at me that way. You know they never would have bothered if it hadn't been worth their while. The stories varied in detail except about how the twins came up with a king of hearts they shouldn't have had and won everything."

"I know this comes as a shock," May said, "but think it over, Ellie. Believe us, those boys just don't know how to cheat. They can't handle the cards good enough."

"There's something else to consider, more in the area of human nature," Gert said. "Men like a good story as well as women. More, with most of them. They'd much rather pass on bad news than good because that's the way to get most folks listening. My guess is after a while, the way you were putting the questions to them, they got the idea you wanted to hear nothing but bad about the O'Malleys. It gave you someone to blame for everything that happened."

Ellie sat back in her chair. "That's ridiculous. I wanted only the truth."

Gert shook her head. "Now ain't the time for lying to yourself."

"I'm not lying—"

She swallowed the rest of her protest and looked away. Could the sisters be right? Had she fed the answers she wanted to the men she questioned? Possibly. But she had been sure she was on the right track in her investigation. There were too many coincidences to have believed otherwise.

The coincidences were still there. She had been told right away, by just about everyone, that the O'Malleys were poor gamblers. That was why their winning came as a surprise.

One of the witnesses had put it best: "There's more to those Irishmen than we suspected. Could be they've been taking lessons from that slick gambler of a nephew. Could be the three of 'em are more alike than we thought."

Hadn't the Dollarhides warned her that innocent-looking men were the most dangerous? Surely that went for the supposedly inept ones as well.

Ellie sighed. All of this took a lot of cogitating, and as much honesty as she could manage. Gert and May pulled away from the table and let her think.

"You want a cup of tea?" May said after a few minutes of silence.

Ellie shook her head. She needed to concentrate. Thinking was hard when feelings kept getting in the way. The main feeling she had right now was that in the future she would be getting revenge for her father's troubles without the help of anyone. She could do it if she had to. She had no choice.

"I know it's a lot to take in all at once," Gert said. "Don't be hard on yourself. You didn't go wrong on purpose."

"You're human," said May.

Ellie gave a bitter laugh. "Cal said very much the same thing." She glanced at the bedroom. "Not very long ago."

She didn't at all like the look that passed between the sisters.

"He doesn't think you're my aunts," she added, giving them something else to think about besides how she and Cal were getting on.

It was the Dollarhides' turn to get indignant.

"He don't think we're good enough?" May asked.

"He says we don't look anything alike. And he doesn't believe I have a fiancé named Bertrand."

"I always thought that part of the story was a little suspicious," said Gert.

"But it's the only thing we told him that's true. Not the part about following him out to Texas, of course, but the fact that he exists."

Gert smashed her cigar out in the jar she sometimes used for ashes and waved away the smoke. "A strong lie is better than a weak truth any day,

136

especially where men are concerned. I know you weren't taught that by your real aunt, but she was a spinster, wasn't she, and I'd bet my last bottle of hair dye a virgin, too. Experience has led me and May to understand the ways of the beasts."

Ellie was not about to get into a conversation with the former madams about Aunt Abigail's lack of a sex life or the habits of men. Remembering far too well what she had been learning from Cal lately, she would rather remain in ignorance all her days.

"Maybe, just maybe," she said, "the O'Malleys won the land by a stroke of unexpected luck, but no one wanted to believe it. The talk about cheating was already going on when I arrived in town. I may have encouraged the talk, but I didn't put the idea in anyone's mind."

"That don't explain the shooting," Gert said.

"You said yourselves bad news is better than good. So the bad news spread and Papa believed it. They could have gunned him down if they thought he was going to accuse them."

"That's another point that's troubling us. Those boys don't know any more about guns than we do. All that shooting behind the house got to them as much as to us. They were the ones to suggest we go to the saloon."

"You're looking cynical again," said May. "All right, they mentioned they would sure like to go, and we said it was all right with us as long as they didn't leave us behind to go deaf. Gert said something about it being a new experience, and I said there wasn't nothing else to do in Glory and I didn't see how it could hurt."

Ellie nodded dumbly, rubbing her temples to get at the headache that was fast developing.

"Maybe I will take that tea," she said.

After May placed a steaming cup in front of her, the sisters disappeared into the bedroom and without saying a word closed the door. They were giving her more time to think.

That was what she did, fast and furious. Gert and May had already been won over by the O'Malleys, and there seemed little she could do to change their minds. She couldn't go along with them. The brothers were fighting a possible charge of murder, a charge from which they had run, so naturally they would pretend to be stupid about cards and guns.

And the sisters were lonely for companionship. If she tried to explain her thoughts to them, they would come up with more reasons she was wrong. Ignorant though she was in a lot of ways, she knew women made excuses for men. For years, she had been excusing Bertrand's dalliance with the widow, hadn't she?

She finished the tea and laid her throbbing head on her folded arms. A short while later, when she heard Gert and May bustling about the room, she sat upright. Her head reeled from the sudden movement, and she took a moment to speak, understanding the need to tread carefully. She liked the Dollarhides. They weren't her aunts, but they were her companions and her friends.

"I wasn't sleeping. There are too many things to think about for me to relax. The one question I can't answer is, what are we going to do now?"

Gert came over and began to rub her shoulders.

"You're tighter than a 60-year-old virgin. Relax, honey. You'll make yourself sick."

Her strong grip hurt at first, but after a minute the rubbing began to feel good.

"May and I have been talking things over. We think the boys know something about what happened with your daddy, even if it's not what we were thinking at first."

"They did win the title in a suspicious game," May put in. "And they did run to Texas when rumors spread about what they were up to."

Ellie felt her headache begin to ease, or maybe it was the heaviness in her heart that was letting go. She had so many ailments, it was hard to keep up with them all.

"So we stay and find out exactly what they know," she said. "I'll just have to write Bertrand and tell him I'll be a little longer than I'd planned."

"Right," the sisters said in unison.

"And the title to the land?" Ellie said.

"We'll still get that for you," said Gert. "Those boys don't belong in Texas any more than we do."

"Don't forget Alden Fowler's offer. They could still sell out to him."

"They could," said Gert.

"But they won't," said May, "not if we handle things right."

Ellie actually managed a smile. "That's the most encouraging thing you've said all afternoon."

"Good."

"Ellie-girl, am I hearing a little spark in your voice?" Gert said.

"You sure are, sister. I'm hearing the same thing," said May.

"It's a very little spark," Ellie said, "but I think it'll get stronger."

Gert beamed. "Eat some of my stew and you'll be ready to take on Cal Hardin himself."

"I said it's a very little spark. Don't douse it right away."

Ellie spoke lightly, but in her heart she both feared and accepted what she had to do: take on Cal Hardin the way she had originally planned. Well, maybe not take him on through seduction, which lately seemed far too possible and eminently dangerous. But she could stall him while they got the deed, and maybe when that was done, somehow the truth would come out.

Between open honesty and outright lying, she already had him guessing, unsure of who or what she was. In truth, as far as her feelings were concerned, honesty seemed to work the best. At least it got him the most confused.

And he had, she reminded herself with more than usual frankness, backed off when he might very well have got her into bed. How much easier it was to feel confident when he wasn't anywhere near.

"We got faith in you, honey," Gert said. "A lot more'n you've got in yourself. We're going walking with the lads tonight, and we were thinking in a few days we might have us a little soiree. If that's all right with you. We'll ask Sir Simon—he seems like a right decent sort—and the O'Malleys, and Mr. Merse and that quiet daughter of his. There's even a few men at the saloon that might clean up all right. We could ask them, too. If we're going to stay here for a spell, we might as well feel at home."

"I'll never feel at home in Texas, but if that's what you want, that's what you'll get. I'll do the cooking. I'm really good at it."

"We were thinking you'd agree," May said. "That's why we hired us some help. Consuela is her name, Consuela Gomez. Merse recommended her, and she seemed real pleased to get the work. She's got a thirteen-year-old son that'll help out, too. There don't seem to be a Señor Gomez around, so I imagine she could use the money."

"And none of it will cost you a thing," said Gert. "We took a fair amount of cash off those boys today. They had a good time, and they'll have a good time for as long as we stay, but we don't come cheap. Never have and never will. They're the ones paying the way."

The next few days were spent cleaning and washing and cooking and making sure invitations went out in a proper fashion.

"We want to do things right," Gert proclaimed.

In the evenings the sisters strolled with the boys, and Ellie wrote in a journal she had begun, mostly about what she had seen and heard since leaving Virginia, leaving out any mention of Cal except in the most impersonal way.

Late one night, while she was lying on her cot by the window and watching the clouds dance across the moon, she heard the Dollarhides and the O'Malleys enter the other room. They were

141

laughing and whispering, but after Gert poured their visitors a drink, the laughing eased off and the whispering turned to outright talk.

Mostly they were talking about Glory and how different Texas was from the States. When Gert turned the conversation to Cal, Ellie knew she was meant to hear what was said. They were providing more proof the O'Malleys weren't the rascals she had supposed, though the subject hadn't come up for days.

She thought about tiptoeing close to the door, but that would be too much like outright snooping. Instead, she sat up and turned her attention away from the moon. Where moral and ethical issues were concerned, she was learning to draw a very fine line between right and wrong.

"How come he never married?" Gert asked. "Fine-looking man like him ought to have a half-dozen children by now."

"Maybe he does," May said. "Only he don't know it."

"The lad has no plans to marry, nor to bring more Hardins into the world."

Fin's rough-edged voice was easy to identify. His brother Fitz always sounded smoother, maybe because he didn't speak so much.

" 'Tis a long, sad story," said Fitz. "And not ours to tell."

"Of course not," Gert said. "Let me get you another drink."

"We don't mean to pry," May said, "but we're getting to like you boys and we're concerned about people who matter to you."

Ellie heard nothing for a few moments, and then Fin began to talk.

"His mother was our dear sister, as you know. May she rest in peace. Born in Ireland, like the pair of us. Poor immigrants we were, I can tell you. Our parents died early. We were all the kin each other had. Until she married, of course, and gave us Cal."

"She passed on?" May asked.

"Aye. She wasn't but a few days in her grave when we left and came to Texas. We had come into the title of some land, you see, though not by nefarious means, no matter what was said, and we'd brought harm to no one. It isn't in our natures and never has been. The vigilantes are wrong there."

Both twins launched into another reminiscence about the terrible night when the guntoting riders had frightened them half to death. Gert was the one who steered them back to where she wanted.

"Have you no other nephews or nieces?"

"None," Fitz said. "Though Cal has a brother and sister, by way of his father. Raymond Hardin took on three wives, one at a time, you understand. Margaret O'Malley was the first."

"But you said she just passed on."

"They were divorced," Fin said, all the disgrace of the word in his voice.

"Oh, my," May said. "How terrible."

"Tragic, more to my mind. He called her a whore. Pardon my language, ladies. I don't mean to shock you, but Raymond was a blunt man. That's the way he saw her, though he was wrong, of course. She wasn't, no more than the two of you."

"Cal was eight at the time," Fitz said. "The arguing must have gone on something fierce, and then Hardin stormed out and got the divorce on grounds of adultery. He was a traveling man and he claimed she sold herself while he was gone."

"Our poor dear sister had always been a mite impetuous, you might say," Fin said. "She was already in the family way when she and Raymond were wed. Years later, when he started throwing charges around, he claimed the boy was not his, though anyone could tell he was, just by looking at him. But a man in a rage of injured pride is nay a thinking man. He was cruel. The boy never forgot."

"And what about your poor sister?" May asked.

"Times were hard for her. She was remarried, this time to a weakling named Alfred Broussard, but he died on her. The only thing she got from the union was excommunication from the church."

It was Fitz's turn. "Cal took to roaming the streets, earning money however he could. We tried to help, but we were barely feeding ourselves. Cal was like his father, stubborn and proud, even as a wee lad. He got into fights defending his mother. He became a right fine bare-knuckled boxer, and as he grew, he made money from his skills."

"We taught him the skill of gambling," said Fin. "There was nothing he wouldn't try. The Negroes on the dock taught him a shell game and a few other tricks. For a time he even went in for tumbling, leaping and flipping and twisting about as if he had nary a bone in his body, then passing a hat to get whatever coins he could. But he decided he preferred boxing."

"By fifteen," said Fitz, "he was able to set us up in a little house with Margaret near the river in the Vieux Carré. 'Twas no small matter, the Irish being scarcely welcomed there. But we settled in with nary a problem and he took to the road, already a man, sending money back when he could. He's done right well for himself. We're proud of the lad, though he's little enough proud of himself."

" 'Tis a strange thing," Fin said, his voice low and thoughtful. "Raymond Hardin had run away from someplace back East when he was the same age. We tried once to tell Cal he was more like his father than he knew, but he would have none of it."

"King Cal," Fitz said, sounding equally thoughtful. "Margaret named him for an Irish king. The name suits. He's proud and sure of himself and he's done well by way of making money. But he'll never marry. And he'll never bring more Hardins into the world."

"Aren't you worried about him all by himself out there in that cabin?"

"He likes being on his own. We learned long ago he can take care of himself."

They went on to speak of other matters, but Ellie ceased to listen. Staring into the dark outside the window, she pictured a little boy growing old too soon, and an unexpected sadness settled in her heart. But she could allow nothing stronger than sympathy to accompany the sadness, nothing that might approach affection.

Cal was what he was. He would never change.

Any woman who was fool enough to let herself care for him was in for heartbreak. Especially a woman who wanted a husband and children of her own.

Cal thought of his uncles but of no one else besides himself. A man like him—if there were any others—would prefer above all else to spend his time with beautiful women as self-serving as he, wanting nothing more than momentary pleasure.

Ellie wasn't beautiful and she honestly didn't think of herself as self-serving. But as she had told him earlier, to his way of thinking she was available. For him, that would be enough. She had a strong enough sense of survival to know that he was fire and she must be very careful to keep from getting burned.

Her thoughts went along the same path until at last she fell asleep. She woke early the next day with a start and slapped a hand over her mouth to keep from crying out. Something was wrong. Something was terribly wrong. It took a moment to realize what it was.

Cal needed help.

She lay still for a moment and tried to put her thoughts in order. Where her panic had come from, she had no idea. Cal's helplessness was impossible to imagine. He needed nothing. He wanted no one. But the certainty he was in trouble remained, cutting into her consiousness like a knife.

Heart pounding, she sat up on her cot. Across

the room Gert and May were snoring peacefully in the double bed; outside the window at her head dawn was breaking, the sky streaked with ribbons of dark clouds lit from behind by the muted early sun. Somewhere a cock crowed. Otherwise, the world was still.

She had awakened with peculiar notions before, remnants of absurd dreams, but nothing approached the absurdity of this one. In all her life she had never felt such a powerful premonition.

Cal needed help. He needed her.

It was her single most ridiculous idea yet. He couldn't possibly be in any kind of danger that required her presence. But the urge to go to him was irresistible. She could no more ignore it than she could will herself not to breathe.

Grabbing the clothes she had laid out the night before, she tiptoed from the room and dressed, then poked the banked coals in the fireplace to life and added a couple of logs. The heat from the fire failed to warm her. Cal had been out alone at the cabin for five days now. The vigilantes could have shot him and no one would know. He could have fallen and injured himself. A thousand things could have gone wrong.

She didn't care, she told herself. If she had been in danger, he wouldn't have worried about her. But she and Cal were not alike, and there was only one way to prove it, to him and to herself.

As soon as Consuela arrived, she asked to borrow her son Antonio for the day. The boy, not far past his thirteenth birthday, was all arms and legs and smiles and talk, but he knew how to fire a shotgun and he would be company for the ride.

147

He helped load up the wagon with supplies from Merse's Mercantile, and with Ellie's bay mare tied to the back, they headed out for the Indian trail that would take her to the Double T.

Throughout her preparations, Gert and May had said not a word except that they would be working on details of the soiree scheduled for the following evening. If looks passed between the pair, Ellie refused to see them.

During the two-hour ride to the cabin, Antonio chattered half in English, half in Spanish, but he could have been speaking Greek for all she knew. Too, a hundred cows and a like number of horses could have roamed past them without her knowing. Her thoughts remained on what lay at the end of the trail.

The cabin sat squat on the top of the rise, quiet and deserted, its chimney bare of smoke. Not even the mongrel dog was there to lift his head in greeting. She didn't know whether to be more worried or relieved. Leaving Antonio to unload the supplies, she rode out on the mare to find Cal.

She rode slowly over the rolling grassland, past thick stands of oak and elm and scattered patches of prickly pear and mesquite. Clouds were forming dark and thick overhead, and the November wind was turning cold. She gave the mare her head and they moved with a strange sense of purpose. An hour after beginning the ride, she felt the edges of despair. He was lying somewhere out of sight, injured, maybe dying. The only thing that gave her encouragement was that she saw no buzzards circling overhead.

She was about to turn back when a *thwacking*

sound drifted from a line of trees by one of the county's wandering creeks. The mare needed little urging to pick up the pace. Ellie saw Cal standing with his back to her at the edge of the moss-draped trees, swinging an ax at a fallen log. Nearby the dog lay sleeping, and on down the slope, close to the creek, Cal's gelding chomped at a patch of grass.

Her first impulse was to cry out with joy, but when she took a good look at him, the cry died in her throat. He was naked to the waist, his shirt and jerkin hanging from a branch of an oak. He wore brown trousers and boots and a sheen of sweat that glistened with each ripple of his muscles as he worked. Methodically he swung the ax, showing no sign he realized she was within twenty yards of him. The dog lifted his big brown head, slapped his tail once against the ground, then returned to his repose.

Half-clothed, Cal looked bigger, more muscular than she would have supposed he would. She allowed herself a moment to study him, the broad shoulders and the contours of his back, the tapered waist, the fit of the trousers over taut buttocks and long legs. His dark hair was damp against his neck, and when he swung the ax, she saw the power of his arms.

Such arms could crush her if they chose. A smart woman would have been afraid. But Ellie felt only relief that he appeared to be all right. All right? He looked magnificent, so much so that she yearned to rub the slick sweat from his body and be held in the circle of his heat.

That was when reason took over, and with it a

sudden rage. What was she thinking of? How dare he be all right? Any man worth worrying over would have had the decency to be hurt. She was about to tell him exactly that when the gelding neighed and the mare whinnied in return.

Cal slowly lowered the ax and turned; his eyes locked with hers, their expression unreadable. The stubble of five days darkened his long, lean face; his sweat-slick chest was as finely contoured as his back. He looked as wicked as she had ever seen him—and more tempting than any man had a right to be.

She could not breathe.

"Have you been there long?" he asked.

Typical Cal, hinting that she had been staring at him while he worked. She found her breath. "At least an hour," she said. She had meant the response to be flippant, but it came out sounding dangerously like the truth.

He dropped the ax and headed toward her.

"Let me help you dismount, Ellie, and I'll show you how glad I am you're here."

Chapter Nine

Ellie dropped to the ground before Cal could get to her. He had known she would, but goading her was something he couldn't resist, especially when she showed up in the middle of nowhere just as he had finally managed to get her off his mind.

The ever-surprising woman was wearing a more substantial bonnet than usual, a head-covering contraption that actually might do some good against the sun and wind, and her cloak covered her from bonnet to boots. Only a few square inches of skin showed, the ivory smoothness of her face, but she managed to look sexier than any bare-breasted beauty he'd ever seen.

Pulling a kerchief from his pants pocket, he wiped his hands and face, then tossed the damp square of cloth aside. She watched the kerchief's fluttery fall as if it somehow sealed her fate.

"So you've been watching for an hour, have you?" he asked. It had been two minutes at the most. He had known the instant she arrived. "I'm going to have to get another guard dog. Baron isn't getting the job done."

At the mention of his new name, the dog's tail thumped.

"Baron?" Ellie asked.

"Why not? The Double T is his empire."

Ellie tugged off her riding gloves and thrust them inside a cloak pocket. "Why not indeed. He serves a king. Isn't that what barons do?"

"What are you talking about?" he asked, half listening, momentarily distracted by thoughts of removing a layer or two of her clothes. What would she look like in nothing but bonnet and boots? The image made him decidedly uncomfortable.

"I'm talking about Baron's master. You. King Cal."

It took a minute for her answer to register. When it did, he reined in his imagination, as irritated with himself as he was with her.

"You've been listening to my uncles."

"A little."

More than a little. Once they got started on a subject, Fin and Fitz had no idea how to stop.

"What else did they tell you? And while we're at it, what the hell are you doing out here alone?"

Was that a blush stealing onto her face? He was catching her at something; he just didn't know what the something was.

She looked to the right, to the left, everywhere but at him.

"Couldn't you put some clothes on?" she asked. "It's getting cold."

"I was thinking about taking more off. When I'm naked, I heat up the most."

Her eyes widened, so deep and brown that a thousand emotions roiled in their depths, none comforting to either of them. He was beginning to think of it as her doe look—only the doe was staring down the barrel of a gun.

Maybe that was just what she was doing, figuratively speaking. He wanted more than ever to find out why she had been at the cemetery in New Orleans and why she hated him so much.

If *hate* was the right word. She didn't kiss as if she hated. Or maybe the fervency of her responses had been because she resented the pleasure he brought to her.

Lord, women were complicated, and none more so than Ellie Davenport. He wasn't even sure that was her name.

"I know you're just trying to upset me," she said. "Quit being childish and get dressed."

The order was so absurd, he almost laughed, except he wasn't in a laughing mood. He hadn't been a child in years; even as a boy he hadn't enjoyed the luxury of childishness.

He stepped close. She stepped back.

"Think of what I'm doing as man-play."

"Mr. Hardin!"

"What happened to Cal? After all we've meant to each other, Mr. Hardin sounds far too formal."

"Does it?" Her eyes narrowed. "All right, if you want me to touch you, that's exactly what I'll do."

She slapped her hands against his chest and put

all her weight behind shoving him away. He didn't move, except to grab her wrists and hold her hands in place.

"Is this your version of woman-play?" he asked. "You'll have to tell me the rules."

She kept her eyes downcast. "There are no rules. This isn't a game."

"Isn't it?"

In answer, she twisted her hands against him in a vain effort to get free. The heat of her palms shot through him straight to his loins. He fought against dragging her hands down his sweaty chest and lower, letting her feel her effect on him.

"If you're trying to make me let go," he growled, "you're going about it the wrong way."

She held as still as a rock. So did he. A minute crawled by while he stared at the top of her plain black bonnet. He wondered what she would do if he really did begin to rub her hands against him. She was holding herself so stiffly he would probably break a tiny bone.

It was another of Ellie's mysteries that she could be as fragile as a flower and as tough as an iron nail at the same time.

"If you promise not to hit me again, I'll let you go."

She snorted indelicately. "Promises don't mean much out here. The other day you promised not to kiss me until I asked."

"Good point. But you needed a better sampling before reaching a decision. That's all I was giving you, an example of what I can do."

She looked up at him. Encircled by the black bonnet and a few wisps of yellow hair, her face was lovely and finely drawn and filled with an anguish he couldn't begin to understand. One so strong, it rocked him back on his heels.

And made him angry, too. He didn't want her to affect him, not even in a lustful way.

"What else can you do?" she whispered. "What have you done?"

He gave her an honest answer. "Anything and everything."

"Except settle into a permanent home. Except marry and father a child."

The last remnants of tenderness toward her hardened behind his protective shell. "You really have been listening to my uncles."

"These are things you told me, Cal. Shouldn't I have believed you?"

"It's back to Cal, is it? I'd like to say I was making progress, but I'm not sure that's true."

He let go of her wrists. Unsteadily she stepped away.

"If you want to wipe your hands on your cloak," he said, "go right ahead. I've been working up quite a sweat. Most women find sweat unpleasant."

"I'm not most women."

"No, you're not. I'm not sure you're even Ellie Davenport."

The doe look returned. "Don't be ridiculous."

"I thought I was being childish. You ought to stick around to point out the error of my ways."

"I don't have that much time. You wanted to know why I'm here? I brought you supplies. We . . . your uncles hadn't heard from you in so long that we . . . they were worried."

155

"You . . . they shouldn't have bothered. I get by."

"You're right. You get by. I won't forget it again. I won't forget anything."

He turned to get his shirt and buckskin jerkin from the nearby oak branch, slipping them on slowly, taking his time about tucking in the shirt. The last thing he did was strap on his holster and gun.

Like hell she was here to bring him supplies; her purpose was something else, something far less kind. As he shifted to face her once again, hard questions formed in his mind, questions that went back to New Orleans.

One look at her, and he forgot them all.

She was holding one hand close to her face, as if she were inhaling his scent, tasting his taste. He could have sworn her tongue was on her palm. Their eyes met, and she dropped her hand, practically flinging it away as though it were no part of her.

But she had been caught, and she knew it, caught in an act both furtive and flagrant and of such familiarity that it stunned him. Without drawing near, he could feel her small, pale hands stroking him, burning him, wrapping around his heart.

But he didn't have a heart, not one that could be touched by anyone. If he had any sense, he would be running as fast as he could, as far as he could, putting miles between them. Instead, he came at her fast, giving her no time to do the running. When he took her in his arms, she held herself stiff, but she didn't fight to get away. Thunder sounded in the distance. She lifted her head; he bent to place his lips close to hers, but he didn't touch her. Instead he waited to hear the words *kiss me*.

"You really are all right," she whispered.

They were not the words he would have chosen, but there was wonder in them and something that sounded like relief.

All right? Like hell he was. And neither was she. They were both shaking like the leaves on the trees. Before he could do something to her, she did it to him, brushing her mouth against his. Sparks ignited, as if lightning had dropped from the incoming dark clouds to tear through them. He parted her lips with his tongue and tasted her as she had tasted him.

Once again her hands touched his chest; this time she moved them voluntarily, easing them up to his shoulders and around his neck. There was tentative shyness in the moves, and boldness, too, an eagerness to learn what she did not know.

The combination was almost the undoing of them both. He wanted to take her there on the ground, sharing a sex as wild as the land surrounding them. Instead he held her close and covered her face with kisses.

"Who are you?" he whispered.

Her answer was a shudder that trembled through her and into him.

Impatiently he pulled at the wide tie holding her bonnet in place and tossed the hat aside. He licked her throat. "What devil sent you here?"

She shook her head. "Please don't talk."

Thrusting his hands into the falling tumble of

yellow hair, he kissed his way to her ear. "Who are you?"

"You're bad to do this to me," she said with a catch in her voice.

"I'm bad. And good." He kissed her eyelids. "Admit it."

She clung all the harder to him. "And good."

"Who are you?" he repeated.

"A crazy woman."

"You're driving me insane. Do you realize that?"

"No."

"Yes."

He spoke the truth. No longer caring who or what she was, he ran his hands down the front of her cloak, moving inside its folds to cup her breasts. Her sharp intake of breath told him more clearly than words that she had never been touched in such a way before.

He wasn't breathing too well himself. Usually he liked overblown women, but Ellie's subtle curves made him feel very much like a man. His hands roamed down to her waist and around to her back, giving him an intimation of how she would look without her clothes. Good, that was how. Damned good.

He also realized something else.

"You're not wearing a corset," he said.

"What?" she said, nuzzling against him, paying no attention to anything except where they touched.

"I like you without it."

"Without what?" she said. And then, "Oh," in a very small voice. "The corset, you mean."

He looked down to see the dazed, languid look in her eyes grow focused as reality struck.

"What are we doing?" she whispered. "This isn't why I came out here."

She held still, her body stiff, as if she had pulled inside herself for protection against his hands and his words.

He was hot and hard and hungry, but he couldn't bring himself to do anything other than let her go.

They parted to stare at one another. She hugged herself as a few splats of rain hit the ground around them and stirred the fallen leaves. Lightning rent the air, and scant seconds later thunder rumbled across the sky. Both horses whinnied, and even Baron lifted his regal head to whine.

She wrung her hands at her waist. "About the corset," she said, as if that were the only consideration that mattered. "I dressed fast this morning. I woke up with the stupid idea that you were in trouble."

"What do you mean, trouble?"

She stared past him toward the trees. "I'm not sure. But it seemed serious. Don't ask why I didn't send for your uncles. To show you how truly stupid I was, it seemed that I was the only one who could help."

At last she looked at him. Her eyes were wide with a look of puzzlement that he would have sworn was genuine. If he had come up with a thousand reasons for her presence, his rescue would not have been among them. She didn't seem to understand the explanation any more than he.

"Don't stare at me like that," she said. "I know far better than you that I'm not making sense. You're nothing to me, just as I am nothing to you."

She lied. He was something to her, all right, something important. Otherwise she wouldn't have been at a New Orleans cemetery seething with a hatred meant for him. And she certainly wouldn't have followed him to this godforsaken land.

"Let me get this straight," he said. "You came to offer help? All by yourself?"

"Antonio Gomez rode with me."

"Who the hell is he?"

"Consuela's son. She's the housekeeper Gert and May hired a couple of days ago for the soiree."

"Of course," he said, as much puzzled as ever. "The soiree."

"It's something my aunts are planning for tomorrow night."

"Is Antonio a big strapping brute with a bandolier across his chest and pistols strapped to his thighs?"

"He's thirteen, but he's got a shotgun he knows how to use."

Cal shook his head in disgust. "Riding out here with a child is no better than riding alone. Worse. You could end up defending him instead of yourself."

"Were you still a child at thirteen?"

"My situation was different. I had to grow up fast."

"Tony doesn't have a father, either. Not so far as I know."

Somehow they had come full circle, edging along why she was here and how she'd made the ride, returning all the way to a past he was trying to forget.

Cal let out a long, slow breath. "What else did my uncles tell you?"

"Don't get upset with them. They didn't tell me anything directly. I overheard them talking last night. I wasn't a very nice person. I didn't let them know I was near."

"And you woke up certain I was in trouble."

She took a moment to answer. "Maybe you are, Cal, and you just don't know it. The only thing I'm sure of is that I cannot help you. I doubt if anyone can."

She leaned down to retrieve her bonnet and in the doing grabbed up his kerchief as well. Without bothering to twist her hair into a knot, she tied the bonnet in place, but instead of handing him the kerchief, she thrust it into a pocket in her cloak.

Lightning and thunder struck again, this time one quickly upon the other, and the sky opened to a heavy, hard rain. Grabbing the reins of the mare with one hand and Ellie's arm with the other, he hurried them into the protection of the trees close to the creek. For once Baron moved fast, keeping close to his master's heels.

They stood close to one another, but neither spoke. Tiny drips of rain worked their way through the thick-leafed trees. He took the oilskin coat from the roll at the back of his saddle, but when he tried to throw it over her shoulders, she shook him off.

Ignoring her protest, he draped it over the two of them and held her against his side. She didn't fight him, but neither did she snuggle close.

"This ought to let up soon," he said. "There's already a break in the clouds."

She said nothing, continuing to stare into the downpour. But he felt her tension and, too, her weariness. He had no doubt she wanted him, though she clearly didn't like him very much. That made two of them. More often than not, he didn't care much for himself.

Ellie's trouble was that she didn't understand her new feelings. She needed protecting, no matter who she was, from herself as well as from him.

Him as a protector? Saint Callaghan? It was a role he could never play, no matter how tempting it might be.

And then he caught himself. Tempting? What in hell was he thinking of? Suddenly he felt the same kind of tightening in his gut he'd experienced on his visit to New Orleans, as if she ought to mean more to him than she ever could.

In that moment he didn't give a damn who she was or why she had been at Margaret O'Malley's funeral. In some inadvertent way he, or maybe even his uncles, had offended her. It would have had to be inadvertent since most everything about her remained a mystery.

All he truly cared about was getting away from there. Why he continued to hold her with gentle solicitude, he had not the vaguest idea, except that for the moment and in the storm she felt right in his embrace.

Which made her the most dangerous person he had ever met.

From across the creek, in another stand of trees, Alden Fowler sat on horseback and through the heavy rain observed the tender scene. Bile rose in his throat. He wanted to pull his shotgun from its scabbard and shoot them both.

He'd thought for a minute that the two of them were going to give in to their primal urges right there in the leaves and dirt. Even the whores he hired were more fastidious. Unless he paid them to do things out of the ordinary. Which he sometimes did.

The woman he was using now could scarcely be called a whore. She wasn't even much of a woman, more like a dummy doll who did what she was told.

There weren't many so-called nice women like Eleanor Davenport, ladylike on the outside but churning inside for a man. In all his forty-plus years he had met only one, his long-dead wife. He was surprised to think of Ruthanne now, though he shouldn't have been, what with the similarities between her and the Davenport woman.

Most anywhere he and she had found themselves alone, she had been willing to touch him and let him touch her, more than once practically pulling down his drawers when she came upon him alone in the barn. Some of the time she had embarrassed him, catching him when he wasn't ready, demanding things he couldn't deliver, making him feel less than a man.

But there were other times. . . . It was those other times that troubled him the most. She was gone, he reminded himself. And that had been a long time ago.

He needed to forget the past, what with the present giving him all the problems he could handle. Maybe he ought to shoot Cal Hardin and use his woman. She would eventually have to die, of course, but not right away.

If he thought such actions would get him title to the Double T, he would be cradling the shotgun in an instant. But Hardin did not own the land. And he didn't know Hardin's uncles well enough to judge whether they would sell out after his death and go back to New Orleans.

Above all else, he must end up with that title.

Damn Buck Shannon anyway. He had made returning to Louisiana difficult for the inept O'Malleys. If he were going to shoot anyone, it ought to be Buck.

Except that he needed him a while longer. There was no one else he could trust.

He sensed more than heard his hired gunman ride up behind him. He glanced Shannon's way, nodding in greeting. Rain dripped from Shannon's sodden hat, and his leather duster hung limp and wet against his thickset body, but he showed no sign the storm bothered him.

The man had come to Fowler's attention a year before on one of his rare trips into town for a game of cards and a few drinks. Fowler wasn't a gambling and drinking man, but he knew such occasional sallies gave him the appearance of an ordinary Texan. Sometimes he picked up information about who was moving into Victoria County and who was moving out, and what land might become available to him.

There was certain land he had to have. Only he knew which parcels and why.

On that particular day, he'd gotten crosswise with a disgruntled drifter, a loser who claimed, rightly enough, that he'd been cheated at the poker table. He tried to draw; Buck Shannon gunned him down before the fool's pistol cleared the holster. More than the quick draw, Fowler had been impressed by the cold, flat expression in the killer's eyes, as if he had done nothing other than swat a fly.

The few witnesses to the scene had shown no inclination to interfere. The bartender pronounced that the dead man had got no more than he deserved and offered a shot of whiskey to the man who dragged his carcass out for the buzzards. A fight had erupted over who would handle the chore.

Fowler liked coldness in a man. Caring too much was the cause of all trouble. He hadn't cared for anyone in years. Land was what lasted. It was the only thing that could be depended upon.

Shannon had more in his favor than just coldness. He had a nondescript look that helped him blend into crowds. Average in height and build, brown-haired and brown-eyed, his craggy face hidden beneath heavy whiskers and a moustache, he looked like a hundred other men passing through Texas. That made him difficult to describe.

Except for the flatness in his eyes.

And so Fowler had hired him, eventually sending him to New Orleans. Today, after following the lusty Eleanor Davenport until she came upon Hardin, Shannon had gone on another mission. Sitting back in his saddle, Fowler awaited his report.

Shannon reined his horse close beside Fowler. "There's no one at the cabin except a boy," he said in a gravelly voice. He spat. "A Meskin."

"Did he see you?"

Shannon shrugged. "Nope. He was too busy dragging things from the wagon and putting the horse inside the barn."

Fowler considered the situation. "We need to send Hardin a warning."

"Shoot him. That's warning enough."

"The way you shot Henry Chase? The way you tried to gun down the O'Malleys?"

"Chase got me riled. And like I told you, with the others I was trying to put the fear of death into them."

"You frightened them all the way to Texas."

"It'll work out. They ain't about to stay."

"The women seem to have given them courage."

"Say the word and they're all dead."

"And have every Ranger in the Republic down on us? Not to mention every do-gooder from San Antonio to Lavaca Bay. Even in this godforsaken land, that kind of carnage would do me more harm than good."

"I can handle the Rangers and anyone else who tries to interfere."

Fowler let the bragging go without comment.

"Women have a weakness for children," he said, and for just a moment a few more forbidden memories flashed across his mind. He had to keep those memories away. They wouldn't do him any good.

"Hurt the boy," he growled, thrusting the memories aside. "Miss Eleanor Davenport won't come out here to entertain Hardin again."

"Entertaining him, eh?" Shannon sat forward in the saddle. "What was she doing exactly?"

"She just about spread her legs for the bastard."

Shannon chewed on his moustache. "Next time I'll be watching."

"There won't be a next time. Not if you handle the boy right."

Slowly the gunman drew his attention away from the pair on the far bank, his eyes narrowing to small dark pins.

"I can kill him."

"Just hurt him. That'll be enough. Maybe they'll think it was vigilantes, the way they did the other night. You're sure those men you hired have moved on?"

"They're gone. Don't worry. I didn't have to shoot 'em. I just looked at 'em and they got the idea leaving was a good idea. They're probably deep into Mexico by now."

Shannon reined his horse once again into the storm, leaving Fowler to stare across the creek at the couple who were giving him so much trouble. Shooting them was still tempting, but he didn't want to arouse suspicion. It would be best if they simply moved on.

If that didn't happen, he would do what he had to do. He had goals in mind and didn't care how he reached them. Top of the list, at whatever the cost, was owning the Double T.

Chapter Ten

The rain had eased to a fine mist when Ellie and Cal set out for the cabin. For Ellie it was not a peaceful ride. The sleeves of Cal's buff linen shirt lay damp against his arms, and his trousers. Well, she simply couldn't give them too close a look. His only other protection against the weather was a water-spotted leather jerkin and a black felt hat. He had refused to wear the oilskin coat, insisting it was for her.

She found it easier to give in than argue. Arguing with Cal was dangerous, for that was when she came closest to blurting out the truths she didn't want him to know.

It was the second-most dangerous thing she could do around him. Number one was letting him get near. She couldn't allow herself to remember the liberties he had taken every time they were alone, liberties she had invited, touches and kisses she hadn't wanted to stop.

There was something terribly perverse in her nature; otherwise she wouldn't have felt so devastated each time he pulled away. This afternoon had been the worst, primarily because he had pulled so far away, not only physically but emotionally, turning more private and secretive than she had ever been. By the time they were mounting the horses, she knew he planned never to touch her again, at least not in any way that might bring him pleasure.

Somehow she had failed him, or at least disappointed him. Good, she told herself. It was nothing more than she had expected and all that she could have asked. Her whole purpose in being here was to get what she wanted from him and watch him leave. What she truly wanted had nothing to do with touching. She couldn't believe she liked it so much.

Her nature was perverse indeed.

As they rode away from the creek, for the first time she noticed a stack of logs near where he had been wielding the ax.

"Getting ready for the winter?" she asked, determined to keep her questions light, though it wasn't easy with him sitting the saddle so comfortably a scant few feet away and his shirt so caressingly damp.

"The wood's not entirely for burning," he said. "I was thinking to build a corral."

He sounded almost embarrassed by the admission.

"But you don't own more than a couple of horses."

"True."

"So why the corral?"

Shrugging, he looked around the landscape, and she noticed the way his wet hair curled against the collar of his shirt.

"It passes the time. Besides, someone will make good use of this country one of these days. It won't be abandoned."

Ellie's heart caught in her throat. "Are you thinking of Alden Fowler?"

Cal's sweeping gaze settled on her. "You sound as if that bothers you."

She gave smiling the best effort she could, but his eyes made lying hard. "I'm just too practical, I guess. I hate to see anyone's efforts help someone else."

"Ellie, if you and the truth have more than a passing acquaintance, I'd be surprised."

It was her turn to study the landscape. "You still don't believe I rode out to help you."

"I still don't."

"I can't blame you," she said. "I scarcely believe it myself."

They rode on in silence for a while. When she recognized the trail leading to the cabin, she realized that on her long search for him earlier she must have been circling needlessly. She was about to speak lightly of her scouting skills when Baron started to growl deep in his throat. She didn't know the docile giant could make such a feral sound. The skin at the back of her neck prickled.

"What's wrong, Baron?" Cal asked.

The dog trotted on ahead, then stopped dead still, his broad head pointed in the direction of the cabin. It wasn't in view yet, but it would be at the top of the next rise.

"You said you left a boy there alone?" Cal asked.

"That's right." Fear struck her. "You don't think something's happened to him, do you?"

His answer was to slap reins against his gelding's flanks and take off at a fast gallop, the dog leading the way. The mare reared. Ellie got her under control and took off after the gelding.

They covered the quarter mile to the cabin in short order. Cal dropped to the ground while his horse was still in motion and darted onto the porch.

"Cal!" Ellie called.

He threw an impatient look over his shoulder at her.

"Baron," she said, pointing to the dog.

The mongrel's attention was directed toward the barn. He barked once. Cal flew off the porch. Dismounting, Ellie had to scurry through the mud to keep up with him.

He threw open the barn doors to a scene that would forever burn in her mind. A man she'd never seen before stood with arm raised over the sprawled, bloody figure of the boy Antonio, a whip in his hand. He paused and blinked into the sudden light.

With a growl as fierce as Baron's, Cal hurled himself at the man, wresting the whip from him and tossing it aside. Gripping the stranger's coat, he threw him from the barn into the mud outside the open doors.

The stranger staggered to his feet and went for his gun. Cal kicked him in the groin, and when he doubled over, knocked the weapon from his hand. Stunned by the sudden violence, Ellie watched in horror as Cal's fists landed again and again on the man's body, his face, any place he could come in contact.

Baron circled the men, snapping and snarling, his hackles raised. It was all happening so fast. She felt as helpless as she did horrified. And then she remembered the boy.

With a cry, she came to her senses and ran back into the barn, praying he was still alive. He lay facedown on the hard dirt floor, much too still, the back of his shirt shredded by the sting of the whip, the welts and the blood obscenely exposed. As she knelt beside him, her trembling hand went out to touch the wounds, but she stopped short, fearful of causing more pain.

"Antonio," she said softly.

His answer was a low moan, and relief flooded through her. But only for a moment. Hurriedly discarding bonnet and oilskin coat, she tried to turn him. His moan became a cry of agony so wrenching, it tore at her soul.

What had she done? She was trying to be so careful not to touch the open wounds. The answer lay in the arm twisted and limp at his side. With the torn clothing and blood demanding attention, she hadn't noticed anything else.

She brushed at her foolish tears, but still they came. She leaned close to kiss the boy's cheek.

173

"You'll be all right," she assured him. "It's over. The man's gone."

But of course his travail wasn't over. She needed help. She couldn't move him alone.

"I'll be right back." Again she kissed his cheek. It was the only comfort she knew to give.

Outside, the scene was equally devastating. Cal hunched over the prone body of the stranger, kicking and pounding, his boots and fists landing anywhere and everywhere they could reach. With each blow the man grunted and tried to rise, but Cal was a madman. He'd kill the stranger if she didn't do something.

In panic, she glanced around her. Her eyes stopped at the trough. She stumbled in the mud as she ran to get the bucket. Scooping up the rain-freshened water, she ran back to toss the bucket's contents in Cal's face, but he paid her no mind.

She screamed his name. Nothing. He was a man she did not know. She swung the bucket as hard as she could against his side, fearing to hurt him, yet knowing nothing else to do. But he was oblivious to any pain she might inflict.

At any moment she expected him to pull his gun and shoot the stranger. For Cal's sake, she had to stop him.

And then she spied the stranger's gun lying by the open barn door. Wiping it on her cloak, she held it aloft and fired. The weapon was far more powerful than her pepperbox; she felt the recoil down her arm. In the echoing explosion, Baron's snarls became a whimper as she threw the gun aside.

Cal's brief hesitation gave her the moment she

needed. Throwing herself against him, she hugged him as hard as she could and held on for dear life, sobbing uncontrollably against his chest.

Gradually he grew still.

"Is he dead?"

For a moment she didn't know whether he meant the man or the boy. But of course he meant Antonio.

"No," she managed as she stilled her sobs. Brushing at her tangled hair and tears, she looked up at him. "But he needs you. He's hurt."

The fallen man groaned, but neither looked at him as they turned toward the barn. Inside, Cal stared for a moment at the boy's striated back, then knelt beside him.

"The welts will heal," she said. "But his right arm . . . he's right handed . . . he won't be able to—"

Her eye fell to the whip, lying like a dead snake on the far side of the boy, and her voice broke. She had spoken all that she could. Cal's expert hands surveyed the misshapen limb. This time, the boy did not cry out or even moan.

"He's passed out," Cal said. "Get one of the beds ready. I'll bring him in."

He looked up, but she could read neither anger nor agony in the hollowness of his eyes. It was as though all feeling had burned out of him in the fight. If it could be called a fight. It had come dangerously close to being a slaying.

Outside, like a sentinel, Baron sat at attention by the door, but the man was gone—gun, hat, everything. Even signs of the struggle were hard to discern in the mud. The rain had ceased altogether, and she thought she heard the sound of a horse in the distance. Scooping up Cal's hat, which had fallen in the fray, she pushed all thought of the stranger from her mind and hurried to the cabin.

One small and bitter irony struck her. She had brought medical supplies with her in the wagon, not knowing if she would have to use them on Cal. But it was a young, brave boy who would benefit from her fear, a boy who had endured great pain because he had so cheerfully accompanied her on a strange, senseless mission of mercy.

All of her premonitions had been for Cal. All of them had been wrong.

Later, when Antonio's arm had been set in crude splints, when his back was tended and wrapped in strips of petticoat, when he rested as comfortably as possible on a straw mattress across the open dog run, Ellie served Cal a cup of steaming tea and sat beside him at the table.

At the edge of the fireplace, chicken simmered in a cast-iron oven, and there was a pan of biscuits waiting to be added, along with the few vegetables she had been able to buy at Merse's store. The biscuits were as much a treat as the peas and potatoes, flour being a commodity in short supply.

With the room redolent of stew and blazing mesquite logs, the scene was almost domestic, except that their thoughts were on the injured boy. If anything, Cal seemed more distressed than she.

She was doing the best she could to bring him

comfort, refusing to consider the why of what she did. Hours ago she had given up trying to understand her reactions to him. All she knew was that despite his physical strength and private nature, he had a vulnerability about him that touched her heart.

At the moment it mattered not how culpable he was in what had happened to her father. She simply couldn't bring herself to believe he had truly been responsible for the tragic happening in New Orleans.

Gripping the hot cup, he stared into empty space. She noticed a sprinkling of gray in his disheveled dark hair, as if it had appeared only today. The gray seemed out of place in a man of thirty-two, a man of such power and strength of will that he ought never to age. But his whiskers were dark as night, shadowing the harsh lines of his face, and he had a faraway look in his eyes that made her feel very much alone.

She took a sip of tea. "Was Antonio able to talk any? He wasn't when I was in the room."

Cal pulled himself from his thoughts and looked at her. "He didn't know the man. That was about all."

"Did you know him?"

He shook his head.

"I thought maybe . . . because he upset you so much, he was someone you had met."

"You want to know why I did what I did?"

"I'm not prying. I'm just trying to understand."

He laughed harshly, without humor. "You know everything else about me. You might as well know this. When I was fifteen, my father took a cane to me. In public, where everyone could see."

"Oh, Cal." She reached out to touch his hand, but he pulled away.

"He had reason. I had lit into him first."

"I'm sure you had good cause."

"He called me the son of a whore. It seemed good enough reason at the time, but there are others who say I was wrong. Raymond Hardin had wives and children who had reason to detest him, but he always had friends."

Ellie could think of nothing to say that could possibly give him comfort.

"I was hustling money on the dock. He came by with a half-dozen cronies. The sight of him laughing and strolling in his fancy suit got to me. He'd already disowned me, so to goad him I called him father. And then we were both yelling and fighting. I was a good scrapper, but I was no match for his cane."

He swallowed the tea. "This needs sweetening."

"I've got some sugar—"

"O'Malley sugar. That's what I want."

It took her a moment to realize he meant whiskey. She found the bottle on a shelf next to the stove, but by the time she set it beside him, he no longer seemed interested.

"He'll bear scars," he said. "Inside and out."

"Do you?" The question slipped out before she had a chance to think. "When you were working out there, I didn't see them on your back."

His lips twitched, and when he looked at her she saw a familiar glint in his eyes.

"That's not where they are. I'll show you if you like."

But Ellie was learning too much about him to let his taunting get to her.

"No, you won't. You talk about taking off your clothes, but I'll bet you never get completely naked with a woman, not in full light. You're much too private to let anyone see you as you really are."

The glint died. "Who made you so smart?"

"Being smart has nothing to do with it. I'm guessing most of the time."

A log snapped in the fire. Suddenly she was very much aware of how isolated they were. She knew he didn't plan to hold her again—it was one of her guesses that seemed very much right—but these were extraordinary circumstances, and for all her flashes of wisdom, she didn't really know him at all.

She looked past him to the window by the front door. "It's getting dark. I should ride back to town."

"Like hell you will."

"But his mother needs to be told."

"She'll have to wait."

"She'll have a bad night. And so will Gert and May."

"I doubt it. They'll think you're lying out here in my arms. Isn't that what we're supposed to be doing?"

Guilt made her start, and she stared at him in what she hoped resembled disbelief. "I can't believe you said that."

"Relax. I'm guessing. Maybe I'm not as good at it as you."

And maybe you are.

179

Worse, he probably knew it. She pushed away from the table, prepared to stir the simmering stew, when a knock sounded at the door.

Ellie started. "He's come back—"

"I don't imagine so. He's probably not moving much right now."

"Of course not. I wasn't thinking."

The knock sounded again. She went to answer. Cal moved fast and caught her by the sleeve.

"How you have survived this long is a mystery to me," he said with a shake of his head. "The man who whipped the boy is not the only bastard around."

Grabbing up the rifle by the door, he called out, "Who is it?"

"Alden Fowler. Your neighbor. Just making a friendly call."

Cal glanced at her.

"He's harmless enough," she said. "You ought to let him in."

She didn't mean what she said. Fowler was the one man who could tempt the O'Malleys out of the land with a more alluring offer than either Gert or May. And that made him far from harmless.

Cal opened the door slowly and gestured for their visitor to enter. Fowler's eye went first to the rifle, and then to Ellie.

"Sorry," he said in far too oily a tone to bring her peace of mind. "I didn't know you weren't alone."

Liar, she thought. He had probably been looking through the curtainless window for who knew how long. For once, she and Cal hadn't given unwanted onlookers something to see. It was little enough for which to be grateful, but she seized on it.

Fowler doffed his hat as he came into the room. Ellie retreated to the fireplace, but not before noticing that he tracked mud onto the otherwise clean floor. Even Cal had taken off his boots once he had carried his patient to the other room.

Alden Fowler was a widower, she reminded herself, and while she was at it, she told herself not to be petty. This was a hard land and this was a bad night, and she couldn't expect Virginia manners, even under the best of conditions.

What really irked was that the peace between her and Cal, temporary and uneasy though it was, had been interrupted by a man she didn't much like.

Using a folded cloth as a pad, she lifted the lid of the cast-iron oven and stirred the chicken in its rich broth. Maybe she could get Antonio to swallow some of the liquid, she thought, for a moment forgetting their visitor. Carefully she added the vegetables she had waiting on the hearth.

"If I'm interrupting something, I apologize," Fowler said.

"What would you be interrupting?" Cal asked.

She could have throttled him with her cloth.

Instead, she stood and, with hands on hips, said, "Mr. Fowler means maybe we're having a tryst. I know that sounds ridiculous, given the fact that we hardly know one another and I'm betrothed, but appearances do make us look guilty." She shifted her gaze to Fowler. "We've got trouble, Mr. Fowler. A young boy was badly beaten here today. He's asleep on the other side of the cabin. He'll live, but he'll be a long time getting well."

Fowler's surprise looked genuine enough. "Beaten, you say? How? By whom?"

"We don't know. I rode out from town with him to bring supplies and went to look for Mr. Hardin. We returned to find him—"

She'd been too brave too long. She turned fast, unwilling to let anyone see her tears. "Please excuse me. It's been a long day."

"Of course, of course," said Fowler. "Your distress is certainly understandable. This is terrible, simply terrible. Cal, were you able to get a look at who did it?"

"A passing glance," Cal said.

"What did he look like? Was it anyone you'd seen before?"

"He was a stranger. Medium height and build, brown hair, brown eyes, bearded."

"But that might describe any number of men."

"Mostly I remember he was mean. I won't forget him. And I don't imagine he'll forget me."

"He must have been a drifter," Fowler said, "though why anyone would beat up a child is beyond me."

All the talk, all the empty words, got to Ellie. They did nothing but bring the horror to her once again. She turned to smile brightly at the men.

"Mr. Fowler," she said, "would you do us a favor?"

"If I can," he said, twisting his hat in his hand.

"It's a very big favor, I'm afraid. I'll be cooking

biscuits in a few minutes. You're welcome to stay and eat your fill. Then I would very much appreciate your riding into town to let my aunts and that poor boy's mother know what's going on."

"Why, of course I will," he said, but he didn't look too pleased about it.

"Assure them Antonio will be all right. He's young and in good health and he's being very brave. What he needs is rest and quiet, and we'll see he gets plenty of both. And chicken broth. My aunt always said there's nothing like chicken broth to cure whatever ails."

"Which aunt is that," Cal said, "Gert or May?"

She ignored him. "If you don't like traveling in the dark, you can wait until morning."

"Nonsense. The rain has ceased and the wind has died down. I know the way well enough, having ridden the trail under far worse conditions than these. Besides, here in Texas we have to help our neighbors."

"That's exactly what I was thinking."

She looked at Cal, who stood tall and straight beside the door, the rifle still in his hand. She thought of all he had been through today, and her heart twisted in sympathy—not because he appeared to need it, but because he managed to look completely unmoved.

It was a mask he had been wearing since he was a boy.

"Do you have a message for your uncles?" she asked.

She knew her sympathy was in her eyes, but his mask remained in place.

183

"Just tell them to stay put and enjoy the soiree tomorrow night. Also tell them the vigilantes haven't returned. They'll readily believe I've got everything under control."

Chapter Eleven

Cal had lied about being in control. As if he ever was, outside of making money. His usual answer to problems was to keep moving on. Whatever power he could claim had been doubly taken from him today—by the cursed memories that came at him unexpectedly, and by a hundred-pound, flat-chested pixie who had trouble keeping to the truth.

Still, he kept himself outwardly civilized, beginning at supper with Fowler rambling on about how Texas needed decent law enforcement to protect its citizens, through a long night helping Ellie care for their suffering patient, to the next two impatient days in which he staked out the boundaries for the corral beyond the barn while he watched for the approach of a bearded stranger bent on revenge.

On the second day Ellie found a shirt and pair of britches one of his uncles had left behind. Small as the clothes were, they swallowed her, but she belted and folded the extra material until they fit, allowing her to wash her muddied gown and, while she was at it, his laundry as well.

He had to hide his underwear, else she would be washing it, too.

Maybe he should have told her what she was doing to him as she bent over the washtub while wearing the trousers, but he'd never had much of a conscience, and around her he didn't have one at all. He went so far as to lend her one of his shirts in which to sleep. But that was as far as he would go to preserve her modesty.

Each night, picturing her in the shirt, he tried to sleep on the horsehair sofa while she and Baron took up quarters close to the boy. He came up with some interesting details about her and that shirt, filling in with his imagination what he hadn't actually seen or felt. The view of her in the trousers helped.

Both day and night Antonio's arm frequently gave him trouble, but when Ellie touched him and told him stories, he settled down without a complaint. Cal wasn't sure how much of the stories the Spanish-speaking youth understood. He suspected it was more the sound of her voice than the tales themselves that soothed him.

Even Baron got into the healing act, resting his big shaggy head near the boy's left hand where he could be petted and coddled. After the first night, he hopped onto the bed, jostling the mattress, but Antonio managed a brave grin through his pain.

"No es una problema," he said, and so there Baron remained.

The morning of the third day, Cal stood in the middle of what might eventually be a corral and listened to the approach of wagons. The sun was halfway up the cloudless November sky, and a brisk breeze stirred the air with a hint of winter. Loosening the pistol in its holster at his side, he retrieved the rifle resting against one of the wooden stakes and hurried back to the cabin to await whoever was coming to call.

He doubted it was trouble on the way. Trouble had a habit of arriving when he wasn't prepared.

Ellie joined him on the porch. Today was dress-wearing day, the plain brown high-collared cotton she'd worn when she caught him chopping wood. She hadn't bothered to pin up her hair, and it was hanging loose against her shoulders and halfway down her back. Why he kept noticing the details of her was beyond him. Clearly he didn't have enough else to do.

Together they watched a strange parade of visitors make its way up the rise. There were four wagons in all and a couple of outriders. Gert and May led the way, with Katya Merse, the store-keeper's daughter, wrapped in cloak and bonnet, sitting like a brown quail between them on the wagon seat and looking as though she would take flight if anyone dared glance her way.

In the bed of the wagon sat a solemn Mexican woman Cal took to be Antonio's mother, Consuela. A colorful serape covered her head and shoulders; the black eyes peering out at him took up half of her lined brown face.

Fin and Fitz, huddled in fur-lined coats, were in the second wagon, along with Sir Simon Pence, as always in morning coat and cravat. The O'Malleys had never been ones to endure much cold. The Englishman clearly was made of sterner stuff.

Each of the two remaining wagons held a man and a woman he had never seen before, by the looks of them farmers or ranchers from the county and their wives.

The two men on horseback were likewise strangers, though one of them, a burly man with thick side-whiskers and moustache, looked vaguely familiar. The second was clean-shaven and lean.

Cal waited for the creaking of wagons, the stomping of hooves and the dust to settle before he spoke.

"Your boy's all right," he said to Consuela. "At least he will be after a little more healing."

She didn't look as if she believed him, and he wondered if she understood his English.

"It's a good thing you came, Consuela," Ellie said. "I've been doing the best I could, but he needs his mama, that's for sure. He's sleeping now, but I have a feeling he knows you're here."

A satisfied look began to steal onto the woman's face.

"But as for the rest of you," she said, a sweep of her hand taking in all the wagons and riders, "I think you'll be a surprise." She saved her smile for Katya Merse. "I'm so glad you're here, too. It gets lonely being with just a couple of men."

The young woman stared at Ellie for a moment,

then looked down at her hands. Cal didn't think she looked quite so withdrawn as she had when he'd seen her in the store.

"We figured since the three of you couldn't come to the soiree," Gert said, "we'd bring it to you. Only now, thanks to Consuela, we're calling it a fandango."

May nodded toward the last two wagons. "We spread the word," she said, "and these good people met us on the road."

"Mr. Hardin," one of the men in the wagon said, "we heard about the trouble. We're not used to such goings-on, even out here in the wilderness, and we come to let you know we're on the lookout for the bastard that done it. Pardon my language, Lucy, but any man'd beat a boy ain't worth shooting."

"But we can hang him right soon enough." This time it was the man in the last wagon who spoke. "I know we've not met, Mr. Hardin, more's the pity. We ought to be holding together instead of keeping to our land. Wright Whitfield's the name, and this here's my wife Barbara. We got us a baby on the way, so you'll pardon if maybe she throws up from time to time. She don't mean nothing by it."

"Wright!" she said, giving him a solid poke in the ribs.

"Well, you don't. It's always best to get matters out in the open—otherwise they'll be thinking it's something you et."

"Long as we're making ourselves familiar to you," the first man put in, "the name's Abe Patchett, and this here's the little woman Lucy."

By no means could the smiling Mrs. Patchett be described as little, but then neither could her strapping husband. Together they filled the wagon seat. On the other hand, the Whitfields could have invited another couple their size to ride alongside.

Cal's attention shifted to his uncles, who were looking alternately sheepish and proud and were for once strangely silent. He could understand the *sheepish*, since they knew how much he hated crowds. It was the *proud* that made him uneasy, and when he considered their silence, he figured that trouble had got here after all.

"Nice to see you paying a visit," he said.

"You sent word you were taking care of things," Fin said.

"We always listen to what you say," Fitz added.

Trouble indeed.

Ellie went down the steps to her aunts' wagon. "We need to get Consuela inside to her boy."

The two horsemen scrambled to help the distraught mother from the wagon, along with Gert and May.

"You get on in there, Consuela," Gert said, "and we'll see to the party fixings. That is, if our having a good time won't upset the lad."

"He'll be glad of the company," Ellie said. "I've just about run out of stories and petticoats."

Silence fell. She looked around her. "For bandages, I mean," she said.

Cal stood watching in silence. He figured she was getting out of her predicament alone better than she could if he were calling attention to himself.

"We didn't figure no hanky-panky was going on," Gert said. "Otherwise we'd have been here defending your virtue two days ago." She glanced at Cal. "We figured right, didn't we? Alden Fowler kind of hinted maybe we should get on out here, but he was talking with a smirk and we decided he just wanted to stir things up."

Cal was tempted to smile at Ellie and let her answer her aunt, but he had just enough chivalry in him to respond.

"You figured right. Your niece is as innocent and pure right now as she was the day she arrived."

Ellie's sharp glance said she didn't care much for the phrasing of the disclaimer, but she let it go without comment.

"And she is one hell of a nurse." He bowed to Lucy Patchett. "Pardon my language, but it's the truth."

The next half hour was spent getting Consuela inside to her son, who, as always, was being guarded by Baron, and unloading the wagons of enough supplies to feed the entire Republic.

When they were done, Gert placed herself in the doorway to the kitchen/parlor side of the cabin. "Fin and Fitz, pump us up some water. We'll need a dozen buckets. The rest of you men get about your man-business while we tend to our chores. And that means you, Sir Simon. We won't let nothing happen to Katya. But don't none of you go far. We'll call you when we're done."

Such orders were not to be ignored.

The uncles disappeared around the back of the house, and the two riders introduced themselves as George Holloway and Dub Krause.

Cal studied the big man, Holloway. "I've seen you before."

"At the poker table. It's a weakness, for sure." Holloway spat tobacco juice from the side of his mouth. "Miss Gertrude and Miss Mayveen are trying to help me break it. Never met women like 'em anywhere."

"They're helping him all right," Krause said. "By taking his money. Those women took to cards like some men take to whiskey. It seems to come natural to them."

"Holloway and Krause are looking to buy land and settle in," Wright Whitfield said. "We need settlers here, and families. We're glad to see you and the uncles move in, though I understand the O'Malleys have been stirred up by the goings-on. Can't understand those vigilantes shooting up your place. We ain't never had trouble like that before."

Simon Pence spoke from outside the circle of men.

"Could it be the Double T is cursed? Perhaps the ghosts of men who have died here wish to keep it sacrosanct."

"That's an idea that hadn't occurred to me," Cal said. "Being from England, you would be the expert on ghosts. Let me know if you see one."

"I will take on the assignment as an honor and a duty," Sir Simon said. "I promise to be ever vigilant."

After the horses were unhitched and watered, Cal led the men past the barn with instructions to tether their stock to the stakes. They were joined by Fin and Fitz.

"I was thinking about putting a corral here," he said.

His uncles looked at him in surprise, but he simply shrugged. Anything he said would give them encouragement about staying, and that remained out of the question, particularly after the attack on Antonio.

"There's work to be done here for sure," Whitfield said. "Seems like the sun don't set but I got chores piled on top of chores waiting for the next day to hurry on around."

Cal looked at Whitfield and Patchett, then on to Holloway and Krause, zealots one and all in a cause he didn't understand.

"I'm working to pass the time. What's your purpose? You have no market for your stock or your crops, you've got a government deeply in debt, your money's worthless, and there are damned few signs civilization will ever make its way out here."

Cal didn't purposely intend to give offense, but he didn't much take to the blindness so many Texans suffered from concerning their homeland.

"All well and true," Whitfield said, showing no sign he was offended. "I guess we're here just to live. Build a new country. Have children and pass the land on to them."

"I have no interest in any of that," Cal said.

"You got woman trouble?" Holloway asked. "Sometimes that keeps a man from wanting to settle down."

"You have to have a woman to have trouble."

Cal knew that every man, including his uncles, was thinking of Ellie Davenport. She was passing through his mind, too.

But they were all too gentlemanly to bring up her name. Besides, surely her aunts had passed on the news that she was waiting for her long-lost fiancé.

"You sound like maybe you're thinking of leaving," Abe Patchett said.

Cal looked at his uncles. "It's a possibility."

"Alden Fowler made us an offer," Fin said.

"I'm not surprised," Patchett said. "He's bought up several parcels in the county. Don't know why. He already owns more than he's working."

Whitfield spoke up. "Seems to me it has something to do with his wife and boy. Comanches got 'em a few years back. Killed the boy outright. The woman—well, I've heard stories, but it was long before Barbara and me come out, so I don't know nothing for sure."

"They got the Merse girl, too," Patchett said. "A few years later. They held her captive awhile, then let her go. They say she hasn't been the same since. That's why she's so quiet. I wouldn't know, of course, not having been here then. I don't guess any of us were."

Sir Simon stirred. "She is not the object of gossip, is she? It would be a shame if she suffered further harm after all she went through."

"Folks are curious," Whitfield said, "but not in a mean way. A few minutes ago I was telling you how we ought to stick together. Knowing what we've been through is part of the sticking. Maybe back in England folks go their separate ways, and some in these parts do, too. But they're not the settling kind. They don't do a land much good."

Cal felt all eyes on him, as if he were being accused of something for which he should offer a defense.

Whitfield wasn't done. "You put down stakes for a corral, didn't you, Hardin? Could be you're putting down roots, too."

"Our King Cal?" Fin said.

"Putting down roots?" Fitz said.

Cal shot them a leveling look. "You're raising issues I don't want to go into." He looked at the other men. "My uncles like to jest, as you've no doubt noticed. But I was serious about the problems you're facing. Exactly how do you plan to make this living out here? How do you plan to survive?"

He didn't care about hearing the answers, or so he thought, but it got them away from him and onto a subject that was clearly dear to their hearts—Texas.

For the next half hour they talked about the wild cattle and horses that were there for a man to claim, if he had the skill and the desire to go after them. They talked about crops that succeeded and crops that failed. They talked about shipping goods and stock out of Lavaca Bay, and they talked, too, about the dangers that faced anyone who remained and, as Patchett put it, "fought the good fight."

They had answers aplenty for him. Against his will, Cal found himself interested. It was his erstwhile rancher uncles who barely gave the talk any mind.

"We'll be just fine if we get us a government that'll help instead of hurt. All President Lamar wants to do is run up debts and fight Mexico and fight the Indians and bring in more slaves. I don't know your feelings about the matter, Cal, but some of us Texians don't hold with owning other folks."

"That's right," put in Patchett. "Old Sam Houston might be a drunk, but he's got the way of things right. Make peace with the Indians and Mexicans and keep more slaves from being brought in. When election time rolls around next year, there's plenty of men'll be lining up to vote Houston back in as president."

Cal would be one of them—if he were staying, which he wasn't.

When a dinner bell rang from the porch, Whitfield and Patchett were the first to head to the cabin. Sir Simon and Cal brought up the rear.

"Those men truly believe what they say," Simon said. "About making a living here, I mean."

"The world is full of fools."

"I number myself among them, but I wonder about these Texans. Do not underestimate the power of passion. By that, of course, I refer to more than sex."

Cal understood the different kinds of passion far better than the Englishman could ever guess. It had been passion of a sort that had led him to nearly killing the stranger three days past. It had been passion that drove him to strike his father so many years ago, and a different kind of passion that distanced him from the remaining Hardins in New Orleans.

It was perhaps the sexual kind of passion that moved him the least. As much as he enjoyed women, the enjoyment had, most certainly, no lasting effect on him, not like the passion that came with hate.

He was the last to walk onto the porch. Through the open door to the left, he saw candles scattered everywhere, though it was the middle of the day. He saw, too, platters of food on the table and more people than the room had been built to hold.

Behind him, across the dog run, another door opened, the one to what had become the sickroom, and he turned to watch Ellie walk out to join him. The sight of her stirred him as none of the talk had done.

She wore a yellow gown cut low enough to show the subtle curves of her small breasts and tight enough to cling provocatively to her tiny waist. With her milk-white shoulders bare, her neck long and slender and her face framed by falls of yellow ringlets, she took his breath away.

The dress was the same one she had worn her first day in Glory. She looked better in it than she did in the trousers, quite an admission for him to make.

His first impulse was to grab and kiss her. She might appear the picture of innocence, but he remembered the way she had reacted to his kisses before.

But somehow the time had passed for grabbing and forcing kisses upon her, no matter how sure he was that she would enjoy what he did. Over the past few days, beginning at the creek and continuing to today, something had changed between them, though he didn't know exactly what it was. For his own well-being he had pulled back from furthering his involvement with her, but that wasn't the answer entirely.

Maybe they'd learned to respect one another.

Or maybe they'd learned the wisdom of keeping a distance between them. They both understood that any relationship they developed would be short-lived.

What hadn't changed between them was the way he grew hard just looking at her. Too bad the sun shone so brightly. Once he stepped from the shadows of the dog run, all she would have to do was look down and she would see clearly enough his problem.

For the first time in his life he wished he had dressed up for a woman, put on a coat and a clean shirt instead of the work shirt and leather jerkin he had taken to wearing around the ranch. He was usually impeccably groomed because that was his nature, but out here, more often than not alone, he hadn't seen the need.

He saw it now.

Behind Ellie, the makeshift curtain they had hung over the bedroom window cast the room into near darkness, but he could make out Consuela hovering over her son, oblivious to the rest of the world. Baron had been banned to the floor at the foot of the bed.

"My aunts insisted I change for the party," she said.

"Remind me to thank them."

"Please, Cal—"

"I know. You're no beauty and I wouldn't notice you if I passed you on a New Orleans street. That's your version. Mine is, I'd see you in the middle of a crowd no matter where we were. And so would every man who wasn't blind."

"That's the Irish in you coming out," she said, but there was a small smile fighting to find its place on her lips.

Cal felt a tightening in his gut that had nothing to do with his arousal. There she went again, getting too close and making him feel too tender. He knew danger when he saw it. Right now it wore a yellow dress.

To hell with respect. It came with too high a price.

"We could go into the barn," he said. "With so many people here, we wouldn't be missed. It wouldn't take long. When I'm properly motivated, I can be quite fast."

She didn't play coy or pretend she didn't understand.

Her smile died before it was truly born, and the light that had come into her eyes died as well.

"Why do you enjoy shocking me?" she asked.

She sounded far calmer than she usually did when he came on strong.

"Because it's easy to do."

"Then it's time it got harder."

Cal had a response for that, but he wasn't sure that in this case she would understand. On the other hand, with the education he was giving her, perhaps she would.

She brushed past him and hurried into the candlelit room. Gert and May came up to greet her.

Evelyn Rogers

They were dressed in the black dresses they had worn for the ride, but without their bonnets their hair looked fuller and redder. Since he'd last seen them a short while ago, their eyelashes had grown longer and blacker, as if they'd stuck a couple of baby tarantulas over their eyes.

Clearly they had been at several paint pots in addition to setting out the food. The air around them was redolent of spices and corn and roasted meat. Lucy Patchett, looking formidable and very much at ease, stood at the end of the table serving the plates of food.

Cal need not have worried about his condition being noted, not with everyone's eyes on Ellie. Holloway and Krause paused in their eating to give her an extra thorough glance. By the fireplace Sir Simon nodded in approval and whispered something to Katya Merse at his side.

Ellie looked nothing more than embarrassed by all the attention.

"We've been heating this food for close to an hour," Gert said. "You men eat up before it gets cold."

It was an order they didn't dispute.

Cal looked down at Ellie. "This is more than I expected. Are we celebrating something I don't know about?"

If she was still upset by his crude remarks, she wasn't showing it.

"Remember that poker game?" she said. "I meant to tell you earlier that my aunts beat your uncles at cards. That was the original reason for the soiree. Sorry, the fandango."

"I hate to disappoint you, Ellie, but anyone can beat my uncles at cards."

He'd meant the comment as a jest, but the solemn look that passed over her face suggested she'd taken it far more seriously. Whatever bothered her, she shook it off.

"I should have asked you a moment ago, but I forgot," she said. "Would you mind removing your gun?"

It took him a minute to understand what she was talking about. In the last few days the pistol had become a part of him and he'd forgotten he was wearing it.

"I've left mine packed away for the night, in case you're worried," she added.

"I wasn't. I looked you over pretty thoroughly, remember?"

"I remember. I also remember what you said."

She made him feel as gracious as a goat. The last thing she needed was her pepperbox, not when she could stab him with a gentle riposte.

He untied the thong around his thigh and unbuckled his belt, slipping the holster free and setting it on the floor beside the door where he could get to it fast if the need arose.

He leaned close and whispered so only she could hear, "You've unmanned me."

She blinked no more than once. "Not yet I haven't. You won't be jesting when I do." She left him to help Lucy Patchett with the serving. Wright Whitfield's pregnant wife Barbara was nowhere in sight. With the smell of food heavy in the air, she was probably outside throwing up.

Gert stepped up and took him by the arm. She

smiled across the room at Fin, and the tarantulas moved up and down. "Let's get you fed. Consuela fixed something she calls *tamales*. Be sure you take off the corn husks before you dig in. We got two pans of them. That one over there's got lots of peppers. *Muy picante*, she says. Very hot."

Cal stared past her to where Ellie was dishing up food onto plates. He understood heat very well.

He turned his attention to the room, to the Texans talking and eating together while their women served; to Simon, attentive and protective, and Katya Merse, pale and quiet as ever in a dress that hung loose upon her and with her hair plaited in tight knots above her ears; and on to his uncles, who stared at the thick-lashed Gert and May as if they were moonstruck.

Suddenly it all became too much, too close to being domestic, too dangerously near to becoming permanent. The walls closed in. He would eat later. Right now breathing was more important.

Grabbing his holster and gun, he went out into the light of day. He whistled for Baron, but the dog did not come. Lacking anything better to do, he walked toward the would-be corral, but he couldn't get away from the laughter that echoed from the cabin and the image of Ellie that burned in his mind.

Out here he was still too close to a crowd of people enjoying the company of their neighbors and good food. He had been near such crowds a hundred times in the past, but he'd always kept his distance, a part of the gathering and yet apart.

These people were harder to leave. At any moment, his uncles would break out the whiskey. With the possible exception of May and Gert, the women would cluck their disapproval, but the men would be grateful. There was an innocence about their having a good time, coming as it did in the face of difficulty.

Cal had always been serious about his solitude, but never more than today. Never could he remember feeling more alone. The bad thing about the feeling was that it bothered him very much.

Chapter Twelve

Everybody was coupling up—Gert and Fin, May and Fitz, and of course the Patchetts and the Whitfields. Even Sir Simon had strayed from Katya Merse's side only to get her a plate of food, though the silent young woman had scarcely given him more than a brief look of gratitude.

Still, keeping to themselves by the hearth, he and Katya were as much a couple as Gert and Fin.

That left the two bachelors, George Holloway and Dub Krause, eyeing Ellie with the possible purpose of staking a claim. She realized that her mistake was in putting on the yellow dress and pinning her hair up in curls, as if she were trying to impress somebody.

Who would she impress? George Holloway? Dub Krause? Certainly not Cal. She had been smart enough not to be surprised at the reaction she got from him when he saw her in the dog run. Instead, she had been disappointed. Expecting everything he said, she had still hoped for something else.

She felt like a foolish woman who got dressed up and went to the wrong party at the wrong time in the wrong place, something Aunt Abigail had done when she was young. But Ellie hadn't gone simply to the wrong house. She had traveled to the wrong world.

Both Holloway and Krause were consuming their food with immoderate speed, swallowing the tamales whole, barely bothering to toss aside the shucks. Taking care not to look their way lest they think she was signaling them, Ellie set her plate aside, sent a silent apology to the other women for not helping clear the dishes and eased out the door, first to slip across the dog run to check on Consuela and her boy and then to stand on the front porch.

The afternoon air had chilled beneath a paling sun. She wondered how cold it got in this part of Texas. As close as Glory was to the coast, she doubted it ever froze. She would hardly need the heavy fur-lined cloak she'd left back in Virginia.

Ellie stopped herself. Of course she would need the cloak. She would be back on her farm outside Richmond sometime this winter, long before the frosts were over.

She told herself she was out there on the porch to get a breath of fresh air, but her eye went unerringly past the barn to the open field, settling onto the lone figure of Cal. He looked so small and still in the distance, yet strong and straight and absolutely unbendable as he stared across the rolling land.

Mostly he looked lonely. But that was a condition he chose. The anger and the violence his loneliness could unleash must dictate his solitude. She didn't know for sure; all she could do was guess. He would mock her if he knew, but she doubted he would tell her she was wrong.

"Cal."

His name was a whisper and a summons on her lips. As she watched him, a warmth flooded through her that was like nothing she had ever experienced, and her heart swelled so that her breast could scarcely contain it. She felt as if heated honey were flowing through her, as if she had drunk far more than her fill of a very heady wine.

She let all of the sensations take control, because she wanted them to and because she had no choice. It was time to accept a truth that was impossible and unbelievable and far more foolish than her inappropriate dress and hair.

She loved him.

Outside of her family, Ellie had never loved anyone before, not truly, uncontrollably loved in the way a woman could love a man. But if love was a warm hand stroking the heart, a sensation of sympathy and understanding that cried out from the soul, a yearning of exquisite pain for something the eye could not discern, then she was so very much in love that she felt giddy from its power.

Like anything newborn—puppies, kittens, chicks—she wanted to cuddle this infant love close and protect it from the world, let it thrive in the warmth of her secret contemplation, and above all else, keep the knowledge of its birth from everyone.

That included Cal. More than anyone else, he must never know how she felt. He neither wanted nor knew how to accept tenderness. What would he do if he knew what she was thinking now? What if she gave in to the impulse to fly from the porch and grab his hands and dance a dance of joy around the open field?

The joy wouldn't last long. He would tell her, rightly enough, that she had lost her mind, but if that was the way she felt, he might as well take her into the barn and let them both get something good out of it.

Cal the Romantic he wasn't. But that was not why she loved him. It was his hurts and his losses and his unrecognized vulnerability, as well as his strength, that made her heart swell at the same time it broke in two.

Tears welled up in her eyes, but when she heard the door open behind her, she brushed them away.

"You must be cold out here," Gert said as she came up to stand beside her.

Ellie smiled brightly at her visitor. "I hadn't noticed."

Gert nodded toward the field. "He's a man to heat a woman even from a distance."

"What makes you think—"

She stopped. Some truths were so obvious that denying them made little sense.

"Lordy," Gert said with a sigh, "a cigar would taste mighty good right now."

"Go out to the barn if you don't want anyone to see you. No one would know."

"I'm getting too old to sneak around. Besides, that Miz Whitfield, being pregnant and all, would smell the smoke clear back to the cabin."

Ellie nodded, partly listening, partly concentrating on Cal.

"We were about to start some singing," Gert said. "Lucy Patchett's idea, but the men don't seem too opposed. Her husband Abe brought himself a fiddle. All we got to do is come up with a song we all know. We might even dance a jig or two, make it a real fandango. You want to join us?"

Ellie shook her head. "I don't have much of a singing voice. And as for dancing . . ."

She let her voice trail off and thought a moment of dancing with Cal. He would be good at it, practiced and charming as he whirled her about. And she would be so happy, her feet would scarcely touch the ground.

But the dancing was only a dream.

"At home I would be playing a harp," she said, her feet very much anchored on the ground. "I would have brought it with me but it was too large to pack."

The joke was feeble, but Gert was gracious enough to laugh.

"I didn't much think you would be joining in. George and Dub'll be disappointed."

"Make my excuses, will you?"

"In a minute. The air smells good out here."

GET YOUR 4 FREE BOOKS NOW— A $21.96 Value!

Mail the Free Book Certificate Today!

Get Four Books Totally FREE — A $21.96 Value!

▼ Tear Here and Mail Your FREE Book Card Today! ▼

PLEASE RUSH
MY FOUR FREE
BOOKS TO ME
RIGHT AWAY!

Leisure Romance Book Club
P.O. Box 6613
Edison, NJ 08818-6613

AFFIX
STAMP
HERE

They both stared toward the faraway field. "Is there something you want to get off your chest?"

"I don't know what you're talking about."

"I was thinking, naturally enough, of Cal Hardin."

Ellie's cheeks burned. "What could I possibly have to tell you?"

"Several ideas popped into mind. Nothing going on between you two, is there? Now don't look offended. A good-looking man like that and a pretty thing like you, out here with only a boy as company and him kept mostly to bed, there's bound to be feelings stirred."

"Didn't you say just a while ago you knew there wasn't any hanky-panky between us?"

"That was talk for the others. Now it's just you and me. I know I'm not your real aunt, but at times I have trouble remembering it. You hired me and May because we understand men. I got to thinking maybe you would like a little extra advice about the gender."

Ellie had a hard time looking Gert in the eye, and it was just as hard to continue staring out at Cal with the other woman standing so close and watching whatever expression might cross her face.

She gave the barn a steady perusal.

"Cal has more problems than any woman can deal with. I'd be the biggest fool in the world to let my feelings get stirred."

"Yep, that's what I was afraid of. You've gone and fallen in love."

Ellie stared at Gert in astonishment. "That is

209

the single most ridiculous—" She broke off with a sigh. "Is it so obvious?"

"Just to May and me. We've been expecting it, understand. Soon as we got a good look at him that first day in Glory."

"Then you're both smarter than I am. I just figured it out myself. Right here on the porch."

"Sometimes the ones about to be caught in a love affair are the last to know what's going on. And then it's too late."

"Cal is hardly caught, and it's hardly a love affair. He doesn't know how I feel, and he's not going to." A new worry struck her. "You haven't said anything to his uncles, have you?"

"Give us credit for a little sense, Ellie. The O'Malley boys can be charmers when they want, but they've got the discretion of a couple of puppies."

Gert fell silent. Ellie dreaded what was coming next.

"So what are you going to do about it?" Gert asked.

"Nothing."

"You still thinking he had something to do with your daddy's death?"

"I never thought he was directly involved. Not that he couldn't kill a man." She shuddered, remembering the one-sided fight outside the barn. "But he wouldn't shoot anyone in the back, and never in cold blood."

"What about Fin and Fitz? You think they gunned your daddy down?"

Ellie shook her head. "I am totally confused. It seems now maybe Papa wanted to get rid of the land and lost it on purpose. But if that's so, why was he killed?"

"You're asking a question I'm not sure has an answer. Not in Texas."

"What you say makes sense. And yet I can't help thinking the answer lies here. I guess what's really bothering me is the possibility I'll never know what it is."

Gert patted her hand. "Honey, you got problems all right. You let me and May know if there's anything we can do to help."

The squawk of a fiddle came from the cabin. Ellie recognized the song as a rough version of "Rosin the Bow."

"Guess I better get back inside," Gert said. She glanced through the open door. "I'll be damned. Lucy Patchett is smoking on a pipe. Sister and I'll be firing up those cigars after all."

She was halfway through the door when she stopped and turned. "Oh, I almost forgot." She pulled a tattered envelope from her pocket and held it out to Ellie. "This came to Merse's store yesterday. It's for you."

The letter was from her fiancé, Bertrand Randolph. In all her maunderings about Cal, not once had Bertrand crossed her mind. She fingered the letter. Without opening the envelope, she could almost recite its contents. His boys were missing her and so was he. He wanted her to come home and see to their wedding, which she would probably have to do. Eventually.

She was totally without honor, completely without shame to forget him so easily and yet still plan on being his wife. Her betrothed was a good man who would always treat her with respect. She, on the other hand, once they were wed, would always lie in his arms and think of another man.

The last remnants of first-love giddiness fled. Loving wasn't like enjoying a walk through paradise. Loving was treading through the fires of hell.

Later in the day, the Patchetts and Whitfields left for home, and the two single men, Holloway and Krause, headed for town, riding alongside the wagon holding Simon Pence and Katya Merse.

Gert and May elected to stay with Consuela; they had brought cots along with them for just that purpose. Fin and Fitz stayed, too. Along with Cal, they found themselves relegated to the barn.

Over the next two days, with so much female attention, especially from his mother, Antonio continued to improve. Even Cal began sitting with him on the porch in the evening and encouraged the boy to teach him Spanish; he in turn vowed to have the lad speaking the King's English before he was done.

"Do you speak, Señor Cal, of Señor Samuel Houston?"

"I've never heard Sam speak," Cal said, "but he'll do as well as anyone."

On such occasions Ellie stood in the background, listening, watching, and thinking how sad it was that Cal would never have a family of his own. He truly seemed to enjoy talking with the boy.

A week to the day after Antonio's beating, Consuela announced it was time to take her son to his own home. Cal wasn't around for the announcement, or for the news that Ellie and the rest of them would be going, too. Shortly after dawn, he had taken a wagon to the creek to begin loading up the logs for the corral.

The knowledge that she might leave with so much unanswered between them proved too much. To get the answers, she would have to find him and do some talking of her own. So be it. It was time she did some revealing, too.

"It's dangerous out there for a woman alone," Gert said.

"We'll hitch the wagon and go with you," said May.

But Ellie held firm. "I'll be fine. The man who hurt Antonio knows enough not to get near the Double T."

This time when she saw Cal wielding the ax, he was fully clothed, even down to wearing his gun. It was probably for the best. This way she could concentrate better on the business at hand.

Pausing in his work, he watched her approach. Having been banished from the sickroom, Baron lay on the ground beside him and greeted her with a thump of his tail.

"Is everything all right?" Cal asked.

"At the cabin, yes. They're getting ready to take Antonio back into town. I'll be going with them."

She hadn't expected him to beg her not to leave, but she would have appreciated more than a narrowing of his eyes.

"Tell Antonio I said *adiós*."

213

"It's for the best." As if he had protested anyone's departure. "This way you can get back to being alone."

Again, she saw nothing but a pair of blue and very piercing eyes that hid far more than they revealed.

She dismounted and tethered the mare to a branch of the oak tree near where he worked. Leaning on the ax, he watched her without saying a word. He had a way of watching a woman that made her want to throw herself into his arms—or else run like the devil as far away from him as she could.

Ellie had started her journey as the running-away kind. She wasn't anymore.

Loosening the fastening of her cloak, she threw the sides over her shoulders and planted her hands on her hips. She was wearing her plain brown dress, and her hair, free of a bonnet, was bound in a tight knot at her nape.

Facing him, she felt her courage flee, but she took a deep breath and looked him straight in the eye, which, all things considered, was probably better than looking at the open throat of his shirt or the width of his shoulders, or just about anyplace else.

"My real name is Eleanor Chase."

"I was wondering what it was."

She had expected something a little more on the order of surprise. "Why couldn't I have been a Davenport?"

"You were lying about so many things, I figured your name was one of them."

She had meant to be the aggressor, but some-

214

how he had put her on the defensive. She was the injured party here; all she wanted from him was to know what part he had played in the injury.

It was possible, she decided, to love a man and be irritated with him at the same time.

She let only the irritation show.

"Doesn't the name Chase mean anything to you?" she asked. "Or do you know so many victims of shootings that they all run together?"

That gave him pause for a moment. He let out a long, slow breath. "Your father was Henry Chase."

"That's right. He lost the Double T title in a poker game with your uncles."

"And was subsequently gunned down by an assailant or assailants unknown. Did you think I killed him?"

"I considered the possibility that your uncles were involved. I heard talk that Papa was about to bring charges against them for cheating him out of his land."

"And you thought I helped them get away with it. No wonder you came out to the cemetery to see what a bastard like me looked like."

This wasn't going right in the least.

"You knew that was me in the veil?"

"I finally figured it out, but it took me a while. What I didn't know was why you were there and why you are here."

He considered her for a moment. She refused to look away, but the effort was hard. Maybe she was the running kind after all.

"You must have been close to your father to come all this way," he added.

"I didn't know him. I hadn't seen him since I was born. Before I got married, I wanted to see him again."

"Very tender."

"Please don't be sarcastic with me now. You don't think it's tender in the least. You think it's stupid."

Of course it would appear that way to him, a man who ran from family because in his experience families generally hurt. It must have been quite a sacrifice for him to help his uncles leave New Orleans, the repayment of a debt for the care they had given his mother through the years.

Despite the way he was looking at her and questioning her, she understood his side of things. And she fell a little more in love with him.

He dropped the ax and took a step toward her.

"Whatever I think about your purpose, it makes more sense than your coming out here to meet up with the man you're supposed to marry. Is he a lie, too?"

The letter, Ellie thought. She had forgotten all about it. It must still be in the pocket of her yellow gown, packed away for the ride back into town.

"Don't stall on me now, Ellie," he said.

He wasn't going to let her get away with a thing.

"Bertrand Randolph is very much real. He's waiting for me back in Virginia. He owns the farm next to mine."

Was that a sharpness she saw in his eyes? Was he somehow not pleased she was betrothed?

"How cozy," he said. "And how relieving to know you are a woman of property."

She must be wrong about his feelings. He didn't sound the least distressed.

"I've pretty much told you everything—"

"Except about Gertrude and Mayveen."

Ellie sighed. Here was a part of her story she would rather ignore, but of course Cal was not about to let her.

"Their real name is Dollarhide. You were right. They are not my aunts. I've had only one, Aunt Abigail, and she is no longer living. In fact, all my mother's family is gone. I hired Gert and May in New Orleans to find out how much your uncles were involved in the cheating and killing of my father. Among the stories I heard was how they liked women."

"And the Dollarhide sisters know how to handle men."

"They are not inexperienced along those lines," she snapped, more defensive for them than she could be for herself. "Anything else you want to know about them you'll have to ask for yourself."

"It's my uncles I'm more concerned about. Fin and Fitz, desperadoes. Is that how you saw them?"

"I didn't know. My father was dead, lost to me forever before I could get to know him. He saved my letters, all of them, through all the years, and I had to find out the reason he died. I realize that's difficult for you to understand. But it's the reason I came out here."

She took a deep breath. "That's not all. I wanted to get the title from them, for my father's sake. Never for mine. Gert and May were to convince them to sell. As you can see, there was lots of duplicity all the way around."

"Do you still want the land?"

She shrugged. "It doesn't seem so important now." Other matters had taken precedence, matters like unrequited love. But that was the one thing she was not prepared to reveal.

"So why are you telling me now?"

Because I love you beyond all measure, and you look so good to me with the dark hairs curling at your throat and your damp shirt clinging to your body and all of you so close, I can scarcely think.

But of course she kept the words to herself, instead looking from him to the wagon half-loaded with logs, to the ax lying beside his feet, to Baron, and back into his eyes.

"Because I'm leaving and I want to hear from you whatever you know. Gert and May long ago decided your uncles were too inept to cheat and too innocent to kill."

"I'm sure Fin and Fitz will find that a relief."

"I would appreciate your not telling them about my suspicions. Whatever you think of the Dollarhides, they're kind and loyal women. Fin and Fitz seem to have grown fond of them, and they feel the same about your uncles. I would hate for anyone to be hurt."

"As would I."

Too late, my love, far too late.

She swallowed the lump that had formed in her throat. "So tell me before I leave, Cal. Do you know anything about my father's death? Anything about why he gambled away his land?"

The click of a trigger sounded like an explosion

in the stillness that fell between them. Cal whirled, hand on holster, but the man standing in the shadows of the trees had the draw on him.

His face was bruised and puffy around and through his beard, but Ellie recognized him as the stranger who had beaten Antonio. She could see the meanness in his eyes.

She pressed a fist to her lips to keep from crying out.

The stranger smirked. "Go ahead, Hardin. Draw. Shoot me, and I shoot the woman. From this distance I won't miss."

Hackles raised, Baron growled deep in his thick throat.

"Pull off your dog or the woman's dead."

"He's not my dog," Cal said, keeping his weight shifted forward as if he were contemplating an attack. "I can't predict what he'll do."

He sounded casual, but Ellie knew him well enough to hear the repressed anger in his voice. And when Cal got angry, he was capable of most anything.

Panic fluttered in her breast.

"Then I'll shoot him first," the stranger said. "I'm pretty fast. I can probably get the woman and the dog both."

"No!" Ellie cried.

Ignoring Cal's warning glance, she whistled to Baron. Much to her surprise the dog came to her side and leaned his weight against her.

"Settle down, boy," she said, stroking his head with a trembling hand. "Everything's all right."

Where she got the courage to be so brave, she

had no idea. She was so scared, she could hardly breathe.

The more she thought about what she had done, the more her knees weakened. A man who enjoyed beating a child was holding what appeared to be a cannon and aiming it straight at her, and Cal was standing nearby figuring how he could get into the line of fire and save the day, and she was petting a dog as if this would all go away without anyone getting hurt.

"What's this all about?" Cal asked. "And who the hell are you?"

"A man's got a right to know the man that kills him. The name's Buck Shannon." He glanced at Ellie. "I was hoping to catch you two humping away, but gawddamn, all you did was talk."

"You've been watching us," she said. Above all else, even the gun, the knowledge shook her. Shannon could have shot them at any time. She clutched the hair on Baron's back for support. The dog held still.

"Henry Chase was a fool," Shannon said. "He should have given me the land when I asked him the first time. Then I could have come back here and all would have been well. But he got stubborn. He had to pay."

Ellie squeezed her eyes shut, then opened them again, but the scene remained the same—the man, the gun, Cal poised ready for anything. And Shannon's words still hanging in the air.

"You were the one," she said. "I . . . I don't understand."

She could almost hear Cal's voice going out to her.

I'll get us out of this.

The thought waves were so powerful, she wasn't sure she hadn't heard them spoken aloud.

"Did you know the fool gambled away the land on purpose?" Shannon said. "Just because of a few threats. He thought he was safe. I showed him he was wrong."

"Oh, yes, he was very, very wrong," Ellie said, so terrified she could hardly get out a word. But she couldn't keep quiet. Talking was the only weapon she had.

"He bought the land for me," she said, "and I wondered why he changed his mind. I guess you frightened him. You're a very frightening man. Why, when I saw you with that whip—"

"Shut up," Shannon growled. "Shut the hell up."

"All I was saying—"

"Can't you get her to hush?" he said, looking at Cal.

"Do what he says, Ellie," Cal said. "This isn't a game."

"Oh, I know it's not. It's just that when I get nervous I ramble on, and right now it's keeping me from swooning. It's just a weak, womanly—"

With a long, drawn-out *ooooh*, she slumped to the ground at the moment Cal leaped forward, gun in hand. Two shots rang out, one upon the other, and Ellie lay in a crouch beside Baron, hands pressed hard against her ears.

"He's dead," she sobbed, "he's dead, he's dead."

With Baron licking the tears from her face, she did the hardest thing she had ever had to do. She looked up to see exactly where Cal had fallen, and if he had managed to hit Buck Shannon before he went down.

Cal was standing over Shannon's body and staring into the woods, looking gloriously healthy. She rubbed her eyes, but there he was, standing straight, wary and watchful. He was all right, and Shannon appeared to be dead.

The tears returned, but this time from the ecstasy of relief. She wanted to run to him and cover him with kisses, and she didn't care what it told him about how she felt.

And then she saw what was holding Cal's attention. Alden Fowler stood in the trees beyond where Buck Shannon had fallen, a rifle gripped in his hand.

"I came up on him, saw what was happening, and did what I had to do," Fowler said. "I hope you folks are all right."

In answer to Cal's questioning look, Ellie pulled herself awkwardly to her feet and walked to his side. He draped an arm around her.

"Are you really all right?" he asked.

She nodded, tried to smile, and that was when she fainted for real.

Chapter Thirteen

Ellie came to in the wagon. She was sitting in Cal's lap, his arms around her, his hands gripping the reins. Nestled in his embrace, she snuggled close, only vaguely aware of the passing landscape. He felt warm and solid and comforting, his leather jerkin cool and slick against her cheek. She even liked the uneven bounce and jostle of the ride.

For a minute all was right with her world.

And then she remembered what had led to her swoon. She started to tremble all over again.

"It's over," he said, holding her close.

But it wasn't. She could still hear the gunshots ringing in her ears and feel the terror clawing at her until the moment she knew for sure Cal was alive.

She tried to pick up the sound of his heartbeat,

but he wore too many layers of clothes. Still, she felt his reassuring warmth, and the play of his muscles each time he moved.

"I don't understand," she whispered against his chest. "Who was he?"

"We'll probably never know for sure. Fowler couldn't help us. I'll ask around, but it's likely whatever answers Shannon could have provided died with him."

"Oh, yes," she said, remembering the details just before she lost consciousness. "Alden Fowler shot him. He saved our lives. We owe him a great deal."

"Maybe. At least he offered to dispose of the body. I myself would have left the bastard out for the buzzards."

She tried to sit up and look at Cal, but her head whirled and she gave in to the wonderful comfort of resting once again against his solid chest.

She fingered a button on his shirt. "What do you mean, *maybe* we owe him?"

"Shannon was killed before we could find out everything."

"Are you saying Fowler shouldn't have shot him?"

"I would have preferred he wounded him. I was about to do exactly that when Shannon fell."

Male pride, she thought. It surprised her, coming from Cal, especially in the particular circumstances she remembered all too well.

As far as she was concerned, no matter how many questions occurred to them, they were better off with the would-be killer six feet underground. They might never know Buck Shannon's past, but the fact that he had no future and presented no further danger to anyone was far more important.

They knew enough. For reasons of his own, Shannon had decided he wanted title to Texas land. Her father had possessed such a title. With Shannon's violent nature and probable lack of money, he had known only one way to get what he wanted—through bullying. When that failed, he flew into a rage and shot her father in the back.

He'd tried the same tactic with the O'Malleys, but Cal had been there to spirit them away.

Beating the boy had been a way to get at Cal, maybe even discourage him and make him leave.

Shannon had underestimated his adversary. Cal would be leaving, all right, but on his own terms and in his own good time. And so would she. If her quest was truly over, she had no reason to stay.

This moment of truth should have brought her relief, especially since her father's killer had paid the ultimate price for his crime. But knowing would soon be followed by leaving, not just Texas but the man who was her life.

The realization hit her like the blow of a fist. She had known this moment would come, but she hadn't known how much it would hurt. In her sudden distress, she almost pulled the button off his shirt.

"Relax, Ellie," he said. "You're getting tight again."

She sighed and did the best she could to let the tension ease.

"Remember the first time we met?" she asked.

"Which time was that?"

"In Glory. I don't think either one of us can count the cemetery in New Orleans. I had pretended to faint. You climbed into the wagon and told me I was supposed to be limp."

"Yeah, I remember."

"A great deal has happened since then, yet you're telling me the same thing."

He didn't respond, and she wondered if he was remembering some of the things that had happened. There was nothing in all those intervening weeks she could ever forget.

Neither spoke during the rest of the ride.

The sound of the wagon rolling up to the front of the cabin brought everyone outside. Gert got one look at her in Cal's arms and threw her hands up in dismay.

"Hellfire, what happened?" she cried as she came down off the porch.

"I knew we shouldn't have let her ride out alone," May said, right behind her along with the O'Malley twins.

"I'm fine," Ellie said.

To prove it, she got down from the wagon without help, but she left it up to Cal to do the rest of the talking. Gathering everyone together around the kitchen table, he reported what had happened. Much to her relief, he didn't announce openly all that she had revealed to him. Later he could tell his uncles the truth about who she and her aunts really were, after she and the Dollarhides were gone.

Cal had an avid audience. No one interrupted until he was done.

"This Shannon's the one that did all the shoot-ing in New Orleans?" Fin said. "Saints preserve us, 'tis a wonder we survived."

"There's bad 'uns in the world for sure," Fitz said.

They went on to pass comments back and forth about all the near misses they had escaped. Gert and May kept watching Ellie, waiting for her to speak.

"I guess we'd better get back into town and de-cide what we're going to do," she said.

"What about waiting for your betrothed?" Gert asked.

"He could be showing up any day," May said.

"I don't imagine he will. Not now." She at-tempted a smile. "It's time to leave."

If Fin and Fitz understood the import of what she was saying, they gave no sign. They were still too wrapped up in being safe and proven inno-cent.

But the Dollarhide sisters knew.

"By leaving, you don't mean just out of here," Gert said.

Ellie felt Cal's eyes on her. She looked at him. "No, I don't mean just out of here."

No narrowed eyes, no glint, no frown—nothing showed to prove he was distressed. But he kept very still and watchful, and for once he didn't look wary or cynical.

He just stared. He didn't look away.

Ellie could take only so much before she burst into tears. Such a display would never do. Aunt Abigail had taught her better about being strong.

"Excuse me," she said, pushing away from the

table, "I'd better let Consuela and Antonio know we're about to ride out."

"We got a bed made in the back of one of the wagons," Gert said. "Everything's loaded up except your clothes."

"I'll get them," she said and practically ran from the room.

The men followed her to carry Antonio to the wagon and get him settled. Ellie dragged out the small horsehair trunk of hers that Gert and May had brought with them when they'd come out for their fandango. On impulse she opened it long enough to take out Bertrand Randolph's letter. If she read his pleas and reassurances, she might feel better about leaving Texas.

She would have done anything at the moment to keep from facing Cal.

Taking the covering from the window, she lowered the rawhide panes on their leather hinges and let in the natural light. Alone in the empty bedroom, she hurriedly read the letter. Forcing herself to take a deep breath, she read it again, this time slowly, taking in each surprising word. At last, sure of its contents, she held the letter loosely in her hand and stared out the window.

The main message was simple. Bertrand didn't want her anymore. By now, he should be married to someone else.

She had been tortured with the knowledge that she must honor her promise to marry him, and here he was, casually breaking his vow to marry her.

In her absence, he had found another widow. She couldn't have been gone more than a week before he began his search. If the letter could be believed, and Ellie had no reason to doubt it, this one was a woman of property, childless and eager to take on his brood as her own. In what he must have thought was a generous gesture, he offered to buy her land—using, of course, his new wife's money. Ellie almost felt sorry for her, except for the fact that she had taken another woman's man.

Not that Ellie had wanted him, but the new Mrs. Randolph hadn't known that.

She knew she was being irrational, and worse, uncharitable, but it was the lone comfort she could come up with on such short notice.

She sat at the side of the bed and stared at the letter. For the first time in her life, she was truly alone in the world. No blood kin, no man, no plans. If she agreed to the sale, she would have money, plenty of it, but she would have no home.

Home had always been more important to her than anything else in the world. Home and family and children of her own. Worse, knowing clearly what she wanted and needed for happiness, she had fallen in love with a man who cared nothing at all for what she valued above all else.

She felt cold and hollow inside, too empty even to cry. Self-pity seemed too petty a description for what she felt. First she had seen Cal almost get gunned down, and now this. She was lost, and she was very much alone.

In truth, she was more alone than Cal could ever be, for he chose his solitude. Hers had been thrust upon her by fate, or her own ineptness, or bad luck, or bad judgment. Somehow, no matter how innocent she might consider herself, she was at fault.

All her life she had done the right things to be lovable. She'd learned the feminine arts, she had developed an affable disposition, and she wasn't frightful to look upon. There was little doubt she could return to Virginia and find someone to wed. Bertrand hadn't been the only one to pay her court.

But he had been the easiest to put off, the one Aunt Abigail had preferred. And no one had ever engaged her heart.

If she went back, everyone would look upon her as a spurned woman. That wasn't the worst thing that could happen. The worst thing would be living the rest of her life without love.

Ellie crumpled the letter in her hand, then tore it into a thousand pieces and watched them litter the floor.

A woman couldn't help it if no one truly loved her. Love didn't come to everyone. It hadn't come to her aunt.

She thought of Cal.

But a woman could help it if she had never been loved in the only way a man like him would understand.

In that moment, she knew what she had to do. At least for now. She would quit planning and scheming and dreaming and wishing for things that could never be. She would take what life offered and worry later about what a fool she had been.

Walking onto the porch, she watched for a moment while Antonio got settled in the wagon, his

mother close at his side. She watched as Gert and
Fin took one wagon, and May and Fitz the other.
She watched until they all noticed she was there.

Including Cal.

She looked at them all, and at last she looked
at him.

"You'd better start your journey before the
weather changes. It'll take you a while longer with
Antonio along. You don't want to jostle his arm."

"What about you?" May asked. "Aren't you
coming with us?"

"I realized there are some things I haven't finished here. I'll ride in later. Cal will make certain
I'm taken care of."

At last she had brought a glint to his eye.

"Are you going to be all right?" Gert asked.
"You're sure about this?"

"I'm sure." She managed a small smile. "I've
never been more sure of anything in my life."

Cal wasn't convinced he was reading her right.
After the wagons departed and just the two of
them were left at the cabin, she asked him to take
care of the horses while she went in to prepare
the late-day meal. She sounded friendly, but that
was all. Domestically friendly. The activities he
had in mind for the rest of the day were only re-
motely domestic.

"There's still some ham left," she said. "Biscuits
and gravy all right with you?"

"Fine."

"Make sure. I want you to keep your strength
up. It's been a very busy day."

The look in her eye said it was going to get busier. Surprise, surprise, he hadn't been misreading her. She must be more experienced than she had led him to believe.

After all, she was close to Gert and May, who were, he was sure, not unacquainted with the male physique.

Something about all this was unsettling to him. Maybe it was the practiced way she was going about things. That was it. He had thought her innocent for so long, and now he saw he had probably been wrong.

Probably, hell. No innocent woman in her circumstances, bred to be a lady and betrothed to a gentleman, could so calculatingly set out to take a lover she did not plan to wed.

He wouldn't think about just how Ellie had got her experience or how she had fooled him for so long. It was her idea for the two of them to be here alone. He wasn't forcing her into anything, or taunting her, or winning her over with a kiss.

For the first time in his life, he was letting a woman determine what he would do. Somehow, with Ellie Chase in charge, he didn't mind giving up control.

He still shook when he remembered Buck Shannon's gun on her, and the way she had called to Baron and stood up to that gun. When she fell, it had been as if they were thinking each other's thoughts. She was the bravest woman he had ever met.

And the most exasperating. Her bravery could easily have gotten her killed. He would tell her so, too, right after they had done whatever it was she had in mind.

Before he came in to supper, he washed up by the pump at the back, put on a clean shirt and combed his hair, then went inside to find his plate waiting for him on the table. Ellie was not in sight.

He went to the passageway and knocked on the closed bedroom door.

"Go ahead and eat," she said, her voice muffled.

He looked around him. Night was falling fast. Baron had already taken up his sleeping post between the cabin's two halves. Otherwise he was alone. And he didn't like it.

"What about you?" he asked. "I'd rather not eat by myself."

"There's not much you'll be doing by yourself tonight. Except eating. I had some food while I was cooking."

"I'll eat later."

"Your supper will get cold."

"Then we'll heat it."

He opened the door and caught her sitting on the side of the bed by the flickering lantern and brushing her hair. She was wearing one of his shirts, a white homespun he'd bought at Merse's store. The sleeves were rolled back, but she hadn't been able to do anything about the looseness of the rest of it. The hem rested just above her bent knees.

She had good knees, and good calves, and small ankles and little feet, and he just about climaxed simply from looking at her.

She stood and tossed the brush aside. Her hair was like sunlight falling around her shoulders. If he undressed her, it would curl all the way to her breasts.

It wasn't *if* he undressed her, but *when*. He truly hadn't read her wrong. If her boldness still unsettled him, it was a problem he would have to deal with later. Like the next day, or maybe the next week.

She hadn't said when she was going back to town. And he hadn't said when he would escort her.

"We've something to celebrate, haven't we?" she said, her chin raised as if she needed sauciness to be brave. "The truth. We both know it at last."

"I don't need anything to celebrate to want you."

Her answering smile was small but genuine. She didn't look in the least like a frightened doe. Her eyes were wide and deep and lit with a fire he felt all the way to his loins.

"It's nice to be wanted," she said.

"It's a great deal more than nice." He took a step closer. "Tell me you want me. A man likes to hear it, too."

She looked down at her nightgown shirt and wiggled her toes against the wooden floor. "I thought it was obvious." Again, her gleaming eyes met his. "I want you, Cal. I could think of no good reason not to have you."

His little pixie was full of surprises. Right now she didn't look so little at all. She looked very huggable and as much a woman as any man could ever want.

But she wasn't offering herself to any man. She was offering herself to him. Instinct told him she

234

didn't do it very often. Maybe no more than a time or two in all her life.

He didn't want to think about her being with any other man.

Closing the distance between them, he began to unbutton his shirt.

"Let me," she said, tugging the shirttails free of his trousers, letting her fingers brush against his chest as she finished the unfastening and pulled the shirt from his shoulders, pinning his arms in place.

For all his thick, dark head of hair, he didn't have much of a hairy chest, but what was there she seemed to like. At least the look in her eye said so.

"You're so big. I'm always surprised when I see you undressed. In your clothes you look so lean."

"And you haven't seen all of me yet."

A solemnity darkened her expression as she looked up to him. "Will I see all of you?"

"I usually make love in the dark, but we could keep the light turned up if you prefer it that way."

Her thick lashes lowered, hiding whatever expression might be in her very expressive eyes.

"Whatever you prefer."

Coy and bold. It was an explosive combination.

She dropped her hands, and he eased out of his shirt. She touched him, her strokes gentle and thorough, as if she wanted to study exactly how he was built. Her fingers walked their way to his nipples. The muscles of his abdomen constricted, and his sex became as hard as an oak log.

"You want me to lift that shirt and take you

now?" His voice was so husky, he barely recognized himself.

She lifted her hands as if he had burned her.

"No. I want you to take your time. I won't touch you again."

He grabbed her wrists and held her hands to his chest.

"That's not what I meant. Kiss me, Ellie."

She did, right on one of the nipples, which was directly in line with her mouth.

He let her go and she backed away, fingers pressed to her lips. "I don't know what made me do that."

"Whatever it was, I hope it won't go away."

He lifted her chin and brushed his mouth against hers. She shivered and gripped his arms.

"Cold?" he asked.

"Oh, no." She stared at his lips. "I put clean linens on the bed."

"That's always been a main concern of mine."

"You're making fun of me."

"I'm enjoying everything you do."

"I wasn't sure—"

She looked down, then back up, this time all the way to his eyes. "What I meant was, I have everything ready. I'm ready. If you are."

Cal let out a ragged breath. "Put your arms around me," he said.

"Where?"

"You can start with my neck."

"You'll have to bend down to make it easy for me."

"I want it to be easy."

"I thought it was supposed to be hard."

Was that a blush on her cheeks? He hoped so. He hadn't been with many women who could still blush.

"Ellie, you surprise me."

"I've heard you say things like that. I thought it was right. Maybe I'm not supposed to make jokes."

"You can do anything you like, love."

She backed away and gripped her hands behind her back. "I'd rather you not call me that."

Perhaps an association with another man? He didn't want to know.

"So what do I call you?"

She thought about it a minute. "You're a king and your dog is a baron. How about Princess? I've always wanted to be royalty."

"Princess it is. Now come down from your throne, your highness, and put your arms around my neck."

Her eyes turned bright. "Yes, yes, yes. We've talked far too long."

She practically threw herself at him and planted kisses across his face, then tiny nips at the corners of his mouth, and then a full kiss on the lips.

He held her tightly, lifting her off the floor. He could tell from feel alone that she had nothing on under the shirt. He made the kiss more thorough, parting her willing lips with his tongue and tasting the moist recesses of her mouth. With that small, beginning union of their bodies, he lost himself in her.

Somehow they ended up on the bed, Cal tugging at boots and socks and anything else he was wearing that might get in the way of holding her flesh to flesh. She lay beside him and watched, her wonderful eyes taking in everything. He had been right when he told her he normally made love in the dark, but tonight light didn't bother him at all, allowing him to open the shirt she was wearing and look at her bare breasts.

Before he could get a good look, she pressed herself against him.

"I want to see you," he said.

"You'll be disappointed."

"Is that any way for a princess to behave? Order me to be pleased."

"I don't think it works that way, but all right. You are herewith commanded to be pleased with whatever you behold."

"So lie back and let me behold."

"You're pretty good at ordering, too."

"Don't forget I'm a king."

She lay back and closed her eyes.

"Loosen up, Princess. You're stiff as a board."

"I'm trying. It seems to be a problem with me."

He managed to get the shirt off her and keep his gaze on her eyes, waiting for the lids to flutter open, but she kept them squeezed shut. At last he allowed himself a slow perusal of all that he had been picturing in his mind.

Her breasts were small—he'd known that from feeling them—but her nipples were provocatively large and stiff, her waist narrow, her abdomen flat, her private triangle of hair dark and full.

He looked quickly down to her strong thighs and fine calves. He looked back to her eyes, knowing that if he dwelt too long on certain parts, he would be neglecting the rest of her.

And he didn't want to neglect anything.

He caught her staring at him.

"I am more than pleased, your highness," he said thickly, and then, "Ellie," more softly, and then he didn't want to talk at all.

She put her arms around him and held herself against him, her flesh like heated satin. He draped her leg across his thigh and bent his head to kiss her throat and down to the taut nipples he couldn't get out of his mind. She arched her back and moaned. All he could think of was how bringing her pleasure brought him more pleasure than he could ever remember.

He couldn't touch her enough, couldn't kiss her enough, his hands and lips so hungry for her, he had to will himself not to be rough. She let him be the aggressor, her own touches so delicate, they seemed tentative, almost unsure, but her reaction to what he did to her burned away any impatience he might have felt.

When at last he stroked her inner thighs and eased his way to her sex, she held very, very still, holding on to him so tightly that he thought for a moment she was afraid. When he stopped what he was doing to her, she whispered, "No," against the side of his neck. "Don't stop."

The order from a princess was not to be disobeyed. He brought her pleasure—he could tell from her trembling—but not the ultimate pleasure. He was selfish enough to want that to happen when he was inside her.

He wanted her so much, he couldn't wait. She

was wet and ready. Parting her legs, he rested himself on top of her, rubbed his sex against hers, and plunged inside.

There was too much resistance. Her body was not ready for him. He realized with a jolt that it had never been ready for anyone before.

She cried out against his shoulder, but when he tried to pull back, she held on, squeezing her thighs against his hips, and then it was too late for anything but the pounding and the passion and the ultimate release.

Chapter Fourteen

Ellie hadn't thought about what to do afterward. An hour or two later, maybe, days, even a year, but not right away.

Neither had she thought about the pain involved in what they had just done, or the embarrassment.

She hadn't thought about how very intimate sex between a man and woman actually was.

Keeping herself very still in Cal's arms, she hoped he would think she had fallen asleep. It wasn't likely. He had just separated himself from her and was lying fairly still himself, holding her close as his breathing slowly steadied.

Men certainly got carried away with sex. No wonder they liked it so much.

Had she liked it? She had liked very much giving him pleasure. She had liked the way he liked looking at her. She had liked the feel of his hands and lips on her. She especially had liked the intimate strokes he had ended far too soon, arousing sensation in a place she had barely known existed, the strokes surprising and enthralling, ending just as she was about to—

She didn't know what she had been about to do. The best way to put it was explode. Or burst into flame. Or soar out of the bed and into the dark of night.

But none of those phrases really covered how she had felt. And she hadn't felt that way very long.

"Ellie."

His voice was thick and dark and as probing as his hands had been, but it brought nothing in the way of pleasure.

"What?" she said. It wasn't the most brilliant of responses, but she was feeling far from brilliant at the moment.

"Would you like to tell me what's going on here?"

She stared at the hairs on his chest. There weren't a lot of them, not like a pelt, but they were interesting and they made his torso look very different from hers.

"Didn't we just make love? If there's more to it, you ought to tell me right away."

"Because you don't already know. Because until a few minutes ago, you were a virgin."

He loosened his hold on her, and there was nothing she could do except ease away and look into his eyes. She tried covering herself with her hands and arms; he was decent enough to notice

242

and to pull the sheet over them both.

She didn't know why that made her feel better, but it did.

"I didn't realize my condition"—she could think of no other word—"would be a problem for you."

He propped his head on one hand and stared down at her. She wanted to cover her face with her hair. She contented herself with gripping the edge of the sheet and holding it close to her chin.

"It's a problem, all right. And damned unexpected."

She wondered if he expected her to apologize. She was willing to do almost anything for him except say she was sorry he was the first and only man she had known.

"What do you ordinarily do now? I mean, afterwards," she said.

"My ordinary behavior has nothing to do with us."

"Are you ashamed of it? Is there really something else we haven't done?"

His sigh was filled with exasperation. "Usually I leave. Unless we do it again. You do know what I mean by *it*, don't you?"

He made her angry, and she forgot to be shy. Sitting up, she forgot about the sheet.

"I must have led you to believe I wasn't pure and unspoiled. Aunt Abigail told me most men value unused women very much. That's the way she put it, unused. I guess you're the exception. For that, I am very sorry indeed. Now please go away. Your supper's getting cold."

She brushed her hair from her face, and in the

process, she brushed away the tear that had dared to fall.

But he didn't move. He just lay there, the outline of his body very evident beneath the lightweight sheet, his eyes probing her as thoroughly as any other part of his body had done.

Then he pulled her into his arms and held her for a moment, his hands gently touching her hair, as if he were a lover who truly cared. Easing away, he took one long look at her breasts, covered her with the sheet and got up from the bed.

His sudden departure left her chilled. So he was going to leave her and go eat, was he? He was only doing what she had ordered, she told herself. As well he should. She was his princess.

The thought brought the burn of tears to her eyes.

But he didn't leave. Instead, he strode to the washbowl that sat on the narrow shelf by the window. He moved into the lantern light, graceful and totally without self-consciousness. She couldn't take her eyes away from him. He was beautifully formed, every part of him flowing naturally into the next part, arms and shoulders tapering to waist and hips, rounded buttocks pale and tight, strong thighs, long, muscled calves. Even his feet looked good.

As he stood at the basin, she realized something else about him. There were thin striations across his buttocks, so small she might not have noticed them except that she was studying him so hard.

She closed her eyes to picture Antonio lying on the ground in the barn, a whip raised high above him. She imagined Cal, not much older, lying on a New Orleans dock as a father who didn't claim him caned him for being what he was.

The tears turned from anger and anguish to empathy so strong that it extinguished all her self-concern. She opened her eyes just as he turned, a damp cloth in his hand.

"I told you I was scarred," he said. "Now you are, too."

"You didn't hurt me. Not really. It wasn't anything that lasted."

"Yes, I hurt you, Ellie. You just don't realize it yet."

He returned to the bed and pulled back the sheets.

"There will be blood," he said.

She realized he meant to bathe her. Maybe he thought it was the gentlemanly thing to do, a gesture of atonement for deflowering her. He seemed to have no idea she understood the implications of what they had done.

She jerked the cloth from his hand. "Please don't watch."

He turned his back, and she cleaned herself. Yes, there was blood, but it was a very little bit. Nothing like the blood a cane would raise.

She threw the cloth across the room.

"You enjoyed it, didn't you?" she asked, trying to sound sure of herself and not like a woman desperate for kind words.

He faced her once again. "Very much. Too much."

He made no attempt to explain what he meant, and she was just cowardly enough not to ask.

"So much," he added, "I want to do it all over again. And more."

She studied the sheet. "Since you know I'm ignorant, there's no use pretending I know what I'm doing. What I want to know is, can you . . . that is, is it possible so soon—"

"It's very possible, Ellie." He hesitated. "Are you saying this because of the scars? You saw them, didn't you?"

"Of course I saw them, but if you think I'm doing this because I feel sorry for you, think again. I'd just like to have you with me when there is no pain."

"You want it better?"

"Can it be?"

"For me, I don't see how. But for you, yes, I can make it a great deal better."

Against every ounce of self-control she possessed, she found her gaze traveling from his eyes, down his chest, to the thick hair at the base of his abdomen. When he had first turned, the private part of his body had been lax. She watched it change. No wonder it had hurt her.

Her eyes flew to his. His stare was solemn and not in the least mocking. Her blood turned thick and hot and she felt stirrings inside her she had never experienced before, not without his hands working their magic along the surface of her skin.

Surely he could hear her heart thundering in her breast. Surely he understood the reason for her ragged, shallow breaths.

Lifting the sheet, he crawled into bed beside her and pulled her into his arms. His kiss was light and warm. "Haven't you figured out this is bad for you?" he asked.

Her answer was to return his kiss. She made hers more thorough, in the ways he had taught her. This time her tongue invaded him, and she understood why he liked to kiss her with his entire mouth getting involved.

His hands trailed down her back and cupped her buttocks.

She had to maneuver around a little, but she managed to wrap her arms around him and grip him in the same way. She couldn't keep kissing him, of course; they were far too different in length from one another, so she contented herself with teasing his nipple with her tongue.

Her thumbs rubbed back and forth across the firm, round surfaces of his behind, and she didn't know if she was actually feeling his scars or imagining them. Either way, she willed him to forget forever all the pain they had brought.

"Princess."

She hardly recognized his voice.

"I didn't touch you much before," she said. "I would like to now."

"Later. This is your time."

He broke their embrace. As she rested her back against the mattress, he raised himself over her, pinning her in place. As if she wanted to leave.

With hands and lips, he showed her what the mating of a man and woman was really all about. This time, when his strokes reached her private parts, he didn't stop until all the circling and the soaring and the tingling came together in one enormous outburst of pleasure, so explosive it came close to being pain. Her body shook and took a while to settle down, even while the tingles continued to ripple through her.

She understood the violence of his reaction when they had mated before. She wanted to curl against him and savor the joy in her private thoughts and in the private parts of her body.

But he was not done. Spreading her legs, he settled himself on top of her with his fingers continuing to raise the tingles, and eased inside her much more slowly than before. His thrusts were gentle and agonizingly slow, and at last she begged him to go faster, faster, faster.

He did, and in the doing brought her to ecstasy once again.

When Ellie woke early the next morning, Cal was gone from the bed. She remembered him lying beside her during the night, but she had slept so soundly, feeling so contented in his arms, she had scarcely stirred.

Hurriedly she dressed and went out to find him. Neither he nor Baron was to be seen.

Perhaps it was best. She hadn't known exactly what she was going to say to him, and she certainly had no idea what he would say to her. Embarrassing moments, she had found, were best handled by throwing oneself into work.

Donning Fin's shirt and trousers, she stripped the bed and washed the linens in the tub behind the cabin, hanging them from a rope she had strung up early in her visit. Cal caught her just as she was done. Baron loped out to drink the wash water she hadn't yet tossed out, and she shooed him away.

Wiping her damp hands against her trousers, she looked at Cal, at the full-sleeved linen shirt and leather jerkin, at the gun he had strapped to his thigh, at his hard, pointed boots. He had thumbed his hat to the back of his head, and with his dark hair and his blue eyes and his sun-browned skin, he looked more handsome than any man had the right to look.

Especially one who hadn't got much sleep the night before.

He in turn looked from her trousers to the sheets hanging on the rope.

"What are you doing?" he asked.

Good morning, my precious princess. Let me thank you for the most glorious night of my life.

The words were entirely hers, dreamed up in her mind while she was doing the wash. She hadn't expected to hear them, but *what are you doing* fell far short of the greeting she had hoped for.

"I didn't think you would want to come back to a soiled bed."

There. She hadn't shown the least bit of embarrassment. Cal was the one to look upset.

"What are you doing?" she threw back at him, except that she said it as sweetly as she could.

"I took Baron for a walk."

"He does like his exercise," she said.

He stepped toward her. "Ellie—"

She brushed past him. "Would you mind emptying the tub? I'll get your breakfast. You must be starving."

She went in to scrape his uneaten supper into Baron's bowl on the dog run, then got out the last of the flour and lard for biscuits. He was watching her from the open door. She needed to keep very, very busy or else all her control would be gone.

"You really ought to get some chickens," she said. "Eggs would taste very good this morning, wouldn't they?"

He tossed his hat aside and took a step toward her.

"Ellie—"

"And a milk cow. That way you could have buttermilk and butter and even some hot chocolate if you wanted it. I guess Joseph Merse stocks chocolate. I always like a warm cup first thing in the morning. It gets me going better than coffee."

"Stop it, Ellie."

"I know, I forgot the coffee. I'm sorry. I'll make it right away."

"Damn it, I said stop."

She slapped at the sack of flour. "Don't make this hard for me."

"Please," he said, "sit down so we can talk."

She regarded the bench beside her for only a moment. "I prefer to stand."

She felt petty enough and frightened enough to take whatever small victories she could. She had vaguely imagined a gentleness between them and a moment of tenderness before the inevitable, bittersweet parting, each of them aware of what could never be.

But the morning wasn't working out that way.

"Tell me the truth," he said, and she shivered.

She could learn to hate conversations that began *tell me the truth.*

"Do you still want the Double T?"

It wasn't what she expected. It was a far easier question to answer than she had feared, mainly because she had already asked herself the very same thing.

"No, not really." It wasn't a complete lie. "Papa as much as gave it to your uncles. I'll honor what he did." She laughed softly. "And what would I do with it anyway? I don't know anything about cattle or Texas crops."

I could learn.

But that was impossible. Women didn't make it on their own, especially out here in the West.

A new thought struck her, one so painful she almost winced.

"You're not about to offer it to me in payment for last night, are you?"

"That hadn't occurred to me, Ellie. Last night was something separate and apart, and if you don't know how special it was, you need to be told. I'm a cold-hearted son of a bitch much of the time, but I'm not that bad."

Suddenly she didn't know what to do with her hands. They fluttered around in front of her as if they had lives of their own. Ruthlessly she shoved them into the pockets of her borrowed trousers.

"What about Fin and Fitz? Don't they want it?"

"Owning land in another country was a dream for them, but the reality has proven too harsh. Now that their names have been cleared—or soon will be—they won't have too much objection to returning to New Orleans. They still have the saloon there waiting for them."

"It's nice to have a place to go."

"You have Bertrand Randolph."

She started to say yes, but the lie wouldn't come. Maybe yesterday it would have, but not now.

"I read a letter from him yesterday. He's married someone else. So if you're thinking I would have tried to present myself to him as an unspoiled dove, think again. We're both sort of edging around last night, but the truth is, I knew what I was doing. Well, pretty much. You showed me what I didn't know."

She looked away. If only he had let her bake the biscuits, maybe she wouldn't be rambling so much.

"You know I plan never to get married," he said.

Her hands curled into fists in her pockets and she stared at him in astonishment, feeling a hurt worse than anything inflicted by a whip.

"Is that what you think I did? Do you believe I offered my virtue in order to get a wedding ring? Think again. Like you, I don't plan to get married. I was betrothed to Bertrand only because I gave my word to him and my aunt. Whatever you believe about me, and despite all the lies I have told, I am an honorable person."

"Hot-tempered, too. That isn't what I meant at all. I care for you, Ellie. I don't want you to be hurt by any misunderstanding."

Like hell you care for me. If only in her thoughts, Ellie was learning to be as profane as he was.

"There's no misunderstanding," she said. "What

happened last night was because I wanted to know what being with a man was like, and I figured you could teach me more thoroughly than any other man I was likely to meet."

"I'm trying to figure if there's a compliment in there."

"A small one."

"You're being very tough and blunt, aren't you? But I don't think it's a role designed for you. You were warm and womanly with me, and you brought me more pleasure than I can ever remember. I'm a great one for scoffing at passion. I never thought it could linger beyond the moment. But it lingers today. We have a lot to offer each other, at least for a while. When I leave, come with me. I'll take care of you. I promise. I'm not the kind of bastard to go back on my word."

For him, it was quite a speech with quite a message for a woman to hear.

Ellie sat hard on the bench.

"You want me to be your mistress?"

"If you have to put a name to it. How about my traveling companion? I can show you much of the world."

He meant mistress, like Bertrand's widow who had died.

For him the offer was the ultimate sacrifice, dictated by a conscience that wasn't quite dead. She hated him for it and loved him at the same time.

Her heart, broken by him many times in the last two days, at last shattered into so many pieces, she doubted it could ever be made whole.

To be near him for a year, or two or three, to

have him and not to have him, to give him pleasure at night and take her own joy, then see him walk away to another part of his life she could never share—all this she could not do. It was a life for which she was not made.

It was not, as he put it, a role designed for her.

"Thank you, Cal," she said, being very, very civilized. "I know the offer wasn't easy for you to make. But I'd really rather live my life alone. Now, if you wouldn't mind saddling our horses while I change clothes, we need to get on into town. Don't worry about my trunk. You can bring it in later, or maybe I can hire someone to ride out and get it."

She looked for signs of relief in his eyes, but his eyes were as hard and empty of feeling as blue stones. The only hint of feeling was in the squaring of his jaw, as frequently happened when he was getting upset.

"There are some cold biscuits left over from yesterday," she said. "They'll have to do for breakfast. I will put on the pot of coffee, however. It's the least I can do for you before we leave."

The ride into town lasted the longest two hours Cal could remember. Ellie sat straight-backed on the mare, looking around her as if she were seeing the land for the last time, and he wondered if, after her exertions of the night before, she might be uncomfortable in the saddle.

She would never show it. If his besetting sin was the need to lead a private life, hers was stubborn pride.

She was right not to accept his offer, no matter

254

how sincerely it was made. Going their separate ways, they could each manage to get along; living together, he wondered if either of them would ever know a moment of peace.

He was relieved she had turned him down. He had to keep reminding himself of the fact, what with the memories of the night still very much in his mind. Cal was a man who never outstayed his welcome, and he appreciated women who didn't outstay theirs. Once spent, passion was done.

So why did he keep remembering the feelings she had aroused? Why could he still feel her soft, smooth flesh on the tips of his fingers? Why could he still taste her on his tongue?

And why did he have this roiling feeling inside him and the certainty their story was not yet done?

The only time he spoke was to ask if she needed a comfort stop.

"I'm fine," she said with a shrug, "but feel free to stop if you need to."

They did make one stop, arrived at by unspoken consensus, and that was to water and rest the horses. They were soon on their way.

Ellie left her horse at the stable to be cared for, and Cal decided to do the same. They walked side by side to the adobe house at the edge of town. Cal caught George Holloway staring at them from the saloon, but he didn't bother to wave.

He pretty much figured that within the hour everyone would be guessing what had taken place between him and her.

They walked inside the house to find the sisters and the brothers sitting around the kitchen table, papers spread out in front of them. All four of them were puffing on cigars, coffee cups at hand, and looking in general very pleased with themselves.

"We thought you might be a while longer," said Gert.

"Like maybe a week or two," Fin said with a wink.

Cal shot him a quelling look, but he wasn't sure his uncle got the message.

Ellie took off her bonnet and smoothed her hair.

"I always intended to come back today."

He had no idea whether or not she lied.

"It's good you got here," Fin said. "We've got news."

Fitz gestured to the papers on the table. "These are copies Gert and May wrote out. Sir Simon has taken the originals down to a lawyer he heard about in Victoria. He should be getting there before long."

Cal knew for certain he didn't want to know what the papers were about. He glanced at Ellie. The look on her face said she felt the same.

"The boys here have decided to get rid of their land," Gert said.

Cal didn't know why the news didn't bring him more relief. He had been pushing for this decision since they'd first arrived.

"You recognized life in Texas wasn't for you?" he said.

"That's not exactly what I meant," Fin said.

"Not in the least little bit," May said. "The four of us have decided to open up a new saloon in town. That place down the street isn't fit for even the drifters that pass through here. We expect to offer more amenities and raise the level of the clientele."

Cal and Ellie looked at one another, then back to the smoke-clouded table.

"But you can't," they said at the same time.

"No *can't* to it," Gert said. "May and me have money. And that don't include what we're owed." She waved a hand. "Now don't go looking so surprised, Miss Ellie Davenport Chase. We told our new partners here we ain't your real aunts. We have no intention of taking any cash from you. If you hadn't made us the offer you did, we never would have met the boys."

She smiled at Fin, and May smiled at Fitz. The boys smiled right back.

Fin shifted a sly grin to Cal. "We plan to pay our part. Ever since you bought it, we've been fighting owning that saloon in New Orleans. We decided to fight no more. We're selling out and investing the money right here in Glory. That's one of the papers Sir Simon took to Victoria."

"Maybe you two better sit down before you hear the rest," Gert said.

"I'll stand," Cal and Ellie said in unison.

"You're selling out to Alden Fowler, right?" Ellie asked.

"Wrong," Fin said. "We're giving the place away."

"Who in hell are you giving it to?" asked Cal.

"You and Ellie."

The two of them stared at one another, then back toward the table.

257

"Don't look so surprised," Fitz said. "You heard right."

"It was the boys' idea," Gert said.

"But we went along right away," May said. "Alden Fowler will just have to buy some other property. The Double T is taken."

"Only it's not the Double T anymore," Fitz said. "We wanted something more elegant as a thank-you gift for the nephew who's supported us all these years."

"And as a thank-you to the young woman who rescued us from a life of boredom in New Orleans," Gert put in.

"It's called the Crown of Glory," Fin said with so much pomp, the announcement deserved the roll of a drum.

"For the town," said Fitz. "Get it?"

"Like hell we get it," Cal said. "We're not taking your land."

"Of course we're not," Ellie said.

Fin shook his head, his chin set obstinately. "You got no choice. The papers are already being filed."

"There's no way Cal and I can share anything," Ellie said.

"I'm not so sure that's the truth," Gert said. "Besides, you don't exactly have joint ownership of it all."

"We knew this was a tricky proposition," Fin said. "You're a better man than you think you are, nephew, but you're not quite ready to share your life."

"Not like us," Fitz said and patted May's hand.

"The boys split the property down the middle,"

May said, and puffed on her cigar. "Slap dab down the dog run. It was our idea, Gert's and mine, to give the bedroom to you, Ellie. Cal, you get the kitchen side. You'll have to decide between you who gets Baron. It was hard to split a dog in two."

Cal decided maybe he would take that seat after all. Ellie made the same decision at the same time. They both fell into chairs and dared to look at one another.

The Crown of Glory.

It simply could not be. Never. Not in a thousand years.

Chapter Fifteen

"Uncles, we have to talk," Cal said.

"We're not changing our minds," Fin said.

"We've decided it's for the best," Fitz said. "Yours and Ellie's. What we didn't see for ourselves, being hopeless males as you should know, May and Gert explained."

Neither of his uncles, normal fidgeters, was drumming fingers or twitching or showing the least sign of distress.

Cal gritted his teeth. "Outside, please."

He held the door open. Puffing their cigars, Fin and Fitz passed him, grinned at Ellie and sauntered into the dusty street, Cal close on their heels.

Usually when he backed them down on an issue, they wouldn't look him in the eye. Today two pairs of round green buttons were directed straight at him. Fin even puffed on his cigar.

"When did you take up that habit?" Cal asked over the noise of a wagon rumbling past.

"It's not new," Fin said.

Fitz joined in the puffing. "We're just enjoying it more now."

"We're finding enjoyment in many a pleasure we thought would never come our way," Fin said. " 'Tis our decision to stay and continue the enjoying."

"If that's your choice, so be it. Mine is to get out of here," Cal said.

The uncles kept staring at him with uncharacteristic quiet.

"I mean it. You know I never stay anywhere for long."

"This land is different," Fin said. " 'Tis not just anywhere. It can get into a man's blood."

"So why are you giving your portion of it away?"

"We're nay giving so much as a blade of grass away. We're deeding our precious property to you in thanks for all you've done for us. And we're staying close enough to visit it from time to time. We won't be expecting reports, understand. Half the Crown is yours to do with as you judge best."

"The Dollarhides thought of giving half to Ellie, didn't they?"

"You're a cynical lad. The ideas came, and we don't know who thought of this or who thought of that. We're as fond of the lass as Gert and May."

"And as you should be, too," Fitz said, looking as if he wanted to go on, but Fin quelled him with a wave of his cigar.

Evelyn Rogers

"The important thing," Fin said, "is we all agree on what we're doing."

What they were doing was matchmaking, the whole lot of them. They would have about as much success with him as they would with Ellie. The fact that she was no doubt inside arguing with the Dollarhides over this impossible situation should have brought him satisfaction. For some reason, it irritated him all the more.

"I'm not cynical," he snapped. "I'm looking at the way things are."

"Now there you're wrong," Fin said. " 'Tis a sad truth, lad, but you've always looked at matters the way you believed them to be."

Something in his uncle's voice struck a bitter chord in him. "Don't start in about Raymond Hardin again."

"And why not? He's never far from your mind."

Glancing at one another, the two uncles shared a subtle nod. Matters were far worse, Cal saw, than he could have imagined. He ought to turn tail and run as fast and as far as he could, but when he looked down at the pair, the solemn affection in their expression rooted him in place.

"All right, say what you've got to say and be done with it."

"We've tried before, but we were never sure it was the right thing to do—the telling of everything, that is. Today there'll be no stopping us."

Fin paused, looking away from Cal as if he were staring into the past.

"There was a time Raymond Hardin loved your mother. He was a young and dashing sort and she

262

was fair beyond imagining, though you'd not have known it from her later years."

Fitz shook his head sadly. "They were so very young, little more than children."

"He abandoned her," Cal said.

"Aye," Fin said, "he had the wanderlust. But when he was home, no one could have asked for a better family man." He barely blinked at Cal's scoff. "You loved him, lad, though you'd not be admitting it now. And he cared greatly for you. Proud he was, proud as any man of his son."

"He got over it," Cal said. "And so did I."

Again the brothers shared a glance before Fin continued.

"We've long defended Hardin, as did your dear departed mother. There was reason, and it's time you knew. He was not as constant as a woman has every right to expect her husband to be. But he loved as best he could. He did indeed return from one of his journeys to find her with another man. He'd left her too often, and a smooth-talking gambler came along and took advantage. He had as much pride as you, lad. He went into a rage, beat the man most near to death, and accused poor Margaret of terrible things."

"Including," Fitz said, "passing her bastard son off on him as his own. She was in the family way with you when they were wed."

Cal wanted to call them liars, but there was something in their sad, intense manner, so alien to their usual way, that declared they spoke the truth.

"He broke her heart, but she broke his," Fin said.

"He called her a whore," Cal said.

"Aye, and you a bastard. In his anger he was casting off everything and everyone who brought him pain. But he was wrong in his harsh judgment. Margaret was a one-time adulteress, and you his first-born son."

If his uncles thought to soften his memories of his father, they should prepare themselves to be disappointed. Too many years had passed for him to change; his hatred for Raymond Hardin was as much a part of him as his hands or his eyes.

"Do not think harshly of our sister," Fin said. "She lived the rest of her life in shame."

"I don't think harshly of her at all."

He truly couldn't. Margaret Hardin had been a loving woman, too much so, and her need for love had cost her her happiness. If sex outside marriage was a sin, he was a far worse sinner than she had ever been.

He thought of Ellie, as far from a sinner as anyone in the world. She had given him her innocence because she'd found herself alone. Women were far more complex creatures than men could ever understand.

Complex and seductive, a small voice reminded him. Seductive without even trying to be. This morning he had found himself unable to let her go. The offer to take her with him had been as much for his sake as it was for hers. Little had she understood what it had taken for him to say the words that would bind her to him for even a short while.

She had been the sensible one, the one who saw their natures would never suit. Why that sensibleness had torn at him—still tore at him—he didn't know.

And here two pairs of conspirators were conniving to keep them together. Cal could almost appreciate the irony.

"So what has all this got to do with the Double T?" he said. Let their real purpose get out in the open. Let them admit to the truth.

"No longer the Double T," Fitz said. " 'Tis now the Crown of Glory, you should recall."

"Sorry. The Crown of Glory. Why split it between me and Ellie?"

" 'Tis time to quit your running," Fin said. "Even your father saw the wisdom of that, though he came to it far too late. We're not wanting to see you make the same mistake."

"Quit running and take a wife, you mean."

"We've not that power over you, else you would have long ago been wed," Fitz said.

Fin nodded in agreement. "She's a fair lass and would make a fine mate for a man such as yourself. But we can no more put the notion of wedding her into your head than we can put love into your heart."

Love was a word Cal seldom heard spoken; he wasn't sure he knew what it meant except for a temporary softening of the brain. He had never seen it bring happiness to anyone.

Love Ellie? Even if he were capable of the emotion, he wouldn't give in to it, for her sake as well as his.

"The truth is far simpler, lad," said Fin. "We're giving you a place that will take all the wanderlust out of you. You'll have to work harder than you ever have in your life. Harder than when you were a boy on the docks and boxing lads far bigger than yourself for pennies."

"You've not thought this through, uncles. I know nothing about ranching."

"You knew nothing of boxing, either, or gambling or investing or much of anything, but you learned. You'll learn the ways of caring for land and cattle soon enough. Already you have a feel for horses, as you've often shown us."

"And there's the mongrel dog," Fitz said. "You could scarce be leaving him after he's given you his devotion."

"I asked for him about as much as I asked for the ranch."

"Aye, and he's brought you a part of the pleasure you'll be getting from owning your own place."

Cal looked beyond them, down the dusty main street of Glory, to the far western hills and the sun that rested just above the rounded green peaks. He thought of the land his uncles were offering. He even thought of the logs he had cut and the posts he had put out for the corral.

And he thought of Baron, who was never far from his side. Never in his life had an animal attached itself to him as Baron had done. Dumb dog, he hadn't realized he wasn't wanted.

Something about all the images called to him. They wouldn't call for long. He wouldn't let them. But maybe for a while—

Then he thought of Ellie.

"I can't accept the land. Not sharing it the way you have laid out. I'm not being petty, simply re-

alistic. Ellie doesn't belong out there. She's a hard
worker, I'll give you that, but she's not strong
enough. She was raised to a softer kind of life."

The reason he presented was logical and right,
but it wasn't the main one that ate at him.

He put it as bluntly as he could. "Ellie Chase
and I are different kinds of people. If you think
we're going to live in that cabin together, you're
wrong. We barely survived one night."

His uncles seemed not the least surprised by
what he said.

"Would you be caring to tell us about the
night?" Fin asked.

"We'll listen without asking questions," Fitz
said.

"No, I would not."

"Then offer to buy the Crown from her," Fin
said. "Perhaps she'll sell and you can own both
sides of the cabin and all the land as well."

"All we want is for you to give the land a try,"
Fitz said. "Build it as you built your other stakes.
You'll need a year, we're thinking, but you're not
expected anywhere, are you? There's little need to
deny it. If someone were expecting you, man or
woman, you'd burn in hell before you met that
expectation. You've that much of the Hardin per-
versity in you."

Fin leveled a stare for the final assault. "But
you've not the nature that would make you aban-
don the land, and with it all our hopes. That much
like him, you are not."

His uncles were far more clever than he had
ever assumed. They had planned their arguments
well. No taller than his shoulders, slight of build

and twenty-plus years his senior, they were beating him into the ground.

He looked from one to the other with a grudging admiration.

"A year," he said.

Fitz nodded. "A year."

"It was your mother's final prayer that you would find a place to settle down," Fin said.

Such had been Margaret Hardin's first and most frequent prayer since Cal first ran away from home, but for all its repetition, it was not a weak argument.

"To build a stake, that's all. I'm not settling."

In the denial there was yet an acceptance in his voice that even he could hear, as if someone he didn't know was speaking.

"Whatever you wish to call it."

"Now," he said, more to himself than to them, "all I have to do is convince Ellie to sell me her half."

"If anyone can convince a lass to do what she's not planning, 'tis you."

It was clear Fin was thinking of last night. Cal didn't think it would serve much purpose for him to know that everything that had happened had been her idea.

"I can't accept the land," Ellie said for the third time.

She paced up and down the width of the room, while the Dollarhides sat at the table and smoked. Cal and his uncles were still outside. She was certain his side of the conversation was going much the same as hers. Surely he would have more luck explaining the impossibility of the proposal.

For all the good she was doing, she might as well have been lecturing an empty room.

"Would you like some coffee?" Gert said.

"I'll heat it up," May said.

Ellie gritted her teeth. "No, I do not want any coffee. I don't want anything." She leveled the strongest gaze she could manage at Gert and May. "I don't know who came up with this crack-brained idea, but it won't work."

"Why not?" Gert said.

"Don't look so innocent. You know why not."

"Because you love him?" asked May. "Gert told me, but I was figuring it out for myself. Seems to me that's a reason for staying."

Ellie stopped her pacing. "And what about his not loving me in return? He doesn't. Believe me."

It was Gert's turn to plow into her. "He sure ain't going to love you if you run away."

Ellie glanced nervously toward the door. "Can we not talk about feelings anymore? I'd rather not be overheard."

"What you're saying is, he don't know," May said.

"And he's not going to. I'm sure whatever I'm feeling is just a temporary aberration on my part. There are a thousand other reasons for refusing the O'Malleys' offer. For one, I know nothing about working land like this."

"Dirt's dirt," May said.

"A cow's a cow," Gert said.

Ellie knew things were far more complicated than the sisters let on, but she would get as far

269

arguing about Texas farming and ranching as she had discussing love.

"You're still determined to marry Bertrand?" Gert said.

"He's never sounded like much of a catch to me," May said.

"No, I'm not marrying Bertrand." Ellie took a deep breath. "He's already got a wife."

"The letter?" Gert said.

"The letter."

The sisters grinned.

"Don't look too smug," Ellie said. "I'm still leaving."

"You sure sound determined." Gert's brow furrowed under her pile of red hair. "Things didn't go so well last night?"

Ellie studied the coffeepot on the stove behind the Dollarhides. "I wouldn't exactly say that."

"Good thing. We'd take it for a lie," May said.

"We know our men," Gert said. "Cal's not one to disappoint."

Oh, but he was. Not in any way they would understand, but he had disappointed her bitterly. Not with his lovemaking. She would take memories of that to her grave. It was afterwards, and then in the morning when he had offered to make her his mistress—for a while—that he had driven a stake into her heart.

"You've got half a cabin out there," Gert said, "and half the outdoors. You want to stay away from him, you'll find a way."

"But you've also got the bedroom," May said, unable to keep the grin off her face for long. "The boys came up with that. A woman that controls

270

the bedroom is always the one in charge, and it don't matter how big and tough and bossy the man is. If he don't beat her, that is, and Cal ain't the sort."

Ellie closed her eyes. She could just imagine the four of them hovering around the table, working on the particulars of their plan. She would not have wanted to be present at the discussion for all the tobacco in Virginia.

"We've seen you looking around the land," Gert said. "You like it."

"A little," Ellie admitted.

Gert's eyes lit. "And think what you could do with that cabin."

Images came to mind—of curtains and rugs and polished furniture and even a harp in the corner near the horsehair sofa. First must come a stove, of course, and a decent set of pots and pans—

What in the world was she thinking? Ellie forced the images aside.

"I need to leave. That's the most important thing to me. I've got plans."

"What are they?" May asked.

"I have to do something with my property in Virginia."

"You've got a lawyer, didn't you say?" Gert asked. "Have him sell it."

Ellie didn't mention that she already had a buyer. If she did, they would never give up.

"And then there's my father's quarters in New Orleans. Something has to be done with that. Why, I might decide to settle there and open a sewing shop of my own." The idea hadn't occurred to her before, but now that she was thinking of it, she thought it a splendid idea.

"I'm really quite talented with a needle," she added for argument's sake.

"We knew you would be. That's why the cabin needs you."

"The cabin doesn't need me."

Gert was relentless. "You've got a cabin and a man out there needing you far more than you know."

"Cal doesn't need me."

"He just doesn't realize it yet. That's your responsibility. Let him know. It's best if he figures it out for himself, but every now and then a man has to be told what's good for him."

Gert sounded as sure of herself as she had ever been, and May's firm nod said she felt the same way.

Ellie had done all the arguing she could without breaking into tears.

"The O'Malleys will simply have to sell the land to someone else. Alden Fowler made them a good offer. They ought to take him up on it."

Gert shook her head. "They decided they didn't like him. We agree."

"Why not?"

"Hard to say. Could be the way he was smirking when he brought the news about you two being alone and caring for Antonio."

"And it could be pure instinct," May put in.

"That's not good business," Ellie said.

Gert snorted. "Sometimes decisions have to be made where money isn't a concern."

"And don't tell us we don't know what we're

talking about," May said. "We were business-women, don't forget. We turned a tidy profit using our womanly instincts. And of course a few other womanly parts, but that's beside the point. Others in our profession turned out poor as field hands 'cause they were always counting pennies and try-ing to be smart."

"Admit the truth," Gert said. "You like the land more than just a little."

Ellie thought of her ride into town that after-noon and how a lump had formed in her throat as she looked at the rolling pastures and the creeks and the trees. Everything was so open, so wide and spacious, it made her place in Virginia seem as if it were indoors.

"All right, I like it very much."

"So buy Cal's share of the Crown and hire help to do the chores. No way you want to go back East and face that lying fiancé of yours."

"We'll be here if you get lonely," said May. "But with all the work you'll be doing and the men who'll be hanging around, we don't think loneli-ness is going to be a problem for you."

"Your father wanted you to have it," Gert said. "This way things'll turn out the way you planned."

Not exactly. She hadn't planned on falling in love.

Still, she found herself weakening. Papa had bought the place for her. Maybe he had dreamed of her settling on it and being closer to him than Virginia. Maybe he had just wanted to be a part of her life. Maybe if she stayed, in a way he would be.

"Cal asked if I wanted the title," she said, as

Evelyn Rogers

much to herself as to the sisters. "I told him no, but I could have spoken too fast."

Gert and May kept silent.

Ellie sighed. "I guess I could make him an offer," she said, thinking that she could be reasonable and calm and logical, and even complimentary—the gentle persuasions, Aunt Abigail had called them. Before she could consider the details of her approach, Cal and his uncles strode through the door.

Cal, her temporary partner and always adversary, seemed so tall and brown and leathery, everything that was masculine, nothing soft or malleable about him that she had been able to find. All by himself he could fill a room; with four others staring at her, along with him, she could scarcely breathe.

"Ellie, we need to talk," he said.

Even his voice sounded brown and leathery.

"Yes, we do," she said.

"We'll get out and leave you two alone," Gert said.

May took Fitz by the arm. "I'll bet there's a table waiting for us down at the saloon. If we're gonna open up our own place anytime soon, we need to study the competition every chance we can get."

Chapter Sixteen

After the sisters and brothers had left, Ellie busied herself clearing the table of the coffee cups and jars of cigar ashes, straightening the papers, looking everywhere but at Cal. He stood by the door and watched. It was a habit he had. He must know how much it unnerved her.

But being unnerved was not the same thing as being defeated. Reason, calm, and logic, sweetened with an occasional compliment, she reminded herself, must guide everything she did and said.

She kept to the far side of the table only because she could think more clearly if Cal didn't get too close.

"They came up with quite a proposal," he said.

"Yes, quite a foolish proposal," she said.

"I figured you would look at it that way."

"And you don't?"

"At first it was hard to view it any other way. But then, for the sake of my uncles, I took a second look. They certainly want me to give settling down a try."

"They've been asking that for years, haven't they?"

"For as long as I can remember."

He sounded far too amenable; she had expected anger or, more likely, his usual cynicism. Something was going on.

A spark of hope tingled in her heart. Maybe he liked the proposal because it would keep her beside him in a natural way, one she couldn't refuse. But it was a very tiny spark, and she saw nothing else in his behavior, in the way he held himself back and spoke with caution, that would fan it into flame.

She swiped at the table with a cloth, catching a swirl of ashes that had missed the jar. Out of nowhere came the picture of what he had looked like without his clothes—the long, muscled arms and legs; the firm, tapered torso; the private parts, especially the pale striations on his buttocks.

So vivid was the image that her fingertips prickled with the texture of him and his scent permeated the air. Finding a stain on the table that required her attention, she tried to rub a hole through the wood.

Was he picturing something equally intimate about her? Probably not. The few scars she had were inside. Besides, he had seen the bodies of a hundred women. Maybe a thousand. She had seen only one man.

Concentrate. She had to concentrate; otherwise he would read her mind and she would expire on the spot.

She looked up at him. "They're making a real sacrifice with this offer," she said in as reasonable a tone as she could manage. "I can see why it would be tempting to you."

Oh, how he was watching her, waiting for the least sign of how she felt. With her dignity, her pride, her very survival at stake, she watched him right back, keeping calm though her heart was caught in her throat.

"It would probably take a great deal of incentive for you to walk away from it," she added, "caring for them the way you do."

"That argument says I'm walking. You're the one who wants out. Let's be blunt. How much do you want for your half?"

Ellie's breath caught, and she felt hollow inside, as if his words had cut out the parts that gave her reason to live. There it was, the proof he didn't want her around. She had known how he felt, of course, but she would have preferred him to take a gentler approach.

There was no way she would ever get it. Denied anything like Aunt Abigail's tutelage, Cal had been reared in a far rougher world than she. Ruthlessly she thrust from her mind all thoughts of what had been between them and what the future might hold. Here and now mattered, nothing else.

"I don't want anything for my portion," she said. "How much do you want for yours?"

It wasn't a calm retort, but it was logical, given

the kind of man he was. She took satisfaction in
the strength of it and, more, the look of surprise
on his face.

"You're not seriously considering staying, are
you?" he asked.

She clutched her hands to hide their trembling.
"Maybe."

"You're just being stubborn. This morning I
asked you if you wanted the Double T and you
said no."

"The Crown of Glory."

"Sorry. The Crown of Glory." He strode to the
table and stared at her across its width, so close
that if she stretched out her arm she could touch
him. "Ellie, do not tell me you're seriously considering turning into a pioneer. You haven't the
stuff for it."

"The stuff?"

Calm, calm, she reminded herself. *And try to
throw in a few compliments.*

"The toughness. The will. God knows you
haven't the physical strength."

All of Aunt Abigail's teachings fled. He had finally gone too far.

"So weak little me is supposed to sell out to big
strong you, is that it?"

"Smart you is better off selling out to dumb
me."

"Don't try complimenting me, Cal. That's an old
trick."

"I don't know what you're talking about. All I'm
trying to do is use reason. I've got family ties to
keep me here."

"You never let that influence you before."

278

"That was in New Orleans. I didn't want to spend more time there than absolutely necessary. Texas is different."

"It certainly is. I like it."

"Don't be ridiculous. There's a real depression taking hold here. The money's worthless. People are leaving—"

"Some people. That gives me more reason to stay. I've always liked a challenge."

"Do you also like the hardship? Do you like the danger? There's nothing to say the Comanches won't return. And don't forget the vigilantes."

"Don't you think Buck Shannon had something to do with them? I do. And he's dead."

"There will be other enemies."

Ellie felt as if she were facing one now. Everything he said was true, except his belief that she was weak. He had no idea what her life had been like back in Virginia. Or what it would be like if she returned.

He certainly had no concept of what she was going through now. She had tried to give him gentleness, but it was toughness he wanted and toughness he would get. In matters that truly mattered to her, she could out-tough him every day of the week.

"I'll hire help for the work I can't do myself," she said. "I won't be alone. I really want to buy you out."

"I'm not selling. I'm buying."

"There's nothing to buy."

He shook his head, and at last she saw real anger in his eyes.

"Do you really want to stay out there with me?

279

Just the two of us? This morning I offered to take you with me when I left, and you turned me down. You pretty much told me your curiosity was satisfied. Don't bother looking offended. You wanted to know what being with a man was like. So you found out."

Lies, all lies, she wanted to cry. When she'd told him that, she had been protecting herself. She should have known he would throw her words back at her.

"I was less than truthful with you," she managed. "It wasn't curiosity that made me do what I did, nor even a need to celebrate. I was still too shaken. After what we had been through, I guess I just wanted to know we were both alive."

It was as good an explanation for last night as she could deliver without opening up her heart, and it wasn't totally wrong.

"I didn't want you to know," she added. "I was afraid you wouldn't understand. I wasn't sure I understood it completely myself."

He had the decency to look embarrassed. "Maybe I was too quick to believe you, but then I was having a little problem with my pride when you turned down my offer to let things go on for a while."

"I had a little problem with my pride when you made it. I wasn't after a permanent arrangement. I wasn't trying to trap you. I just . . . wanted you."

She turned away.

He came around the table.

"Don't touch me," she said. "I'm fine." She glanced over her shoulder to show him she was not crying, then shifted to face him straight on.

280

"Now that we understand one another, name your price, Cal. I mean it."

"Name yours."

"I don't have one."

"Neither do I." He thought a moment. "We could go on like this forever. I don't suppose you would flip a coin."

"You're the gambler, not I."

He ran a hand through his hair. "I can't believe I'm saying this, but what if we gave this sharing a try? For a period of time, I mean, until one of us gives up."

Ellie took a long time to answer. He had no idea what he was asking of her . . . or what he was offering. In truth, neither did she.

She closed her eyes a minute and thought of the possibilities. Most of them were frightening, but a few of them were as tempting as his kiss.

"Let's get the details spelled out," she said. "If you give up, you would be willing to sell out to me?"

"Right. And the reverse is true."

"We'd have to divide the chores, based on what each of us could contribute," she said.

"I wouldn't expect you to—"

"Don't start talking down to me again. I think you'll be surprised at what I can do." She leveled a look as tough as she could manage at him. "But that doesn't include allowing you in my bed."

"I didn't think it did," he said, so fast that she wondered if he lied. "Am I supposed to keep you out of the kitchen?"

All her pent-up emotions gave way and she found herself laughing. The absurdity of the whole situation must have addled her brain. How could she find relief in the fact that they wouldn't be parting quite so soon? The next weeks would not be easy, not in any way. They would probably prove the best and worst she had ever known.

And they would keep her truly alive. The Dollarhides knew that, knew her better than she knew herself. She could hear Gert saying right now, "Temporary aberration, like hell."

"They really came up with a devious plan, didn't they?" she said.

He grinned. "Yep. That's Texas talk for yes. I better start practicing if I'm going to fit in."

He looked so wonderful smiling. She had hardly seen him do it before. And she was reminded all over again of the difference in the way they felt about one another. If anything proved to be her undoing, it would be her love.

She loved him, but she didn't necessarily trust him.

"I think we ought to put this in writing," she said. "So that later there are no misunderstandings."

"You want Sir Simon to take it to the lawyer in Victoria?"

"You're getting sarcastic again."

"You realize I don't think this is going to last for very long," he said. "Just long enough to cause a scandal. No one is going to believe we're not sleeping together."

"I can't help what people believe, nor worry about it," she said and meant every word. "Besides, the scandal will die soon enough after you're gone. Before a month is out, those cabin walls will be closing in on you."

"Nope," he said.

"More Texas talk? Then I guess my response is yep, they will. I promise, and I'll put it in writing if you want and take the paper to Victoria myself, that when you finally sell out to me, I will never say I told you so."

During the first few days of shared ownership, no cabin walls closed in on Cal. He wasn't inside long enough.

First, there was the ongoing work at the corral, and then came a thorough study of the barn. Both lay on Ellie's land, along with a couple of rich fields ripe for planting and the run-down chicken coop, but he owned the well behind the cabin, the best grassland, and most of the creek.

Even she had seen the wisdom of each improving the other's property, the purpose being betterment for them both.

Those first two days, she stayed in town deciding on supplies, ordering whatever she needed that Joseph Merse didn't have in stock, buying another wagon and a mule from the stable for the Dollarhides.

She even ordered a kitchen stove, which he thought showed more optimism in her staying power than was warranted.

All this he got in a report from his uncles, who rode out in the new wagon to check up on him.

"We're not checking up on you," Fin had said as soon as he walked out to the corral where Cal was pounding in posts.

"We've come to offer encouragement," Fitz said.

Like hell, Cal thought.

The mid-November weather had turned cold, but sweat plastered his shirt to his back. Brushing a sleeve across his forehead, he paused a moment in the pounding.

"I'd find it very encouraging if you unloaded those logs and scattered them around for me."

"We would do so, lad," Fin said, "even with our bad backs, but we've no interest in robbing you of the pleasure you'll be getting as you develop the Crown on your own."

"Of course," Cal said. "I should have figured that out."

"Your partner sent you a few gifts she thought might be useful to you," his uncle added.

"The makings for soup, cold ashcakes and a keg of nails," Fitz said.

"Don't be forgetting the hammer," Fin said.

"And a fine wool blanket in case the kitchen fire dies during the night."

Fin smiled. "The lass thinks of everything."

Fitz nodded. "That she does."

She had missed out on one point. He wasn't sleeping near the kitchen fire in his side of the cabin. Until she returned, he was sleeping in hers. Since he spent his days working her corral, he thought it only fair to use her bed at night.

The fact that it brought back warm memories was beside the point.

Fin and Fitz climbed down from the wagon and proceeded to unhitch the mule. Cal watched in amazement. He didn't know they knew how.

"Gert and May showed us," Fin said in answer to Cal's raised brows.

"The girls know any number of things useful to a man," Fitz said.

Not even for clear title to the Crown would Cal have asked his uncle to name another of them.

Fin proceeded to water the mule and stake him out to graze; Fitz went inside the cabin to start the soup.

Amazing.

While Cal unloaded a few more logs from the wagon, Fin brought him up to date on what was happening in town.

"Word's spread about the arrangement between the pair of you."

"Our arrangement is nobody else's business," said Cal, thinking automatically of the fact that they would be sleeping in separate rooms.

"Let's not be testy, lad. I'm speaking of the sharing of the Crown, of course. There's nothing else that's of any concern to anyone but the two of you. I thought you'd want to know most of the money is on you."

Cal paused in the unloading. "What are you talking about?"

"The betting money. Most are saying you'll be buying Ellie's portion before she has a chance at yours."

"They're right. I will."

"There's little reason to be cocky, nephew. A small, vocal number of folk say the lass will outlast the lad. It has split the households of both the Patchetts and the Whitfields, with the men siding with you and the wives taking the woman's side."

"So the men are for me and the women are for Ellie. I thought the women were smarter than that. What about you and the Dollarhides?"

"We're remaining neutral, seeing as how the idea was ours in the first place. And you're wrong in thinking the men are all on your side. Sir Simon and George Holloway both are carrying Ellie's standard—figuratively, you understand. It's led to some lively discussion in the saloon. At Merse's the lovely and usually silent Katya was heard by Gert to put up an argument with her father."

"All this in two days?"

"There's little else going on in Glory."

Of course there wasn't, thought Cal. The work was all out here on the land.

"Until we open up our saloon, that is," Fin added. "Things will change soon enough then. There's plans to hold theatricals, for which we'll be needing a stage."

"And more, lad," Fitz put in. "The ideas are coming at us in a flurry now that we're truly on our own. Not for long will Houston be called the cultural center of the Republic. There'll be glory days for Glory soon enough."

"We're waiting for word from New Orleans about the selling of the saloon," Fitz said. "All we need is money to start putting our plans into effect."

Cal could have pointed out that only a month or so ago, they were equally excited about working their own land. But they would have an answer for him. They always did.

"So when is my partner going to get out here

and start contributing her share of sweat?" he asked.

"Are you expecting her to help with the hammering and the pounding?"

"She was the one who wanted to share everything."

Everything but the bed.

Cal could hear the petulance in his voice. He sounded like a damned child. Or a lonely man.

He was neither. He was a loner with a finely honed sense of fairness, that was all.

"She'll be returning to the Crown in the next day or two, never fear," Fin said. "And don't be thinking she'll shirk her share of the tasks. You're underestimating the lass."

"She's underestimating the tasks."

Fin put up no further argument. When the mule was rested and the soup at a slow boil and the sun beginning its downward journey in the western sky, the O'Malleys bade Cal farewell and started the two-hour journey back to Glory.

Cal threw himself into work, ate two big bowls of the soup and most of the ashcakes, fed the remaining soup to Baron and fell into bed not a quarter hour after the sun had set.

He rose at dawn and after a breakfast of hot coffee and cold bread, he made a quick trip to the creek with his fishing pole, then was back at the pounding and the hammering. All the noise he was making didn't cover the creak of the wagon that approached the cabin at midday.

Pausing in his work, he turned to watch Ellie as she guided the wagon toward the barn. She was wearing a sensible bonnet and wool cloak and her brown eyes took up half her face as she looked around for the first time at what was now her property. She looked more child than woman, though he knew that in her case appearances were deceiving.

Even more than young, she looked vulnerable, as if the world would crush her if she didn't protect herself. Or better, have someone to protect her. Why that should irritate him so much, he didn't know.

And what was she feeling now? Her expression gave little hint of her thoughts. It seldom did.

The wagon was piled high with supplies he couldn't begin to guess at. Tethered to the rear were her mare and a very discontented milk cow who looked as if she would deliver little else but sour milk.

"You shouldn't have come out here alone," he said as he strolled toward her. "The ride must have taken you hours."

"Yes, but I'm tough, remember?" She pulled a shotgun from underneath the seat. "I've been practicing the past few days. George Holloway and Dub Krause helped me."

"I hope they did a good job."

"You sound irritated."

"Let's put it this way. Have you made out a will? When you get waylaid somewhere on the trail, am I going to end up sharing the Crown with Great Aunt Matilda Beauregard back in Richmond?"

She rolled her eyes. "You know well enough I have no family left. Besides, I believe there is something in the deed that gives each of us survivorship rights. Simon was explaining it to me.

You die and I own everything; the same thing holds true for you if I don't live past the time you quit."

"Maybe I shouldn't turn my back on you."

"You're safe for the time being. Just don't rile me."

She looked almost laughable, throwing down threats from the wagon seat. But Cal wasn't about to start taunting her any more than he already had. Life over the next few weeks was going to be difficult enough.

Taking off her bonnet, she fingered her hair from her face and dropped to the ground. He didn't offer to help her, having learned her ways, albeit slowly. But he did notice a wince when she tried to lift her arm. Recoil from practicing with the shotgun had done its damage. She would be bruised. Without her spending any time working the land, already her satin skin had been marked. It was an image he didn't dwell on.

She pulled a bucket from the wagon bed. "I'll need to milk the cow. Poor baby. I've named her Queenie if you've no objections. She's half yours."

"Which half? I doubt I got the teats."

He caught a flash of a smile on her lips. "Don't be absurd."

"I'm just getting the facts. You wanted everything spelled out, didn't you?"

She nodded. "Everything. I've kept a record of all that I've spent. We can settle up later. I would appreciate it if you did the same."

She was starting to talk fast. He suspected she was nervous. Awkward. Exhausted. Hell, he didn't know how she felt. He was going by the effect she was having on him.

She stroked the mare's neck. "There, there, Duchess, I'll get to you when I can, but right now Queenie's in real pain."

"Damn it, Ellie, you don't have to do everything."

"Stop ordering—"

She caught herself and he saw the way she was squeezing her hands tight.

"You're right," she said with a little laugh. "It's just that we haven't got all those cursed rules spelled out."

"So we go by common sense."

"Which isn't very common, is it?" For a moment she looked a little lost. "Look at what we've got ourselves into."

She had no idea how close she was to getting grabbed. Held. Caressed. Kissed.

She did not, however, look ready to throw herself into his arms.

Maybe she was right. Maybe she was tougher than he.

As she led the cow into the barn, he concentrated on caring for the horses, then unloading the wagon. Any minute he expected a cry or some other sign of distress to echo from behind the barn doors. But all was silent. She was probably trying to figure out which end of Queenie gave the milk.

Just as he was about to go check on her, she strode out with a bucket of milk. She had shed the cloak and gloves, rolled up the sleeves of her gown, and smudged her face, but the look of triumph in her eyes spoke loudly of her success.

Cal got only a quick glimpse into the bucket. There wasn't much milk there, but that didn't stop her from being proud. Damned if he didn't feel a little pride himself.

What the hell was he doing? She was supposed to get disgusted and leave. Any success she found would only prolong the agony for them both.

Filling the cabin's larder with the newly purchased supplies, stacking them on the shelves and in the corners of the room, Ellie had never felt more tired in her life. And sore. And frustrated. She'd left most of Queenie's reluctantly given milk on the barn floor, she had come up with a dozen things she should have bought and worst of all, there was Cal out in the field, rippling muscles and all, working away as though he hadn't a care in the world.

She and the cow had parted friends, but just barely. And Baron was ignoring her. He would stir himself from the dog run soon enough after she started supper, but not before.

Tomorrow would be better. After she got a good night's sleep. Why she had ever thought to practice with that cursed shotgun, she couldn't imagine. Her shoulder hurt so much, she could barely lift the sack of cornmeal, but of course she had to. And without complaint.

George and Dub—they were all on a first-name basis now—had been all that she could have asked in solicitude. What they should have done was what Cal would have done: told her to put the gun down and never pick it up again.

Of course she wouldn't have followed such an order from Cal. But she might have if it had come from her new friends.

When she went to get water from the well, she found a string of fish in a bucket at the back of the passageway. With grim satisfaction, thinking how surprised Cal would be, she cleaned and fileted every one of them, fried them in cornmeal and hog fat, then dished them up with hot johnnycakes and the cold baked sweet potatoes she had brought with her from town.

It was a feast fit for a king.

When Cal came in, his hair and face damp from the washing at the well, she set his plate in front of him without a word. His look of amazement was all the thanks she needed.

Fair was fair. She hadn't thanked him for working on the corral, had she?

She was too tired to eat much, but Cal gulped down everything on his plate—once he quit looking for fishbones. This first meal together in the home they shared was hardly a festive affair. They didn't even look at one another. Not that he didn't look wonderful—one quick peek had told her that—but with her sunken eyes and unkempt hair, she must look as if the wrath of God had struck her down.

After cleaning up, she barely made it into her side of the cabin. As she trudged across the dog run, she was vaguely aware that he was trying to tell her something, but unless it was that the bedroom was on fire, his words didn't matter.

Sleep mattered. More than anything. And this was only her first day on the Crown.

But she had been so busy the past two days in Glory, working late into the night sewing and planning and making lists and during the day attempting to learn to use a spinning wheel and a loom. Katya Merse was teaching her, mostly by example, rarely by words. Ellie knew what to do with ready-woven cloth of all kinds, but getting the cloth woven was something she had never needed to know.

In Texas the skill would come in handy.

And so would sleep. The ride out to the Crown had been long and miserable. She had stopped to soothe Queenie a dozen times, every pull on the reins another exquisite torment, and then she had arrived to find Cal the Magnificent looking as if he hadn't a care in the world.

The second she got a look at the bed, she knew what he had been trying to tell her. The sheets were a mess, wrinkled and muddy, obviously used by him in her absence. This wasn't his room; it was hers. But she was too tired to be indignant. She was too sore to get undressed, except to pull off her heavy work shoes. No dainty slippers for Miss Eleanor Chase, not anymore.

She didn't bother to light a fire in the fireplace that separated the two halves of the sleeping quarters. Never one to like the cold, she had brought a pile of extra blankets from town. She would simply layer them on and hide for a while from the world.

As she fell into the bed, she realized something else. Cal's scent was on the sheets, a scent not in the least unpleasant, not really sweaty or dirty. It was the scent she associated with him as she held him in her arms.

Smothering herself in the blankets, giving way to free-floating thoughts, she decided it really wasn't a bad thing that he had been there before her. It wasn't a bad thing at all.

Chapter Seventeen

As much as Cal needed to learn about ranching and farming, over the next few weeks he discovered a more immediate need: killing time away from the Crown, away from Ellie Chase.

Today, with December beginning, he'd finally found the perfect excuse for staying away. Only for a day. Maybe tomorrow he could come up with another reason to ride.

Things weren't working out at the Crown exactly as he had planned. It was one thing to talk about splitting the cabin, dividing the chores, and generally staying out of each other's way, and quite another to follow through on all the talk.

He discovered right from the start that ignoring his new partner was asking more of him than he had to give. She was a woman for rules—who would do what, who would spend the day where, when they would eat, when they would sleep, and of course where they would make their beds.

She had offered him the back half of the sleeping side, but the bed was uncomfortably slanted, the window frame let in the cold, and he knew that in the dark of night he would be listening to her breathing. It was the breathing that made him choose the horsehair sofa as his bed.

In all his adult life, Cal had been governed by only one decree, not to let anyone or anything matter enough to alter the manner of his life. Ellie was busy altering everything, not by edict but by example, patterning her life around work from dawn until long past dusk, never uttering a word of complaint. Cal had never been lazy—hell, he had expanded his plans for the corral and all by himself had the log fence well over halfway complete—but he also saw the need for reasonable pacing.

Ellie saw no such need. Demons were after her, as ferocious as his own. She was losing weight, though she had possessed not an ounce to spare, half-circles shadowed her eyes, and she twisted her hair beneath a poke bonnet that must be the ugliest bit of fashion ever designed for womankind. It almost seemed as if she were trying to make herself unattractive, uncommunicative, untouchable.

If that was her scheme, it wasn't working. Every waking moment, and frequently during some strange erotic dreams, she managed to arouse him, even when she was a hundred yards away.

It was little wonder he was close to finishing the corral.

Spending a day riding the countryside, conferring with the Patchetts and the Whitfields, moving on to Alden Fowler's place—all this was supposed to keep him from the devastation of her quiet presence. For the most part, his scheme had worked, but it wasn't until he rode onto Fowler's land that she completely left his mind.

About the most charitable way he could put it was that the Rancho Grande did not live up to its name.

Remembering all the Texan had said about wanting to build a substantial, profitable holding, Cal had pictured a burgeoning empire with hundreds of cattle grazing in the fields, a dozen or more horses in the corral, a barn twice the size of his, at least one bunkhouse for the workers, chickens, hogs, the whole works, as well as fields plowed for planting in the spring.

In short, he had expected the kind of development he envisioned for the Crown, something far beyond the meager beginnings that the Patchetts and the Whitfields called home.

With the exception of an established corral and a couple of horses, what he saw proved to be what he himself already possessed—a small barn in need of repair, a chicken yard with a couple of scrawny hens scratching at the dirt, one pig burrowing into the damp ground beside a half-filled trough and beyond the barn a small plowed field marked by dying stalks of corn.

If the man owned cattle, he was letting them graze on another pasture far away from the trail leading to the main ranch house.

The house itself was the only structure that

showed real improvement over Cal's. Riding up the hill on the black gelding he had named Duke, he gave it a quick perusal. Large and square, its stone walls were fronted by a wide porch and a lone rocker that faced directly east. The windows boasted glass, with lace curtains to keep out the hot summer light and shutters for protection from winter winds.

It should have looked welcoming. He was trying to analyze why it didn't when Alden Fowler stepped out the front door and stood by one of the hand-tooled posts on the porch. His thinning brown hair was slicked back from a craggy face; he was wearing a black suit and paisley waistcoat, ruffled white shirt, and a black string tie knotted beneath a stiff, high collar.

Fancy clothes, Cal thought, for a cattleman and farmer home alone on what should have been a workday.

At least Cal assumed he was alone.

"Welcome to Rancho Grande," Fowler said when Cal reined to a halt.

Cal dismounted and nodded a greeting. "I came asking for help."

Fowler gave him a slight, noncommittal shrug.

"If you've got the time," Cal added, "and it's not too much trouble."

"No bother. I'll take the time." He hesitated a minute. "Weather's mild enough for us to stay outside, if you've no objection."

"None."

At Cal's insistence, Fowler took the rocker. Cal hiked a hip onto the porch railing, shifting his gun holster to a more comfortable position, watching Fowler watching him. If Cal were back at the Crown, Baron would be lying listlessly at his feet. No dog appeared by Fowler's side. Behind them, the house was silent. Cal's eerie feeling about Rancho Grande extended to Fowler himself.

"I understand you've taken over the Double T," Fowler said, crossing one leg over the other. "You and the woman."

Both the Patchetts and the Whitfields had referred to Ellie by name and asked about her health. Cal found the contrast with Fowler unsettling. He rested a hand on the holster. Never had he been put in the position of defending a woman's honor, but now was as good a time as any to start.

"Miss Chase and I share ownership temporarily."

"Don't get my hopes up, Hardin. Don't tell me the Double T will soon be for sale."

"It's the Crown of Glory. And it's not for sale."

A frown flickered across Fowler's face. "A pity. But I'll wait. There aren't many who can endure life out here."

"So you said the first time we met."

Learning firsthand about the hardships, Cal was in no mood to get a lecture from a man who couldn't maintain so much as a decent henhouse.

Coming here had been a mistake, no matter the seriousness of his intent. He had misread the man and his bold talk. It was a mistake he seldom made, but it was hardly fatal. He was about to excuse himself and leave when Fowler spoke.

"You said you needed help."

Cal nodded. Fowler didn't know the half of his situation. In the weeks since taking over the ranch, he had found himself needing more help than at any time in his adult life. He stopped himself at the *taking over* part. Nothing about his daily routine had the markings of a man in charge.

"Wright Whitfield and Abe Patchett gave me advice about getting ready for the spring crops." His gaze shifted briefly in the direction of the dying cornfield. "But neither man is much on cattle and horses. Not on the scale I'm contemplating."

"And you thought I might be."

Cal switched from the cornfield to the rundown barn. He had to bite back an impatient retort.

"I know you're interested in buying land," he said. "What's the purpose if you don't run cattle? Why all the pasturage if you don't put horses out to graze?"

"Investment."

"Investment. I see."

"It's clear to me you do not. And here I took you for a businessman," Fowler said with a smirk. "One who understands how money is made and how fortunes are created."

"So explain things to me. How do you make money buying land no one else wants?"

"Someday there will be a great demand for all of this."

The sweep of Fowler's hand included the cornfield and the barn. Cal figured it would take another hundred years before anyone paid good money for what Fowler seemed to prize.

"How are you making money now?"

"When I came to Texas in '26, I already had a substantial bank account, the combined legacies from my family and my late wife. I'm not ashamed to admit it. The money was honorably come by. I'm almost done investing it. All I lack is one more parcel of land."

Cal didn't need three guesses to figure out exactly where that parcel might be found.

He was about to go on to other topics when he remembered something Fowler had said on an early visit. He had claimed a poor birth and upbringing. Now he was claiming wealth. If he was going to change his stories so much, he ought to keep them straight.

Cal had ridden over to ask Fowler what he knew about rounding up the wild longhorn cattle and mustangs that roamed the county, about breeding other stock with them, about markets for their sale. But Fowler was a talker, not a doer, and a liar as well. Cal was beginning to wonder if the man were even sane.

It could be that the loneliness of the life was getting to him. Not all men were loners like himself. Or his mind could have been affected by lingering grief over the loss of his wife and son in the Comanche raid so long ago. Some men didn't get over things like that.

Whatever the cause, Fowler was not all that he seemed, and Cal saw more sharply than ever that he should have known it. Why he had been anywhere near the creek when Buck Shannon showed up was a question that continued to nag him. More than ever he wished Fowler hadn't gunned down the bastard before the truth of Shannon's deeds could be known.

In the aftermath of the shooting, Fowler swore he'd seen the dead man only once before, briefly, in town months earlier. Cal had no reason to doubt him, then or now. But neither could he explain the squalor of the misnamed Rancho Grande.

The man and his delusions were getting to Cal. It was more than impatience. It was as if he could see something of himself in Fowler, or at least how he might be ten years down the road.

Now that didn't make a hell of a lot of sense. Something—or someone—was playing havoc with the little reason he had left. It didn't take much thought to figure out who that someone was.

"Look," he said, standing, "it's later than I realized. I've a long ride back to the Crown."

"Surely you came to hear more than just my ideas about buying land."

"Next time you can tell me about cattle. That's what I really want to know. Cattle and horses, how to get them, how to sell them."

Fowler stood beside him. "There's no market. And there won't be for a while."

"Then I'll have to find one. Or make one myself."

Fowler's face grew flushed. "That's fool talk."

"Probably," Cal said.

"You let me know when you realize it for sure."

Cal tipped his hat. "I'll keep you in mind."

Which, if Fowler only knew it, was the same thing as saying he would be watching his neighbor, trying to determine if he was an enemy or a friend.

The Rancho Grande didn't linger long in his mind. He'd gone no more than a quarter mile when he started thinking of where he was going instead of where he had been.

He started thinking, too, of what he would do when he arrived. It wasn't that he had forgotten the terms of the agreement with his partner. He'd been going by them so fastidiously that he ought to be a candidate for sainthood.

He had never been considered virtuous by anyone, not even his dear departed mother. Now he decided he had taken all of his partner's edicts that he could, whether they were spoken or not. It was long past time for the joint owners of the Crown of Glory to renegotiate.

Alden Fowler watched his uninvited guest leave, then slowly opened the door to his home.

"He's gone," he called into the shadows.

A woman pattered on moccasined feet from the back of the house, her black eyes sullen and downcast. Her hair was twisted into two black braids that fell across her breasts. A fringed leather top and calf-length skirt covered her squat, solid body. Her cheekbones were high and sharp, her lips full, her skin closer to brown than red.

"Is dinner ready, Squaw?"

Squaw was the only name he had for her, the only one he needed. He'd bought her off a former soldier in San Antonio a couple of months before. He wasn't sure she understood much English, but

303

she did as he said, in bed and out, and she kept to the shadows when anyone else was around. Only Buck Shannon had known of her existence. Alden was glad Shannon was dead, though he had yet to find a replacement gun for hire.

Once he took possession of the Double T—he'd burn in hell before he called it the Crown of Glory—he would be hiring a few men to help him get his own place going once again. He had let it lie fallow far too long. He'd seen the disgust in Cal Hardin's eyes.

All he was waiting for was the final acquisition, and then he would show the world what he could do.

The Indian stepped aside for him to walk ahead out the back door to the separate room that served for cooking and eating. Ruthanne Fowler had insisted on keeping the kitchen separate from the rest of the house.

"It's safer that way," she had said.

All his wife's precautions hadn't kept her from the torture of the Comanches. Her blood still stained the ground that Cal Hardin and his whore claimed for themselves. It wasn't visible to the eye, but he knew it was there, lying in hidden ribbons across the hills and in the valleys, wherever the savages had dragged her, by now a part of the dirt, feeding the roots of the grasses and the trees. He owed it to her memory to possess the land. And he would, no matter what he had to do to get it.

Thinking of his wife, he lost his appetite for dinner. He turned to the squaw. She looked into his eyes and without a word changed direction to the large bedroom where he slept alone. The food Squaw usually prepared tasted like something he would scrape off the bottom of his boots, but she serviced him well enough otherwise.

Closing the door, he took off his coat, laid it carefully aside and dropped his trousers. She lay back on the bed and lifted her buckskin skirt. Otherwise she didn't move. She never did. That was the way he wanted it, him in control. He'd once had a woman of other inclinations. But his wife was long dead and buried, at least all of her remains that he had been able to find.

He pounded hard into the Indian, the only sound in the room the creak of the bed. Not even his crying produced a sob. With each thrust, with each bitter tear that stained his cheek, he saw himself drawing closer to his own inevitable death.

Ellie had been shoveling manure out of the barn for the past hour, and her shoulders screamed in protest. That didn't mean she could stop. She still had a half dozen shovelfuls to go.

Besides, every time she paused in her task, her ungoverned thoughts strayed down paths they must not go, to a tall, lean, solemn-faced man who had, against her will and certainly against his, become her everything.

Her one consolation in this disastrous situation was that he didn't know how she felt, although it seemed strange to her that he couldn't sense the tension in the air. Even on the sunniest day, it was as if an approaching storm lay on the horizon, moving fast in the direction of the Crown.

She would rather be struck down by lightning than show her weakness. And so she worked from dawn to dusk, barely able to crawl into her lonely bed each night, finding sleep as elusive as a moment of hopeful peace.

The more she thought of her situation, the more depressed she became. Which wouldn't get her anywhere near that precious peace. Enough maundering. To work.

Queenie. Now there was a topic she could manage. The close-to-useless cow was definitely spending too much of her energy producing dung and not enough turning out milk. She and Cal were drinking every drop she could squeeze out of Queenie's udders, and that wasn't much. At this rate she would never get to use her new butter-churn.

Ellie sighed, a luxury she allowed herself when her partner wasn't around. The goodness of buttermilk and cornbread would forever be a memory from another life, along with hot chocolate in the morning and the music of the harp at night.

In between the mornings and the nights, she had undertaken a thousand chores back in Virginia, but never had she shoveled cow dung.

In Texas, such was her daily challenge.

The manure was piled outside the barn, protected by the roof's overhang and a heavy, oiled tarpaulin Cal had found crumpled into a small heap at the back of the barn. Someday, when they—or someone—got around to plowing the fields for crops, the manure would be useful as fertilizer. Right now, she couldn't imagine ever putting her shovel aside.

At least she had possessed the good sense to change from her dress to trousers. She had bought two pairs in town; in the evenings when she had been able to stay awake, she had altered them to fit and sewn herself a shirt from one of the precious bolts of cloth Joseph Merse stocked.

Today, shoveling day, was the first time she was trying out her new clothes. She had twisted her hair into a knot at her nape, pulled on her once-fancy riding gloves, and got to work. She was glad Cal was off finding out about ranching and not around to throw out a caustic comment or two.

She stopped herself, and once again was galloping mentally down one of the forbidden pathways that led to Cal. She had to be honest. From the moment he rode off into the first light of this morning's dawn, she had started missing him, and as the day progressed the missing had only gotten worse. No amount of shoveling could ease the heaviness in her heart when he wasn't around.

It was far worse than the torment when he was near.

He truly didn't taunt her much, except by the look of him and the sound of him, and that was hardly his fault. And when he returned, he would have the decency to tell her all that he had learned.

He would, however, have the indecency to look wonderful as he passed on his news. Sometimes when she looked at him, she wanted so much to touch him, her hands hurt.

Enough, her mind screamed. *Work*.

At last the manure was taken care of, though as she cast a baleful glance at Queenie grazing in the nearby field, the knowledge brought her little pleasure. Not for one minute did she think an ounce of that new fuel would be going for milk.

Duchess, munching grass not far from the cow, was doing her own part to add to the fertilizer supply. Ellie was not in a mood to be pleased.

But enough feeling sorry for herself. Late afternoon was already upon her, and a few chores had yet to be done before she started supper. Besides, standing out here without working, she felt the cold wind cut through the thin material of her shirt.

Setting the shovel aside, she went back into the barn and began forking the hay. It was the one resource that the former owner had left behind. With winter coming on and the grasses already growing more scarce, she needed to turn the hay regularly, especially after the few recent rains had brought dampness into the barn.

Even this was not an activity safe from stray thoughts. Memories of the first time she had been in this same spot came back to her. Cal had thought to torment her with the denied pleasure of his kiss. The cad. He had also assumed she would be afraid of mice. In some ways he understood her better than she understood herself. In others, he really didn't know her much at all.

The thought brought a moment's despair. Pulling off her gloves, she flexed her cramped hands and leaned on the handle of the fork. When the barn doors suddenly opened, she jumped.

"Oh, it's just you," she said, her hand on her pounding heart.

"That's not much of a greeting," Cal said. With

the light behind him, she couldn't see his face, but she could hear the sharpness in his voice.

She allowed herself a small smile. Not for all the milk in Virginia would she let him know how deliriously glad she was that he had returned safely.

"I was expecting President Lamar to arrive for afternoon tea," she said, desperately seeking the right amount of insouciance. "I thought I would get a little exercise before baking the cakes."

"So where's the shotgun?" he asked. She could feel his eyes moving over her. "I can't see where you could conceal the pepperbox. Those trousers fit you much too well."

"The guns are back at the cabin."

"Where they're doing you damned little good."

The truth was, she had forgotten all about them, but she didn't feel much like letting him know.

She lifted the pitchfork. "I'm a woman of many weapons."

"So you are," he said, and she could hear the change in his voice. "So you are."

He took a step toward her.

Were those danger signals she heard clanging? It was probably just the pounding of her heart. Not once in the past weeks, since they had taken up their strange form of cohabitation, had he made a move in her direction. Usually he was headed the other way.

She took a step back. "What are you doing?"

"Can't I come into your barn?"

"Don't be ridiculous."

"I'm not able to help it. I'm feeling ridiculous."

She bit her lower lip. "You must have had an unusual day."

"I did."

Another step. The closer he got, the more visible his face became. With a feeling that was both dismay and exhilaration, she watched and waited. The conviction struck that her storm had arrived.

"I've been a very good boy, and Princess, that's just not my way."

He hadn't called her Princess since that night.

She couldn't allow herself to remember.

"Admit it," he said. "For weeks I've scarcely looked your way. Well, maybe I've looked, but that was all. If you think I missed the times you looked at me, think again."

She should have known she wouldn't get away with anything.

"Sometimes I get tired of looking at Queenie," she said.

"Strange. I never get tired of looking at you. Frustrated, maybe, but not tired."

Blood pounded in her ears.

She took another step away and got a firm grip on the pitchfork. "What was so unusual about your day?" she asked. "Was it good or bad?"

What a stupid question to put to him, like the little wife welcoming her husband home, but she had to get this meeting on a basis she could handle. The way things were going, her resolve and control were fast slipping away.

"You'll get a full report," he said. "Later."

The thunder and the lightning were all around her. She raised a hand.

"I don't know what you're doing, but please stop."

"I don't know what I'm doing either, but whatever it is, stopping's not easy."

"The Patchetts—"

"Both fine. So are the Whitfields. They're stubborn, like you, and hard workers."

"You mean they're not quitters."

"Right. Although it seems to me there is one thing you've quit."

"I haven't quit anything," she said, but the answer came too fast.

He thumbed his hat to the back of his head and stared down at her. "Glad to hear it."

The power of his stare sucked all the air from the barn.

"No," she said, and he knew what she meant. "We had an agreement. Why have you forgotten it?"

Something passed through his mind, something dark and private that showed only briefly in his eyes. If all were well between them, she would have asked what that something was and he would have told her.

But all was not well.

"Blame it on Alden Fowler," he said.

Nothing he said could have surprised her more. Except, of course, *I want you because I love you and always will.*

"He still wants the Crown?" she asked, trying to make some sense of what he said.

"A man doesn't always get what he wants."

"Neither does a woman."

"But sometimes both of them do."

He took another step toward her. How had he managed to get so close?

"How about playing a game?" he asked, tossing his hat aside. "It's called I Take Off Your Clothes and You Take Off Mine. The rules are easy. I'll explain them as we go."

"Don't be ridiculous. I smell like cow dung."

"Texas perfume."

She dropped the pitchfork and rubbed a hand against her thigh. "I told you there would be no fooling around in bed. You agreed."

He glanced around the barn. "Tell me if I'm wrong, but I don't see any bed in here."

"We're supposed to get n-n-n . . ." *Naked* was a word that would not come to her lips. "You want us to undress in the barn?"

"We wouldn't be breaking any of our rules."

"Bed was just a . . . a euphemism."

"My, my, partner, you certainly do use big words."

"You know what I mean."

"Do I? I'm never quite sure. For instance, are you objecting to doing what we both want to do because it's not in bed?"

"I'm objecting because this really is a game for you."

"And what is it to you?"

Not a game, she wanted to cry. *Never a game*.

"You have aroused certain feelings in me, certain urges that—" She rubbed at her face, desperate for the impudent words that would not come. "When we eventually part, and it doesn't matter right now who goes and who stays, I don't want to feel ashamed of how I behaved."

"It has never been my intention to hurt you, Ellie. Sometimes I want to throttle you because you don't know what's best for your own safety, but that's not the same as purposely hurting you. All you have to do right now is tell me not to kiss you. You'll have to say it very firmly, however, or I might not hear."

"Once, in this very same place, you told me to ask you for a kiss."

"So have we come a long way or gone backwards?"

"I don't know."

"Neither do I. All I know is that I spent a long time away today, riding and seeing other places, and when I got back to the Crown, it seemed to me the best of the lot. I don't know whether that was simple weariness or familiarity or the fact that you were here. When I saw you forking the hay, wearing a man's trousers and doing a man's work, you were to me the most womanly creature in all the world."

He sounded like a man who had at long last arrived at his home. But it was a home he didn't recognize and, waiting inside it, was a woman he could not claim. He had erected too many barriers for him to ever change.

Dear, dear Cal, invincible and vulnerable both.

He was so close, she couldn't resist putting her hands on his arms. He was dressed in shirtsleeves and the buckskin jerkin, and the kerchief he wore at his throat was the same blue as his eyes.

"You feel cold to me." She touched his face. "Your skin is chilled."

"Strange," he said, "I'm feeling hot inside."

Ellie understood. Her blood must be close to the boiling point.

The heat burned away all reason as her hands worked their way around his neck. She gave in to what had been inevitable from the day she accepted joint ownership with Cal.

"Kiss me, Cal. I'll play any game you want."

please, selfishly wanting to be pleased, but not worried.

Together they sank onto the blanket. She lay on her back and looked up at him. Narrow beams of sunshine cut through the open slats of the barn walls, casting patterns of light and shadow across his face. She couldn't resist ruffling his hair where his hat had left a crease, seeking out the few streaks of gray she looked upon as his badge of suffering.

He in turn loosened the thick knot of hair at her nape and spread the long tresses against the blanket. She felt his touch down to her toes.

After the initial explosion of the kiss, they both were holding back, as if once the commitment was made, the commitment to sex and nothing more, the pattern of their lives over the next weeks would be set.

Ellie understood. She hoped her lover did as well.

"This isn't a game, Cal," she said. "Please don't tell me that it is."

"It's natural," he said. "An affirmation of life. I believe you called it something like that."

"Affirmation?" she said. Suddenly, inevitable as all this was, she needed desperately to keep it light. "My, my, partner, you certainly use big words."

"I can use whatever words you like."

He would never use the phrases she needed to hear, and so she said, "Please, no talk."

"Not even to call you Princess?"

She worked at the kerchief around his neck and

317

Evelyn Rogers

slowly pulled it away. With a flick of her wrist, she sent it spiraling into the dark.

"Princess is all right."

In truth, it was more than all right. It was all she could hope for, the only answer to a hopeless quest. Here she was, the spinster virgin turned into a wanton. Love could do that to a woman. Love could turn her inside out.

He unfastened the top button of her shirt. "Everything's all right."

Shyness struck. "I wish I had more to offer you."

His gaze traveled up her throat to her lips, to her eyes.

"You're everything I want."

But she wasn't.

"I meant larger . . . you know."

"Breasts? Can I say the word breasts?" He finished unfastening her shirt, pulling it from the waist of her trousers, and laid it open, staring at her white, lace-trimmed chemise. "Ah, another layer." He licked a nipple through the soft cloth. "Regal, that's what you are. You offer a regal peak."

If she hadn't been trembling so much, arching her back, gripping at his shirt sleeves while he touched and talked, she might have laughed.

He licked the other nipple.

"Bountiful and regal both."

"Liar."

"A loyal subject does not lie to his princess. He's damned lucky to lie with her, and he wouldn't want to do anything to change her mind."

"She's not changing her mind."

To prove it, she let go of him long enough to
slip out of both shirt and chemise. If he thought
she sported a pair of royal peaks, then who was
she to argue?

She lay back on the blanket and he ran a hand
up her inner thigh. Her audible gasp brought a
smile to his lips.

"Have you got anything on under these trousers?" He kissed the corner of her lips. "I'm planning ahead."

Underdrawers, she started to tell him, wondering if other women came to him already un-
clothed. But then she remembered he had wanted
to play an undressing game.

"Find out for yourself," she said.

Tugging on the trousers this morning had taken
at least half a minute. In the late afternoon Cal
had them off in a tenth of the time.

"Ah, another layer," he said, staring down at the
underdrawers.

"Disappointed?"

"Challenged."

Cal knew how to meet a challenge. Right away
his hand found the opening slit in the material
between her legs. She almost came off the blanket
when she felt the soft brushing movement of his
fingers against a very sensitive spot.

Too much, she thought, and pulled his hand
away, gripping his wrist to keep him from a return visit. He could easily have broken her hold,
but he honored her wish and held back.

What was she thinking? She didn't want to be
honored. She wanted to be loved. Letting him go,
she worked at the buttons of his shirt. He helped

her and they began their game in earnest, not stopping until they were both naked and wrapped in each other's arms. They kissed and nuzzled one another, stroked and kissed again.

Ellie felt as if she were floating in hot honey, one second languid, the next roused to feats of tremendous energy, letting him kiss and fondle wherever he wished, then returning the favor. He truly made her feel royal and special and beautiful, and for a while he made her feel loved.

By the time he was running his hand once again up the inside of her thighs, she was running her hand up the inside of his. She took his sex in her hands before he could touch hers. She enjoyed his sharp intake of breath almost as much as she enjoyed the hard, slick feel of him beneath her fingers.

"Show me how to hold you," she said.

"You're doing just fine," he rasped.

Regal, indeed.

When he reached her special place, she didn't feel so regal. She felt pure joy, instinct driving her to whisper a soft little *oh* again and again and at last not whisper at all as his fingers worked their special magic. Just when she thought she would fly into a thousand pieces, he stilled his fondling. So did she, but they did not let each other go. Staring up at him, she saw raw passion in his eyes; she could not imagine what he read in hers.

It seemed the most natural act in the world to part her legs and pull him down on top of her. He eased inside, and then they both went wild. She curled into his strength and his power, giving way to the tender violence that shook them both, wanting to laugh and to cry and to extend the ecstasy forever, yet impatient for what she now knew to be the ultimate release.

It came upon her too fast, and then it came to him. The world rocked with the explosion, and then the gradual, inevitable slowing, and at last the clinging together and the slow easing back into reality.

But it was a reality that had changed. Unlike the time before when she had lain with him, she had no need to say or do anything. All she needed was to hold him in her arms and know that for this little while, the barriers between them were down. She was his, and he was hers.

Over the next few weeks, Cal felt like a thorough bastard half the time and for the other half, like a man possessed. He couldn't leave Ellie alone. No matter how hard they each worked during the day, in the late afternoon they found themselves in the barn locked in a hot embrace.

She never invited him into her bed. He never asked. The barn became a symbol of the drive that brought them together, certainly not respectable or acceptable by the standards of the outside world, but in the very fact of its illicit nature irresistible, inevitable, and as necessary to them both as the air they breathed.

He tried to tell her she could be with child.

"So be it," she said. "My condition will never be a shackle on you, Cal. I'm in a free, new land, and I will live my life however I choose."

But he knew she didn't understand the consequences of such carelessness, the ostracism, the hard times that would come to her and any child she might bear.

His child. The thought filled him with a dread so powerful, it went beyond explanation. Her pregnancy was a thing that simply must not be.

When he could, he spilled his seed into the hay—they had soon forgone the luxury of the blanket—but it was an effort that took more will than he had ever possessed.

He was bastard enough to be glad they were experiencing a mild winter, dry and clear, the temperature nowhere near the freezing mark. With the heat they generated in the barn, however, he figured a snowstorm wouldn't have kept them apart.

The Patchetts and the Whitfields called upon them one Sunday afternoon, and Ellie proved herself an able hostess, serving up tea and coffee and small, flat cakes of cornmeal and molasses with the aplomb of a Boston matron.

"It was all that training from Aunt Abigail," she explained to him when he complimented her that evening in the barn.

"So what are you learning in Texas?" he asked.

"To be wanton," she said, and she showed him exactly what she meant.

Two days later, Gert and May rode out with his uncles. In the wagon bed was a special gift for his side of the cabin: the wood-burning cookstove Ellie had ordered weeks before. The women stayed while Fin and Fitz rode back to town and he went off to scout the herds of longhorns and mustangs that he planned to gather in the early spring.

He had no idea what the women talked about

while he was gone, but when he returned and settled himself down for the food they had prepared, he felt himself the object of great scrutiny, like a bug pinned down by a scientist.

Setting out Cal's plate, Ellie asked about the cattle and horses he had seen.

"There are hundreds out there," he said, "waiting for someone to round them up and brand them."

"I'd like to ride out with you the next time you go and see them for myself."

"Don't be—"

The look in the eyes of the Dollarhide sisters stopped him. Ellie's tilted chin also had its effect.

"Your sidesaddle makes for an awkward ride," he said.

"Gert and May brought me a gift, too. A regular saddle for Duchess. I'm wearing trousers most of the time now anyway. All I need is practice."

One time in the barn she had said the same thing about sex. The glint in her eyes said she was remembering those words as well as he.

"The next time I ride out, I'll be gone several days," he said. "There's Queenie to think of, if nothing else."

"I've already got a solution for that."

She didn't offer more information, and he didn't ask. Her solution arrived the next day in the form of Antonio Gomez, who rode out with Fin and Fitz. The boy had regained full use of his broken arm, and if he harbored any fear about returning to the scene of his beating, he gave no sign of it.

Evelyn Rogers

This time the gift that was brought for Cal came in two parts—a mule and a plow.

Possessions. They were surrounding him. In a past life the only possessions he'd wanted were money in his pocket and a ticket on the next departing train. It was the uniqueness of the situation that was keeping him from restlessness. Or so he told himself. Ellie had issued him a challenge and he wasn't ready to back down.

Eventually one of them would leave. He still figured it would be her, when she grew tired of the private thoughts he never revealed, when her passion lost its powerful edge. After she was gone, he would finish out his year, then offer the Crown of Glory for sale.

Not that he was making any money off the place. For now it was a drain on his reserve funds. And it had to be on Ellie's, too, but she didn't complain. She was the one who paid for the supplies they bought in town. Never once had she asked him for repayment, except to say she was keeping accounts. She had even bought two extra blankets and sewn them each a warm coat.

"You'll do neither of us any good if you get sick," she had explained when she placed it beside his plate one evening at supper.

Nobody had ever made him anything before. His first instinct had been to come around the table and hold her and thank her, but something held him back. Here was another possession, a tie to this place and this land.

After the four visitors departed, sisters and brothers both still talking about their own plans for a new saloon, Ellie set about clearing a place

324

for Antonio in the barn. She carried out extra bedding and asked Cal to bring out her emptied trunk for the boy to use as storage for the few belongings he had brought with him.

With Antonio getting acquainted with Queenie in the field, Cal approached Ellie in the barn.

"He'll be in here," he said.

"Right."

"It's his place."

"He'll have to share it with Queenie, Duke and Duchess on the nights we're here."

"This isn't going to work."

"Why not?"

"I don't feel right leaving him alone when we're gone."

"Neither do I. That's why George will be joining him in the next few days. I sent a message in with Gert asking if he would hire out for a few days and start plowing the fields. Later we can hire Dub, too, if we see the need, and if you don't mind their borrowing your mule and plow."

"It's going to get a little crowded in here."

"There's plenty of room. If the weather turns really ugly, they can sleep by the kitchen fire. They all understand the situation. I explained it clearly enough the last time I was in town."

"I'd have a passing interest in exactly what you told them."

A definite glint lit her eyes. "You would, would you?" she asked.

"Princess, could you be baiting me?"

"A little. I seldom get the chance."

She turned solemn. Today she was wearing a

dress; she had the edges of the skirt bunched in her clenched hands.

"I made a one-sided, arbitrary, high-handed, regal decision," she said. "Everyone assumes we are sleeping together. Your uncles, Gert and May, and I'm sure even George. Antonio, too, most likely, but I'd rather think he's not dwelling on such things."

"Get to the decision, Princess."

"With so many people moving in, the only place for you to spend each night is in my bed."

"There are two beds on your side of the cabin. I could sleep in the bed in the back. Or I could continue sleeping on the sofa. I've sort of grown attached to the thing."

"That's your choice. My bed or the sofa. Unless you choose to snuggle beside Baron on the dog run. But afternoons in the barn are definitely out."

"Baron snores louder than you. Your bed it is."

And that was how Cal found himself slipping deeper into the nest that Ellie was building. He doubted she knew what she was doing, other than making the best of life as it was playing out for her.

As far as he was concerned, she was certainly making life comfortable for him. Temporarily. He kept reminding himself of that fact, though the word was beginning to have a hollow ring. With her in his arms, he got the best loving and the best sleeping of his life.

The fact came upon him gradually that he didn't want it to end. Not ever. But all the good times in his life had been impermanent, and so was his life with Ellie.

Whenever time allowed, Antonio resumed Cal's Spanish lessons. Cal saw the necessity. Outside of Comanche braves, the best horsemen around were the vaqueros, the men from Mexico who could work wonders with the wild herds. He would need them in the spring when the roundup of the mustangs began. He wanted to speak their language and learn from them as much as they could teach him about taming the beautiful beasts that flew across the land.

He wanted, too, to visit a ranchero south of Goliad, a vast holding that was the property of a long-time Texan who had once been a citizen of Mexico. Cal had heard that the señor knew much of raising and selling cattle, having done both since long before the Revolution, a battle in which he had fought on the Republic's side.

Most people in the States thought the Revolution had been fought on a strictly Americans-versus-Mexicans basis. But men and women from south of the Rio Grande had taken positions on both sides during the war.

Texas was a land of riches, both in people and resources. The fact that it was going through hard times only made the battle to establish it more challenging, the prize all the greater because it had been hard-won.

Damned if he wasn't turning into a patriot. A Texian, as the people sometimes called themselves.

Temporarily. He had too many memories, too

many restless urges, to think of settling down. And Ellie would soon be moving on.

Still, he was rascal enough to enjoy her company when they finally set out on a three-day journey to scout out the wandering herds. There was one stallion in particular he wanted as his own. He had learned enough to know that each herd of horses confined itself to roaming over a certain area of land. It didn't matter who owned the land. On an open range, unbranded cattle and horses belonged to anyone who could claim them.

He found the white, wild-eyed mustang the second day out, when he and Ellie topped a hill. A herd of fifty horses grazed in the field below them. Beyond lay the banks of a tree-lined creek.

He talked of breeding the stallion to a mare he wanted to bring in from Louisiana. He knew a horseman north of Baton Rouge who would be willing to sell him prime breeding stock.

"I've got a lot to learn about such matters," he said.

"Yes," she said. "You do."

They were both wearing the blanket coats she had made. Her usual bonnet had been changed for a hat not unlike his own. She had twisted her hair into a single thick braid that rested against her back, and she was riding astride, not making a single complaint.

Neither had she complained the night before when he suggested they lie together wrapped in a blanket, under the stars, and make love. As a matter of fact, she might have been the one to do the first suggesting. As if he were her possession, and she was his.

Possessing and being possessed were not so
bad after all. Maybe he could at last truly forget
the ravages of his past, the ties that he had fought
so long to break.

Maybe. But he had held himself apart for so
many years, he didn't know if he could change.
The revelations of his uncles about Raymond
Hardin hadn't done the job. If anyone could help
him, it was Ellie.

The biggest *maybe* of them all was that maybe
she could be talked into staying for a long, long
while.

He was in a strange mood when they rode back
onto Crown of Glory land, restless and settled at
the same time, contented to be discontented for
as long as his time with her would last. He hoped
she felt contented in the same way.

As they neared the cabin, he heard laughter
from the field beyond the barn. He and Ellie rode
slowly toward the sound.

Two boys were chasing a squawking chicken
through the patches of dying grass. Antonio saw
them first and came running.

"Look, Señor Cal, Señorita Ellie, your neighbors have brought you a gift. I have repaired the
fence and built a henhouse for you while you
were gone, but the chicken is *estúpido*."

He lapsed completely into Spanish, but Cal
barely heard what he said. His attention was directed at the second boy, who was older, taller,
closer to being a man. The recognition between
them was instant, and his blood ran cold.

His brother Cordoba Hardin bowed slightly
from the waist, then stood straight and stared

back, the laughter gone. From the corner of his eye, Cal saw Ellie reach out for him, then withdraw her hand.

When he'd seen Cord months before at the New Orleans cemetery, he had thought it was for the first and last time. The boy had done nothing to him, but neither did he matter in his life. Why his presence today should cause such a reaction, he didn't know, except that seeing him was like being a boy again himself, under the power of a tyrant father, under the power of a hatred he could not let go.

He knew that life was unpredictable, but he had thought to erect walls around himself, invisible barriers that would hold out the past. He had foolishly thought that here, for a while, he and Ellie were creating a new world that had nothing to do with what had gone before.

Cordoba Hardin's presence proved him wrong.

Chapter Nineteen

"What the hell are you doing here?"

Cal's question snapped out like a whip, so sharp and fast that Ellie jumped.

There was only one person in all the world he would greet in such a way—another Hardin, the half-brother she had learned about the night she overheard the O'Malleys' conversation with Gert and May.

Gripping the reins, she looked from brother to brother, Cal in the brown blanket coat she had made him, his hat pulled low over thick brows, his body stiff and straight in the saddle, his jaw squared and hard as granite; and the boy, his shoulder-length black hair tousled, his black shirt too thin for the cold December air, his black trousers torn at the knee.

Other than the Hardin blue eyes, there was little physical similarity in the two. The boy's face was far more sharply hewn than Cal's, his hair and skin darker, his limbs long and gangly, not yet muscled like a man's. But he held himself as stiffly as Cal, and he had the same proud stance as he stood, legs apart, in the middle of the corral.

The two Hardins were no more than a dozen feet apart, with only the log fence of the corral separating them, yet for all the familial warmth passing between them, they might have been at opposite ends of the universe.

Antonio, Baron, and even the squawking chicken fell silent as the brothers stared at one another, and for a moment the world seemed to stand still.

Ellie's stomach tightened into a hard knot. This couldn't be happening. One minute she was riding up to the cabin, her heart singing a rare song of hope, and the next minute discordant notes were clanging in her ears.

The younger Hardin was the first to move. He grabbed a black wool jacket that hung on a corral post and slung it over his shoulder.

"Don't worry," he said, matching Cal's sharpness. "I'm gone."

"No!" Ellie cried out, surprising herself as much as anyone. Instinct governed her now, and a fear she did not understand. The only thing she understood for sure was that the boy must not be allowed to leave.

Without a glance at Cal, she slid from the saddle and ran to the corral, bending to slip through the fence. Hand outstretched, she walked up to him.

"Please don't go. I'm Eleanor Chase," she said, then added needlessly, "I own half the Crown."

The boy looked over her shoulder at Cal, then back to her, and again she was struck by the pair of Hardin eyes that stared out at the world with wariness, an expression Cal had worn a thousand times.

The boy took her hand. His shake was firm, his hand large for one so young, his slight bow unexpectedly formal.

"Cord Hardin, *a su servicio*."

"You speak Spanish," Ellie said, wishing she could come up with some more intelligent remark, wanting at the same time to break the tension of the moment.

Wanting, too, to go back to the closeness she had felt with Cal over the past few days and knowing in her heart that time could very well be gone.

"My mother taught me," Cord said. "She was from Córdoba, Spain."

"Hence your name."

"She was of noble blood."

Cord looked past her again to his brother, as if daring Cal to argue with what he said.

"She died, did she not?" Ellie asked.

He looked at her again, still proud, still wary, and nodded.

"Are you here alone?"

Another brief nod.

"Does anyone know you're here? Your family perhaps?"

"I have only a borrowed family."

That would be Raymond Hardin's third wife

and the infant half sister, as best Ellie could recall.

But the boy was wrong. He had a brother, whether the brother recognized him or not.

"It sounds as if you ran away."

"I am fifteen."

He said it by way of explanation. Fifteen was the same age Cal was when he left New Orleans, the same age his father had left his own home. To Cord it must seem a perfectly natural reason for leaving, and it probably would to Cal . . . if he ever admitted the bond between the two.

"You must have found out in New Orleans where Cal had gone."

Cord ran a hand through his coarse black hair. "It was not hard."

"And you came to find him."

"Yes, I came to find him. As I said, it was not hard." The boy shrugged into his coat. "My mistake. The chicken is not the only one here who is *estúpido*."

He stood tall and straight. Dressed all in black, with his ebony hair wild and long and thick, he looked like a child playing at being a man and finding the process more difficult than he had expected.

She would have given all her worldly possessions to have a brother seek her out in such a way.

In that moment she made a decision she knew would forever affect her relationship with Cal. She had given up everything for him—her pride, her future, her reputation—but she could not deny all that she valued. She could not give up her soul.

"When I said don't go, I didn't mean for just a while. I meant stay for as long as you want."

She sensed more than heard Cal's mutter of disgust. When she turned to explain to him what she was doing, he was reining the horse away from the corral.

"Cal," she called, but he was gone, clouds of dust and anger in his wake. Baron ran after him for a short distance, then reversed his path and returned to the corral. Cal rode on alone, to what destination she could not imagine, and, probably, neither could he.

Making excuses for him came to mind, but she knew that whatever she said would not keep Cord from seeing the truth. He must want a home very, very badly to risk rejection as he had done. Her heart went out to him. The two of them were much alike.

She looked at the boy. "He'll come around," she said, hoping it was the truth.

"It doesn't matter to me one way or the other. I'm just passing through."

She glanced at the leaden sky. "Winter's really going to hit us, maybe tonight. Can't you feel the sting in the air?"

His jaw squared just like Cal's. "I can take it."

"Of course you can. I didn't mean to imply otherwise. But you would be helping me if you stayed. I know you don't know me, don't know anything about me—"

She could see by the sharp look in his eyes that he understood her relationship with Cal, understood it and judged her harshly for it, but she could not stop.

"—but Antonio can tell you my meals are passably good. Nothing like you're used to, I'm sure, but better than you could get on your own. When the weather warms, you can leave."

"I do not stay where I'm not wanted."

"I want you. I need help here with chores I can't handle. I've already hired Antonio. I'll hire you as well." She smiled. "Stay on my half of the Crown. I own the barn."

"Señorita Ellie," Antonio said, "Cordoba has been staying with me and Señor Jorge for two days past. He knows the barn."

"And I'll bet he knows Queenie, too."

"Sí. He gets much milk from the cow."

"More than I do?"

"Sí."

"Thank goodness. Now maybe we can get some butter. And with the chicken, we can get some eggs." She put as much lilt in her voice as she could manage. "If things keep rolling along the way they are now, before you know it we'll be civilized."

Cord looked at the barn, at the cabin on the hill behind her, at the log fence, at her trousers, and lastly into her eyes. He started to say something, then changed his mind and shifted his gaze to the distant hills.

But not quickly enough. She caught a glimpse of the lost look he was trying hard to hide. Civilization must seem very far away from him right now, and the adventure he had sought empty and cold.

She wanted to cry for them both, but crying would push him away and would do her little good. She reminded herself that she was tough and she was strong, and more, she was needed by both of Raymond Hardin's sons, whether they knew it or not.

They needed her as much as she needed them.

At that moment a chill wind swept from behind her, blowing her hat across the corral. It was Cord who ran to fetch it, barely beating Baron in the chase, while Antonio went for the frightened chicken.

When she took the hat from Cord, she grabbed his hand and held on. He didn't try very hard to pull away. At fifteen he was already taller than she was by a couple of inches. He would be a very handsome man, as handsome as his brother, but in a different, more exotic way. If something were not done, like his brother, he would also find comfort only in solitude or short-term affairs.

Like Cal, he would miss out on the greatest thing that life could offer. He would miss out on love.

"Regardless of what you think of me or my land or even your brother—don't flinch, that's what he is—we all need you here." She spoke from her heart and she didn't try to hide the burning of tears in her eyes. "It's very important that you not leave. It's going to take some of us a while to realize it, that's all."

Wherever Cal rode off to, it kept him away for the rest of the day. He didn't return until late, after Ellie had fed the boys and settled them in the barn for the night, along with the Crown's meager stock. She was sitting by the fire debating whether to eat her own meal or wait a while longer for Cal when he walked into the cabin.

Shaking off his hat, he hung it on a peg. Droplets of moisture clung to his hair and to his blanket coat, but he had wiped his boots off outside and tracked in only a trace of dampness.

She rose slowly to her feet, wanting very much to go over to him with a welcome embrace. Instead, she remained where she was, with the table and a world of uncertainty between them.

"I didn't know it was raining," she said, as if that were the most important matter of the moment.

"It just started," he said, holding back as much as she.

"Come by the fire and get warm."

He didn't move. "Wright Whitfield says a blue norther's on the way."

She thought about the boys. She had extra blankets. They might need them tonight. Under normal circumstances the barn was warm enough, but if the weather got too bad, they would have to come inside.

"You saw Wright?"

"He was rounding up some strays that had wandered onto the Crown. George was helping him. I joined in."

"George was supposed to be here with Antonio."

"He didn't see any reason to stay close since the boy had company. He's gone on back to town before the storm hits."

Cal spoke calmly, but she could see the tendons

in his neck tighten and his eyes turn as hard as blue stones.

She didn't want to think about what she must look like, stark and pale and mumbling inanities. Everything between them was so strained she wanted to scream.

"Please, Cal," she said, gesturing toward the fire. "Supper's waiting. I put off eating until you got here."

Without waiting for him to respond, she took the plates from where they had been warming on her new stove and set them on the table, poured them each a cup of coffee, and sat.

"It's only dried beef and cornbread, but I opened a jar of pickles to—"

"Ellie, stop."

She picked up her fork. "I can't stop. I'm so nervous I'm about to scream."

"He's still here, I take it."

There was no need to define the *he*. "In the barn with Antonio."

"Because you asked him."

Because you need him.

But of course she didn't tell him the truth. "Because even I knew the storm was coming. I wasn't about to let him strike out for God knows where with only a light coat and no destination in mind."

Her hand shook so hard, she set down the fork.

"Surely," she added, "you can have no objections."

"You have no idea how I feel."

"So tell me."

He looked at her for a moment, started to

speak, then looked away. A log snapped in the fire, scattering ashes and sparks, and the sound of the wind penetrated the room.

Shoving away from the table, she got up from the bench.

"I'm not hungry. I'm going to bed."

"Your room will be cold."

"I started a fire earlier. It will be warmer than in here."

She started for the door. Cal caught her by the wrist.

"He can't stay long. As soon as the weather settles, he'll have to go back to New Orleans."

"He won't do it."

She didn't know how she could be so certain, but she was. Maybe it was because she saw how much the two brothers were alike.

"He won't have a choice. I'll make him leave."

She stared down at the grip Cal had on her, then stared him straight in the eyes.

"He can stay on my land. I don't think you need worry you'll be running into each other. He doesn't like you any more than you like him."

Where she got the courage to speak in such a way, she didn't know. But then, she had already alienated him. What else did she have to lose?

Cal released her wrist. Without a word, without a glance into his eyes, she left him and hurried to a bed that was once again lonely, hurried to what must be the first of many sleepless nights.

Cal watched her go. Damn her. Damn Cord. Damn the world. He should have known the peace he had begun to feel wouldn't last. A cold, hard son of a bitch, that's what he had been and what he remained. Cord was little more than a child. Of course he had to stay—Cal was about to say so when Ellie had jumped in—but on the first clear day, whatever the cost, his half brother would be taken down to the coast and thrown onto the nearest ship bound for New Orleans.

Hell, he might even hire the Dollarhide sisters to escort him home. If his uncles' situation was any indication, Cord would have a difficult time getting away from them.

As the only other Hardin around, he was obliged to get Cord back where he belonged. It was best for the boy.

And it was damned sure best for him. Cordoba Hardin was a responsibility he was not prepared to accept over the long term.

Suddenly he was ravenous. Ignoring his own plate, he tore into Ellie's food, eating everything, sopping up the juices with the cornbread, but he found no satisfaction. He was halfway through his own food when he heard a whine at the door. He opened it to let a shivering Baron inside.

Giving in to the inevitable, he set his plate on the floor near the hearth. Baron didn't need to be told the food was for him. The mongrel cleaned the plate in two swallows, then settled into his usual brown lump in a draft of warm air.

Glancing at the dog in envy, Cal paced. Why was he so restless? He knew what he would do about Cord; there was no indecision there. He was in the cabin safe and warm, protected from the howling wind. And the food had been filling.

Maybe too much food was the problem. Everything he had eaten lay like a rock in the pit of his stomach.

He paced some more, then in disgust threw himself on the sofa. His boots hung over the edge; he tugged them off, then shifted so his bare feet were closer to the fire.

Ellie was the matter. She was interfering in matters that were none of her concern, siding with the boy as if the two brothers were enemies instead of strangers. With a storm coming, Cal would never have cast him out; he wasn't a monster.

But Ellie had looked at him that way.

He can stay on my land.

Where had she gotten that? They hadn't talked *my land, your land* since the first days of their partnership. They would be talking about it now. And they would be thinking *my life, your life*, the differences between them growing deeper and wider every day.

Cal felt as if someone was carving away at his insides with a sharp, pointed knife. The wind rattled the shutter on the window and shook the door. Muttering a string of profanities, he tugged on his boots, grabbed his coat, and strode into the storm.

The way to the barn was dark and wet. He threw open the doors to see two miserable boys huddling beside the slight warmth of a lantern.

"Get your blankets," he said, then grabbed the lantern, waiting only long enough for them to put on their shoes before he retraced his steps to the cabin.

To his side of the cabin.

"The two of you can sleep with the dog in here."

He left them and invaded Ellie's bedroom.

She sat up in bed, the covers tight at her throat. The glow from the fireplace sent a flickering warm light over her, across her flowing yellow hair, her parted lips, her thick-lashed, shadow-brown eyes.

"I brought them in," he said. "Antonio hasn't been well."

"I heard you go after them. And I heard Baron whining, too. Is the dog all right?"

"He's a hell of a lot better than I am."

He stared at her a moment. She didn't look surprised that he was there, nor that he had seen to the boys.

"You knew I'd get them," he said.

"I was going out if you didn't."

"Still, you figured I would."

"I didn't know for sure. But I opened the door to the back room in case someone wanted to sleep in there. I didn't want it to be too cold."

"They're sleeping in the kitchen."

In two strides he was closing the door that separated the two halves of the sleeping quarters. Moving slowly to the center of the room, he started taking off clothes. Ellie sat with her back against the wall and watched.

"I'm sleeping in here," he said.

"So I see."

A gentleman would have asked if the lady objected. But Cal wasn't a gentleman, certainly not tonight, and Ellie had renounced being a lady the first time she invited him into her bed.

He knew he wasn't being fair. She was a lady

in the purest sense of the word. A stubborn, interfering, provocative lady who took pleasure in sex the way every woman should.

She was a woman to cherish. If he had been any kind of man other than the man he was, he would have given her his life. It was his curse and her good fortune that such could never be. He could give only that part of him he could not crush or deny—his passion and whatever pleasure it could bring to her.

Maybe she was right. Maybe he was a monster.

In that moment he didn't like himself very much. For her and for her alone, he wished he could be all that she deserved.

Naked, he eased into the bed and took her in his arms. Somehow, with all his undressing, he hadn't noticed she was slipping out of her gown. He must be worse off than he had supposed.

"You're cold," she said as she pressed her bare flesh against his.

"You're hot."

Her brown eyes softened. "Cal—"

"No," he said, wanting no talk.

Suddenly he was as ravenous as he had been at the supper table, but for a nourishment far different from food. He was tired of thinking, tired of running, tired of everything but the woman he held in his arms. Anger boiled in him. He wanted to punish her for being what she was, and worse, for understanding him.

He chose a slow kind of torture, kissing her, then licking her lips, then kissing her again when he sensed she was about to speak. She felt tense under his hands, willing to do whatever he wanted but holding back something he could never have.

Cal wanted all of her. Knowing Ellie in every sense was the only way to forget himself, and punishing her had nothing to do with it. He touched her, kissed her, fondled all of her, her body as much a part of him as his arms, his legs, his eyes . . . his heart. The more he touched, the more he wanted, until his lovemaking became a kind of frenzy.

She gave as good as she got, anticipating every touch, every kiss, opening her body to him, yet retaining the essence that was hers and hers alone, demanding and yielding, nothing held back, her hands burning their way across his chest, his abdomen, between his thighs, her tongue tasting his hot skin, her teeth taking little nips after each kiss.

He attempted once to speak.

"Princess—"

"No," she said, and swallowed his words as she covered his mouth with hers.

They moved in unison, their lovemaking a physical eloquence that took the place of words. When she parted her legs, he thrust inside her, eagerly, hungrily. Much too soon they climaxed together. With the wind and the rain lashing the cabin, he held her tightly and she clung to him, as much a part of him as any human being had ever been.

They did not let go, not for a long while. She seemed small enough for him to wrap his arms around her twice, yet pulsating with sufficient spirit to light up the stormy night. Lying like this with their bodies entwined, he felt a sense of belonging that was as close as he could ever get to coming home.

The feeling was an illusion. Cal knew it as well as he had ever known anything. Worse, it was an illusion they both shared, though the words of affection and comfort would never be spoken between them. She had her pride. And he had his.

Their eventual parting was inevitable. The kindest thing he could do for her was to begin the separation right away, keeping his distance from her whenever he could, allowing her to separate herself from him.

But right away did not mean tonight.

He stroked her small, high breast, rubbing the taut nipple against his palm. Tonight he would love her in the only way he knew how.

Chapter Twenty

The winter storm spent its fury during the night, and early the next morning Cal rode south toward Mexico, past Goliad, his destination the ranch of Miguel Alejandro, a long-time cattleman whose fame had spread throughout the western half of the Republic.

With the creeks high from the rain, the going was slow; he didn't arrive until noon the second day. Even in the seasonal grayness, with the grasses turning brown and the trees bare of their leaves, he could see the splendor of the ranch, the herds of fat cattle, the pastures of horses, the plowed fields waiting for spring seed.

Alejandro's sprawling hacienda, nestled in a protected green valley, was the most splendid of all his holdings, with its red tile roof and white-washed adobe walls and half-dozen outbuildings scattered around the house like chicks with a mother hen.

Three of Alejandro's men met him on horseback when he was halfway down the incline leading to the house. Like Cal, they were armed. In broken Spanish he was able to tell them he was there to learn about their employer's methods of achieving success.

He spoke sincerely. A native of Mexico, Alejandro had moved to Texas before the turn of the century and forty years later had been a supporter of the Revolution. Although some Texians resented his success—especially those newly come to the Republic from the East—Cal had heard nothing of substance that would impugn the rancher's integrity or ability, or his loyalty to the young country.

One of the men broke away and rode toward the house. Alejandro was outside the heavy, carved front door by the time Cal dismounted from his gelding. The rancher greeted him with a slight bow and a handshake. An image of Cord greeting Ellie with a similar bow flashed through his mind, unsettling him more than it should have.

The fifty-year-old cattleman was slight and dapper in his brown leather pants and waist-length tooled leather jacket, his short hair dark, his brown eyes wary and welcoming at the same time.

"You have come to learn of my success?" Alejandro asked after Cal had introduced himself.

"Yes. I have a small place in Victoria County, but I'm hopeful that it will grow and prosper."

That much of the prosperity would benefit another owner was a detail he kept to himself.

"If my visit comes at an awkward time," he added, "I will not impose upon you longer."

"There is no such thing as an awkward time for visitors in this wide land." Alejandro stepped aside, gesturing for Cal to enter his home. "My wife has no doubt ordered a grand meal for you as we speak." His dark eyes glinted with humor. "She understands my need to talk about myself."

Over the next few days Alejandro did just that, showing Cal his methods of ranching, with both cattle and horses, and with people, too, inviting the participation of his foreman, his workers, and his two sons and three sons-in-law who lived with their families at the ranch.

Here was a real Rancho Grande, Cal thought, unlike the pitiful holdings of Alden Fowler. In naming his place, Miguel Alejandro had settled for a more modest Alejandro Ranch.

For dinner each evening Cal joined the family, which included Señora Alejandro, a woman whose grace and charm matched her husband's, and the Alejandros' daughters and daughters-in-law. Included were a half-dozen grandchildren, who dined alongside the adults in the large dining room that was the heart of the hacienda.

The meal was a lively affair, with much talking about the day's activities, arguments among adults and children alike, all settled peacefully or without acrimony allowed to continue over until another day. Cal had never been with such a group. The closest had been the celebrants that Gert and May had gathered at the Crown weeks

Evelyn Rogers

ago for its first—and probably last—fandango.

On that day, he had chosen to stroll the confines of the corral alone. On these late afternoons he could not be so rude, so separate, yet as he sat amidst the Alejandro family, he thought of Ellie and how she would enjoy such company. If he were not around to darken her day.

Except for rare moments on their three-day ride across the Crown, never once had he made her laugh. Only rarely had he made her even smile. Now that Cord had arrived, his presence a reminder of the family man Cal would never be, he could not see her smiling for him again.

Whatever pleasure he brought her came during their time in bed. But a man and a woman could not spend their lives in bed, no matter how much they might like to do so.

When Cal left Alejandro Ranch, it was in the company of two vaqueros who would help him track the white mustang stallion and his *manada* of mares. His saddlebags were stuffed with enough food to last a week, and in his pocket he carried a signed agreement for Miguel Alejandro to sell him cattle breeding stock after the beginning of the new year.

It took three days to track down the horses, another day to round them up into a makeshift pen built for the purpose of capture, and two more to lead them back to the Crown. All the while Cal learned from the vaqueros their methods of handling the wild animals, their gentleness, their slyness, their calm assumption of control.

By the time the white stallion was confined in the Crown's sturdy corral, along with a dozen of the best breeding mares from the original *man-ada*, Cal felt both humbled and encouraged that he could manage the same feat with men he trained himself.

Ellie, Cord, and Antonio were on hand to watch them ride in. From the moment she stepped into view outside the barn, Cal had difficulty pulling his gaze away from her. The day was brisk, but she was wearing only her plain brown gown, her hair twisted into a single braid against her back. As small and vulnerable as she was, in that moment he saw her as the best of womanhood, representing the strength, the endurance, the loyalty that women offered, and the beauty and grace, too. Her eyes were wide, deep, and watchful, and when they rested upon him, he felt as if she were stroking him with her hands.

How could he ever leave her? How could he let her go? The questions, never before asked so bluntly, pounded against him, but he had no answer except that it must be so.

The vaqueros reluctantly joined them for a meal inside, but there was no laughter, no disagreements, only occasional talk. Briefly Cal told Ellie of the past week and a half, the talks with Miguel Alejandro, the roundup of the horses, the return journey, leaving out the family gatherings at Alejandro Ranch, keeping the details centered on ranching business alone. Her questions were brief, some put to him, some to the vaqueros, and the meal passed with Antonio occasionally serving as interpreter. Cord never said a word.

The vaqueros insisted on leaving after they were fed, refusing a bed for the night as well as the money Cal tried to force on them.

"We offer our services in honor of Señor Miguel," one of them said. "We wish you well. You will make a fine *mesteñero*, Señor Hardin."

A fine mustanger was what he said. Cal knew he could give no higher compliment.

All through the meal and the parting of the vaqueros, Cal felt Cord's eyes on him, shifting only when they were outside, in the direction of the corral. When he went down to the band of horses, planning in his mind the taming of the stallion as the vaqueros had described the process to him, it wasn't Ellie who accompanied him. It was Cord.

He knew she was giving them time together. It was a time he did not want.

Standing at the side of the corral, his arms resting on the top rail, one booted foot propped against the lower, he thumbed his hat to the back of his head and caught sight of Cord standing close by.

"I am good with horses," the boy said.

"Don't tell me Raymond taught you. He barely knew one end of a horse from another. The only thing he could figure out was how to tell the stallions from the mares."

Both brothers watched the stallion, but Cal could have sworn he caught a brief twitch of Cord's lips, as if he fought a smile.

"My mother taught me. She was killed by a horse."

Cal didn't think that was the best argument for the boy being good with horses, but he kept the thought to himself.

"A riding accident, I heard," he said.

"A fool drove his carriage into her path. She could not rein away in time to save herself."

"You saw it?"

The boy nodded.

"How long ago?"

"A long while, though it seems like yesterday. I was eight years old."

Cal had been the same age when his father abandoned his first family and sought another. It was another link with this boy who was his half brother. It was another bond he did not want.

"I will help with the horses," Cord said. "I want to earn my keep."

"Milk the cow and help Ellie," Cal said. "That's work enough until you leave."

The boy stiffened. He was wearing his coat and the trousers with the torn knee. Someone—Ellie—had patched the tear, but the rent was still visible.

Before Cal could stop him, Cord slipped through the rails of the corral and walked toward the restless, milling mustangs. The animals were wild, capable of stampeding even in a confined area, of rearing and biting and kicking. Cal started to go after the boy, but something happened that held him back.

As Cord approached the horses, he began speaking in a low tone of voice, the mixture of Spanish and English words drifting across the evening air like the hum of bees. The horses separated as he moved amongst them, providing him a path. At the edge of the *manada,* the stallion stood still, head raised, his dark eyes wide and his nostrils flared.

Cord did not go near the stallion, letting only

his words reach the untamed beast. For a full minute, boy and horse stared at one another; then the boy turned and strolled toward Cal as if he walked among wild horses every day in the week.

"You know little about me," he said when he came to a halt on the opposite side of the fence. His chin squared. "Our father treated me no better than he treated you. After my mother died, I was put into a home for orphans and he was gone, grieving, he told me, for his dead wife. I seldom saw him. When he remarried, he decided to reclaim me. But I did not wish to reclaim him."

The boy spoke stiffly, formally, like a man reciting from memory the history of someone else. But he was still a boy. Cal saw the hurt in the depths of his blue eyes, and he saw, too, the hate. He recognized both hurt and hate as his own.

"When I saw you at the cemetery," he continued, "I thought we could be brothers. Someplace besides New Orleans." Cord slipped through the fence. "Do not worry. I will not stay much longer. I never intended to make my life with you."

He walked past Cal, his stride steady as he disappeared inside the cabin.

Whether the boy spoke the truth, Cal couldn't guess. He spent a long time alone by the corral, thinking of the similarities and the differences between them, the waste of empty years that neither could do anything about. He was a man; he ought to be able to help a boy. Hell, through the years he'd done his share of helping homeless children in the cities of the East, giving money if not his time, though it was nothing anyone knew anything about.

He didn't know why he had done it, except that he had been compelled by an urge he could not name.

He was likewise compelled to see that Cord was cared for—someplace else. He saw himself as a man without chance of redemption, a loner all his days. The knowledge had never hurt before. His problem was that he had let people get too close.

When he returned to the cabin, the two boys had already bundled up their gear and retired to the barn. Ellie was in her room, and Cal headed for the sofa, pulling off his boots and socks as he went, tossing his holster and gun aside. His back was to the door when he heard it open and close. He sensed her presence right away.

He turned to see her standing by the hearth. She was wrapped in a blanket, her hair brushed long and free. The air was warm in the tightly constructed room, the only light provided by the flickering flames of the fire.

She carried extra blankets. She dropped them by her bare feet, along with the blanket that was her sole garment. She stood before the golden bath of warm light without saying a word. She didn't have to. Her nakedness spoke far more eloquently to him than words ever could have done.

"I thought you didn't like to be cold," he said.

"I'm not cold," she said. "Well, maybe a little bit. That's where you come in."

Cal had meant to stay away from her . . . for her own good. But his good intentions fled into the night.

She knelt to spread the blankets in front of the fire. When she rose to her feet, he was there before her. She unbuttoned his shirt and tugged the tails from his trousers, then kissed his chest, pulling him down to the blankets where they both knelt facing one another, their heights closer to the same than when they stood.

She rubbed her breasts against his bare flesh, pressed her satin thighs against his roughly trousered legs, held her hips to his until he knew she must feel his erection. He cupped her buttocks and held her tightly in place.

"This is what you do to me, Ellie."

"I came to you tonight. That's what you do to me."

When at last their lips met, Cal was beyond analyzing right from wrong. The kiss was long and thorough and as satisfying as any kiss had ever been. When he undressed, she helped him, her hands more often than not getting in the way, but he didn't tell her so.

Their mating was quick, too quick, but she would not slow down for the niceties of touching and stroking. Thrusting and plunging were what she craved, and so did he. They made love twice more during the night, snatching brief periods of sleep in between, and after the last time falling into a deep slumber, entwined in each other's arms.

Cal woke at dawn, alone in a tangle of blankets. Wrapping himself in their warmth, he gathered his clothes and went across the dog run to find her. She was already dressed, this time in trousers, her hair in the single braid.

"I've got some water in the basin for you to

wash up and shave," she said, as if the night had never been.

She spoke brusquely, too much so to sound like herself.

"What's wrong?" he asked.

"What could possibly be wrong?"

"I don't know. That's why I asked."

She looked around the room and out the raw-hide window to the blurred light of day. "It's nothing, really. I sometimes wonder what Aunt Abigail would say." She shrugged. "And then I remember that I'm the one whose opinion matters."

Before he could respond, she added, "I'll fix breakfast and get the boys. While you were gone, I got a few more chickens from the Whitfields and George brought me out supplies from town. We'll have biscuits and butter to go with the eggs and bacon. I don't know about you, but I'm starved."

Ellie kept the daytime hours as busy as she possibly could. She and Antonio worked on an improved henhouse; the two brothers worked at taming the mustangs, beginning with the mares.

Gert and May, visiting with the O'Malleys on the second day of Cal's return, queried her about how things were going. Something in her quick "Fine" must have told them the opposite was true; they didn't ask again.

Along with the Dollarhides and the twins, George and Dub rode out from town to watch the taming, offering their advice, and on the third day Antonio's father, Juan Gomez, showed up to hire out his services, which were formidable and, Cal admitted, very much needed when they finally decided to take on the stallion.

Gomez had ridden up from Mexico, where he had gone when his father fell ill. The father had died and the small family farm had sold, Gomez explained to Ellie. After a year-long separation, his reunion with his son was brief but warm, neither shrinking from the *abrazo*, the embrace that so much embarrassed Texas men.

As if by mutual consent, Cal did not visit her every night, and she did not visit him. Two nights, three, even four would go by and then one of them would appear to the other. On those nights, whether in bed or before the kitchen fire, their lovemaking was wild. He called her Princess. She called him King. It was as if real names, real feelings, did not exist.

Every morning she was up first, leaving the bedroom for him to shave and dress. Once she returned for a forgotten item and saw him holding the coat she had made him. He wasn't putting it on, he was just holding it close, and she tiptoed away before he could know she was there.

She didn't give much thought to what she had seen. In her heart she knew they were growing further apart.

Winter curtailed much of her outdoor activity, and with the growing team of men taking over whatever tasks she might have tended to, Ellie found herself performing the more traditional chores of her sex, cooking and washing and mending. In the evenings she wrote entries in her journal, expounding on the activities and the plans for the Crown, avoiding matters of the heart.

As the years went by, she might forget the details of her work. Never would she forget her love.

More than ever she longed for her harp. A silly, womanly weakness it was, but still, she would have liked the delicate music to fill the empty corners of a house that was not a home. Too, she would have liked her books. As a substitute, she related to Antonio and Cord the myths of Greece and Rome that she had read as a child, and she told the stories of Shakespeare's plays as best she could remember them, recalling only snatches of the poetry that brought the stories to life.

Antonio listened to everything she said. At first, Cord pretended to be bored, and then he began to question the absurdity of the myths and the exaggerated drama of the plays, and the three of them got into rousing arguments about what the stories might mean.

Cal sat to the side or else worked in the barn or, when the weather permitted, simply disappeared for an hour or two. Juan Gomez returned to town to be with his wife.

The day came when Cal announced that a separate cabin should be built to house the workers they would be needing if the Crown grew as he wanted.

"As I want, too," Ellie said. "I'll share the expenses. We'll put it in the back where it can straddle our separate property."

He didn't argue. She wished he had. At least it would have been a talk with passion about something other than sex.

Evelyn Rogers

Men were hired from town. Wright Whitfield and Abe Patchett volunteered their help. Fitz and Fin showed up with Gert and May, the four of them bringing furnishings to go inside the new cabin.

"Our contribution," Fin said. "There'll be a time soon when we'll be wanting help with the saloon."

It was all accomplished quickly, and Ellie announced they would hold a Christmas feast to celebrate its construction. She looked upon it as a final gathering of the friends she had made and a silent good-bye to the man she could not win.

After the new year she would claim that the ranch work was too hard, and she would deed her property over to Cal. She would settle in New Orleans, in her papa's shop. It was the one place in all the world she knew Cal would never visit.

Perhaps Cord would go with her. She would ask him later, after she had talked to Cal.

And so she began to count the days she would remain on a rugged piece of land that she had come to love, and she counted the nights as well. Since leaving Virginia, she had become quite an actress. Cal had no idea that she had written to her lawyer instructing him to sell her property and belongings in Virginia to the highest bidder, whether or not it turned out to be Bertrand.

He was to sell everything but the harp. Gert took the letter into town for her with a promise to send it on its way.

The holiday dawned beautifully warm and sunny; a host of people came, everyone Ellie had invited except Alden Fowler. Cal kept his distance from it all. Katya Merse rode out with her father

360

and Sir Simon. The Merses brought a small tree to decorate with the tin and paper ornaments Katya had made. They brought, too, small gifts for everyone, mostly jars of food from the store, explaining that the tree and the gifts were customs of their native Germany.

Cal had shot a wild turkey for the meal, his lone but important contribution, and Abe Patchett brought the loin of a newly slaughtered pig. Sweet potatoes, peas, corn, hot bread, wild plum pies—the meal was truly a feast.

Much was made of the upcoming birth of the Whitfield baby. Ruthlessly Ellie suppressed thoughts of motherhood. She was not in a family way, for which she should be grateful. Gert cornered her by the barn and asked her outright if she might be. She made no attempt to be offended by the question. She simply told her no.

"Well, something sure as hell is going on," Gert said, puffing on a cigar.

"Yes, we're having a Christmas party. I'll expect you and Fin to lead the singing later."

When the Christmas feast was done and the singing began, Fin and Fitz came up with some Irish ditties that might best have been kept from mixed company, but no one took offense. Gert and May were the loudest to join in. Barbara Whitfield swore she didn't mind the smoke from their cigars, especially since the door was cracked open, and Lucy Patchett fired up her pipe.

Discounting an occasional pang of longing, which Ellie attributed to the season, all went well. Except that Cal kept his distance from the talk and the laughter and the singing. Cord, too, watched the proceedings from the side of the room.

A pox on all Hardins, Ellie told herself in a most unchristian way, and she put on a brave smile that fooled everyone but the Dollarhides.

Except for the Whitfields and the Patchetts, everyone stayed the night. The Gomez family were chosen as the first residents of the new cabin. The rest of the women took the bedroom side of the dog run, the men the kitchen side. At mid-morning the day after Christmas, the departures took place—first the Gomezes, including Antonio, and then Sir Simon with Katya close to his side on the wagon seat.

"I will ride with the always kind Dollarhide sisters," Joseph Merse said. "The young people need time alone. The Englishman is good, I think, for my precious German child."

Cord went to the barn to continue the work he'd begun on the new stalls for the stallion and the two mares that showed signs of being pregnant. Cal simply disappeared, riding the white stallion, leaving Ellie alone for the first time in a long while. Donning her trousers, she set to work cleaning the kitchen.

Just as she was preparing to start the afternoon meal, the clatter of horse and wagon invaded the quiet cabin. There was something frantic about the noise, and she knew right away that trouble was riding toward the Crown.

She ran out to a sight that would forever burn in her mind: Simon Pence slumped on the seat of the wagon, his face bloody, frock coat torn and bloodied like his face, his pale eyes wide with anguish.

"He's got her," he managed before drawing in a few shallow, panicked breaths. "Help . . . I couldn't . . ."

Ellie flew off the porch, crying out, "Cal," knowing he couldn't hear, and then, "Cord!"

The younger Hardin ran from the barn to help the injured man from the wagon. Sir Simon slumped on the ground at their feet, and Ellie knelt to wipe the blood from his face with her apron. He had taken a blow to the side of his head, and his right arm bled where a bullet had pierced his flesh and passed on through.

Over his protests, they helped him inside, with Simon muttering all the while about helping *her*.

Ellie tied her apron around the arm to stop the flow of blood.

"Who's got Katya?" she asked.

Sir Simon tried to rise from the sofa. "Alden Fowler," he rasped. "I couldn't . . . oh, God. . . ."

And then he slipped into unconsciousness.

Images of Katya flashed in her mind, of the fear that never quite left her eyes, of the brave attempt she was making to be with people again. She couldn't imagine why Alden Fowler had captured her, but she knew he meant her harm.

Cal had been right when he'd said the man was not quite sane.

Barking orders to the boy, Ellie set about doctoring the Englishman's wounds. When she had done all she could, she thrust her pepperbox pistol into her trouser pocket and grabbed the shotgun she had practiced using two months before.

"Saddle the horses. We'll look for Cal."

She whistled for Baron, who was never far away. "Take care of Sir Simon," she said, stroking the dog's head. "The way you did Antonio."

She could have sworn the dog understood.

"I need to leave," she said to no one in particular. She looked through the rawhide window in the direction of Alden Fowler's Rancho Grande. "Someone has got to help that poor girl."

Chapter Twenty-one

Ellie's mare Duchess and the gelding Duke, ridden by Cord, flew across the paths and pastures of the Crown, but nowhere were Cal and the white mustang to be found.

With the shotgun across her lap and the loaded pepperbox crammed inside her pocket, Ellie came to a decision fast.

She leveled as stern a look as she could manage at Cord. "Go back to the Crown and wait for Cal. Tell him what's happened."

"No."

"You have to. Sir Simon may still be unconscious. He needs help. When Cal returns, he won't know where we've gone."

"He'll figure it out. I'm going with you."

Ellie had no time to argue. Besides, Cord was a Hardin, which was a stronger weight on him

Evelyn Rogers

than his youth. He wouldn't listen to anything she said.

She had never been to Alden Fowler's misnamed Rancho Grande, but Cal had described the way. Digging her heels into the mare's flanks, she took off. Both horses seemed to sense their riders' urgency, and their hooves scarcely touched the ground as they raced side by side across the pastures.

Somewhere along the way Ellie lost her hat, and her hair streamed wildly in the wind. The important thing was she held on to the shotgun. She hadn't taken time to put on her blanket coat, but she felt no cold, not with her blood pumping hotly in close-to-panic fear.

The fear was not for herself or even Cord, but for Katya Merse.

The moment she could see Fowler's cabin, she reined to a halt. All looked serene from the top of the rise where she and Cord had stopped. Smoke curled from the chimney, the lone sign that someone dwelt inside.

Suddenly indecisive, she rubbed a gloved hand against her thigh. They had only to ride down one incline and up another and they would be there. But what if Fowler saw them and hurt the young woman? What if he decided to shoot Cord? He could fire out the door and there was no way she could stop him.

If Cord hadn't been with her, she would have known what to do: ride right up to Fowler's front door and demand to see Katya Merse. She would throw down the shotgun. He wouldn't know about the pepperbox.

366

But Cord was there, close by her side. Weeks ago she had asked him to stay at the Crown. Today he needed her protection as much as Katya.

"We need to separate," she said, taking out the pepperbox from her pocket and passing it over to him. "Circle wide around the house and see if you can sneak in. I'll try a diversion at the front."

"A good plan, Miss Chase. Too bad it won't work."

It wasn't Cord who'd answered. She looked over her shoulder to see Alden Fowler sitting astride his pinto mare. Above the white collar of his shirt, his broad, flat face was scratched and bloodied, and he wore a cold, mad look in his eyes. The look frightened her as much as the shotgun he had leveled straight at her. It must be the gun he had used to kill Buck Shannon, the gun he had used to wound Simon Pence. Ellie had no doubt he was near the point of killing again.

The two of them had been concentrating so hard on the house that they hadn't heard him ride up. Her heart pounded in her throat.

"Let Cord go," she said. "It's women you want, not boys."

"You do not know what I want, Miss Chase. Please," he said, gesturing with the gun, "throw down your weapons and ride slowly in front of me." He glanced at the boy. "It would be a mistake to disobey me. I will shoot you dead."

She could see Cord's pride and anger fighting reason. He glanced at her. She pleaded with her eyes, and reason won. They did as they were told, guiding their horses slowly down the hill and up the rise to the square stone structure that was Alden Fowler's home.

All lay quiet before them. The wind picked up, moving the empty rocker on the front porch slowly back and forth. It looked as if a ghost sat waiting to welcome Fowler's latest prisoners.

In unison she and Cord dismounted and walked onto the porch. Fowler came close behind them. Cord whirled and Fowler hit him with the stock of his gun, catching him close to the eye. The boy fell. Blood seeped from the split skin and trickled down his cheek.

With a cry, Ellie knelt to tend him, but Fowler gestured with his gun for her to back away. Cord dabbed the cut with the back of his hand.

"I'm fine," he said. "The *bastardo* did not hurt me."

Ellie was so frightened, she couldn't breathe; worse, she couldn't think. Ignoring Fowler, she extended a hand and helped Cord to his feet, and the two of them walked inside the house.

"In there," Fowler growled, gesturing toward a door to the left of the entryway. The door opened onto a parlor, the first real parlor Ellie had seen in a long while. Directly opposite the door, Katya Merse sat bound to a chair close to the fire.

Her normally tidy knot of hair was in disarray, her dress was torn at the shoulder, and her cheek bore an ugly bruise. A dirty cloth was tied around her mouth, but her eyes said more than words ever could have conveyed. There was a desperate wildness in their depths, and Ellie was reminded of a rabbit she had once freed from the sharp jaws of a trap.

Without waiting for permission, she hurried to the woman and untied the knot holding the dirty cloth in place.

Katya spat out threads from the frayed gag, and next came a spate of German invective that scoured the stone walls.

Fowler looked unimpressed, but Katya did not stop. It seemed as if the months of silence had given way to stored-up anger for all the torture she had suffered at the hands of men.

Ellie whirled on him. "What have you done to her?"

"Nothing. The Comanches got to her first."

"I didn't fight them hard enough," Katya said. "I will not make that mistake again."

Cord started for him. Fowler trained the gun onto the bound woman. "A step closer and I shoot her."

"He means it," Ellie said. "He's killed before."

Fowler's thin lips curled into a smile. "You must mean Buck Shannon. The man was a fool, albeit a useful one. I hired him to get me a deed. It was a simple task. He brought nothing but trouble down on my head. He deserved to die."

"You," Ellie said, barely above a whisper. "You had him kill my father."

"That was one of Buck's mistakes."

"Why? Why any of this? Surely you didn't want to use Papa's land for a working ranch. Cal said you don't work what you already have."

Fowler's smile died as he stared at Katya. "She understands. She knows the depredations of the savages. Except that what they did to Ruthanne was far worse than what they did to her."

369

He looked at Ellie, but his gaze turned inward, to a vision that played out only in his mind.

"They stripped the skin from the soles of her feet. And they made her run. She was tied behind a pony. She had no choice. Her blood stained the soil. I will own every inch of land where they dragged her poor, broken body."

Katya shuddered and bowed her head, the fight taken out of her, and Ellie wondered what memories were assaulting her. She put a comforting hand on the young woman's shoulder. From the corner of her eye she spied Cord taking a slow step toward Fowler.

"And your boy?" she asked. "You had an infant son, didn't you?"

"His death was merciful and quick."

Cord pounced, but Fowler was too quick, catching him again with the stock of his gun, this time in the mouth. The boy went sprawling. Blood spurted from the cut lip.

Only the gun pointed at her heart kept Ellie from rushing to his aid.

"*Schweinehund!*" Katya hissed.

"I'm growing impatient with you all," Fowler growled. "First Squaw ran away, and then I find myself burdened with a replacement who has been used by the Indians." He looked Ellie over. "And you dress like a man. But I know you are a woman. Maybe later it will be you. In the meantime . . ."

He studied his three captives. Pulling a knife from his belt, he slid it across the floor to Ellie. "Cut her free. If you try anything, I'll shoot the boy."

Ellie picked up the knife. The ivory handle was warm from Fowler's body, and the steel blade glinted in the light from the fire. Taking a deep breath, she sawed at the ropes that bound Katya's hands and feet. She was slow, awkward, trembling from fear and anger, but at last the young woman was rubbing at her wrists and flexing her unbound feet.

"Out," Fowler said, motioning with the gun for Katya to leave.

Wide-eyed, Katya looked from him to Ellie, then Cord, and back to him. "I cannot leave them here."

"Damn you, woman, I said out." Fowler was practically shouting. "Get Hardin. Tell him I have his woman and the boy."

"No!" Ellie cried. "He's not part of this. You want a woman, don't you?" She fingered her wildly tangled hair and smoothed her shirt and trousers over her figure. "No Indians have touched me. Let Katya and the boy go, and I will do whatever you want."

"You'll do that anyway, regardless of who stays or goes." He glanced at Cord. "The boy stays. The woman goes."

He rubbed at the scratches on his cheek, breaking the scabs, dabbing his blood with his fingertips. "I ought to kill her. Later, maybe I can get her again."

Slowly Katya stood. Swaying, she took Ellie's hand to steady herself. When she was able to straighten and stand on her own, she turned her cold, angry eyes on her captor.

"You are a bad man, Herr Fowler. You hurt

Simon, and then you threatened me with talk about what you planned to do to me. But you are also weak. There is nothing you can do that has not already been done. What will keep me from riding far from here, disobeying your orders about Callaghan Hardin?"

"If Hardin is not here within two hours, I will kill the boy. Two hours more and the woman dies. Not, of course, untouched. Perhaps you do not fear me, but she does."

The women stared at one another. Fowler had almost got it right. Ellie was afraid, but not for herself. Her terror was for the two Hardins.

She did the only thing she could. She hugged Katya, and she didn't care where Fowler pointed his gun.

"Take care. Simon is all right. He's at the Crown."

"And Herr Hardin?"

"I don't know." Ellie looked at Cord, still sprawled on the rug just out of reach of Fowler's legs. "I honestly don't know."

"I will find him," Katya said.

"Ride Duchess. She'll get you back to the Crown. Maybe Baron can help you find him."

The women stared at one another, and then, sparing Fowler nothing more than a final look of contempt, Katya was gone.

In the ensuing silence, Ellie was aware of the crack of logs in the fire, of Cord's breathing, of the pounding of her heart. She heard, too, the sounds of hoofbeats on the hard ground as Katya rode away.

Don't find him, her mind screamed, and then

she thought of the danger that would mean to Cord. She should have faith in Cal's ability to save them. When he put his mind to something, there was nothing he couldn't do.

Fowler looked from Ellie to Cord and back to her. "Which of you does Hardin care for the most?"

It was a question Ellie refused to answer, even if she could. And yet she thought she knew the answer. It would come as a surprise to Cord.

"It doesn't matter." Fowler sidled past the fireplace and took his place beside Ellie. He pointed the gun toward her forehead, brushing her skin with the cold metal.

"Sit," he ordered. "We have a long wait."

Slowly, fearful of making a sudden move, Ellie sat in the chair where Katya had been bound. She looked at the ropes by her feet and wondered if she could somehow put them to use. Fowler kicked them away, missing the knife she had covered with her boot, and gestured for Cord to come to her side.

"On the floor," he said. "I won't have you throwing yourself at me again. It would only cost the woman's life. I would say your sister-in-law's life, but she's not your sister-in-law, is she? Your brother and she have not bothered to wed. They are, you must agree, an abomination. At least one of them must be destroyed."

Cord's reply was in Spanish.

Fowler rolled his eyes. "Doesn't anyone speak English around here?"

"You can't stand like that for hours," Ellie said. "What if you—"

373

The front window shattered, and she swallowed her words with a cry.

"I know you're out there, Hardin," Fowler said, his voice raised. "I expected you. Throw in your gun or the woman's dead. My finger's on the trigger. The last impulse of mine will be to fire."

Silence.

"Now!" Fowler barked. "I will give you until the count of five, and then there will be only the boy to rescue."

Before Fowler got to *one*, the gun came through the window, landing on the shattered glass, and Cal climbed through after it, crouching, slowly pulling himself upright.

He glanced at Cord and then at Ellie.

"Don't worry, Princess. I've come to take you home."

Chapter Twenty-two

Cal smiled at Ellie, glanced once again at Cord, making sure both were all right, then gave his attention to the bastard who held them at gunpoint.

With his gun hand empty, he had nothing but words to rescue them. He must be as crazy as Alden Fowler to attempt the use of reason with the man. If he went wrong—

He wouldn't allow himself to consider the possibility.

"Are you wanting to die?" he asked Fowler.

"By your hand?" Alden sneered. "You offer no threat."

"If not me, someone else will get you. If you harm either of these two, that is."

"No man chooses to end his life unnecessarily. Somehow I will survive."

"Then what is it you want? The Crown? You'll

get it. I'll sign over my share right now, and I don't imagine Miss Chase will balk at signing over hers."

"I thought that was what I wanted. For years the idea of possession has consumed my days and stirred me in the night. Right up until the moment you invaded my home. Looking at you now, I see the error of my dreams."

"Let me get this straight," Cal said, stalling, his mind racing. "You've changed your mind about wanting the Crown, is that right?"

"Why should I want it? I see the truth now. You have soiled the sacred ground with your presence and your changes and with the people you've brought onto it. For that, someone must pay. Later, if I change my mind, I will claim all that you own."

He looked down at Ellie and past her to Cord. An evil smile played on his lips. "Here is your chance to play God. You choose. The woman or the boy."

For a moment Cal didn't understand what he'd said, the proposition being too inhuman even for a madman like Fowler.

But Ellie understood. He could read it in her eyes.

And Cord understood. He sat straighter beside the chair, as if to say *choose me.*

The realization came as a shock unlike any Cal had ever experienced. He looked at Cord, at the torn trousers, the bloodied face not yet formed into manhood, the blue eyes darkened with wisdom beyond their years. Here was his last link with the Hardin clan, some illustrious citizens, some thieves, most simply men and women with the weaknesses that came from being human. They were a passionate breed. He had come late in life to understand that same passion in himself.

And he looked at the woman who had brought that understanding to him. Ellie sat straight-backed in the chair, giving no sign she cared one way or the other about the gun pointed at her head. Her yellow hair was wildly tangled from the fast ride to Fowler's, but he saw no signs of blood or bruising that would indicate she'd been hurt.

Like Cord, she held wisdom in her eyes, but hers was a gentler, more imaginative kind of intelligence that saw beyond the here and now into the unseen realm of possibility.

She had seen possibilities in him; otherwise she never would have stayed in Texas. Fool that he was, it had taken him too long to figure that out.

In her simple shirt and unseemly trousers, she was the most seemly woman in all the world, and the most courageous. As she met his gaze, she did not blink and she did not plead for her life.

Like Cord, her eyes said *choose me.*

Fowler growled in impatience. "I repeat, which one do I shoot, the woman or the boy? Surely the choice is not difficult. You care for one or the other or maybe both, but not with equal fervor."

Fowler backed away, easing the point of the shotgun from Ellie's temple, and Cal wiped from his mind an image of what a load of buckshot from that weapon could do.

"Stand," Fowler ordered.

Cord rose nimbly to his feet. Ellie stumbled, landing briefly on her knees; then she stood beside the boy. She mumbled, "Sorry," as if she owed the madman an apology. Both Cord and Ellie kept their eyes on Fowler. If they were trembling—and, given his own condition, they had to be—they didn't show it.

"Take the ranch," Cal said. "This will be your last chance."

Fowler snapped out his answer. "Choose."

He shifted behind the two captives, positioning himself between them where he could take down either one.

"Choose," he repeated. "Now."

Ellie closed her eyes for a moment, and then stared at Cal, her arms held stiff and straight at her sides. "You don't have a choice. You must save your brother. He is family, Cal. And family means more to you than you know. If you let him die, you will never forgive yourself."

"No," Cord said. "Don't treat me like a child. I am the one who should die."

"Shut up," Fowler growled. "Enough of this nobility. I'll kill you all if I have to."

Cal knew with certainty that he planned to do just that, no matter what choice was made, but first he wanted to play his ugly game.

Enough of Fowler and his madness. He looked at Ellie.

"I love you."

She blinked once and her beautiful brown eyes widened. "What did you say?"

"I know it's a hell of a time to make a declaration. I don't know whether you care for me, but I think you do."

His words, not threats of death, brought tears

to her eyes. "It's not a bad time to tell me, not at all. Tell me again."

"I love you. A long time ago you had a dream about my needing you. You were right. You don't have to tell me how you feel, not if you don't want to."

She didn't have to speak. He saw her answer in her eyes. But he also saw something else, a determination that chilled his soul.

"Don't—" he began, but she was already moving, tossing something to him, throwing herself onto Fowler's gun at the exact moment Cord did the same, each intent on self-sacrifice for the other.

Buckshot tore into the rug, and the explosion echoed against the room's stone walls. Cal caught the knife Ellie had thrown, and with a snap of his wrist sent it flying back across the parlor. His aim was true. The knifepoint pierced the skin just above Fowler's stiff collar, the gun clattering to the floor as he grasped the ivory handle. Blood turned the front of his white ruffled shirt to crimson.

Staring in disbelief at Cal, he attempted to speak, but the only sound that emerged from his mouth was a hideous, voiceless burble. He fell to his knees as if in supplication, then toppled forward, embedding the knife in his throat.

Cal was the first to move. He grabbed Ellie and pulled her away from the dead man, and then he grabbed Cord and held him close. Woman and boy each filled an arm. He hugged them as near as he could to his heart, and he did not let go until long after the gunshot had faded into memory.

*   *   *

"How did you get there so fast?"

Ellie was sitting close to Cal on the horsehair sofa at the Crown, still half in a daze and at the same time wondering how he had ever fallen asleep on the uncomfortable furniture.

Cord sat at his other side shifting nervously, obviously wanting to get up, but Cal kept pulling him back.

"Something told me you were in danger. Remember when you felt the same thing about me?"

"I remember. You weren't exactly impressed at the time."

"That was before I understood the real ways of the world. Up until then, I knew only making money and arranging deals and keeping on the move."

Ellie peered around him to Cord. "Remember everything he says today. After a good night's rest, he may change his mind about all this."

Cal kissed her forehead. "You'll see. What is it your Shakespeare said? 'Tomorrow and tomorrow and tomorrow'. That's when I'll prove myself."

"You know Shakespeare?" Ellie elbowed him but none too hard. She wanted every excuse she could come up with to touch him all that she could.

"You never asked."

Ellie rolled her eyes. She was going to have to do a lot of forgetting. One of the lessons Aunt Abigail had taught her was that men did not like to be reminded of their shortcomings. Especially when those shortcomings were matters of the past.

"Cal rode up like the hounds of hell were at his heels," Sir Simon said. He was sitting at the table, his head bandaged; behind him, Katya busied herself at the stove.

"I told him what had happened," he added. "The man was out the door before I could finish speaking."

Katya put down her stirring spoon and turned toward the sofa. She had bound her hair once again in its neat knot, but there was a light in her eyes that had not been there before and a trace of militancy in her stance.

"What is to happen now?" she asked.

"We'll have to send word to the Texas Rangers," Cal said. "We left—"

"You can say it," Katya responded. "You left the body where it fell. There are men in the county who will see that he receives a proper burial beside his wife and son. He was a victim of the war with the Comanches as much as anyone."

"You feel sorry for him?" Cord asked.

"No, never. But I understand him. For too long I would not think of all that had happened. He forced me to remember. Out of memories came a strength I had been lacking."

She put her hands on Simon's shoulders. He covered a hand with one of his. "You should have seen her fight him. He had me down, and she came at him with her nails. Like one of the Valkyries. I'd be more of a fool than I already am to let a woman like that get away."

He spoke lightly, but Ellie could see the love in his eyes when he looked up at her.

A smile played on the young woman's face, small yet radiant. It brought out all the natural beauty she had been hiding for so long.

"When I asked about what was to happen," Katya said, "I did not mean about Herr Fowler. I meant about the two of you."

Ellie felt a blush coming on. Once Katya had decided to speak, there seemed to be no topic that she would not broach.

"We came to an agreement," Cal said.

"Another one?" Sir Simon asked.

"A different one. Since Katya used Ellie's horse to ride back here, she had to ride back with me on the stallion. Somehow I got her to accept my proposal of marriage."

Ellie was so proud of him, she could have burst. He hadn't choked on a single word. *Marriage*, the way he had said it, was still singing in her ears.

"It was the only way he could figure out to get my half of the deed," she said.

"Texas law says a woman retains ownership of any property she brings to a marriage," Sir Simon said.

"I knew I liked this country," Ellie said. "And what about you two? You said you wouldn't let her get away. Would you like to be more specific?"

The Englishman shuddered. "I'll have to find employment. Then we will wed."

"Nonsense," Katya said. "I care for you now. You can have part ownership in the store. Papa will be very much relieved to have his woebegone fräulein off his hands."

Ellie could see trouble brewing.

"I'll hire you," said Cal.

"We'll hire you," said Ellie, then looked at her beloved fiancé. "Doing what?"

"Miguel Alejandro told me of another Englishman near Houston who's running a beef factory. It's quite an operation. They soak the cut-up pieces of beef in brine, then pack it in salt and send it down to Galveston to be shipped to the West India Islands. You could run such a place in Glory, using the beef supplied by me and other ranchers in the county. Are you interested?"

"*Ja*," Katya said before Simon could answer.

Ellie would have felt sorry for the man except that he had needed direction in his life. He would get all that he needed from his wife.

"The deals have already started, haven't they?" she asked the man who was giving direction to her.

Cal looked at her and winked.

Suddenly she wanted very much to be alone with him.

When she eased from his arms, he made no move to stop her. She took her coat from the peg by the door. "I need to check on Queenie."

Baron, lying close to the fire, thumped his tail against the floor but he made no move to follow her. He had stayed by Simon's side until Cal arrived, but he was not needed anymore. All was well with his world once again. He could safely return to being a lump.

Cal caught up with her by the corral. The wind was blustery, and there were signs of another storm in the air, but she did not feel the cold.

He stood beside her and took hold of her left hand. "I have my mother's ring, given to her by my father. At least, Fin and Fitz have it. I wanted to throw it away, but they wouldn't let me. Those two are smarter than I ever realized."

"Of course they are. They saw right away the value of Gert and May."

"Tell me the truth, Ellie. If you want a new ring, I'll buy you the biggest diamond in Texas. Hell, I'll send to New Orleans or New York or wherever you want."

Behind them the barn door creaked open. They turned to look at Cord, carrying a bucket.

"Don't mind me. I was afraid Ellie was going to milk Queenie and we wouldn't get enough for butter."

"Show some respect for your sister-in-law," Cal said.

Cord's eyes met hers. "I respect her. She'll make the best Hardin of us all."

With that, he disappeared inside the barn, closing the door behind him.

At last they were alone. Cal took her in his arms. "We're going to build an empire together, love. It won't be easy, but with you beside me, the Crown of Glory cannot fail."

She felt his lips brush against hers, the first kiss since they had become engaged. She trembled in anticipation, so full of love and yearning that she felt six feet tall.

The sound of an approaching wagon ended the kiss before it had really begun.

She opened her mouth to whisper an obscenity, then held back. Mistresses of empires, princesses and their ilk should show a little dignity. She must, for instance, get out of her trousers. Cal would help her there, later, if they ever got truly alone.

The two of them turned to watch a crowded wagon bounce up to the front of the Crown's cabin. People poured onto the ground—Fin and Fitz, Gert and May, and Joseph Merse.

Ellie waved. "Katya's fine," she called to the solemn father. "So fine, in fact, you won't recognize her."

Under the sharp perusal of the Dollarhides, she tugged at Cal's hand. "I'll claim that kiss later," she said softly, just to him. "I love you more than life itself, and I'll prove it later tonight if we can find a place to settle. Until then, we need to tell the other people we love that despite our doubts and doleful predictions, we're going to have our happy ending after all."

Epilogue

The first of the next generation of Hardins came into the world on September 1, 1841. The proud parents named him Henry Houston Hardin for Ellie's father and for the outspoken hero of San Jacinto, who was once again President of the Republic.

"If Hank's anything like his mother, he'll be outspoken, too," Cal remarked as he held his son for the first time.

Propped up in the high feather bed that had been Cal's purchase for the cabin, Ellie wished she had some way to preserve the picture of father and son. Later she would describe it as best she could in her journal, now well into its second volume. So much was happening, she scarcely had time to record it all.

Cal had said he wanted to build an empire. She

had long ago learned that since his redemption on that terrible, wonderful winter day just over nine months ago, he seldom said anything he didn't mean.

He'd bought breeding stock from Miguel Alejandro, gotten some fine mares from New Orleans, and he'd begun to help Sir Simon to set up his beef factory. Most important of all, he had married her a week after the proposal had been made and accepted.

The man was a wonder. If he ever went into politics, he could take Sam Houston's place when Sam retired.

He swore empire-building was a full-time job. That and caring for his family.

Cord was still around, but he was showing signs of restlessness. Ellie figured it was the Hardin wanderlust. Someday he would have to find a good woman to settle him down.

"I have a gift for you," she said as Cal paced back and forth with Hank.

He stopped to look at her. "I have everything I need."

"The important things, yes. But you've been doing most of the empire-building lately. I want to do my share."

"I'm thinking dynasty right now."

"For that, we'll need land."

"We've got the Crown."

"Let me hold Hank for a minute. There's a small box under the bed. Could you get it, please?"

Reluctantly he settled the baby in her arms, kissed her forehead, then pulled out the box.

"Open it."

He pulled the folded paper from the box and quickly scanned it.

"We own the Rancho Grande?"

"I had to do something with my money. Since neither Fowler nor his wife had any heirs, the property went to the government. Let me never deal with officialdom again. I started trying to make the purchase months ago."

"And here I thought all you were doing was growing a baby."

"Women never do just one thing at a time. Haven't you learned that yet?"

Cal waved the paper. "But this far more than doubles our land."

"I know."

She stared at him expectantly, hoping he approved. Her biggest fear was that he would associate the calamities of the past with the land on which the calamities had occurred.

His eyes glinted, and he tapped the paper against his hand. "There's some good grazing and farmland there."

Ellie sighed in relief. "Yes," she said simply. She should have known her husband was far too practical a businessman not to see the advantages of her gift.

He grinned at her. It was an expression she saw often these days.

"You did this and I didn't know."

"Right."

"I have a surprise for you, too." Tucking the paper into the pocket of his leather jerkin, he went to the door and called for Fin and Fitz.

Gert and May were the first to come into the room.

Then came Fin and Fitz carrying Cal's special gift. It was her harp, delivered to the Crown all the way from Virginia.

"Oh," she said, unable for the moment to say more. Except, of course, to look up at her husband and whisper, "Thank you."

Next to the people surrounding her, it was the most beautiful sight she had ever seen.

Cord edged into the room. She smiled at him. "I told you that we were going to be civilized, didn't I? I never heard of a harp in a savage land."

"You get out of bed as soon as you can," Gert said. "We want you to audition for the grand opening of the Palace. It's only a month away, remember. Juan Gomez brought the thing all the way from the ship at Lavaca Bay, and the boys helped him get it out here this morning. They can sure as hell—" She stopped herself. "They can sure get it back to town for a few days."

She glanced at May. "With the babe around, we got to stop the cussing."

"The smoking, too," May said.

"You lasses may even have to accept our proposals of marriage," Fin said.

"And make us the happiest pair of Irishmen on earth," Fitz added.

"Maybe," Gert said.

"We're not making any promises," May warned. "We're partners in business. I don't know if marriage and business mixes right well."

"Yes, they do," Ellie said.

"She's right," Cal said.

"Look at Simon and Katya Pence," Fin said. "Those two are having a fine time setting up Cal's beef factory. Simon even helped round up those pesky longhorns last spring."

Ellie knew he had been more observer than participant, but still he had tried.

"I didn't mean the Pences," Ellie said. "I was thinking more of the Hardins. We're in this empire building together." She smiled at her husband. "And we're certainly going to have to cooperate if that includes the dynasty my husband is planning."

"That's right," Cal said.

Henry Houston Hardin chose that moment to cry, and Cal hustled everyone from the room. Then he settled into the rocker he had bought her and watched as Ellie began to nurse their son.

She stroked the baby's cheek, encouraging his suckling, but she didn't have to stroke for long. Cal rocked and watched.

"So what else is happening on the Crown?" she asked. "I don't want to be out of things for long."

"I hired George and Dub. Permanently, this time."

"We'll have to build them quarters. We've already got the Gomezes living in the back."

"George and Dub won't be at the Crown. The Guadalupe needs another ferry. Someone was bound to put one in, and I figured, why not us?"

"They'll run it?"

"Right."

"Good thinking, partner."

"The only reason I didn't talk it over with you was that you were busy getting ready for the baby.

I didn't want to worry you with the details."

"It's no worry, Cal. We're a partnership, remember."

"I'd like to see me doing my share of feeding our son."

"All right, I concede. We have our separate responsibilities."

"And the shared ones, too. As soon as you're finished, let me put the lad into his cradle. I'm not rushing you, understand. Your body has to heal. But I'd like to discuss this dynasty idea. What good is an empire without a family?"

Ellie could not have agreed more.

BETRAYAL Evelyn Rogers

By the Bestselling Author of
The Forever Bride

If there is anything that gets Conn O'Brien's Irish up, it is a lady in trouble–especially one he has fallen in love with at first sight. So after the Texas horseman saves Crystal Braden from an overly amorous lout, he doesn't waste a second declaring his intentions to make an honest woman of her. But they have barely been declared man and wife before Conn learns that his new bride is hiding a devastating secret that can destroy him.

The plan is simple: To ensure the safety of her mother and young brother, Crystal agrees to play the damsel in distress. The innocent beauty has no idea how dangerously charming the virile stranger can be–nor how much she longs to surrender to the tender passion in his kiss. And when Conn discovers her ruse, she vows to blaze a trail of desire that will convince him that her deception has been an error of the heart and not a ruthless betrayal.

___4262-2 $5.99 US/$6.99 CAN

WICKED
Evelyn Rogers
An Angel's Touch

"Evelyn Rogers delivers great entertainment!"
—*Romantic Times*

Gunned down after a bank robbery, Cad Rankin meets a heavenly being who makes him an offer he can't refuse. To save his soul, he has to bring peace to the most lawless town in the West. With a mission like that, the outlaw almost resigns himself to spending eternity in a place much hotter than Texas—until he comes across Amy Lattimer, a feisty beauty who rouses his goodness and a whole lot more.

Although she's been educated in a convent school, Amy Lattimer is determined to do anything to locate her missing father, including posing as a fancy lady. Then she finds an ally in virile Cad Rankin, who isn't about to let her become a fallen angel. But even as Amy longs to surrender to paradise in Cad's arms, she begins to suspect that he has a secret that stands between them and unending bliss....

_52082-6 $5.99 US/$7.99 CAN

THE FOREVER BRIDE — **EVELYN ROGERS**

"Evelyn Rogers delivers great entertainment!"
—Romantic Times

It is only a fairy tale, but to Megan Butler *The Forever Bride* is the most beautiful story she's ever read. That is why she insists on going to Scotland to get married in the very church where the heroine of the legend was wed to her true love. The violet-eyed advertising executive never expects the words of the story to transport her over two hundred years into the past, exchanging vows not with her fiancé, but with strapping Robert Cameron, laird of Thistledown Castle. After convincing Robert that she is not the unknown woman he's been contracted to marry, Meagan sets off with the charming brute in search of the real bride and her dowry. But the longer they pursue the elusive girl, the less Meagan wants to find her. For with the slightest touch Robert awakens her deepest desires, and she discovers the true meaning of passion. But is it all a passing fancy—or has she truly become the forever bride?

_4177-4 $5.50 US/$6.50 CAN

TERMS OF SURRENDER

SHIRL HENKE

"Historical romance at its best!"
—Romantic Times

Devilishly handsome Rhys Davies owns half of Starlight,
Colorado, within weeks of riding into town. But there is one
"property" he'll give all the rest to possess, because Victoria
Laughton—the glacially beautiful daughter of Starlight's first
family—detests Rhys's flamboyant arrogance. And she hates
her own unladylike response to his compelling masculinity
even more. To win the lady, Rhys will have to wager his
very life, hoping that the devil does, indeed, look after his
own.

_3424-7   **$4.99 US/$5.99 CAN**

Cassandra Clayton can wield a blacksnake whip as well as any mule skinner and cuss as well as any Denver saloon girl. There is one thing, though, that she can't do alone—produce a male child who will inherit her freighting empire. Steve Loring, wrongly accused of murder and rescued from the hangman's noose, is just what Cass needs and with him she will produce an heir. But Steve makes it clear that silver dollars will never be enough—he wants Cass's heart and soul in the bargain.

_4201-0 $5.99 US/$6.99 CAN

Dorchester Publishing Co., Inc.
P.O. Box 6640
Wayne, PA 19087-8640

Please add $1.75 for shipping and handling for the first book and $.50 for each book thereafter. NY, NYC, and PA residents, please add appropriate sales tax. No cash, stamps, or C.O.D.s. All orders shipped within 6 weeks via postal service book rate. Canadian orders require $2.00 extra postage and must be paid in U.S. dollars through a U.S. banking facility.

Name_____

Address_____

City_____State_____Zip_____

I have enclosed $_____ in payment for the checked book(s).

Payment <u>must</u> accompany all orders. ☐ Please send a free catalog.

DESPERADO
SANDRA HILL

Major Helen Prescott has always played by the rules. That's why Rafe Santiago nicknamed her "Prissy" at the military academy years before. Rafe's teasing made her life miserable back then, and with his irresistible good looks, he is the man responsible for her one momentary lapse in self control. When a routine skydive goes awry, the two parachute straight into the 1850 California Gold Rush. Mistaken for a notorious bandit and his infamously sensuous mistress, they find themselves on the wrong side of the law. In a time and place where rules have no meaning, Helen finds Rafe's hard, bronzed body strangely comforting, and his piercing blue eyes leave her all too willing to share his bedroll. Suddenly, his teasing remarks make her feel all woman, and she is ready to throw caution to the wind if she can spend every night in the arms of her very own desperado.

_52182-2 $5.99 US/$6.99 CAN

FRANKLY, MY DEAR...

SANDRA HILL

By the Bestselling Author of *The Tarnished Lady*

Selene has three great passions: men, food, and *Gone with the Wind*. But the glamorous model always found herself starving—for both nourishment and affection. Weary of the petty world of high fashion, she heads to New Orleans for one last job before she begins a new life. Then a voodoo spell sends her back to the days of opulent balls and vixenish belles like Scarlet O'Hara.

Charmed by the Old South, Selene can't get her fill of gumbo, crayfish, beignets—or an alarmingly handsome planter. Dark and brooding, James Baptiste does not share Rhett Butler's cavalier spirit, and his bayou plantation is no Tara. But fiddle-dee-dee, Selene doesn't need her mammy to tell her the virile Creole is the only lover she ever gave a damn about. And with God as her witness, she vows never to go hungry or without the man she desires again.

_4042-5 $5.50 US/$6.50 CAN

Dorchester Publishing Co., Inc.
P.O. Box 6640
Wayne, PA 19087-8640

ENCANTADORA
GAIL LINK

"Gail Link was born to write romance!"
—Jayne Ann Krentz

"Husband needed. Must be in good health, strong. No older than forty. Fee paid." Independent and proud, Victoria reads the outlandish advertisement with horror. When she refuses to choose a husband from among the cowboys and ranchers of San Antonio, she never dreams that her father will go out and buy her a man. And what a man he is! Tall, dark, and far too handsome for Tory's peace of mind, Rhys makes it clear he is going to be much more than a hired stud. With consummate skill he woos his reluctant bride until she is as eager as he to share the enchantment of love.

_4181-2 $5.99 US/$6.99 CAN

Dorchester Publishing Co., Inc.
P.O. Box 6640
Wayne, PA 19087-8640

Please add $1.75 for shipping and handling for the first book and $.50 for each book thereafter. NY, NYC, and PA residents, please add appropriate sales tax. No cash, stamps, or C.O.D.s. All orders shipped within 6 weeks via postal service book rate. Canadian orders require $2.00 extra postage and must be paid in U.S. dollars through a U.S. banking facility.

Name_____
Address_____
City_____ State_____ Zip_____
I have enclosed $_____ in payment for the checked book(s).
Payment <u>must</u> accompany all orders. ☐ Please send a free catalog.